The Life
and
Times
of
Tom Watson

by

RAYNETTE MITCHELL

Mitchell Media

First published in 2025 by Mitchell Publishing

Cataloguing in Publication entry is available from the National Library of Australia

http://catalogue.nla.gov.au

Raynette Mitchell/The Life and Times of Tom Watson

ISBN 978-0-6488426-6-8

for George Basil,
And Alice and Ash,
with love

·❤·❤·❤·❤·❤·

Contents

Preface   VII

1. CHAPTER 1   1

2. CHAPTER 2   11

3. CHAPTER 3   25

4. CHAPTER 4   37

5. CHAPTER 5   55

6. CHAPTER 6   61

7. CHAPTER 7   75

8. CHAPTER 8   87

9. CHAPTER 9   103

10. CHAPTER 10   113

11. CHAPTER 11   125

12. CHAPTER 12   135

13. CHAPTER 13   151

14. CHAPTER 14   163

15. CHAPTER 15   173

16. CHAPTER 16   181

17. CHAPTER 17   189

18. CHAPTER 18   203

19. CHAPTER 19   221

20. CHAPTER 20   237

21. CHAPTER 21   255

22. CHAPTER 22   265

23. CHAPTER 23   275

24. CHAPTER 24   295

25. CHAPTER 25   315

26. CHAPTER 26   329

27. CHAPTER 27   339

28. CHAPTER 28   347

29. CHAPTER 29   357

30. CHAPTER 30   369

Acknowledgements   389

Afterword   391

Also by   393

Author Bio   395

PREFACE

Although The Life and Times of Tom Watson is book 2 in the series, Secrets Have Consequences, it does not follow on from the first book—The Life and Loves of Karen Romano. It's more a spin-off from that first book.

Whilst writing Karen's story, I became very fond of a secondary character, Tom Watson, who was a friend of one of the main characters in Karen's life. I found I couldn't let go of Tom, and thought about him a lot, wondering how his life would turn out. I wondered if he would follow his dream of becoming a professional musician, or would he take the safe option and end up a big-time executive in the computer industry?

How could I not write Tom's story?

It is not necessary to read the books in order, and each of them is complete in itself, but you, the reader, will get a better picture of the characters' lives if you read both books. I am currently writing books 3and 4 in the series.

Raynette Mitchell

Chapter 1

Jim Watson's first reaction, when he was summoned to the Office of the Vice President of the hugely successful IT company for whom he worked, was impending doom. There had been a spate of redundancies in middle management lately and he presumed the worst.

He took a deep breath as he patted down a stray wisp of hair on the crown of his head and, with chin up, affected his most managerial face as the secretary ushered him into the VP's superbly appointed office

'Sit down, Jim. I've got a proposition for you.' Jim sat, somewhat relieved—this was not usually how the company handled redundancies.

'We're putting the finishing touches to a new custom-built office and warehouse complex in Sydney, Australia. It will be an important part of our Asian operations, and I'm looking for someone to organise the move and run the division for a year or two.'

'I'd like to offer you the job. It's a big step up from your current position of Divisional Manager, but I know you'll handle the added responsibility well. And of course, it comes with a commensurate salary and benefits. What do you say?'

Jim relaxed and replied, 'I've heard rumours about the new complex being built in Sydney. I believe it'll comprise the latest in warehousing and distribution, with office organisation even beyond what we've got here.'

He smiled as he stood and extended his hand across the desk. 'I accept.'

Jim, not only chuffed with the promotion and the financial benefits it brought with it, was also excited by the prospect of living in Sydney, Australia. He had visited Australia several times and had enjoyed the atmosphere and some of the best living conditions in the world.

He imagined his son, Tom, would be happy about the move. But he had doubts about his mother Enid's reaction. It would be a huge upheaval for a woman of her age to move to another country, away from her friends and the support group which had formed around her following the death of her beloved husband a few years back.

Enid had moved in with Jim and Tom three years ago when Jim's wife, Carolyn, died in an accident. Tom had been eight at the time and had been badly affected by his mother's death. His grief was ongoing—until his Gran gave him a guitar for his ninth birthday after talking with Mr. O'Brien, the music teacher at Tom's school. He had told her Tom was exceptionally talented and should be encouraged.

Since moving in with them, Enid had reared Tom as her own and had been a steadying influence in his young life. Her age and wisdom meant she was aware of what 9-, 10-, 11-year-old boys get up to and Tom had been guided through these years with a firm and knowing hand. He was a good boy, but any boy growing up through those formative years without a mother could have easily been led the wrong way. Enid's experience and intelligence had ensured Tom learned life's lessons without too much heartache and angst.

As Jim drove his now 12-year-old son to his guitar lesson the following day, he glanced across at Tom and said casually, 'I've been offered a promotion with H.P. in Sydney, which means we would have to move to Sydney for a year or perhaps two. What would you say to living in Australia for a while?'

This question caught Tom by surprise. He'd heard of Australia and he knew Sydney was its biggest city. He also knew Australia had some deadly reptiles and insects and kangaroos, but that was as much as he knew of the place. It wasn't as if he had many close friends here he would miss, but music had become a large part of his life and he would miss his music teacher, Mr. O'Brien. He rubbed the left side of his face with his open hand as he stared out the window of the car and thought for a long moment before replying, 'Sounds OK. Will Gran come with us?'

'I haven't mentioned it to her yet. Let's tell her about it at dinner tonight.'

The conversation over dinner was difficult. Jim Watson had worked hard for this promotion at Hewlett-Packard and the transfer to Australia was a reward for his management skills and loyalty to the firm. He wanted this promotion, but he also wanted his son and mother to be happy about the move.

When Jim set out the prospect and what it entailed, he could tell Enid was surprised, and disappointed.

Enid took a deep breath and regained her composure. She stroked her hair back off her face as she composed the sentences in her head before she spoke.

'The opportunity of living in another country for a few years is one any 12-year-old boy should grab with both hands,' she said, taking hold of Tom's hands and smiling into his eyes. 'What an experience! You'll learn about a different place to what has been your comfort zone for 12 years. You'll make new friends, hear various accents, taste different foods, and discover another culture. Oh, Tom, it will be the making of you.'

Jim shifted slightly in his chair, his heart full of gratitude for this wonderful, wise woman and the words she had chosen. He watched Tom intently for his reaction.

'Do you think so, Gran?' Tom smiled shyly. 'I reckon it sounds like fun. Will you come with us?'

'I'm a bit old to take on a new country, so I won't come with you to Australia. But imagine what fun it will be when we get together at Thanksgiving and Christmas? There'll be so much to catch up on; it'll be like a month-long party.'

So, Jim had his answer. He let out the breath he had been holding and said, 'It'll just be you and me looking out for each other, Tom. Do you reckon we can make a go of it?'

'I read somewhere there are some good guitarists in Australia. It would be great if we could get to see some of them.' He looked at his father expectantly.

So much for looking out for each other, thought Jim. *I'll fade into the background in no time at all.* He smiled and tousled his son's hair. 'So, it's agreed. Gran will stay and look after this house, and you and I will go on a big adventure to Australia. They'll wonder what hit them when we get there!'

Jim and Tom bustled down the aisle of the plane, shuffling and struggling with their hand luggage between the rows of seats, as all the passengers tried to get off it as quickly as possible. As Tom reached the Exit door and stepped out onto the landing of the steps which led down to the tarmac, he shielded his eyes from the bright sunlight. The air was so clear he could see for miles as he surveyed the scene before him. Sydney airport. At last. He didn't think they'd ever get here.

Packing up seemed to take weeks even before they'd left the house. The flight from San Francisco to L.A. hadn't taken long, but once they landed in L.A. it took another hour to find the right departure gate for the flight to Sydney. Then there was a 2-hour delay because of a "technical adjustment." The flight seemed to go on forever, but at least it was broken by a short stop-over in Honolulu.

As he stood there taking it all in, he was filled with an elation he had never felt before. The start of their Big Adventure! *Mum would have loved this,* he thought, as he descended the steps in front of his father. She would also have said: 'Seize the day, Tom. Enjoy every moment. You may never pass this way again.'

As they made their way to the luggage carousel and stood waiting for their suitcases, Tom looked around at the milling crowd, then glanced up at his father. 'This airport is a bit bigger than I thought it'd be. I love how they talk,' he said, grinning at his father.

Jim looked down and winked at him. 'Wait until you see where we're going to live.'

Their bags were among the first ones to come off the plane, and once they were sure they had the right luggage, they made their way to the taxi rank outside the terminal where a line of cabs was waiting.

The driver of the first cab in the line hurried around the cab to where Jim was picking up the largest suitcase. 'Here, I'll put those bags in the boot for you, mate,' he said, taking the suitcase from Jim.

'What did he say?' asked Tom quizzically.

'He means the trunk, but they call it the boot here,' replied Jim.

'Weird! Anything else I should know?' laughed Tom. 'Oh, you'll catch on soon enough,' said Jim as they climbed into the back seat of the cab.

'Double Bay, thanks driver,' said Jim as the taxi edged into the traffic.

'Been here before?' asked the cabbie, glancing in the rear-view mirror at them.

'I've been here a few times, but this is a first for my son. We'll be living here for the next year or two.'

'Well, you're in for a treat,' the cabbie replied, turning and looking in Tom's direction. 'You're only a stone's throw away from Bondi, the best beach in the world.' He said, proudly. 'It's only a few K's from where I'll drop you.'

'What did he say?' whispered Tom, turning to his father.

'He means we're going to be close to Bondi Beach. It's a beautiful beach, even if the size of it is a bit overwhelming at first.'

Tom continued to stare out the window of the cab, amazed and delighted at everything he saw. The streets were narrower than they were back home and there were no freeways, which probably explained why there was much less heavy traffic. The buildings were so different from each other. Some seemed quite old, while others looked brand new with lots of glass and colourful signage. And where were all the black people? Everyone they passed on the sidewalks or in parks seemed so "Australian", and there were buses everywhere! It didn't seem as glitzy as San Francisco; it felt smaller and more comfortable. Tom relaxed as he enjoyed the cab ride. This city of Sydney felt welcoming, more like a country town back home.

'I know Double Bay is on this side of the harbour, but would it be possible to cross the Harbour Bridge then come back so Tom here can see the harbour from the bridge?' Jim enquired of the driver.

'No worries,' replied the driver, delighted to be their tour guide for the next half hour.

The number of cars on the road increased as they approached the city. Pedestrians scuttled out of the way as traffic lights turned green and cars and trucks picked up speed. They drove in a complete circle through a tunnel before emerging into the sunshine once again as they approached the Harbour Bridge. *This is so exciting,* thought Tom, *if the kids from school could see me now! Although, it's strange how they drive on the left side of the road. Feels dangerous.*

And onto the Sydney Harbour Bridge. 'You could not have picked a better day to see the harbour,' said the cabbie, 'but it looks terrific in the rain too.' *Sure is different from the Golden Gate back home,* thought Tom.

Tom was spellbound. It didn't matter where you looked, the harbour dominated. The blue water sparkled in the sunlight and sailboats and ferries dodged each other as they made white ribbons of wake in the blue water. His view was suddenly interrupted as a train sped past in the opposite direction. So much happening at once, so much to see, much busier than San Francisco Bay.

'On the left, which is the western side of the Bridge,' said the cabbie, slipping into his Tourist Guide persona, 'the Harbour eventually becomes the Parramatta River. On our right, the Harbour flows out into the Pacific Ocean between North and South Head, about fifteen K's from here.'

'They use kilometres here, instead of miles,' Tom's dad whispered in Tom's direction. 'That's what he means by K's.'

'Oh no, now I've got to learn about kilometres as well as all the other weird words and their meanings. I thought I'd pick up here where I left off back in California. I didn't realise it would be a whole new learning curve.'

'Aw, mate, you'll catch on in no time,' laughed the cabbie.

Tom relaxed back into the cab seat and consciously opened his mind and his heart to this wonderful new adventure. Even though it had been a long flight and he was physically tired, he was aware of a feeling of excitement as the adrenalin flowed and he was carried along in the pleasure of the moment.

Once on the northern side of the harbour, the cabbie made a right-hand turn, and then another, and they found themselves back on the Bridge, heading south.

The Harbour looked even bigger and more spectacular from this side of the Bridge and Tom drank it all in with relish. *I'm going to be living here*, he thought to himself gleefully. *Tom Watson, how did you get so lucky?*

'Ah, you wouldn't be dead for quids on a day like today, would ya?' smiled the cabbie. 'God's own country.'

Tom glanced over at his father and they both stifled a laugh.

Fifteen minutes later, they pulled up in front of a small, white cottage nestled between two bigger and more imposing mansions, on a pretty tree-lined street in Double Bay.

'This is it. Your new home away from home. I hope it's every-thing you want it to be,' said the cabbie. He walked around to the back of the cab, retrieved their suitcases and Tom's guitar case from the boot, and placed them on the footpath.

'Can I put this on a credit card?' asked Jim as he dug a card out of his wallet.

'No problem, mate,' the cabbie replied as he swiped the plastic card through the small machine. 'Sign here.'

'Would you have a pen I could use? I must have left mine on the plane,' said Jim as he felt his pockets.

'Sure, Mate. Here, use my biro.'

At which point Tom dissolved into laughter as he picked up a suitcase in one hand and his guitar case in the other, pushed open the front gate, and walked up the path to the front door.

'A Biro!!! Must remember that one. That's the best yet.

Chapter 2

Tom had trouble getting his head around the fact that the school year began in January in Australia, in the middle of summer. In America, Christmas was in the middle of winter, and the hot weather was in June, July, and August.

He turned 13 in early January and entered that no-man's-land, where kids transitioned out of their childhood and into the adult world, not always smoothly.

Joe Elphick and Tom Watson started at Eastern Sydney Boys' High School on the same day, when school went back at the end of January after the Christmas holidays. Neither boy noticed the other until day five, when Joe saw Tom shoving a guitar case into his locker as the bell rang, signalling the start of another school day. He casually walked over to Tom and, staring hard at the guitar case, said, 'So, what do you play?'

As Tom closed the locker door and turned the key, he glanced at the stocky, pimply faced youth who had sidled up to him. 'Uh, m-mostly pop,' Tom stammered. The boy had caught Tom off guard, and for a moment, he was unsure of what to say. Although he'd seen him around, he didn't know his name or anything about him.

'I play the piano. I'm pretty good. Wanna jam sometime?' The cocky attitude softened a little, and he smiled. 'Ah, the name's Joe, by the way.'

'I'm Tom. Pleased to meet you.'

'See you in the music room after last period this arvo. We'll have a bit of a jam,' said Joe, as he picked up his school bag and turned to walk away. There was no question in his statement; it was more like an order. He had a certain swagger in his walk, which amused Tom, reminded him of a bossy rooster.

'Sure,' was all Tom could reply, as each boy went on his way to their first class of the day. *Well, that was interesting,* thought Tom. *Hope he's as good as he says he is. Guitar and piano, great basis for a group.*

They met up in the Music room when lessons had finished and to Tom's delight, Joe displayed a natural talent for the piano. He was as good as he said he was. He had a great sense of rhythm and worked beautiful chords into anything he played, plus he seemed to have an extensive repertoire of tunes. He chattered endlessly, which saved Tom from having to make conversation—not one of his strong points.

'Where did you learn to play the piano?' Tom was interested to know how a thirteen-year-old boy could play so well—had he learnt from a classical teacher or was his a natural talent?

'Both my mom and dad play piano. Mom's a teacher at the Conservatorium. She started teaching me when I was three. Dad plays in the Sydney Symphony Orchestra.' Joe suddenly looked bashful. 'How could I not be good with a such a background!' Joe laughed an embarrassed laugh. 'What about you? Had any formal training?'

'My Gran gave me a guitar for my birthday a few years ago and signed me up for lessons from a local teacher near where we lived in the States. I loved it from the first lesson. Our choirmaster at school was a terrific singer and musician, and he used to encourage me to practice and to try new stuff all the time. I really miss him since we came to Australia at the end of last year.' A wistful look crossed Tom's face as memories of Mr. O'Brien filled his mind.

'Well, never mind. You've got me to encourage you now. Play on!' Joe ran his fingers over the keys with an intro in the key of F Major. 'You know any Bee Gees numbers? Their stuff is cool.' Tom picked up on the intro and recognised the start of 'More Than a Woman' which had been a huge hit for the Bee Gees a few years before.

Fifteen minutes later, as they played up a storm, the door opened and an unusually tall, thin boy poked his head around the door, his fair, thick hair falling over his eyes. He subconsciously bent his head forward to compensate for his height.

'You guys sound like you could use a drummer. Mind if I join in?'

'We're only allowed to use this room for twenty minutes today and we're nearly out of time. But you could meet us here tomorrow after last period for another session.' Joe looked over at Tom as he spoke. 'You're OK for tomorrow arvo, aren't you, Tom?'

'Not tomorrow,' replied Tom. 'Better make it Thursday.' *I could get sick of this bossy rooster routine real quick*, thought Tom.

'What's your name?' he asked, looking up at the head poking around the door.

'Josh Curran.' Josh stared hard at Tom. 'You're Tom Watson, aren't you? The American kid.'

'Yep. And this is Joe.' Tom poked Joe in the back. 'What's your last name, Joe?'

'Elphick,' said Joe quickly.

'Great. See you guys here, Thursday afternoon, after last period.' Tom said as he placed his guitar in its case and flipped both locks.

The minute the last class finished on Thursday afternoon, Tom raced to his locker, grabbed his guitar, and ran down the corridor to the stairs at the far end, taking them two at a time. He reached the Music Room at the same time as Joe, with Josh no more than twenty seconds later. The three boys burst into the room and Joe opened the piano lid as Tom retrieved the guitar from its case and Josh made himself comfortable at the drum set in the corner.

'Hey Tom, do you know Sweet Dreams Are Made of This?'

'Absolutely,' replied Tom, and banged out a riff in the key of C Sharp Minor as an intro.

'Aw, great number,' smiled Josh and joined in at the same time Joe began.

Within the first minute, Tom slipped into the magical aura of making music and remained there for the rest of the afternoon. This was what he had dreamed of from his first lesson on the guitar—making music with like-minded people, and in his wildest dreams—becoming rich and famous doing it!

He looked around at the other boys. There was Joe, dishevelled, untidy, his uniform grubby, his shirt hanging out of his trousers, but playing the piano like he was knocking on heaven's door. His eyes were closed and he was in another state, a natural, comfortable state, where he belonged, swaying in time with the beat, feeling the rhythm, his fingers tripping lightly and gracefully over the keys.

Josh smiled as he found the beat. Although he lacked Joe's class, he made up for it with enthusiasm and gusto. He reminded Tom of what a praying mantis playing the drums might look like: all arms and legs, but with a head of blonde, shaggy hair covering half his face.

And then there was Tom, in his happy place, playing his guitar as if it was an extension of his arms. Here he could let his feelings take over completely, didn't have to speak, just be. This was where he was most at peace, his mind empty of thoughts of anything other than the next riff, the progression of chords leading into the next passage, at one with the world in this little room, with these soul mates.

Together, the three of them made a surprisingly good sound.

Word spread around the school—a trio of kids made music in the Music Room after school most days—and it wasn't long before another boy approached Tom to join the group.

'You're Tom Watson, aren't you? My name's Mario. I heard you and a couple of other guys jam in the Music Room after school. Can I join you? I play bass guitar. I haven't been playing long, but I'm desperate for more experience playing in a group.' All this came out in a rush in one breath. He was obviously keen to play with them.

Mario was a handsome boy, and his noticeably short curly dark hair matched his dark brown eyes, which were surrounded by crinkly laughter lines. He spoke with what sounded like a slight Italian accent. His school uniform was immaculate and looked like it had been hand-tailored, his pointy-toed shoes shiny and Italian-looking. Tom liked him immediately. 'Sure, we meet in the

Music Room after last period most days. I reckon bass is what we need. See you later today.'

Mario grinned broadly and, gripping Tom's arm, said: 'You won't regret it. Thanks, Tom.'

'You're late getting home from school today, Tom. It's after seven. Everything OK?' Tom's father looked up from watching the evening news on the TV and Tom instantly felt guilty when he saw the half-worried, half-angry look on Jim's face. In a flash, he realised he'd forgotten to tell his dad he'd be home late today.

'Sorry, Dad, I forgot to tell you this morning I was going to be late. I arranged an extra jam session after school today with the other kids in the group. Looks like I'm kind of the leader now. We're trying to come up with up a name for the group. Got any suggestions?' Tom thought it might appease his father for the worry he had caused him to include him in the guessing game for the band's name.

'Well, if Queen and Prince can make it big, how about Kings of Sound?'

Tom smiled. 'Yeah, I'll pitch it to the other guys and see what they reckon.' Not exactly what Tom had in mind—Kings of Sound was as far away from INXS or AC/DC as you could get. They were looking for something quirky, different, memorable, and Kings of Sound wasn't it.

'I'll be home around this time on Mondays, Wednesdays, and Thursdays. We've got the use of the school gym three afternoons a week after school for two hours now, which is much better than the Music Room, much bigger, and great acoustics.'

'So, you're taking your music seriously? You'll be playing gigs soon at this rate. I'll have to come and have a listen.'

'You'll get to hear what we sound like at the end-of-year concert,' said Tom over his shoulder as swung his guitar over his back and took the stairs to his room two at a time. *But you won't like what you hear,* thought Tom. Volume! Lots of volume. That's what made them sound terrific. Not only did it make the band sound fabulous, but it also drowned out the odd wrong note or forgotten words.

Tom was pleased with the way the group had developed. The four of them got along well together—if Tom kept the Rooster in check. They had been playing together for a few weeks when Tom called Joe 'Rooster' one afternoon, partly by accident and maybe to see what reaction it would get.

'Who're you calling Rooster?' said Joe indignantly.

'You. You remind me of a rooster,' Tom replied and laughed. Mario chimed in: 'I like it. Rooster Joe.' To which Josh added: 'Yeah, Rooster it is!'

And Rooster it was, from that day on. Even Joe got to like it. And he never found out that in his head, Tom usually added 'Bossy' before Rooster.

The group still hadn't decided on a name. They'd tossed around lots of ideas, but either nothing sounded quite right, or all four of them couldn't agree.

One Thursday afternoon, Tom, Josh, and Mario set up, tuned the equipment, and were happily practicing when, after the third number, Mario commented 'Rooster's late today. He's never late,' just as Tom dropped his pick on the floor.

'Damn! It's gone under the piano.' He crouched down at the side of the piano and, putting his eye to the floor, spied it half buried in the dust, as Joe burst into the room, bringing the lingering smell of cigarette smoke with him.

'Sorry I'm late. I had to run an errand for Mr. Green.' Rooster panted, sliding onto the piano stool and opening the lid at the same time.

'Liar, liar, pants on fire!' said Mario, pointing at Rooster and laughing. 'You've been smoking down behind the toilets!'

Rooster looked crestfallen. 'Is it that obvious?'

Down on the floor, Tom had heard nothing after 'Pants on Fire.' His brain had locked onto the expression, and he'd stopped listening. All he could concentrate on was—*great name for a band! Pants On Fire. That's it!*

'That's it,' he exclaimed as he retrieved the pick and stood up. 'That's it! That's what we'll call the band: Pants on Fire.'

The others all stopped what they were doing and looked at him., their young minds ticking over in consideration. At last, in a burst of exuberance:

'That's good,' said Josh, 'incredibly good.'

'It's great,' said Mario, punching the air with his fist.

'Not bad,' said Rooster, brushing the last of the cigarette ash off his tie, trying to look unimpressed, even though he thought it was a terrific name for the band.

The group practised loud and long, putting in many hours in the school gym each afternoon. They played a few gigs locally and by the following year, were even getting the occasional write-up in the local newspaper. The first gig was at the school captain's eighteenth birthday party, at which they were a huge success and played until nearly midnight. Another gig was at Mario's cousin's engagement party, where an incalculable number of relatives had cheered them on. Tom was even recognised by a young woman in the main street of Double Bay one Saturday morning. He was embarrassed at first when she told him she'd seen them perform before kick-off at a recent local football match, but he was also secretly thrilled and couldn't help smiling as he continued his trip to the deli for milk for breakfast.

You're a Rock Star, boy! He thought as the smile grew into a broad grin.

And he tripped up the gutter as he crossed the road, completely destroying the illusion.

During their weekly phone call, Tom kept his Gran up to date with his life. At age 14, he was doing well at school and seemed to be popular with his peers, probably because Pants on Fire had become well-known in the Eastern Suburbs of Sydney. Gran was genuinely interested in everything Tom did, but she particularly loved the idea of his success with his music. She was so proud he had kept up with the guitar she had given him and had attracted similarly disposed boys around him, had even formed a band. She told anyone who would listen all about her popular and successful musician grandson in Australia.

Jim was also proud of Tom and his achievements, but even though Tom was doing well with his studies, Jim would have liked him to spend more time studying and less time playing his guitar. Still, he couldn't exactly criticise Tom when he achieved such good grades.

During their second year in Sydney, Jim was promoted to Vice President, Asia, and agreed to remain in Australia for the next five years. Tom was secretly pleased with this decision; the band was growing in popularity and had accumulated a small following of loyal fans, mainly female.

The two men returned to Palo Alto to spend Christmas with Enid and Lola, who flew in from Arizona for the few weeks they were there. It seemed Gran had acclimatised well to life in California—she certainly didn't miss those Washington, DC, winters—and had made some good friends, had even joined a couple of local women's groups. She wasn't as disappointed as Jim and Tom expected when the time came for them to return to Sydney to begin the five-year stint.

The weekly phone calls with Gran resumed, and life settled down to a comfortable routine for Tom of schoolwork and band practice, mostly after school in the Gym, but occasionally at one of the boys' fathers' garages, although the noise was sometimes a problem.

The trip to California to spend Christmas with Gran and Lola became a yearly tradition, one the whole family anticipated with relish. Every year it was the same—lots of presents, every family meal a joy, many nights spent sitting around the fire chatting, catching up with the past year's happenings. Christmas dinner was a banquet which took days to prepare—and days to get over—and Tom was asked to play every tune he knew for Gran and Lola. The house was always warm and friendly during this holiday season and full of love, with rarely a cross word spoken between the four of them.

Back in Sydney, Pants on Fire continued to develop. Josh announced some bad news when he arrived at the Gym one day—his family was moving to Queensland, and he had no option but to go with them.

'Ah, never mind, Josh. You'll find another group to play with up there, if you can find anyone who isn't surfing every spare minute. I've heard that's what they're like up there. Beach mad.' This was Rooster's way of making Josh feel better about his planned move. In reality, Rooster wasn't at all sorry Josh was leaving. They could replace him with a better drummer. He had always thought Josh held them back from being great rather than simply good.

And as Rooster had hoped, Andrew Strauss, the replacement drummer, was sensational. The band took on a new life and their bookings picked up. By their third year, Pants on Fire was getting roughly one gig a month. And their followers were growing in number at a surprising rate.

The band's sound had changed over the past few months, and although Tom didn't mind the slightly different tone, it wasn't the same as the original sound. Late one afternoon, shortly before they were due to finish up, Joe suggested they could play 'Smooth Operator,' a song made popular by Sade a year or two before. Tom loved the song but hadn't played it before, but Joe handed the sheet music around and said: 'You'll pick it up from this. Great number.'

Joe had obviously played it before—many times. The others picked it up easily from the music, and the four of them soon fell into a melodic rhythm, combining to make a sweet, soulful sound.

'Nothing personal, Rooster, but I wouldn't want to play too much stuff like that,' said Mario as he was putting his bass into its case. 'I didn't feel the floor vibrate and the walls kinda didn't even move when I hit the base notes. Nice tune, but not exactly rock music, is it?'

That was when Tom realised—Joe had been slipping into jazz mode more and more recently, which was changing the sound of the entire band. He'd been using more and more diminished 7th and minor chords in his playing lately. Pants on Fire was not a jazz band!

The following week, during lunch break, Rooster took Tom aside.

'Tom, there's something I've got to tell you. I've decided to leave the band to concentrate on a career as a jazz pianist. I feel like I'm letting you down, but I know this is what I've got to do. I've loved playing with you, and Pants on Fire, and I hope we'll remain friends, but this is something I've got to do for myself. I know jazz will become my life.'

Tom was bitterly disappointed to lose the Rooster—he'd been an original member of Pants on Fire, one of the foundation rocks on which the band had been built—but he also knew in his heart, Rooster would make a brilliant jazz musician.

'I'm really sorry to see you go, Rooster, but I understand. This music thing runs through our veins, and we've got to answer the call when it comes. We'll miss you.'

Tom was quiet for a minute, conflicting thoughts filling his head. He would miss the Rooster's quirky personality and stupid sense of humour, but he also admired him as someone who could see their future so clearly and had the guts to go for it.

'There is one thing I would ask: can you teach me a few basic chords on the keyboard before you go? I reckon I could pick it up enough to get by until we can replace you—which shouldn't take long, you were never much good anyway,' he said, laughing and making a silly face. He grabbed Rooster in a headlock and punched him on the arm—a genuine sign of affection between two teenage boys—as they ambled out of the cafeteria.

Chapter 3

The 1980s formed a large part of the collective memory of Generation X. Although the decade became known as the 'Me-First Decade', the 'Yuppie Decade', the world's future was shrouded in the fear of a nuclear face-off between the two superpowers, the United States of America and Russia.

The explosion of the space shuttle, Challenger, shocked the world. Like the assassination of John F. Kennedy a generation before, it was a defining moment in this generation's history.

In a terrorist attack, Pan Am Flight 103 was destroyed over Lockerbie, Scotland, killing all passengers and crew.

Wall Street buyouts were all the rage, signalling a 'Decade of Greed,' and environmental issues were debated more seriously. The Cold War eventually ended as the old Soviet Bloc crumbled. One by one, the nations of Eastern Europe threw off their Communist governments. The Berlin Wall finally came down, and the nation of East Germany ceased to exist within a matter of days. The Chinese government violently put down a student protest in Tiananmen Square in Beijing, ending hopes for democracy there.

The pleasure-seeking indulgence of the 1970s was re-evaluated. Many drugs which were considered recreational in the '70s, were found to be addictive, deadly substances. Even though reports of celebrities entering rehabilitation centres, and the horrors of drug-ridden inner cities became widely known, newer and more dangerous substances, such as cocaine, exacerbated the world's drug problem.

The sexual revolution was rocked by the spread of Acquired Immune Deficiency Syndrome, or AIDS. This deadly disease was most commonly communicated by sexual contact and the sharing of intravenous needles. With the risks of promiscuous behaviour rising to a mortal level, monogamy and 'safe sex' with condoms eventually became 'the norm.'

It was the decade of 'Image.' Stars like Madonna and Michael Jackson based their success on the 'look' as well as the music. Michael Jackson made one of the most successful music videos ever, even though it ran for over thirteen minutes, and 'Thriller' became the first music video to be inducted into the United States Library of Congress' National Film Registry, while Madonna's 'Material Girl' typified the values of an increasingly materialistic decade.

The video cassette recorder (VCR) allowed consumers to record television shows and watch them at a later, often more convenient, time and view feature films in the privacy of their own homes.

Young Urban Professionals, or yuppies as they became known, replaced the socially conscious hippie of the previous decade. Yuppies sought executive, middle-management jobs in large corporations and spent their money on upscale consumer products like Ray-Ban sunglasses, Nike Sneakers, and BMW cars. The health and fitness industry exploded as many yuppies engaged in regular fitness routines and gyms flourished. Although they were self-centred and materialistic, yuppies were a generation of young men and women who were plagued with anxiety and self-doubt. They were successful, but they weren't sure they were happy.

But the biggest change in the lifestyle of the 1980s was the computer. Businesses could use computers to manage inventories, payrolls, and mailing lists, but in doing so, replaced large numbers of staff with machines. Silicon Valley in California, home to many of the firms that produced the processors and wrote the software that made these computers run, became the symbolic heart of the technological economy. As a flow-on, the internet became the most defining invention of the age and ultimately created the biggest change to everyday life for a huge percentage of the world's population.

Yes, it was a good time to be a teenager, living your formative years in Australia in the '80s!

Mid-way through Tom's final year of high school, the President of Hewlett-Packard phoned Jim to pitch a proposition to him: if Jim would move to Melbourne and run the Asia-Pacific region for the next four years, the company would then bring him back to the States and promote him to Vice President Worldwide. Jim didn't care which part of Australia H.P. wanted him to operate from, he liked Australia and would have been happy in any of its cities, but he was extremely interested in the carrot at the end of the four-year stick—Vice President Worldwide. There was just one thing standing in the way of such a move happening soon—Tom's education. The middle of this, his final school year, would not be the best time to make such a move. To have to do the second six months of this year, leading into the final exams in November, in a strange new city, with virtually no support system in place, was too big an ask of a teenage boy, even one as self-confident and good-natured as Tom.

Rather than answering him immediately, Jim asked the President if he would give him forty-eight hours to think about it.

The President suppressed his surprise at Jim's reply—he had half expected him to accept the proposition before he'd even finished asking the question—but he couldn't help admiring a man who was not so easily bought. In the position of Vice President Worldwide, Jim would face some tough decisions, some involving many millions of dollars of the company's money. A wise man would consider the consequences assiduously before making those tough decisions.

Jim hung up the phone and sat in his office looking out the window over the bushland to the north of the building, thinking about what he would say to Tom to get the result he wanted. After ten minutes spent in deep introspection, he decided to sleep on it and discuss it with him tomorrow.

Tom was very involved with his band and his music. It would be a wrench to move interstate and give up that camaraderie and attachment to the other boys for the sake of his father's job. It was, however, important to Jim that Tom come with him to Melbourne. Seventeen was too young to live in Sydney on his own.

By the time he spoke to Tom about it tomorrow, Jim was confident they could work it out to their mutual satisfaction.

'Yumm. Thai takeaway. Nice!'

Tom ripped into the containers and helped his dad spoon the food onto plates on the kitchen countertop. Tom would have eaten Thai takeaway every night of the week, but he knew his father wasn't that keen on it.

'My favourite, Thai Special Fried Rice!' he exclaimed, licking the spoon and savouring the smell of the oriental spices in the rice as it mixed with the Red Curry Duck on the plate.

'Yes,' replied his father, 'the place will smell of Thai food for days.' But he couldn't help smiling at the look of delight on Tom's face as he savoured that first mouthful of the curry.

Where did teenage boys put all this food? Jim thought, *they must have hollow legs!*

'I had a phone call from the States this morning,' Jim said casually as he helped himself to another Spring Roll. 'They've asked me to move.'

Tom froze momentarily, then dug into more fried rice. 'Well, we always knew that was on' he said, using Australia lingo he had picked up during his time here. 'We've been here three years longer than first planned.'

Jim blinked. He hadn't looked at the situation from that angle. He stole a sidelong glance at Tom and went on. 'Actually, they don't want us back in the States yet. They want me to transfer to Melbourne for four years with a guarantee of returning home to the States after that.'

Tom stared at his father in confusion. 'But what about my finals? What about the band?' His voice held an undertone of irritation.

'That's why we're talking about it now,' Jim said calmly. He knew from experience that it was important not to become emotional or to rush in when negotiating. It was also important to listen carefully to any opposing argument.

'I don't think it's a good idea to move anywhere right now, but what would you think about moving when you've finished your exams? I understand what your music and the band mean to you but that would give you some time to settle into Melbourne, check out the music scene down there, before you start university next year.'

Tom fell silent. He felt rattled. The band was the shining light in his life, how could he walk away from it? On the other hand, it had crossed his mind—many times—that eventually they would return to the States, at which time he would have to walk away from it.

'But Pants on Fire is playing at the End-of-Year dance the week after final exams. I can't miss that.'

'I may have to spend the odd week or two in Melbourne between now and then, but I reckon I could get them to agree to me officially starting there say, mid-December. That would give you a couple of months before university starts to become acclimatised to Melbourne and the music scene down there.' Jim knew the mention of 'the music scene down there' would pique Tom's interest which was why he mentioned it more than once.

And it did. Tom had heard about the pub bands in Melbourne, how a huge part of the night life of that city revolved around the live music played in pubs. Most of these venues were prepared to give unknown bands a gig, a foot in the door, which sometimes led to the big time—a record contract or a regular booking, or even a tour. The ones in the city, in the suburbs, in the outer suburbs, all drew good crowds to have a drink or a meal and enjoy the music.

The absence of poker machines in clubs meant people were lured by live entertainment rather than gambling.

'I guess that could work,' said Tom tentatively. 'What do *you* think about moving to Melbourne?'

Jim could tell Tom was warming to the idea and knew his answer was important. He thought for a moment as he recalled the wording he'd prepared for this situation. He placed his plate carefully on the countertop and wiped his mouth with one of the paper napkins which came with the take-away food before replying:

'I think a move like this takes you out of your comfort zone and opens you up to new ideas and objectives. I also think it gives us an end date for moving back to the States rather than it being 'sometime in the future.' Don't get me wrong, I've loved our time here in Sydney, and I've accomplished everything the firm asked of me, but I would look forward to the next challenge in Melbourne.'

Then added:

'Have you decided what you want to do at university yet?'

He was concerned that Tom was taking a laid-back attitude about his future and wished he would decide which course he wanted to take. The timing was even more critical when it involved enrolling in a university in another state.

'Not yet. I've looked at a couple of things, but I haven't made up my mind. Plenty of time.'

Jim was pensive for a minute or two, thinking about Tom; watching a boy grow into a young man was as interesting and complex as it was life-affirming. Tom, the little boy with the dark curly hair, the one who was always so happy and laughing, talking non-stop about everything in his life, until that fateful day of the accident when they had both lost the force of nature that was their wife and mother. That was when Tom had changed, knocked sideways by the loss of the one person who completely understood him, loved him unconditionally, and gave his life meaning as well as fun and foundation. That was when he had virtually stopped talking and had withdrawn into his own world. It had taken years for him to move on from the loss of his mother, and his music had helped more than anything anyone could say or do.

And here he was, nearly eighteen, the dark curls long now, longer than Jim liked, and unkempt, resting on his shoulders like a shaggy black mane. Almost 6'1" in height, taller than Jim had expected, bright blue eyes in a darkly handsome face, the infectious lop-sided smile revealed even white teeth, the black clothes he loved to wear gave him the appearance of an upstanding raven, glossy and regal. He wore many silver rings on his long-fingered, pale-skinned hands, which caught the light as he played his guitar, compounding the enigma that was Tom Watson. It was no wonder the girls loved him, swarmed around the band wherever they played, calling his name, waiting around for him after each gig. But they wasted their simpering adulation on him: Tom was only interested in the music.

His knowledge and mastery of music and guitars had developed exponentially ever since he received that first three-quarter size guitar from his grandmother. By the second year of playing, he had progressed to a 6-string steel guitar, and now owned another three electric guitars, including his pride and joy—a Fender Telecaster—which the family had chipped in and given him last Christmas.

As he matured through puberty, Tom remained unpretentious. Jim was ever grateful he hadn't developed that teenage know-it-all personality that seemed part and parcel of the teenage years. He genuinely liked people and rarely argued, accepting others' opinions, even if not always agreeing with them. His friendly nature and ability to fit in made him popular among his peers, and of course, being the lead of an up-and-coming rock band only increased his approval rating.

Jim loved and admired Tom and was prouder of him than he could easily express. But it still bothered him that Tom was more musical than academically minded. He also realised that whatever Tom wanted to do with his life to be happy was more important than his father's ambitions for him. Jim, the quiet achiever with a business mind like a steel trap, was, at heart, a realistic and wise man.

He snapped back to the present and changed the subject from the move to Melbourne and university courses. He didn't want to push the discussion any further right now. They could make a final decision tomorrow.

They agreed to move to Melbourne a day or two after the school dance at the end of November.

There were three separate trips to Melbourne for Jim between their conversation and the move, plenty of time for Tom to be on his own, to quietly study for his final exams. But instead, he left the studying until the week before exams and spent that valuable study time with the band, practicing and polishing their repertoire for the dance.

On one of these occasions when Jim was out of town and Tom was alone in the house, he began experimenting with chords on the keyboard he'd bought when Rooster gave him some lessons before he left the band. Before long, he was picking out a melody to go with the chords. He played the tune a few times, tweaking it here and there, adding a couple of more complicated chords until he felt he'd polished it enough to call it a proper song. But songs needed lyrics. That part was harder, but within hours, he felt he had captured enough lyrics to make it worthwhile. Although he had written many arrangements for the band, this was the first time he'd written the whole thing—melody, chords, and lyrics. He jotted down the notes in a simple arrangement and put them away in the guitar case. It would be interesting to hear what it sounded like when the band played it the next day at practice.

Their first attempt was better than he had expected, and the other guys loved it.

'I wrote some lyrics to go with it. How about we do it again and I'll sing?'

The other guys whooped and whistled: 'Yay, go Tom, let's hear you sing.'

They fell silent as Tom sang, each playing their instrument 'sotto voce' to allow the voice to feature.

'Wow, that was terrific,' said Mario. 'Got any more like that?'

'Yeah, man, that was really good,' enthused Jason, who had replaced the Rooster. 'Great voice.' Praise indeed from a boy who rarely commented, barely even spoke, but was the most gifted pianist Tom had heard since Rooster.

'Not yet,' replied Tom, 'but I'm working on it. I'll try and write another two or three for the dance, although the punters usually want familiar cover stuff.'

Jim had flown to Melbourne the week before the school dance, intending to be home the night before the dance on Saturday. He had timed it that way so he could be there to wish Tom well for the End-of-Year School Dance, which he knew was important to him. Plus, he was looking forward to hearing all about it on Sunday. Unfortunately, as he arrived at the airport for his plane home, there was a major outage at Sydney airport. It had been hit by a vicious electrical storm and all flights into Sydney were cancelled. All computers and electrical equipment at Sydney airport were damaged and out of action for at least 36 hours, which meant he couldn't get home until Sunday.

The first plane he could get was the three-thirty out of Melbourne on Sunday afternoon. At least he could spend Saturday in the office and tie up some loose ends to prepare for next week's move.

Not so bad, really.

Chapter 4

The End-of-Year dance was a major event on the school calendar and the students had decked out the gym like a gala ballroom with bunches of red and green balloons tied to the rafters, a decorated Christmas tree standing tall in one corner. The final year girls from Eastern Sydney Girls' High and their partners were invited and went all out to dress for the occasion. Some boys even wore tuxedos or dinner suits, their hair slicked back and gelled, practically unrecognisable. The girls looked gorgeous with their formal hairdos and 'special occasion' makeup, their long full skirts gracefully sweeping the floor and swishing back and forth as they moved. Some wore daring low necklines, which caught every boy's attention. Even Tom took notice.

'Check out the red dress,' whispered Mario, poking Tom in the ribs with his elbow. 'Now she's hot!'

'Yeah, nice,' replied Tom. Mario rolled his eyes and sighed, thinking to himself, *this guy could have any girl in the room and all he can say is 'Yeah, nice.'*

The boys scrambled up onto the stage and plugged in their equipment and amplifiers, leaving a mass of wires and electric cords in their wake. As they were tuning up, the M.C. for the night unhooked the microphone from its base and, striding from one side of the stage to the other, trailing the mike cord, announced:

'Come on People, put on those dancing shoes! It's time to celebrate the end of the school year on the dance floor. How about a round of applause for Pants on Fire—undoubtedly the best band in the Eastern Suburbs.'

The applause was ear-splitting, with much whistling and whooping, as Pants on Fire broke into the intro to 'You're the One That I Want' from the hit movie Grease.

And the night was up and running.

Nothing like playing to your home crowd, Tom thought, as the buzz took hold and the adrenalin pumped through his veins. At the beginning of the second set, Andrew called to Tom: 'Now would be a good time to play one of the ones you wrote. Why don't you announce it and see what sort of a reaction it gets?'

Tom was suddenly self-conscious: he felt the sweat break out on his hands and his breathing sped up. To his horror, he felt the deep pink blush creep up his neck, over his chin and finally settle on his cheeks. As he looked out over the crowded dance floor and into the glare of the lights, he momentarily froze - it was one thing to play your own composition at band practice with trusted friends, another thing altogether to put your heart and soul out there on full display for a large audience of your peers to judge.

This is it. The moment of reckoning. It's now or never, thought Tom as he stepped up to the mike and, standing tall, even though his knees felt like they were going to give way beneath him, and hoping desperately not to make a complete fool of himself, took a deep breath and announced:

'This next number is one I wrote especially for tonight. It's called 'Out into the World.' Hope you like it.'

There was subdued applause as the boys played the intro. It was the first slow number of the evening, a softer, more melancholic song, and several couples wandered out onto the dance floor and began to dance more closely than was necessary. As the band got further into the number and Tom gained confidence in his singing, more couples moved onto the dance floor. By the time they had reached the last bracket of the tune, the floor was crowded with young people, some of whom were obviously enjoying the chance to get up close and personal with members of the opposite sex. As the band finished the number, the dancers broke into spontaneous applause, some shouting their approval.

'Great song.'

'More like that please.'

'Good job, Tom.'

'Didn't know you could sing!'

Wow, it was a success. They genuinely like it. Tom breathed a sigh of relief and pride. He could hardly wait to sing another one. *I want more of this*, he thought to himself. *I wonder what it would be like to be a professional muso.*

Before long, even with the huge ceiling fans whirring at top speed, up on stage, it was like being in the tropics in the middle of summer. And the spotlights which shone on them made it hotter. The boys' faces glistened with sweat, and Tom felt light-headed. He glanced across at Mario who was looking decidedly un-Mario-ish, his usual impeccable clothing sweat-patched and dishevelled, his dark curls wet and clinging to his forehead, sweat forming little rivulets down his cheeks before dripping onto his shirt.

As the night wore on, the heat on stage became even more intense. They were half-way through the final set when Tom couldn't stand it any longer. He put his guitar down on the floor, pulled his shirt off over his head, and threw it on the floor behind him. He picked up his guitar and continued playing, bare chested, without missing a beat.

Whistles and whoops, louder than before. Heavy foot stomping. It took a minute for him to realise — it was the girls who were making all the noise.

At about half-past eleven, after five encores, they eventually finished playing for the night and packed up as the crowd began to drift out the doors of the gym into the cool night air. By now, ties had come undone and were hanging loose. Most of the boys had removed their coats and some of the girls were wandering around swinging their shoes in their hands, enjoying the feel of the slightly damp grass under their bare feet. The crowd had dispersed into small groups who were now standing around chatting about what a great night it had been. Nobody wanted to go home yet. It had been such a terrific evening, who would want it to end?

Rooster ambled over to where Tom was stuffing the rest of the sheet music into his bulging guitar case.

'Yo, Tom.' It was clear he'd had a great night. He was bare-foot, unbuttoned shirt hanging out of his pants, with his black bow tie tied around one wrist.

'Hey, Joe, how are you?' replied Tom, delighted to see his old friend. 'It's great to see you. How's the jazz thing going?'

Joe nodded to the others. 'Hi guys.' he called out, before turning back to Tom.

'Great. Great, Man. You sounded good tonight. Been practicing?' He laughed as he punched Tom on the arm. 'Hey Man, my brother's got a party going back at our place, a few of us are going there now. Why don't you guys join us? Would be good to have a catch up, maybe even a bit of a jam. Whaddaya reckon?'

After playing a gig for five hours, Tom's energy was zinging, and he didn't want to come down from that level yet. The thought of a party at any other time would have produced a definite NO, but right now, he was up for it. And his dad was away until tomorrow, so there were no time constraints. The others all had reasons why they couldn't make it. There were other parties going down that night at various kids' places, including ones to which Tom had been invited, but he'd always enjoyed a chat with Rooster, and that thought made his decision an easy one.

'Why not? Sounds good, count me in. What's your address?'

'You got a vehicle?'

'No, I got a cab here tonight, with all my equipment—three guitars, amps, music, the trolley. Oh, the cab driver was thrilled—NOT!'

Rooster picked up two of Tom's guitars and, in his usual bossy manner, announced: 'Come on, I'll take you in mine.'

Tom called out to the others, 'See you for one last session in the gym on Monday arvo, and then it's Adios Amigos.'

There were embarrassed murmurings and shouted insults as they all made light of the possibility that they'd never see each other again. It was easier to joke about saying goodbye to friends of five years than to admit how much they would all miss each other.

Tom and Rooster trundled off to the car.

Until the moment they drove up to Rooster's house, Tom did not know where he lived. Cars were parked up and down the street, but Rooster drove up the driveway and into the garage as the automatic door opened—exposing an area big enough for six cars, a sleek black BMW parked in one corner.

'Jesus, Rooster, I didn't know you lived in a mansion! Bloody hell, Man, this is some garage!'

Rooster gave an embarrassed guffaw. 'I don't talk about it. My parents play down the fact that we're rich. They're Socialists at heart, although you'd never know it,' he added with a glance around the garage.

'There's a couple of guitars in the house and a piano so you can leave your stuff in the car. I'll lock it up. Your equipment will be safe in here.'

Once in the house, Tom looked around in amazement, his mouth hanging open as he surveyed the vastness of the living area. An imposing curved staircase dominated the entrance foyer. The huge double front doors made of dark stained timber and glass stood open, exposing the marble floor, which appeared to flow through the entire living area downstairs. Two kids Tom recognised from school wandered in through the front doors and Rooster turned away to speak to them, leaving Tom to wander through the house alone.

He entered the kitchen — it could have been a kitchen in the biggest and best restaurant in the country by the size of the room and the display of appliances. A uniformed waiter holding a tray of champagne flutes offered Tom a drink. He took a glass and savoured the deliciousness of the contents as he shook his head gently to make sure he wasn't dreaming. *Probably the best French champagne,* he thought, and smiled as he continued his discovery tour, nodding hello to some others he passed, until he entered what was referred to as The Lounge Room—more like the richly furnished lounge of an expensive hotel. He stopped dead in his tracks and gasped in awe.

There, in a corner of the room, on an elevated area akin to a small stage, in all its shining, opulent glory, stood the most highly polished, magnificent, full-sized grand piano Tom had ever seen. The lid was fully open and rested on a lid prop, exposing the inner workings of the piano—the soundboard, the hammers and strings, the dampers. The key lid was also open as if beckoning someone to come and caress its keys and release the perfect sound only a grand piano of this quality could make.

Tom stepped closer to have a better look at 'the real deal.' He had only ever played electric keyboards, but had often wondered what a grand piano would feel like. Was it *that* much different to play? Was the tone *that* much different to the ear? He carefully placed his half-empty champagne glass next to the magnificent white floral arrangement on the antique console near the piano and slid onto the padded seat of the matching black piano stool. He brushed his right hand over the keys. *Yep, the ivory keys certainly felt different to the electric keyboard 'black and whites.'*

He glanced around to see if anyone was watching him. He was surprised to see how many people were in the room, but nobody was taking any notice of the guy sitting at the piano, so he played an arpeggio. *Yep, the tone was about one hundred times finer and more mellow than his electric keyboard.* At a guess, he was sitting at a Steinway worth somewhere in the vicinity of $200,000.

He couldn't resist continuing to caress the keys and began to play one of the tunes he had written recently. To his ear, it sounded like a symphony. The cadence and subtlety of tone was mesmerising, and he continued to play, lost in the silky feeling of the music which emanated from this superb instrument. *Oh, you could become addicted to this.*

Out of the corner of his eye, he saw Rooster walking towards the piano, carrying a black and white Fender Stratocaster guitar in one hand.

'Hey Tom, how about we play something together?' and, handing the guitar to Tom, said: 'Here, try this for size. You're on my patch now. Let's play some jazz.' He added with a wicked grin.

In one fluid movement, Tom stood up and Rooster took his place on the piano stool. As Tom placed the strap around his neck and released his curled fingers across the nickel-plated steel strings, Rooster played a smooth jazz intro to 'A Whiter Shade of Pale.'

'You know this, you know you do,' laughed Rooster. 'C Major—couldn't be easier.'

The two young musicians slipped into jamming mode and became oblivious to many of the guests who had gathered around the pair to listen to the music. Although it was a classic pop song, Rooster and Tom put their own spin on it and it took on a new life as quintessential jazz. The crowd broke out into spontaneous applause.

As the pair finished, a tall, extremely attractive girl brought over a fresh glass of champagne for Tom and a beer for Rooster. Rooster pulled a small table out from next to the piano. 'Here, put your glass on this. Mom would have a fit if anyone put a glass down on her precious piano.' Tom took a mouthful of champagne and placed his glass on the small table as one of the guests called out: 'How about Smooth Operator?'

The two boys replied as one: 'Good choice!' and so began a bracket of four or five songs with wide appeal.

Tom was enjoying himself immensely. This was the way he loved to play his guitar, loosely, informally, from the heart, and he realised sadly, that he was going to miss this feeling when he went to Melbourne—this intimacy, this almost secret kinship with another musician, playing in their own little world. He also realised how much he'd missed chatting (well, listening mostly) with Rooster, his relentless good humour, even his bossiness.

They had been drinking between each number, and Tom was feeling a dangerous combination of headiness and elation. As they finished The Girl from Ipanema, an older man approached Rooster and handed him a small plastic bag. Rooster slid around on the piano stool as the other man pulled up a couple of chairs for Tom and himself.

'Yo, Dave, thanks Man. I see you've already got one rolled. Oh, this is Tom, Tom—Dave. Tom's new to this party scene, Dave, maybe he'd like what you've got there.'

'Sure,' replied Dave. 'Smoke, Tom?'

'I don't smoke,' replied Tom with a gentle wave of his hand, although his interest was piqued by the plastic bag out of which Rooster took the makings of a roll-your-own.

'Oh, don't worry, Tom,' said Rooster, 'it's not a cigarette, no tobacco or nicotine. Harmless, but you'll like how it affects you're playing. Heightens the senses, so to speak. Go ahead, try it. You'll be glad you did.'

Tom hesitated for a moment. He'd heard Rooster smoked weed occasionally but had never felt the desire to try it himself. Not that he'd ever been offered any. But his defences were down. Here was his chance, and why not? As Rooster said, it's harmless, and he had to admit, he was curious.

He took the pre-rolled joint Dave offered him, vaguely noticing that Rooster was already part-way through rolling another. Dave leaned in and clicked a cigarette lighter under Tom's smoke as he put it between his lips. The blue flame of the lighter flared and Tom inhaled as the flame caught the paper and it glowed into life.

He had tried a couple of cigarettes with Josh down behind the school playing fields a year or two ago and hadn't liked it, the taste of the tobacco acrid in his mouth, but this, this was much softer and the sweet, pungent smell was almost aromatic. He coughed as he inhaled the second puff.

Nice feeling, Tom thought, *to be at a party where people were friendly but not overwhelming*. In fact, he was feeling quite mellow.

The three of them chatted for 20 minutes as they smoked, although later, Tom could recall none of their conversation.

'Have another drink and we'll play some more,' said Rooster as he disposed of the tiny end of what was left of his smoke.

Tom took a long drink of champagne before picking up the guitar. He felt energised and relaxed at the same time and couldn't wait to play. His fingers felt sensitive, free, a mind of their own, and when he played the first riff, it was the best riff he'd ever played. *Wow, I didn't know I was capable of that.* Rooster was playing like a man with four hands. Together, they sounded like a symphony orchestra, and the surrounding crowd applauded appreciatively.

After a few more numbers, Tom leaned close to Rooster's ear and said: 'Got any food around here?' Before adding: 'What we need is another drink.'

'Absolutely,' said Rooster. 'I'll be back.' and he disappeared towards the kitchen. As soon as he'd walked away, a tall, attractive girl sat down on the piano stool and eyed Tom up and down. 'Hi, I'm Louise.'

Tom took her to be five or six years older than he was. She looked self-assured and used to getting her own way if appearances were anything to go by. The husky voice with the beautifully rounded vowels was breathy and sensual, and Tom looked more closely at her as he replied, 'I'm Tom.'

She had a languid manner about her; her heavily made-up smoky eyes looked out from beneath hooded lids, her cupid bow's mouth with its glossy finish, mesmerizing as it slowly curved into a Mona Lisa smile. She dipped her head slightly and glanced up at him from under the kohl-rimmed eyelids.

'Oh, yes, I know you're Tom. Everyone knows you're Tom. Rooster tells me you're going to be famous one day. Can I get you another drink?'

'I, uh, think Rooster has gone to get us a drink. And something to eat. I'm starving.'

'Would you like to have a look at the rest of the house, Tom?' Louise breathed, leaning in and casually placing her hand on his knee. She crossed her legs in such a way that Tom couldn't help but notice her thighs above her extremely short dress—firm and golden and smooth. A sudden thought entered his head and would not be silenced: *I wonder what it would be like to run my hand up the inside of her thigh?*

'Sure.' Tom mumbled just as Rooster returned with a fresh bottle of champagne tucked under one arm, a six-pack of beers swinging from one hand, and a plate bearing enough delicious looking finger food to feed half a dozen people in the other hand.

'Bugger off now, Louise. Tom and I are busy. You can show him the house later. We've got things to do.'

Undeterred, Louise stood up, and the smile widened to reveal perfect white teeth. 'I'll be back, Tom. Don't forget.' And in a cloud of delicious exotic fragrance, she disappeared into the crowd.

After devouring three curry puffs, several sausage rolls and countless small, perfectly constructed and precisely cut sandwiches, plus half the bottle of champagne, Tom picked up his guitar. Rooster turned on the stool, and gliding his hands over the keys, played the first couple of chords of Dancing in the Dark. Tom morphed into '1940s Supper Club' mode, and they played old numbers from the '40s and '50s, some guests even coupling up to dance intimately in the now dimly lit atmosphere of a party in full swing.

Five or six songs later, Rooster suggested they take a break, and the pair meandered out onto the back terrace to get some fresh air. A soft breeze found its way from the harbour to the back garden, bringing with it the heady perfume of the jasmine which covered the back garden wall. They were alone out here and, taking the plastic bag from his trouser pocket, Rooster extracted the makings of a smoke. He offered the open bag to Tom.

'Can you show me how to make one?' Tom asked tentatively. 'No problem,' replied Rooster, and proceeded to give Tom his introduction to rolling a joint. Rooster lit up and handed the joint to Tom, who melted into a blissed-out state much more quickly than before. The two of them sat on the back steps and enjoyed the night, Rooster prattling on about old times and how Tom was going to be famous, no doubt about it, while Tom listened with a broad grin on his face.

A while later, both boys stood up and stretched. As they made their way back inside, they bumped into a group of people on their way out, one of whom was Louise.

'Well, hello Tom, I was just looking for you and here you are! C'mon, I said I'd show you around the house.' And she took Tom by the hand and led him towards the staircase. Tom noticed one strap of her dress had slipped off her shoulder and she held an open bottle of champagne in her other hand. He felt himself blush when that previous thought ran through his mind again as he allowed himself to be guided up the stairs by this intriguing woman.

'Let's start with the room at the end of the hallway.' Louise almost hurried to the last door, which she opened with a flourish. 'As you can see,' she said with a husky giggle, 'this is a bedroom.' She gently pulled Tom into the room and silently closed the door. In one movement, she placed the bottle of champagne on the dressing table, wrapped her arms around Tom's neck and kissed him full on the mouth—much to Tom's delight. Drawing her to him, he parted his lips and felt Louise's tongue slide onto his, as they shared a lingering and sexually titillating kiss.

Louise deftly pushed Tom back against the wall and before he knew what was happening, she had his belt undone and her hand inside his pants.

His voice reflected a cross between panic and anticipation as it caught in his throat: 'Careful, Louise, someone might come in and catch us like this.' The effects of the weed hadn't completely worn off and he was torn between the fear of someone walking in on them and a state of extremely heightened sexual excitement.

'Don't worry, they wouldn't dare,' she whispered, as she placed one of his hands between her legs.

'Christ, you're not wearing any knickers.'

'All the easier to fuck you.' She murmured against his lips as she pushed his pants down around his knees and gripped his buttocks.

That did it! That was it! He could wait no longer, and within seconds, he was inside her.

Tom had been out with a few girls before and had even made out with a one or two who hung around the band from time to time, but they had always stopped him before he could go 'all the way.' He had never actually had full on sex before this moment. His mind was a blur as he raced to an uncontrolled climax. Louise dug her nails into his back as he shuddered in the ecstasy of the ultimate moment, wringing wet and panting, not only from the physical exertion, but from the intense sensation of what had just happened.

'Congratulations.' Louise took a step back and appraised the tall, darkly handsome young man. 'That was as good as I thought it would be.' She took a deep breath. 'Here, have a drink.' she smiled as she handed him the champagne bottle and smoothed down her dress.

'Did you plan that?' Tom asked in amazement.

'Absolutely! You are hot, Tom Watson. H.O.T.'

A smile spread across Tom's face and widened into a huge grin.

'Really? You're not bad yourself.'

He handed the bottle back to her, and she took a swig as he straightened his clothing and did up his belt.

Louise smiled, shyly. 'We could do this again if you like. I'll slip my phone number into your pocket before you leave.'

'Sure. That would be great. I'll ring you,' said Tom, glibly. *Wasn't that what you said in this type of situation?* 'Come on, we'd better get back to the party before we're missed,' and they sauntered down the stairs as if she was a Real Estate Agent showing a prospective buyer around the house. At the foot of the stairs, Louise turned and headed for the kitchen, gently nudging Tom in the opposite direction.

Entering the Living Room, a waiter carrying a tray of champagne-filled glasses approached Tom. He took another glass and downed the contents before a small group of guests stopped him and insisted on telling him how much they had enjoyed the music and inquiring if he intended to make music his career, as Joe does. As Tom chatted with them, a thought made him smile inwardly: *I wonder what they'd say if they knew I'd just had sex for the first time in my life!* He suppressed a chuckle as he moved on.

Minutes later, another group caught his attention. 'Hey Tom, can we get you a drink to show our appreciation for the music?'

'Sure.' A woman in the group passed him another glass of champagne, but by the third mouthful, he suddenly felt overwhelmed with tiredness, exhausted, and absolutely wasted.

He found Rooster, who was arguing loudly with two other guys about politics, and interrupted him when one of them stopped to take a breath.

'I need to call it a night. I'm buggered, Man. I need to get home and into bed, it's been a long day. Thanks for inviting me to the party. I can't remember ever enjoying myself so much.' He ran his hand through his dishevelled hair as he tried to concentrate on what he needed to say. 'Can I call a cab?'

'No need,' replied Rooster jovially. 'You look wrecked. I'll drive you home. Your stuff's in my car anyway. I stopped drinking a fair while ago so I should be OK. Besides, I need an excuse to get away from these two idiots, neither of whom knows what they're talking about. They're both stoned.' He slapped one of them on the back as he turned to Tom.

'If you're sure that's OK with you. I'd appreciate it.'

The two found their way to the garage and slid into the car as the automatic door opened. In less than a minute, they were on the road to Tom's place.

The streets were empty. Tom had lost track of time; he'd completely forgotten it was the early hours of Sunday morning. They were turning into Tom's Street when Rooster said:

'I hope Louise didn't annoy you too much. Don't feel bad; she annoys everyone. She can be a pest.'

Tom glanced at Rooster. 'No. She didn't annoy me. How do you know her, where does she fit in, how come she was at the party?' he asked, trying to sound casual. Tiredness was overtaking him and he was only minutes away from falling asleep, desperately trying to keep his eyes from closing, when Rooster's voice brought him back to the moment.

'Oh, I thought you knew. She's my sister. She's married to that dickhead, Geoffrey, who you met earlier.'

Tom's eyes flew wide open, and he twisted his head to look out the car window, hoping Rooster couldn't see the look of shocked horror on his face. Wild thoughts raced through his pounding head.

Sister!

Married!

Christ, what have I done?

Thank God I'm moving to Melbourne in a couple of days.

Chapter 5

Early Sunday morning, Jim received a call from the airline advising him that Sydney airport was now back in business after yesterday's blackout and asking him if he would like to catch an earlier flight than the three-thirty. He said if there was one around ten-thirty in the morning, he would take it. This would get him home by one-thirty at the latest, about five hours earlier than he had expected.

Which was why he arrived home unexpectedly early on Sunday afternoon.

Tom, who had passed out on his bed fully clothed in the early hours of the morning, stirred at the sound of a loud crash downstairs, followed a short while later by his father's heavy footsteps on the stairs. He glanced at his watch and saw it was only one-twenty. What the hell??? His dad wasn't expected home until five-thirty and he'd left all his equipment in the hall inside the front door, too tired to put it away this morning when Rooster dropped him off. If there was one thing Jim was a stickler for, it was putting away whatever you had used when you'd finished with it. *That crash must have been dad tripping over the equipment. He'll be annoyed, angry even,* thought Tom as he tried to get up.

But the throbbing pain in his head wouldn't let him. He fell back down on the bed, now feeling nauseous and faint, the foul taste in his mouth surpassed only by his blurred vision.

'Water, I need water.' He mumbled, slowly getting his legs over the side of the bed and looking around for the glass of water he always kept on the bedside table.

Jim opened the door and put his head around the doorway. 'What's with all the stuff in the hall? How many times have I asked you to put everything away before you go to bed?' Pause. 'But then you haven't been to bed, have you? How was the dance? You look the worse for wear.'

'Yeah, well, you would too if you'd gone to a party after the dance and jammed for most of the night and smoked marijuana and had sex with a married woman—all of which I enjoyed immense-ly!' he screamed to himself in his head. But he said mildly:

'The dance was terrific. Rooster asked me back to a party at his place and we jammed for a bit.' His head ached, and he felt irritable with his father for getting home early—as well as feeling so terribly hungover. He wished he could pass out again.

Jim was also irritable, and sore where he had skinned his shin on an amplifier which had been left at the front door. He was annoyed his son had taken advantage of the fact that Jim wouldn't get home until five-thirty that evening and had stayed out all night. The kid was eighteen, and he wouldn't have objected had he known, but Tom had gone behind his back thinking he'd never find out.

'Well, it looks like you had far too much to drink. I hope there weren't any drugs at this party. And I certainly hope you didn't have unprotected sex with some girl you didn't know.'

Tom nearly laughed out loud. *Oh, if only you knew*, he thought, but the inner mirth quickly faded when he remembered his father had an inbuilt antenna for knowing what was going on below the surface.

'Get up and have a shower, then come and move all your stuff out of the hallway. I'll make us a cup of coffee and fill you in on the next couple of days.' The anger had gone out of Jim's voice, and he had resumed his usual calm persona.

Tom breathed a sigh of relief and dragged himself up off the bed and into the shower. By the time he'd dried off and put on some clean clothes, he felt almost normal, pleased with himself it hadn't taken him long to recover from a drug-induced, far-too-much-champagne/not-enough-sleep hangover. Once downstairs, he collected all his musical equipment from the hall and stacked it in its usual place, smiling all the while as he recalled Louise's seduction of him in every lurid detail. What a night it had been!

Two cups of freshly brewed coffee sat on the kitchen island countertop. Jim was perched on a stool scanning the Sunday papers and Tom pulled a stool up to the opposite side of the island and took a sip of the steaming liquid which tasted like nectar of the Gods given the current circumstances. 'So, tell me about the dance,' Jim said, folding the paper and putting it aside.

'Dad, it was terrific. They loved us, wouldn't let us go until we'd played five encores. Everyone had such a good time, which was why I went to Rooster's party—I wanted to hold on to that feeling for as long as I could.' Tom was silent for a moment as he remembered how good it felt being on stage, playing to a wildly appreciative audience who were generous with their applause and accolades. He went on: 'We played some great older numbers from your era, absolute classics. I'd forgotten what good music had been produced during that period.'

Jim smiled. He didn't like being patronised by his son, but he was genuinely glad Tom had enjoyed his end-of-year activities. It was a milestone in his coming of age—almost 18, no longer the schoolboy, soon to be a student at a leading university, and beginning to make his mark on the world.

'It sounds like it was a memorable ending to your high school years, something you can look back on in the years to come.'

Jim took a mouthful of his coffee and continued: 'And now onto the next chapter in the life of Tom Watson. The plan is for the two of us to finish off the packing tomorrow, although most of it is already done. The removalists will be here at ten o'clock Tuesday morning so we'll need to be finished by then.'

Tom interrupted: 'I'm meeting up with the others tomorrow afternoon to say goodbye. I'll be out for a couple of hours, be back by about five. Also, Dad, I don't want the removalists taking my equipment in their van, can we take it in the car with us?'

'If it'll fit. The move is all about compromise, Tom. We might have to make some allowances along the way but don't worry, we'll be here while they load everything.'

Tom made to interrupt again, but his father put his hand up to stop him. 'Let me finish please.' He opened up a large map and smoothed it out on the kitchen counter. A bright red permanent marker line snaked its way down the map from Sydney to Melbourne on the coastal road. Jim turned the map around to show Tom.

'This is the route we're going to follow,' he said, running his finger along the red line. 'We'll drive down the Princes Highway. H.P. is sending the cleaners in at one o'clock on Tuesday so we can leave as soon as they arrive. I reckon we should get to Narooma by about seven o'clock that night, in time to check into the motel and get some dinner. If we leave Narooma by about nine on Wednesday morning, we should arrive in Melbourne by six on Wednesday night. I've booked us into the Hyatt in Melbourne on Wednesday night as the removalists won't arrive at the house in Richmond until about ten o'clock on Thursday morning, so we'll meet them there.'

'The plan looks good on paper. I hope it works out OK,' said Tom, not quite convinced.

Chapter 6

The unknown is always interesting.

Tom had given little thought to Melbourne ever since he found out they were going to move there at the end of the year. What with studying for final exams and preparing for the end-of-year dance at school, he had not had the time nor the inclination to wonder what Melbourne might be like as a place to live. He knew it was the second largest city in Australia with a population of around three million people and that it was well-known for its many parks and gardens, but that was the extent of his knowledge of the place. He had also heard Melbournians were mad about Australian Rules football, regarded it almost as a religion, but this information meant little to Tom—he wasn't interested in any form of sport, much less football!

They had arrived in early December and although the drive from Sydney had not been the perfect road trip Jim had planned, the two men had eventually unpacked. The house in Richmond was in direct contrast to the previous house in Sydney. A warehouse conversion which had been done out in the latest open plan style, it was modern minimalist and furnished accordingly; whereas the

Sydney house had been a cosy cottage, furnished in an eclectic and comfortable style.

Both Jim and Tom were surprised by the new 'house,' unpleasantly at first, but it quickly grew on them. It was summer, and the openness of the place was a cool and inviting haven from the intensity of the summer heat. Jim's predecessor had purchased the warehouse building on behalf of the company two years ago as an investment property, a wise choice indeed. In two years, it had increased in value by almost 40% thanks to its position in the heart of Richmond and the excellent architectural design and workmanship of the warehouse conversion.

The entrance was virtually on the footpath of a cobbled lane. The front door opened directly into the enormous living area with its four-metre-high raked ceiling and sandstone tiled floor on which were scattered three or four large colourful rugs. A couple of leather sofas and three Wassily-type occasional chairs defined the sitting area and the biggest TV Tom had ever seen sat atop a low cabinet of blonde timber on steel legs. One corner of the living space contained a small, well-appointed all white kitchen and larger dining area with a glass-topped table and leather dining chairs. Two bedrooms, each with their own ensuite bathroom, formed the back half of the building. Much to Tom's delight, there was a small shed at the end of a back garden, which, as Jim pointed out, would make a great music room. A garage, accessible from the lane which ran along behind the building, was next to the shed.

With most of the unpacking completed over the weekend, Tom spent Monday checking out the local area. He decided to make his way into the city the next day, and, following a map he'd bought, walked to the Fitzroy Gardens. He spent the next half hour in the shady area and enjoyed the respectful ambience of the beautiful park before continuing his walk into the city.

Once in the city proper, he wandered the streets and lanes for several hours before catching a tram back home, which he enjoyed—no trams in Sydney. He soon discovered trams were a symbol of Melbourne and used extensively; they were by far the best and quickest way to get anywhere within a ten-kilometre radius of the city.

Melbourne soon began to feel familiar. At first it seemed a bit dour—Tom had taken the glitz and glamour of Sydney for granted, had readily accepted the brashness and beach mentality of the eastern suburbs. But this city was different. It felt older, more refined perhaps, maybe even slightly European. The many gardens and parks gave it a certain elegance in a distinct contrast to the brassiness of the glitter city on the harbour.

By the end of the week, Tom thought it was time to investigate some of the live music venues he'd read about. He took a walk along Swan Street on the Friday evening and had crossed the intersection of Lennox Street when he heard strains of music coming from the building on the next corner. He followed the sound of music to its origin at the Corner Hotel.

Outside the pub, groups of mostly young men and women clustered around tables, enjoying the warm evening whilst eyeing up each other and the competition.

He entered the pub and was immediately struck by the buzzy atmosphere of the crowded interior. The room was so much smaller than he had expected. The smell of stale beer, sweat, and cigarette smoke completed the image of an inner-city Melbourne pub.

Members of a live band were setting up in the corner and a few folk had already gathered near the stage in anticipation

Tom absorbed the atmosphere as he meandered through the room, and it excited him, as if something significant was about to happen. He bought a beer and found a place to stand and take in the scene as the room hummed with anticipation.

The sound of instruments being tuned, of drums being checked out, of mics being tapped and tested, was balm for the soul as far as Tom was concerned. At last, the leader stepped up to the mic, and the room fell silent.

'Good evening, ladies and gentlemen. We're The Dandy Rats and we're here to entertain you. AND YOU'RE GONNA LOVE US!!!'

The crowd erupted in thunderous applause. Tom joined in, caught up in the moment, and the band began to play, loudly, and with gusto. He looked around at the expectant faces, smiling with delight, drinking it all in. *I could become a part of this,* thought Tom. *These are my people.* The fellow standing next to him turned unexpectedly and bumped Tom's arm, pushing him into the bar where he was standing.

'Oh, sorry mate, I was getting a bit carried away there,' shouted the man over the music. 'I didn't mean to crash into you like that. But they're great, aren't they?'

'That they are,' said Tom as loudly as he could manage while remaining polite, instantly forgiving anyone who thought the band was 'great.'

The other man sensed a fellow music lover and continued the conversation at top volume, 'Do you come here often? I haven't seen this group here before although I've seen them at other pubs. Their guitarist is the best!'

'This is my first time here,' replied Tom. 'I'm new to Melbourne, just sussing out live music venues. And you're right about the guitarist.'

The other guy picked up his beer and took a swig. 'I heard he's leaving them next week, going overseas to try his luck in the UK, I think. I don't know what they're going to do without him.'

The hairs on the back of Tom's neck stood up. So, the band would be without a guitarist soon. He couldn't let an opportunity like this go by.

'So, which one is the leader?' asked Tom, trying to appear casual.

'I think the drummer is the leader of the group. I know Joe who runs this pub, and he told me the drummer made the booking direct. They don't appear to have a manager.'

Later that night, as the pub rocked to the sound of loud music and an appreciative Friday night crowd, the band played their final number and left the stage to deafening applause and foot stomping. They began packing up their instruments and Tom excused himself from the man's company and approached the drummer. After glancing around at the other band members, he spoke directly to the drummer.

'Great show tonight. Fantastic sound! Have you guys been playing together long?'

The drummer and bass guitarist both smiled at Tom as the drummer replied, 'I reckon about three years. We'll play anywhere, anytime, but we specialise in the pub circuit. Is this the first time you've seen us?'

'Yeah, I'm new to Melbourne, just sussing out the live music scene. I don't suppose you guys know of any group who's looking for a guitarist, do you? I play a mean guitar, keyboard too. I'm looking to get into a band while I'm studying at uni.'

'Is that so?' The drummer glanced at the bass guitarist and winked. 'This is Nat Glasso, our bass guitar, and I'm Johnno Thompson.'

'Tom Watson,' said Tom as he shook hands with the two young men.

'We practice at Nat's place over in Collingwood every Saturday afternoon. Why don't you come along tomorrow, and we'll see how you go?'

Tom managed to hide his excited intake of breath. 'That would be great. Thanks. What's the address and what time do you want me there?'

Johnno wrote the address and time on the back of a much-used drinks coaster he found on the floor as the others finished packing up.

'See you tomorrow, Johnno,' they called collectively, as they lugged their instruments out the back door, Nat with his arms full of Johnno's drum kit.

'Sure. Two o'clock. Don't be late.' Turning to follow them, he looked back over his shoulder at Tom. 'See you at two o'clock too, Tom.'

It was more of a command than a comment. *Looks like I've met another bloody 'Rooster,* thought Tom, as he sidled out the front door of the pub. He made his way up the street in high spirits, grinning from ear to ear. As he turned the corner, he punched the air with his fist and yelled: 'I'm as good as in. I'm going to be a Dandy Rat! Woo Hoo.'

Because Tom had borrowed his dad's car on Saturday afternoon, he could take two guitars and the keyboard. It was two o'clock as he pulled into the driveway of the given address.

'Hi Tom,' called Johnno from the front door, 'Come on through. We're down the back in the garage.' Tom lugged his equipment down to the garage.

Introductions were made and as Tom placed his two guitars on the floor of the garage, he noticed that although he'd arrived right at two pm, the others were already set up and about to start.

'I'd like to sit and watch you guys for a few minutes if you don't mind. Get a feel for your arrangements and rhythm, how you fit together,' said Tom, as he took the initiative and pulled a milk crate out from the corner and sat on it. In doing so, he dislodged some oily rags from their nesting place and the smell of car engines and motor oil wafted up and temporarily overwhelmed him. It was a garage after all, and as he looked around him, he noticed the gleaming black powerful looking motor bike near the roller shutter door. *Wouldn't mind a go on that*, Tom thought to himself before he was pulled back to the present by Johnno, who grinned and said,

'Sure, good idea. We do lots of covers so nothing new there, but we also do a few of our own arrangements. See if you can fit in with them later.' Johnno climbed onto the drum seat as he spoke and reached for his sticks.

That first practice session at Nat's place was an eye-opener for Tom. This was no high school boys' band jamming in the gym after school. This organised group of musicians took their playing seriously and followed their captain's lead with little or no argument. Any 'questions' from the band members to Johnno were phrased as suggestions or comments, and Johnno took all comments on board respectfully. For these young men, their music was not a part-time hobby, it was their *raison d'être*. Although they each had a day job, payment for which kept them clothed and fed and paid the rent, they lived to play music and would have done so for nothing rather than knock back a gig because there was no money in it.

As they played, Tom observed each member individually, not only their playing ability but their demeanour, their body language, and how they held their instruments.

Johnno was not unlike Rooster, short, stocky, not exactly untidy but dishevelled, and wearing the oldest pair of Doc Martens ever, older even than his worn and torn jeans. Tom thought he was 22 or 23. His fair, colourless thin hair looked like it had last seen a comb back in 1980, but it also looked like there wouldn't be much of it left by the time he was 40. He wore a small gold hoop earring in one ear, and a tattoo of what looked like a scorpion seemed to climb up his neck out of his shirt collar, as if reaching for the earring. But all that faded into nothingness when he smiled. All you noticed was the smile. The most devilish, wicked, charming, smile.

By contrast, Nat was like a young boy. But a boy who could play the bass guitar as if it was an extension of his arms. A natural at rhythm and understanding the meaning of deep sound, able to play the right notes at the right time. He wore his long, dark hair with its bleached highlights, pulled back in a ponytail on the nape of his neck. His dark brown, almost black eyes looked like they might hide a secret, and he glanced around the room constantly, perhaps to see who was looking at him. This was no ordinary person who played the guitar, this was someone who lived and breathed music, obvious just from the look of him. He oozed rhythm. When he walked, it was as if he walked to the beat of his inner drum. It was a musical walk. Hard to tell his age, possibly older than he looked, pleasant face, neat and tidy, but above all, his admiration for Johnno showed openly on his face. A person of few words, he let his guitar do the talking.

Mark Tuckerson was their keyboard player—6'3" and skinny, he had to bend his long, lean body at a most uncomfortable angle to get his hands on the keyboard. Although Mark was an accomplished pianist, he had none of the Rooster's flair or natural ability. Mark's style was born in classical lessons and many hours of practice. *His parents must be devastated he plays in a rock band,* thought Tom, *no wonder he doesn't smile.* His fair buzz cut hair went perfectly with his long, unsmiling face which, unfortunately, gave him the appearance of being an inmate out on day release, and not much fun. How wrong that assumption turned out to be!

Joe Epstein was the direct opposite of Mark. At 5'6", Joe was mischief on legs. He played several instruments, none of them particularly well, except the rhythm guitar, at which he excelled. He made up for his not-quite-fabulous ability on the other instruments with his sense of humour. The band clown, Joe could keep things running smoothly if there was ever any tension in the band. He was one of the most likeable people Tom had ever met, completely unaffected.

And then there was Scott MacDonald, the guitarist whom Tom had heard was leaving the band soon to travel overseas. The shock effect of his short black hair and bright turquoise eyes set him apart before you even noticed his handsome face and toned physique. He wore a similar black T-shirt and black jeans to those he'd been wearing last night but the black cowboy boots were different—today's boots had high Cuban heels—and with the added black leather sleeveless jacket over the T-shirt, the look screamed 'Rock Band Guitarist.' He oozed confidence, which was amplified when he played guitar. He was good, and he knew it: knew he was good looking, knew he was cool, paraded it for all to see. Yes, he was going to smash it in the UK. They would wonder what hit them when Scott arrived on the scene over there. Tom disliked him instantly.

The band's name amused Tom, and he wondered who invented it. They were anything but Dandy, but the Rats part seemed appropriate.

He was mesmerised by their look, their sound, their performance. Even in practice, they were to be taken seriously. Collectively, they reminded him of the Rooster. He had taken his music seriously enough to make it his vocation, and within the first five minutes of absorbing the essence of this group of men, on this Saturday afternoon, in a weatherbeaten and much used backyard garage, Tom made a life-affirming decision to become a professional musician. He wanted to be a member of this band.

The moment they finished the current number, Tom jumped up from his milk crate, knocking it over. His words tumbled over each other as they spilled out of his mouth.

'Let me show you what I can do.'

He picked up his guitar and played his favourite riff. He'd tuned the guitar before he left home, so he knew it was ready to go and, without waiting for acknowledgement, he played as he had never played before. The others quickly picked up on the tune and joined in with their own arrangements of the number.

This was different. This was nothing like Pants on Fire. This was soul deep, heartfelt sound. This band played with purpose, as if their lives depended on the next chord, the next number, the next bracket. Tom's spirits soared in sync with the music.

At the end of that first number, Johnno smiled as he carefully placed his sticks on the smallest drum. He stood up from his drum seat and walked around to where Tom was standing. He extended his hand to Tom and grinned, as he said,

'That was pretty good. Let's play some more and see what happens.'

Pretty good? thought Tom. *That was sensational!*

But he kept that thought to himself and, as he shook Johnno's extended hand, replied casually: 'Glad you liked it.'

Johnno turned to Scott: 'Hey, Scott, how about you get us some beers from the fridge in the house while we listen to Tom without your back-up.'

Scott looked slightly miffed. 'Sure,' he muttered, as he placed his guitar on its stand and walked out the side door and up to the house, continuing to mutter to himself. Embarrassed, Tom stood still and waited to see what would happen next. Johnno suggested he take Scott's place in the pecking order and announced the name of the next number in the practice session. *Why should I feel embarrassed?* thought Tom. *I'm not the one leaving the band to seek greener pastures, as if Melbourne's not good enough for him!*

Forty-five minutes later, Scott wandered in with a carton of beer and set it down on the milk crate. 'Help yourselves, fellas. There wasn't any beer in the fridge in the house. I had to go up the street to the Bottle Shop to get this.'

As Johnno walked past Joe to get a beer out of the carton, he leaned in and whispered: 'That was the idea, mate.'

They had each taken a beer and were enjoying the feel of the cold liquid as it hit their parched throats. 'Ah, playing your favourite music gives you a thirst, don't ya know!' laughed Joe. They all agreed.

After that first hour of playing with a professional band, Tom was on a high; the music, the cold beers, the camaraderie, had energised and excited him. He couldn't hold back any longer. 'I heard Scott is going overseas soon. To the UK I believe. I'd like to apply for the position of guitarist with the Dandy Rats.' Nothing like being straightforward, his dad always said. If you don't ask, you don't get.

Johnno glanced around at the others as he smiled and said: 'I reckon that's not a bad idea. This is how it goes: I organise our gigs and control the money. If we're lucky we can get four gigs in a week, but the occasional week goes by when we don't have any. Each band member gets $100 per gig, and we pay Rodney, our Roadie, $50 a gig to set up our lighting and sound. I bank any leftovers. We're building up a fund to cover some of our expenses if we ever get to go on tour.'

'We've got a gig on Wednesday night at the Tote, at Collingwood. Six-thirty for a seven o'clock start. Don't be late.'

'Don't worry. I won't be.' And putting on his serious face to suppress his excitement, he shook hands with Johnno. 'And thanks.'

But inwardly his mind was spinning: *$100 a gig. four gigs a week. Go on Tour! This is a dream come true!* And then: *Thank you Mr. O'Brien. I'm glad I took notice when you were prattling on about practice, practice, practice.*

'Now come on you guys. As you were!'

Chapter 7

Because the move from Sydney to Melbourne had happened in December, it wasn't possible to organise a trip back to the States to spend Christmas with Gran and Aunt Lola. This turned out to be fortuitous for Tom as the gigs came thick and fast during the week leading up to Christmas; six gigs, including two on the same night at different venues. Fortunately, Tom had always enjoyed playing Christmas songs which was just as well as they played an awful lot of them during that week.

January was slower, but at least it gave them a chance to play some new stuff at practice. Tom was itching to play some songs he had written and get their opinions.

'I've written a couple of songs and I'd like to know what you guys think of them. I've sketched out some rough arrangements. Do you reckon you can follow them?' Tom handed around his arrangements and notes, which were scribbled in blue biro on scraps of writing pad paper. There were a few surprised looks and comments, but yes, they could follow the arrangements.

They played the tune Tom had written for the end-of-year dance. Although it was a bit rough the first time, and Tom had to make a few alterations to the arrangements, by the third try, the various instruments melded well, and Tom was satisfied they were on the right track. Johnno was quietly excited by what he was hearing and suggested they put a bit more time into it to get it exactly as Tom wanted it. On the fourth rendition, Tom sang the words—and transported the song to another level. There was a moment of silence when they finished, followed by a collective exhale of breath and a spontaneous round of applause.

'That is definitely included in our repertoire from now on. Got any more?' Johnno's enthusiasm had caught on and the other guys nodded in agreement.

Tom's head was always full of music stuff. The band was getting two, three, sometimes four gigs a week, and he spent most of any spare time he had practicing and experimenting with writing music and lyrics in his music room in the back garden. He preferred to compose on the small keyboard his dad had given him one Christmas rather than on one of the guitars: he could transcribe melody and bass more easily from keyboard to paper. As he became more proficient on the keyboard, he realised he needed to upgrade to a larger and more sophisticated one, especially as he was now making some money.

Unfortunately, his father was not happy with how Tom spent his days and nights.

'Have you done anything about enrolling at university yet?' Jim enquired during breakfast one weekday morning. Jim was ready for work and pouring himself a cup of coffee as Tom wandered into the kitchen in his pyjamas, looking the worse for wear after a late night playing a gig at Frankston. The long drive home had taken the edge off the gig at a hugely popular venue, playing to a great crowd, and he hadn't slept well. He needed coffee, and lots of it.

Tom knew by the irritated tone in his father's voice he needed to think of the answer his father wanted to hear, but his mind wasn't working as fast as usual thanks to the lack of sleep. He'd checked out the universities in Melbourne and surrounds but had made no enquiries about available courses. Tom knew this would not be a pleasant conversation.

'I haven't decided which course I'll take but I intend to finalise all of that today.' Nothing could be further from the truth. He'd agreed to meet up with Johnno and Joe later today to look at a new place opening in Brighton. They were hoping to be the opening night act.

'As I said before, Tom, you don't have to decide your entire future right now, but unless you're enrolled, you'll miss out on university altogether this year and you'll be a year behind everyone else. University starts at the end of February here, so you'd better get off your arse and act quickly or you'll end up doing Ancient Greek!'

'Sure, Dad. Don't worry. By the time you get home today, I'll be all set up and ready to go.'

'I'm getting tired of hearing nothing but the band and where you're playing and what you're playing. You're here to get a degree for your future career, Tom. The band is only a hobby thing.'

As soon as Jim left for work, Tom got on the phone. After several phone calls, he learned that even though most of the courses he was interested in were closed for applications, he could still apply to Science and Mathematics and, because of his pass mark, would probably be accepted. With panic beginning to set in, he decided then and there to enrol in Science and Mathematics at the University of Melbourne. It was not his first choice, but at least it would keep his father off his back. Tom was not especially clever at maths, he much preferred English, but he reckoned he could scrape through. At least he had his own computer, which he knew inside and out. He also knew computers and computer science were the future and, if nothing else, a degree in science would guarantee him a job with his father if his music ever failed him.

Having got university enrolment out of the way, he showered and dressed and was ready and waiting when Joe called to pick him up at two-thirty, as arranged.

The university year began in February, and although Tom found it monotonous, he had to complete his part of the deal he had made with his father when his dad had been transferred to Australia five years ago. The best part of university was that he made a friend of one of the other guys who was doing the same course as he was. He and Paul McElhone were both 18 and of a similar nature; neither was outgoing, although Tom was more gregarious than Paul. They often had a drink at the pub around the corner from campus after last class and a lifelong friendship was forged over many beers, over many afternoons.

Tom's life became a mix of university by day—three or four days a week—and gigs at night, if he was lucky.

He was developing his own style and wore black jeans and a black T-shirt or sweater every day, and rarely left home without the customary silver rings on several fingers of each hand. He liked how they caught the light when he played his guitar, but more importantly, each one evoked a certain subliminal memory or feeling.

The day before they left the States for Australia, Gran had given him the small plain signet ring, which he wore on the smallest finger of his right hand. He subconsciously touched it many times during a gig, as if saying, 'Thanks Gran. You made this possible.'

The lady at the Thrift shop in Paddington where he bought the large silver and onyx ring he always wore on the middle finger of his left hand told him it would bring him luck in his chosen career, and he repeated the prophecy to himself every day as he slipped it on his finger.

But his favourite ring was the wide Florentine silver band into which a dragon had been carved. It belonged to his mother's grandfather who, the story goes, had won it in a card game in China in the 1800s. The story had passed into family folklore and had been embellished with each telling until it reached the stage where one man had been shot during the card game, another thrown into jail and left to rot there by the Chinese. The ring had been passed down to each generation, gaining intrinsic value and fanciful tales on its journey to Tom's hand.

Early in the year, he had even found himself a girlfriend, one of the girls who swarmed around the band during, and especially after, a gig. Jennifer was a pretty brunette with an overt sex appeal, as experienced as Tom was innocent. The short skirts she favoured complimented her long, lean legs, and the leather jacket she often wore was always left undone, subtly revealing a skimpy and revealing singlet top. Jennifer had mastered the art of attracting men in her early teens and had practiced and polished that art until it shone. She had set her sights on Tom and had not let up until she got him into her bed following a drunken party at her flat one Friday night.

It was never a serious relationship as far as Tom was concerned, which was why he wasn't bothered when, after a short-lived fling, she brushed Tom aside and moved on to Nat, the bass guitarist. Jennifer had soon discovered Tom was only exciting when he was onstage and in his own world, adrenalin pumping, ignoring the surrounding crowd. Once he was removed from that spotlight of intoxication and glamour, he was just another average, boring bloke. Tom suspected Jennifer would be disappointed when she discovered Nat had even less to say than Tom and was even more involved in his music than the other band members. Tom smiled when he wondered how quickly Jennifer would find out she came a poor second to Nat's guitar—on a good day!

But of course, for Tom, there was always another girl to move into the space Jennifer had vacated. Amy was a petite blonde with enormous eyes and big hair and spoke with a lisp. She was cute and eager and made more of an impact on Tom, but he soon found her paranoid fear of falling pregnant off-putting. Their relationship didn't make it to the three-month mark.

Then one night, while they were playing a gig, a couple of girls Johnno knew in his day job and a few of their friends invited the boys to join them at their table for a drink between sets. Tom took the last vacant seat next to one of the girls and, as a way of beginning a conversation, she asked,

'How long have you been playing with the Dandy Rats?'

It was a question he'd been asked many times before, usually by groupies who followed pub bands from place to place, hoping to crack on to one of the members.

'Oh, a few months,' he replied, as he took a mouthful of his beer. He set the glass down on the table without looking at her.

'My name's Ann, by the way, Ann Thompson,' she said, extending her hand to him. 'What's yours?'

'Ah, Tom, Tom Watson.' He took her hand and held it for a moment. It was warm and soft but with a certain firmness, the fingers long and slender like his own, and he noticed she wasn't wearing any rings. Tom turned his head to get a better look at her and inadvertently looked directly into her eyes. She held eye contact with him for a moment, which he found disconcerting, especially as he was still holding her hand. Releasing his grip, he looked away and took another sip of his beer as he tried to think of what to say next. He need not have worried; Ann was a natural at small talk and deftly put him at ease.

'So, tell me, Tom Watson, exactly how easy is it to write music?'

She smiled directly at him as she spoke. Tom felt slightly discombobulated. He turned on his chair and looked her up and down, trying not to make it too obvious, which didn't altogether work. She was lovely. Her short, curly blonde hair framed a pixie-like face. She had a wide, amiable smile, and her bright blue eyes twinkled mischievously. He relaxed when he saw she was wearing a T-shirt and jeans, normal attire for a pub-goer, about as unlike a band groupie as you can get.

They were deep into a conversation about lyrics and Tom was enjoying leaning in close to her mouth so he didn't miss a word of what she was saying. If he leaned in even further, he could catch a whiff of a fragrance he could only describe as 'pretty.' A memory of his mother scooted across the back of his mind, and he smiled inwardly as a warm and pleasant feeling washed over him.

'Ay, Lover Boy, come on. Sorry to drag you away, but it's time to play some music.' Mark laughed as he dragged Tom's chair out from the table and pulled him to his feet. 'This is our last set for the night. You can come back and talk to the lady when we've finished for the night. OK?'

Tom had already decided to ask her out at the first opportunity when they'd completed the gig.

It was early November when Jim suggested he and Tom think about Christmas and start planning their trip back home to the States. 'Let's talk about it on Saturday morning over breakfast.' Tom could tell by his father's tone it wouldn't matter what Tom may have planned for Saturday morning; this discussion was non-negotiable.

As they sat at the breakfast bar on the Saturday morning, Tom splashed some cold milk onto his breakfast cereal before adding half a dozen fat strawberries. He glanced over at the calendar Jim had spread out in front of him and was alarmed at the number of days blacked out in December. The blacked-out area looked huge—most of December—from where he sat.

'I think we should go for at least three weeks this year. We missed out last year because of the move, and the women have been complaining about not seeing you for ages. I know you speak with your grandmother every couple of weeks, but she and Lola want to spend some time with you, hear all about how you're doing at university, the band, and everything else you're involved with.

What do you reckon if we left December 12 and got back around January 4?'

Tom did a quick calculation in his head—*just over three weeks away from home, on average six gigs a week at this time of year, at $100 a gig. Great—a holiday in the States would cost him $2,000 in lost earnings. Plus, Ann had been getting antsy lately, saying he wasn't showing her as much attention, complaining that he'd changed since she had first started dating him. Honestly, women! They're more trouble than they're worth! He had a feeling this holiday was going to cost him dearly.*

'Gee Dad, that's a long time to be away. I understand what you mean, but I'll lose a lot of income. You know I don't get any holiday pay or anything.'

'Let's not lose sight of the bigger picture here. Remember, Tom, you're here to get your degree, and the university is on holiday, so you won't be missing out on any study. Your music and the band is a hobby. The fact you make a few dollars from it is incidental.'

Tom could see his father was obdurate on this point and it would be futile to try to convince him otherwise. He hoped Johnno would be more understanding when he told him he'd be away for three weeks, and that they would need to find a fill-in lead guitar for that period.

Unfortunately, Johnno's reaction was the opposite of what Tom was hoping for.

'Are you fucking joking?' Johnno's thick black eyebrows dipped in the middle in a glare that made little kids fear for their lives. He waved both arms in the air and Tom suspected smoke might explode from his ears any minute. 'Where do you think we're going to get a fill-in at this time of year? You know we take holidays in the middle of the year when it's quiet. You also know how many gigs I've got lined up for us over Christmas. We've got a better fucking chance of finding a full-time replacement for you.'

Silence. The air was charged with Johnno's anger. The glare did not soften as he brought his arms down and thumped them into place on his hips and continued the death stare at Tom. His reaction shocked Tom, but he remained calm and stood very still, although his insides felt like swirling liquid. Johnno knew Tom was important to the band, he'd built up quite a following with his original stuff, and the girls loved him, but Johnno was angry—he'd put so much effort into locking in a lot of gigs over the holiday period. He'd been running this band for a few years and couldn't back down because one guitarist bucked his system.

'It's all or nothing, Tom—either convince your father you can't go to the States or find another band to play with when you get back. The music industry is fickle enough as it is without messing us about by going away at the wrong time of year. We'll keep you on until you go away. Hopefully, we will have found another guitarist by then.'

Johnno's outburst set Tom back on his heels. This was his first taste of rejection in his young life, and he was crushed. So, this is what it felt like to get the sack! He also knew his father would never budge on the trip to the States for Christmas. In short, he would no longer be a Dandy Rat come December.

The following morning at breakfast, Tom told Jim about John-no's reaction. He was still hurting and angry until Jim offered his take on the situation.

'Can I make a suggestion?' Jim asked as he buttered his toast. He stalled for time by adding peanut butter and honey to the slice of buttery toast and licking his fingers. He didn't always have time for a decent breakfast, but he had a major board meeting this morning and could handle it better on a full stomach.

Tom glanced up from his cereal at his father standing on the other side of the breakfast bar. 'What?'

'Speak to a lawyer quick smart about royalties and how you go about receiving them for your compositions when they're performed in public. I'll cover the cost. He can also tell you about copyright and music licencing. These things can be important, especially when you're working in the creative field. It could also be important when you're negotiating with a new band next year. If they're half-way professional, they'll realise you're serious about your music.'

Tom stared into his breakfast bowl, mostly milk now he'd eaten all the last bits of cereal, the spoonful of milk half-way to his mouth. He placed the spoon gently back into the bowl as he raised his head and looked at his father.

'I'd never thought of that. But you're right. I'm sure The Dandy Rats will continue to play my songs. We've built up a bit of a following of people who really like my songwriting. Some of my stuff is even being requested. Thanks, Dad.'

'One thing I've learned, Tom, is you always protect yourself in any business dealings. Writing music is one thing, making money from your original compositions is a whole other ball game. It pays to dot the i's and cross the t's early in the piece. Don't wait until the shit hits the fan.'

Chapter 8

Within two days of getting back from the States after a wonderful time regaling Gran and Aunt Lola with tales of the band, university, breaking up with Ann, and what he wanted to accomplish in the next year, Tom was out and about checking out bands on the Melbourne pub scene. Damn! They all had surprisingly good guitarists.

By day four, he was feeling despondent, and he didn't even have Ann to cheer him up. She had been a good listener, always offered her shoulder to cry on when he had a bad day, and then there was her bed—that big soft queen-sized bed with the pale blue girly sheets with pink flowers all over them and the multitude of colour co-ordinated pillows. The bed and pillows filled the bedroom in her one-bedroom flat; the bed she would lead him to, whispering how she knew ways of making him feel better (even if he felt good at the time).

But the relationship with Ann changed forever one night during the week before he left for America. The band had sat around drinking and talking music after the pub closed. They didn't include Ann in their conversation, the in-house jokes, the childish skylarking. She was on the outer, like all the other girls she'd seen in the same situation over the months she had been seeing Tom, and which she had secretly vowed to never become. Well, she was sick of it. Tired of sitting around in grungy pub lounges like a stale bottle of beer, waiting for the band to finish their gig for the night, waiting for Tom to drive her home and crawl into her bed, occasionally falling asleep within minutes of his head hitting the pillow, ignoring the lovely young woman lying beside him.

Which is exactly what happened on that particular night. Ann poked him hard in the ribs and Tom woke with a start.

'Oooow! What was that for?'

'Sit up, Tom. I want to talk to you. Now!'

Oh, please, not again, thought Tom. *I'm too tired for this right now.* But he sat up and faced her, and mentally prepared to be ticked off for something he didn't even know he'd done, or not done.

'I'm sick of it, Tom. You make me feel like the fifth wheel when you're with the band—unnecessary and in the way. It's like you're all in some of 'special club' for 'special people.' And you're not special. None of you! You're like kids, playing at being rock stars.'

'I want an actual relationship with a regular guy. I want to enjoy the next stage of my life. Tonight was the last straw.'

'I've been thinking about this for a while. Would you please get up and leave? I've made up my mind, I intend to move on with my life. It's over between us, Tom. Please don't contact me again.'

'But...what brought this on? What did I do?' stammered Tom. He looked bewildered, in a fog, trying to work out what had gone wrong. From the first time they went out together, she knew his music was the most important thing to him. It wasn't like she had just found out. *I'll never understand girls,* he thought.

Ann got up and walked over to the doorway and switched on the bright overhead light, as if signalling the end of the relationship. Even from the bed, he could see she was crying.

'I have nothing more to say about the matter. It's over, Tom.' She sobbed. 'Close the door on your way out.' And with those last words, she hurried to the bathroom and slammed the door loudly and with a definite finality.

The following day, as the realisation dawned that Ann had meant what she said, he rang Paul.

'Hi Paul. Have you got time to meet for a coffee?' He hadn't told Paul exactly when he and his father were going to the States and thought that could be a good excuse, but he really wanted to get Paul's take on the incident last night with Ann. Maybe Paul would see it differently and could advise him on the best way to deal with it.

'Sure. I can be at the Aroma Coffee Shop by eleven. See you there.'

But Paul didn't see it differently. Paul understood it even less than Tom did.

'You know I know absolutely nothing about women. They terrify me. And this is a perfect example of what I mean. You never know what they're thinking, never know what they want you to do. They expect you to read their minds, like it's an inbuilt trait men are born with. I would be the last person on earth to offer relationship advice.'

He placed his cup back in its saucer and looked thoughtful for a minute or two, then offered good advice:

'Why don't you go to the States and have a wonderful holiday. It'll be the New Year when you get back; you can make a fresh start. New band, new woman.'

Now that sounded like a plan.

So here he was, trying to make his 'fresh start.'

The Dead Parrots were playing the Village Green Hotel in Mulgrave the following Friday night and during the band's break, Tom struck up a conversation with the bass guitarist. The Dead Parrots was an undisciplined and shabby looking group of guys playing some good music.

'Have you guys been together long?' He had grown tired of trying to think up different ways of starting a conversation and had now resorted to using the same opening line, no matter the circumstances.

'I'm Izzy Rowan,' the bass player extended his hand to Tom, grinning broadly. 'You're Tom Watson, aren't you? Played with The Dandy Rats? Write your own stuff? You sing as well, if I remember correctly.'

This was not the answer Tom was expecting. He'd only been recognised a few times and was not used to being spoken up to—well, that's what it sounded like to him. There was a certain respect in Izzy's voice.

'Yeah. We've parted company and I'm looking for another group. Is your guitarist permanent?'

'The guitarist is, but we're currently without a lead singer and I'm filling in until we find the right bloke. Singing is not exactly my forte. In fact, I don't like the singing bit. I like to improvise on the bass, but I can't do that and concentrate on singing. I'm not a natural singer.'

Then quietly, out of the corner of his mouth: 'I'd actually prefer to play jazz, but there's no money in that right now.'

Tom chuckled as he imagined this rough-looking guy, in his too-long jeans and long, lank hair, playing jazz with Rooster in his fancy house.

'We need a keyboard player/Singer. Tony over there is moving back to New Zealand on the weekend. Don't play keyboard by any chance, do you?'

'I do.' Tom was warming to this guy. He seemed genuine, almost normal, unlike some of the mad musos he'd come across lately.

'Wanna audition right now? Can you play Whiter Shade of Pale, know the words?'

Before Tom could reply, Izzy spun around and called to Tony across the table.

'Yo, Tony, can you sit this one out? Tom here is going to fill in for a few minutes, see if he can stand the pace.'

And then to Tom, 'Come on, check out the keyboard' and they made their way to the tiny stage. The keyboard was better than Tom had expected, even had a chair! 'I'll introduce you to the other guys after this number.'

The other three band members settled into their positions as Tom played an intro to Whiter Shade of Pale.

The Dead Parrots were a more relaxed group than The Dandy Rats; they enjoyed their music rather than being a slave to it. At one stage, the drummer played a solo, and Tom was hugely impressed. *Great drummer*, he thought. *Eat your heart out, Johnno Thompson.*

Following on from the instrumental intro, Tom began to sing.

The atmosphere in the room changed. It was as if the audience was listening to the words for the first time, enjoying what they heard. The applause, when the song ended, lasted for ages.

Tom grinned as he turned and faced the audience. Placing one arm across his waist, the other behind his back, he bent forward from the waist and took a small bow.

More applause.

When the applause had died down, Izzy yelled out to the audience,

'What do you reckon? Do you think we should hire him as our new keyboard singer when Tony goes back to NZ?'

A collective and unanimous 'YYYYESSS!!!' was heard loud and clear.

Tom and Izzy looked at each other and laughed.

Izzy grabbed the microphone and, looking directly at Tom, spoke into the mike:

'You heard them. Do we have a new singer?'

'Absolutely!' Success enveloped Tom like a warm blanket on a cold night as he shook hands with Izzy and the other band members. He was back in business as a working musician, and it felt great.

Within that first week of working with the Dead Parrots, Tom told Izzy he wouldn't be available to play for the three weeks over the next Christmas because he had to go back to the States to see his family. He explained this was what had caused the break-up with

The Dandy Rats, and he wanted to make it clear from the outset those three weeks away were non-negotiable.

'Well, thanks for letting me know, Tom. At least we've got plenty of lead time to find a fill-in for those weeks. Shame it's the busiest time of the year, but I'm sure we can work around that.'

Tom breathed a silent sigh of relief. He needed to get that potential problem out of the way quickly, and he had been worried about how Izzy would take it. Little did he know how excited Izzy was to have Tom join their band. He was aware of Tom's following and knew it would be a tremendous help in securing gigs. And he didn't want him on that keyboard forever; he was far too good a guitarist to be wasted on keyboard. He wanted him as lead guitarist and singer as soon as possible. They'd worry about a fill-in over Christmas later.

Izzy pulled him aside one night as they were packing up and, in a serious voice, asked,

'Tom, the punters like your songs. You know, the ones you write. D'ya reckon you could knock out a few more? Anyone can do covers, but not many other bands write their own stuff, so the original stuff is important if we want to get ahead of the game. If we can expand our repertoire of original songs, we can increase our following and that gets us more gigs.'

'Not as easy as it sounds, Izzy,' replied Tom. 'Between uni and playing three or four nights a week, there's not a lot of time left over for writing. And writing good stuff takes time. Anyone can write rubbish, and we don't want that, now do we?'

'No, we do not. Anything I can do to help?'

'Writing comes more easily when I'm relaxed and feeling mellow. Weed helps the creative juices flow; I always feel like we're wasting it when we sit around after a gig and smoke a few joints. I've also noticed my best stuff happens after a few drinks.' Tom was half joking, but he realised Izzy was serious even though he laughed as he replied,

'Well, it looks like I'd better keep you stocked up with booze and weed.'

'Let me know the next time you've got some spare time to write, and I'll come around to your place and we can get stoned together. I reckon that's how the Beatles do it.'

'Sure.' Tom grinned as he thought: *Glad I had that lock put on the Music Room door!*

Over the ensuing months, Tom, with Izzy's help, had written some of his best songs 'under the influence.' Without a doubt, the combination of vodka and weed had the desired effect on his creative ability. Or so it seemed.

As his repertoire of originals expanded, so did the band's following—as did their bookings and their income. As the number of fans increased, so did the number of women, and Tom was never without a pretty girl at his beck and call. Royalties were flowing in since he had acted on his father's suggestion to consult a lawyer, who had advised him to join the Australasian Performing Right Association.

The time Tom had put into studying, combined with his success with his music, strengthened the relationship between him and his father, which had developed into one of respect and admiration. They had floundered for a while there, when Tom was spending too much time on his music and not enough time on his studies, even argued loudly and angrily a few times, but both had made a genuine effort to understand each other's viewpoint and the curve had flattened into a relatively smooth line, with just the occasional corrugation.

What a pity Christmas was the busiest time of the year for pub bands, Tom thought, as he and Jim boarded the plane for the States in mid-December. However, he had to admit; he was looking forward to seeing Gran and Aunt Lola. The only downside to this holiday was that Paul wouldn't be there. Paul was quiet and contemplative, a welcome balance to the other side of his life—his music.

Next year would be their last year of uni and Tom and Jim would be returning permanently to the States. He thought he'd ask Paul to come to the States with them next Christmas—he and Paul could have a fun holiday together in America before they both had to get serious and start working for a living. Paul would love Gran and Aunt Lola and he knew they would welcome any friend of his without hesitation. Yes, good idea. He'd do that.

Not long after Tom and Jim returned from the States, Tom received his exam results—Pass! Over celebratory beers with Paul at the Prince Alfred Hotel later that week, Paul stood up, and holding his glass aloft, proposed a toast:

'Here's to the continued success of Tom Watson.' And as Tom raised his glass and clinked it with Paul's, Paul added: 'I think you're beginning to catch on to this Maths and Science thing—and it only took three years! Your father must be ecstatic.'

Plus, his dad had even come to listen to them three or four times during the year and had told Tom he thought they were 'quite good.' Tom had noticed him clapping wildly in the audience one night but didn't like to mention it, even though he was secretly thrilled to think his father thought he was a good musician.

Jim and Tom had settled into the comfortable Melbourne lifestyle. Paul came to dinner occasionally, and the three men would organise takeout, enjoy a few beers, and chat for a few hours. Life was good.

Life was even better when, around the middle of that year, during one gig they played at the Pier in Frankston, who should walk into the pub but Rooster. The surprise registered on Tom's face as Rooster stood and clapped loudly and enthusiastically after Tom's solo, and he acknowledged Rooster with a smile and a wave. When they had completed the set, Tom found his way to Rooster's table.

The two men wrapped arms around each other in a warm embrace, laughing with genuine delight at the shared joy of this moment.

'Man, it's good to see you. How the hell are you? What are you doing here?'

'Well, I came down to see you perform, didn't I?' replied Rooster, motioning Tom to sit. 'I decided I wanted to see you, have a chat, find out what you're up to these days. I've missed you, Man.'

Tom stepped back and took a good look at his old friend. Yep, same old Rooster—wearing a much loved, and almost clean, T-shirt, tucked into an equally worn, but comfortable looking, pair of jeans. But the shiny two-inch-heeled black boots looked brand new, obviously purchased in Melbourne—Melbourne was way ahead of Sydney in the fashion stakes. It was so good to see his old friend.

'You know what? I've missed you too.'

Tom was surprised at how much he enjoyed being with Rooster again. Rooster had not been lying when he said he had come down to Melbourne to catch up with Tom. he had contacted Tom's dad to find out where Tom would be playing that night so he could surprise him.

They spent the next three days together, chatting late into the night, thoroughly enjoying each other's company, and even met up with Paul for lunch on one of the days. The three men got on extremely well together and forged a new friendship which would strengthen and deepen over time.

Tom had introduced a few of the girls he'd been dating at the time to his father, but one had been 'different' to the others. Carol—she of the long black hair, the goth make-up, the tattoos, including a barbed wire 'amulet,' and nose piercing. The long black boots accentuated the short black leather skirts she favoured, and the black painted fingernails set off the look of 'fragile butch.' Jim nearly laughed aloud when Tom introduced him to Carol but controlled the urge, smiled, and said he was pleased to meet her. But he couldn't hide the stare! Couldn't take his eyes off her—how could a real live person look/dress like that? How long did it take her to apply that black eye make-up? Did she think those tattoos suited her? And he wondered if that nose ring hurt.

Carol was a study in black and white, delicate but powerful, like a combination of soft jazz and heavy metal. Underneath 'the Look,' which took endless time and money to achieve, she had a great sense of humour, a twisted combination of irony, sarcasm, and slapstick, which was incongruous in a person who looked like one of the walking dead. The rest of the band loved her, laughed at her jokes, and liked that she could laugh at herself. She was mad about Tom. Seriously mad about him. She would do anything to be with him. If Tom said, 'Jump,' Carol said, 'how high?' Not that he didn't appreciate her. He did—in his own way—but his music still came first. The thing was, Carol didn't seem to mind. She was happy to take a back seat in his career. Carol was not the love of his life, but until that person came along, he enjoyed her company.

Although Carol knew from the start Tom would return to the States at the end of the year, it didn't stop her from becoming distraught when the time came for them to say goodbye the day before Tom flew out. She had come to his place that afternoon so they could say their farewells in the privacy of his music room.

Tom was upset, but Carol was devastated. She cried, begged him not to go, told him he was the only man she had ever loved, and between sobs, asked if she could come with him. By then, the black eye make-up had smudged into two huge black patches covering most of her face. The mascara on her right eye had melted into a crooked rivulet which dribbled down her face and into the black lipstick; the mascara from the left eye had run sideways and down into her hair. Tom gently wiped her face with a clean tissue and tried to comfort her.

As he pried first her left arm, then her right arm, from around his neck, having first broken her vice-like grip on him, Tom whispered,

'We knew it would come to this. Remember when we first started going out, I explained how I had to go back home to America when uni finished, that my dad's time in Australia would be complete at the end of this year? Well, that time has come.'

'But Tom, I don't know how I'm going to live without you. You mean everything to me.' She declared. The black rimmed red eyes in her tear-stained face looked earnestly into his.

'And you mean a lot to me too, Carol. But we can't always have what we want. This is the reality of our situation.'

She flung her arms around his neck once more and cried into his chest, staining his shirt with her non-waterproof makeup.

'Oh, Carol. I have to go and pack. We need to say goodbye and mean it.'

'I know. You're right, Tom.' She straightened up and fluffed her hair out, smoothed her skirt, and blotted her eyes with a ball of wet tissue. She took a deep breath and smiled a bitter-sweet smile: 'Goodbye, Tom, and good luck. I hope you're an enormous success in America and think of me occasionally.'

With that, she turned and walked away, didn't look back, out the door of his music room, down the steps, and out of his life.

He sat at the keyboard and played the most melancholy tune he could think of. He reached for the almost empty bottle of vodka and took a swig before rolling a joint and completely immersing himself in self-pity.

Three days later, the three men boarded the plane for America—Tom and Jim on one-way tickets, having packed up and left the house in Richmond for the last time. All their goods and chattels would follow them home to the States over the next couple of weeks. It would be good to have Gran there to help them settle into a permanent life in America.

It was hot and windy as Tom stopped on the landing at the top of the steps leading into the plane and looked around—his last look at Melbourne, Australia. He had enjoyed his time in Australia and emotion overcame him as he realised he'd lived here in this country for longer than he had lived in America, and he would miss it. Those years had broadened his outlook on life and had opened his mind to the possibilities which lie ahead. The Australian attitude of laid-back acceptance had rubbed off on him and he knew he was going home a more relaxed and outgoing person than when he arrived. He also thought his mother would have been proud of the young man he had become. An image of her as she was the last time he saw her flooded his memory and melancholy washed over him for a few moments. He raised his left hand and waved—at nobody in particular—and then noticed the quizzical look on Paul's face. He dropped his hand immediately. 'Thought I'd acknowledge the adoring crowds who've come to see me off,' he laughed, as Paul punched him on the arm and shouted above the wind: 'Get a move on. You're holding everyone up.'

Later that night, after dinner, the three of them put their tray tables up and settled back in their seats to prepare to sleep for a few hours. The lights dimmed, and a hush descended over the cabin. Tom closed his eyes, but sleep didn't come, and he let his mind drift back over the past year.

His singing and song-writing career had taken off, and he had developed a loyal following; getting into that band had been the best thing he'd done so far, music-wise. He smiled as he remembered the nights they had sat around after closing time at various gigs, and talked music, smoked a few joints, and developed into a tight-knit group of musos who understood how and what they played.

Tom stirred and moved his legs into a more comfortable position, took a sip of his bourbon night-cap. He glanced over at his father slumped in the reclined Business Class seat and downed the last of the bourbon. Beneath the eye mask, Tom knew Jim was asleep. That man could sleep standing up in a hammock!

Chapter 9

'So, how's the job going?' Jim asked as he, his mother, and Tom sat down to a delicious dinner of roast beef with all the trimmings. Tom suspected, hoped, this was going to be followed by some of Gran's homemade apple pie and ice cream. Gran had always been a superb cook and both Tom and Jim had put on a few pounds since they had returned to live in the States.

'It's going well. More interesting than I thought it would be. I reckon I'd know more about Hewlett-Packard computers than you would at this stage.' Tom smiled and winked at Gran.

'I would hope so,' replied his father. 'That's what you're being paid to do. That's how everyone starts in Sales. Don't ever forget, product knowledge is everything in this industry, Tom. By the end of your indoctrination, you'll be expected to know everything about every computer model we make. And you'll be expected to be able to take any computer apart and put it back together again.'

'And do you know all about every computer?' asked Tom, flippantly, as he helped himself to two more roast potatoes.

'I don't have to. I read Balance Sheets, Profit and Loss Reports, exciting stuff like that.' Jim smiled.

Gran beamed at her two men. She loved having the three of them all together again under the same roof, even though she knew Tom would fly the coop eventually. A young man in his twenties needed to experience living on his own and be independent. But not just yet. She wanted to enjoy him for another year or two. She cleared away the empty dinner plates to make space on the table for the apple pie and ice cream.

After investigating the various departments at H.P., and following Jim's advice, Tom had finally accepted a job in Computer Sales, a coveted division of the company. The money and perks were better than most other areas, and successful sales guys were revered amongst the other employees.

'Tom, would you like another piece of pie?' Gran was already cutting into what remained of the pie in anticipation of his answer.

'I'd love one, Gran, but I've got to go. I'm meeting Bobby and I'm late. We're practicing some new numbers tonight.'

Gran looked at Jim with a quizzical expression. 'Which one is Bobby again?'

'Don't worry about it, Mom. You can get a better grip on their names when they're rich and famous.' Jim laughed, but Gran still looked concerned that she couldn't place Bobby, or any of the other boys in Tom's band for that matter.

During his third week at Hewlett-Packard, Tom pinned up a notice in the staff lunchroom: **Are there any musicians out there? I'm looking for a bass guitarist, a keyboard player, and a drummer, who are interested in forming a band with me.**

Must be exceptional talent! Ha Ha. Give me a ring and we'll talk about it if you, or anyone you know, are interested. Tom Watson.

He was delighted to hear from nine people in a matter of days and arranged to see each one in the canteen after work over the coming few weeks.

After interviewing a few mediocre would-be band members, Bobby Gardener came in and Tom's spirits picked up considerably. Bobby was in his late twenties, six-feet tall, short back-and-sides army-style haircut, wearing a superbly cut navy blue pin-striped suit, shiny black dress shoes, and a grin which displayed blindingly white perfect teeth. Bobby worked in Legal. The deciding factor in Bobby's favour was the Rickenbacker bass guitar he carried in his left hand. This was a young man who took his guitar playing seriously. Rickenbackers didn't come cheap.

When Tom explained what he was intending to set up—a rock and roll band to play gigs in clubs, bars, events—Bobby didn't waste any time. 'I'm your man. I've been playing with various groups for a few years now. The last one broke up a few months ago and I can't wait to get back into it. Not only that, but I've also got a dedicated music room in our back garden where the band can practice. I'm keen, Man. When do we start?'

His enthusiasm was catching and within minutes, Tom was explaining his experience in Australia and how he wanted to replicate a band like The Dead Parrots now he was back home to stay.

One down, two more to go.

A few days later, Zac Robertson was waiting in the canteen for Tom as per their arranged meeting. He had been there for nearly half an hour, did not want to be late. Zac was an arts graduate and worked in the Design department of H.P. but although he could design a good-looking computer, music was his first love. He had contacted Tom the minute he'd seen his advertisement. Zac had an aura about him which stirred something in Tom; he had an energy you could almost see. *I bet he's a terrific drummer,* thought Tom.

'I'll bet you're a terrific drummer,' said Tom. He looked down at his feet as he realised he had spoken his thoughts out aloud.

'You bet I am. My cousin lives in Melbourne and he's told me all about you, all good. I couldn't believe my luck when I saw your ad on the notice board. If you'll give me a go, I guarantee you won't regret it.'

After a brief discussion: 'You'll be hearing from me soon. Real soon,' said Tom as they parted company.

The keyboard player was proving harder to find. Tom had worked his way through the list and hadn't yet met one decent keyboard-player. Despair was hovering in the wings. Until the following evening, when Bobby called him,

'Hi, Tom. It's Bobby Gardener. Have you found the perfect keyboard player yet? No? Well, I know one and he's looking for a job. He used to play keyboard in the band I was with previously, before we broke up. Outstanding player and a nice guy as well. Would you be interested in speaking to him?'

'Yes, I would,' replied Tom, suppressing his excitement, and trying not to let Bobby know how keen he was to meet this guy. 'I've got a drummer, and yourself, of course. Why don't you speak to your man and the four of us will meet at the canteen on Saturday afternoon around two o'clock when it's quiet and we can discuss the whole thing?'

'Sounds like a plan,' said Bobby. 'See you then,' and hung up the phone.

The following Saturday afternoon, four young men sat around in the empty canteen and talked about forming a band. Tom would be the front man—lead guitarist and singer—Bobby Gardener would be bass guitar, Zac Robertson the drummer, and Harry Daben, who, Bobby assured the others, was the best keyboard player in California, would be their pianist. Tom took control in his quiet but determined way.

'First, we need to play together for a few weeks to get a feel for each other's methods. Then we are going to have to practice, practice, practice before we can even think about getting gigs. I'm not mucking around; we need to be good, and we need to feel confident about our arrangements before we hit the outside world. Are we in agreement on this?'

The other three heads nodded vigorously in agreement.

'We can meet in my music room whenever,' said Bobby.

'Thanks, Bobby, great idea. How about tomorrow afternoon?' Tom didn't want to waste any time getting started.

'Oh, and another thing,' said Tom. 'The band is going to be called Pants on Fire.'

Stunned silence.

'Sounds good,' said Zac.

'Yeah, great,' said Bobby.

'That is fantastic. So original,' said Harry.

Little did he know!

And so it was agreed. They would meet at Bobby Gardner's place at one o'clock on Sunday afternoon.

Instruments and sheet music, much of it hand-written, lay strewn around the carpeted floor of Bobby's music room. Six or seven books on the shelves on one wall had been squashed up against the other books to make room for several empty beer bottles and a mug containing the cold dregs of an unfinished cup of coffee.

'You've got to admit, Tom, the sound is getting better and better, the more we play together.' Bobby looked at Tom as he spoke before taking another mouthful of beer. The four of them had been playing for about two hours and decided to end the session and have a drink. All four of them were sitting around on the floor, drinking beer and playing back some recordings of the session.

'Yep, I reckon another two months should do it.'

Zac gasped. 'Two months! You mean to say you reckon we're two months away from being gig worthy.'

'Absolutely sure of it,' replied Tom.

'We've been practicing for about ten weeks now,' replied Zac, 'and I think we sound pretty good.'

'Not good enough, Zac.'

Bobby and Harry joined in the conversation: 'He's right, Zac. We need to be more nuanced, and the rhythm is not quite there. But we're close.'

Tom was secretly pleased with their progress. Bobby had several recording mics strung up and hanging from the ceiling, like baubles on a Christmas tree, so they could play back and listen to the four instruments individually or collectively. He and Tom agreed that separately the four instruments and Tom's voice sounded near perfect, but when the four separate tracks were played as one, the combined sound was not quite right: the drums were either too loud and drowned out the lower range of the keyboard, or Tom's singing sounded like he was trying to compete with the instruments and losing the battle.

Five weeks later, when they met once again in Bobby's music room, Tom couldn't wait to tell the others the good news.

'Good news guys! I got us a gig on Friday night at The Fringe; you know that live music club next door to the University.'

Zac and Harry instantly stopped what they were doing and replied in unison: 'That's fantastic!'

Tom put his hands up in front of him like a traffic cop halting oncoming traffic, took a deep breath, and continued,

'And every Friday night after that for a three-month trial!' His face broke into a huge grin, and he punched the air with his fist.

'You're joking!' Zac could hardly believe it. He couldn't stop smiling as he turned and looked at Bobby and Harry.

'Oh no, I'm not. Every. Friday. Night. For money. With a live audience. And applause.'

'This calls for champagne,' said Bobby, grinning stupidly, as he opened the bar fridge and took out a bottle of French champagne, saved especially for an occasion like this.

'A regular gig. Not even a one-off. Every. Friday. Night.' Harry kept repeating as if trying to convince himself it was really happening.

'Professional musicians.' Zac couldn't contain his delight.

Friday night began a slow but steady build-up of regulars, mostly uni students, who came to listen to Pants on Fire each week. The band that had started out as almost background music, completely unknown, soon turned into Friday night's principal attraction at The Fringe.

A few weeks later, while they were playing covers, someone in the audience requested one of Tom's original songs, which he had sung a couple of times previously. This was the first time one of his songs had been specifically requested, and he knew this was a significant moment in their evolution. 'It would be my pleasure,' he replied to the audience before he gave the thumbs up sign to the others as he whispered: 'Remember this moment, guys.'

Later that night, as they packed up their instruments and the last of the crowd dwindled out of the building, Tom announced: 'I'd like to buy us drinks to celebrate our successful launch into the music industry. What'll you have?' He walked over to the bar and ordered beers for the others and a vodka-on-the-rocks for himself.

'Well, guys, this is a significant night in more ways than one. The Manager just asked me if we'd agree to play here every Friday on a permanent basis.'

'Fantastic,' said Harry.

'That's great,' said Bobby.

'What did you tell him?' asked Zac, who had become a bit more business savvy than the other two during the past couple of months, occasionally asking Tom how much money they now had in the bank, and a few other questions about insurance and tax—which Tom couldn't answer.

'I told him I'd discuss it with you guys and get back to him. I'd like to talk about it at our next practice session at Bobby's on Tuesday.' *That gives me Monday to talk to an accountant and Dad's lawyer*, thought Tom.

'Sounds good to me,' said Bobby.

'Great,' said Harry.

'Yeah. I've got some questions,' said Zac.

The following Tuesday, before they had set up their instruments for practice, Tom suggested they sit down and discuss the band's future.

'I'm thrilled to be offered a regular Friday night gig.' Tom stopped and looked at the other three guys.

'But...' said Zac.

'But I'm reluctant to sign us up to play every Friday night for the next year at the same place, wouldn't matter where it was. I propose I tell the manager that and be as honest and upfront as we can be. If the occasional gig comes along on a Friday night somewhere else, that we want to accept, then we do it. I personally think he'll agree to that. He can see Friday night's live music audience has grown considerably since we've been playing at the club. He'd be a fool to risk turning away paying customers if he tells us to get lost. What do you guys reckon?'

Bobby put his hand up and glanced at the others. 'I for one, couldn't be bothered finding gigs and arranging them around convenient dates and places. I say we let Tom make any arrangements he sees fit. I'm happy to go along with whatever he suggests.'

'You are so right, Bobby.' Zac and Harry looked at each other. 'We just wanna make music. All this administration crap is a pain in the ass.'

'Although the money's handy,' added Harry, grinning at Tom.

Tom relaxed and replied: 'OK, I'll have a chat with him on Friday night and see how it goes.' He took a mouthful of beer and went on,

'How do you feel about playing the first Saturday night of each month at the Blue Door club in San Mateo, for good—I repeat good—money?'

'Great!' said Bobby.

'Great!' said Harry.

'Same deal as the Fringe?' said Zac.

'Of course!' Tom smiled inwardly. Only Zac would think to ask that question.

Chapter 10

The day Tom graduated from the rigorous training program at H.P., he was on his way to his dad's office to tell him he'd passed with flying colours when a tall, attractive woman practically mowed him down as he stepped out of the elevator on the Executive floor.

He was momentarily stunned by the impact but exclaimed, 'I am so sorry.' The big toe on his left foot was screaming in pain where she had stepped heavily on it. He wanted to yank his shoe off and rub the toe to stop the pain, but even though the collision hadn't been his fault, he took a deep breath, smiled, and said,

'I hope I didn't hurt you.' It was only then he noticed she had dropped a folder.

'I'll live.' She replied grimly, stooping to retrieve the dropped paperwork. As she stood clutching the precious folder in one hand, she reached up with her other hand and tucked a stray lock of hair behind her ear. For the first time, she looked directly at Tom. 'You're Tom Watson, aren't you? Your father's looking for you.' And without the hint of a smile or apology, she stepped into the elevator and pressed a floor button. Tom stood staring at the closed doors thinking, *What just happened? Who was that rude woman?*

How did she know his father was looking for him? And would his stepped-on toe ever be the same again?

Tom limped into his father's office and sat down in one of the visitors' chairs opposite Jim, who was busy signing papers. 'I was just nearly run over by an attractive woman at the elevators. She said you were looking for me.'

'Yes, that was Sally, my new secretary. Extremely efficient too. It was she who told me you'd completed your training and are now a fully-fledged salesman. Well done, Tom. Congratulations.'

Jim stood and shook hands with him.

'Thanks, Dad. I just got my first territory—Oakland. It's a huge territory. Hope I can keep up.'

Jim poured coffee for the two of them from the coffee machine in his office and they sat and chatted for a while. Tom purposely avoided any talk of the band or his music, and the atmosphere was one of genuine camaraderie until a knock on the door interrupted them. Sally walked into the office with more papers for Jim to sign.

'Sally, I believe you've met my son, Tom.' Tom stared unblinking at Sally, mesmerised by the smooth blonde hair and electric blue eyes in the dimpled face. 'Yes, we met at the elevator.' she said dismissively, without even looking at Tom. As she turned to leave, she glanced in Tom's direction and added sneeringly, 'Sorry about your foot.'

'It should be okay—in a couple of weeks.' replied Tom sarcastically as she swept past him on her way out.

'She's a piece of work. Where did you get her?' Tom said, as the office door closed and they were alone again.

'H.R. does the hiring around here, but as I said, she's extremely good at her job.' replied Jim.

The following day, as Sally leant against the bench in the executive staff room enjoying a coffee and donut with her friend Kara, she mentioned she had made an idiot of herself the previous day when she crashed into Mr. Watson's son, Tom, at the elevators.

'I accidentally stepped heavily on his foot. Made him wince. I felt terrible, especially since he's gorgeous. Have you seen him? Longish black hair, dark complexion, very 'Heathcliff'.'

'Oh yes, everyone knows of Tom Watson. And you're right, he is gorgeous. Sounds like you didn't make a good impression.'

'No. Compounded by my embarrassment when I walked into his father's office later. I didn't expect him to still be there. When Mr. Watson introduced me to him, I mumbled something and left as quickly as I could. He must think I'm an idiot.'

'Why don't you email him and apologise?' said Kara.

'Good thinking. I'll do it now.' She immediately returned to her desk and emailed Tom, adding a receipt request so she'd know when he'd opened it.

Hi Tom, Sally Boyd here, your father's secretary.

I'd like to apologise for the incident at the elevator and my rudeness later in your father's office. I had other things on my mind. Please accept my apologies and my assurance it won't happen again.

Sally

Two days later, as they were packing up to go home, Kara casually asked Sally about Tom's reply to her email.

'There wasn't any. No reply. Nothing. Zilch. Which is a shame, I'd love to see him again. And I'm not used to being ignored.' *Damn Tom Watson!*

Sally stewed for a few more days. The more time passed, the more she thought about Tom, until it began to nibble away at her concentration on her job. *Should she email him again? Should she phone him? Why hadn't he replied? She knew he'd opened the email when she received the receipt. Damn Tom Watson!*

Another email. Yes, that's what's needed. But she needed an excuse. Mustn't appear desperate.

As she sat thinking about ways to get Tom's attention, the phone on her desk rang. She picked up the receiver and immediately recognised her brother's voice. Before he had a chance to get past 'Hi Sally, how are you?' Sally said, 'Yeah, Hi Mike, can you possibly get me two tickets to the Giants' game at Oracle Park next Friday night?' Mike was in PR for a sports company and was always good for tickets to most of the major baseball, football, and basketball games.

Mike replied in an exasperated voice, 'I'm fine Sally, thanks for asking. We haven't spoken in a couple of weeks, and that's the first thing you say to me?'

'Oh. Sorry, Mike. But can you get the tickets for me?'

In an even more exasperated voice, 'Yeah, sure. I'll have them sent over to your office.'

'Thanks Mike. You're a star. Now, what did you want?'

Twenty minutes later, after re-writing and deleting the first seven emails to Tom, Sally finally hit Send on the one she thought said it best—simple, uncomplicated, to the point:

Hi Tom, Sally Boyd here. How are you?

I just received two tickets to the Giants' game at Oracle Park on Friday night. I was wondering if you'd like to accom-

pany me to the game—my way of apologising for my recent rudeness.

Let me know and we can arrange a time and place to meet. Sally.

Pleased with herself, Sally sat back and took a deep breath. She closed her eyes and concentrated on the tingle of excitement she felt thinking about the prospect of Friday night with Tom Watson!

Unfortunately, the reply email the following day was not the one she was hoping for.

Hi Sally,

Thanks for asking me, but I've got a previous commitment on Friday evening.

Regards,

Tom

Damn Tom Watson! Arrogant prick! Whatever made me imagine I wanted to go out with him? thought Sally, and she deleted the emails from her computer, and her life.

The Oakland territory proved to be much tougher than Tom imagined, although he loved being out on the road after so many months of intensive training. That first sale of four computers to a small importing business on the outskirts of the city put him on a high for the rest of the week. When the customer asked his advice on which software they should buy, Tom was in his element. He enjoyed interacting with people, especially when he knew and understood the intricacies of his subject so well, thanks to all that training.

That first sale was followed by four more in quick succession, and Tom felt a quiet confidence in his ability to sell computers. His Regional Sales Manager was also impressed with Tom's results and made special mention of his success at the Friday afternoon sales meeting.

It was following one of the Friday afternoon sales meetings while he was going through his emails, catching up on correspondence, that he came across the email from Sally Boyd asking him to the game. He'd meant to follow up on it before this and ask her out for a drink after work one night, but it had slipped his mind in those first few frenetic weeks of his new job. He dashed off an email to Sally while he thought of it.

Hi Sally,

Just wondering if you'd like to go for a drink after work next Tuesday. I was thinking of the new Rooftop Bar at the Hyatt. We could maybe even get a bite to eat after.

Let me know if you're free then and we can make arrangements.

Regards,

Tom

A tiny squeal escaped from Sally's lips when she read the email the following Monday morning. She immediately rang Kara,

'Guess who got asked out by Tom Watson?'

'You didn't!'

'I did!'

Sally read out the email to Kara. 'How about that? I knew it would happen, eventually.'

'The new Rooftop Bar at the Hyatt. Ooooo, Special,' said Kara, and the two women dissolved into a fit of the giggles.

When Tom arrived at the hotel, Sally was already there, sitting in the foyer reading a magazine. She hadn't seen him, and he took a minute to have a better look at her. She was gorgeous. Elegant in a sleeveless white summer frock and sandals which set off her slim bare legs, her long blonde hair fell loosely about her shoulders. She appeared to wear very little make-up and even less jewellery, both of which were unnecessary on one so naturally attractive.

Sally became aware of someone looking at her and glanced up from the magazine. She recognised Tom and stood up as he approached.

'Hi, I hope I haven't kept you waiting.' Tom said, smiling. 'Shall we go up?'

They took the elevator to the top floor and entered The Rooftop Bar, which was crowded with office workers from the local IT companies enjoying the open-air atmosphere and cocktails at the newest place to 'see and be seen.' They squeezed their way through the throng and found two high-stools and a small bar table which two geeky-looking young men were vacating. Sally commandeered the stools while Tom found his way to the bar and ordered drinks—a white wine for Sally and a double vodka martini for himself.

It was a warm, balmy evening. The full moon rose in the darkly mottled sky as the last vivid orange-pink rays of the setting sun fell below the horizon. A wandering bar girl placed a bowl of bar mix on their table as Tom raised his glass.

'Nice to see you again, Sally Boyd.'

'Nice to be here, Tom Watson,' replied Sally, as she clinked her glass against his.

Their knees touched under the table, but neither moved away. Sally tilted her head so her long fair hair fell forward to cover the blush she felt creep up her neck and warm her cheeks. By the time they had finished their second drink, both were feeling relaxed and comfortable, happy to be at this place, at this time, on this soft, silver evening.

They talked long into the night, ordered pizza at the bar so they didn't have to break the atmosphere by going somewhere else to eat, and enjoyed getting to know each other.

Tom told Sally about himself, including how he started a band when he was in high school in Melbourne, but he was much more interested in getting to know her history.

Sally told him she was a native New Yorker who had run away to California when she was sixteen to escape her controlling, bigoted parents. She'd struggled at first, waiting tables whilst studying for her Business Administration degree, which had finally landed her the job of her dreams working for his father at H.P. She told him of her friendship with Kara, which meant so much to her.

Tom explained that even though he loved his job, his current band, Pants on Fire, was the most important thing in his life; that they played a regular gig every Friday night at The Fringe near the University, which was why he couldn't take her up on her offer of the big Giants' game a few weeks back.

'Oh, I see,' said Sally quietly, as the realisation dawned that he wasn't fobbing her off when he declined her offer. 'I'd love to come along and see you in action one Friday night.'

'I'd like that too, but there's something you should know. I can't spend any time with you once we've finished playing for the night. That's the band's 'wind down time' and we usually sit around and have a few drinks, talk about how the show went, that type of stuff. Please don't be offended, that's just the way it is.'

'I understand. It makes sense. I guess women get in the way.'

Tom breathed a sigh of relief, glad he'd gotten that one out of the way. The breakup with Ann had affected him more than he cared to admit. On reflection, he realised it had been his fault she'd broken up with him, and he wanted to make sure that situation didn't happen again.

The crowd had thinned out and eventually it was closing time.

'I think it would probably be a good idea to leave, rather than be thrown out,' Tom grinned as he stood and stretched his legs. 'Do you have your car here or can I drive you home?'

'Kara dropped me here on her way home from work, so a lift home would be much appreciated. Thanks.'

It was quiet in the car, a certain tension in the air. Following her directions, Tom pulled up at her flat and walked around to Sally's side of the car. He escorted her up the external stairs to her front door, bright moonlight lighting their way. She had told him about her flat earlier in the evening, how it was above a large garage in a well-to-do neighbourhood. When the husband of the wealthy couple who owned the house had died, the wife had converted the area above the garage into a small but beautifully appointed apartment. The owner thought she would feel safer and less lonely knowing there was someone living close by.

As they stopped at the front door, Sally turned and put her hand on Tom's arm. She looked into his eyes and said,

'I really am sorry I stepped on your foot.'

A shadow passed over his eyes and he looked serious. 'Did you know you broke my big toe?'

Genuinely shocked by this revelation, Sally gasped as her eyes widened in horror. She stepped in closer to him and grabbed his other arm. 'No! I had no idea! Oh, Tom, that's awful. I'm so sorry. Did I really break it?'

His eyes crinkled with humour, and he smiled a cheeky smile. 'Nah. Just kidding.'

She didn't know whether to laugh or smack him, so she did both, laughing as she smacked him hard on the hand. Before her feelings of sympathy disappeared, he reached out to her and added in a cheeky voice,

'So, are you gonna ask me in or what?'

Sally frowned and looked apologetic.

'I'd like to, but I've got an early start tomorrow morning. Big meeting.'

Tom was crestfallen.

'Really?'

'Nah. Just kidding!' she said with a wicked grin.

And taking him by the hand, she opened her door and led him inside.

If the prospect of going out with Tom had affected Sally's concentration before the event, she might as well not even gone into the office in the days that followed that Tuesday night.

She could barely think of anything else—the memory of him leaning over her as she lay sprawled on the bed, undressing her slowly and deliberately, the feel of his hands on her body, the sight of him naked in the moonlight, the feel of his mouth on hers.

That first time they had made love had been so natural and un-complicated; the second time more wanton, lustful. The thoughts filled her mind again and again as she relived every minute of their time together.

It had been after three-thirty in the morning when Tom left, and Sally felt more alive and at ease than she had felt in years. She fell into a warm, restful sleep and was woken by her alarm at seven. She smiled when she saw the message light blinking on her muted phone by the bed. She unmuted the phone and pressed the flashing red light. Tom's voice emanated from the speaker: 'Can't wait to see you again,' it whispered. She replayed the message six times and couldn't stop smiling.

If only he'd left Sally's place earlier, Tom would not have been late for his meeting with one of the largest accounts in Oakland.

The worst part about getting to his appointment late was that Mr. Boyland was now seeing another rep. whose appointment was originally after Tom's. Because he'd arrived early and Tom had arrived late, the other guy was now selling his product to Mr. Boyland.

The best part about being late was he could now sit here in this ridiculously uncomfortable visitor's chair drinking this god-awful coffee the receptionist had made for him and think about last night at Sally's place. The way she kissed him, free of constraints; the feel of her soft, pliable body under his as they made love. He closed his eyes and relived every moment from when she led him through the door to when he left.

Suddenly: 'Mr. Boyland will see you now, Tom.'

In a flash, he was on his feet and handing his coffee cup to the receptionist, following her into Mr. Boyland's office in full salesman mode.

'Morning, Mr. Boyland.' Tom beamed as they shook hands. 'What a perfect day for me to show you how we can make your working life easier.'

Two hours later, Tom, resisting the urge to skip, walked calmly out of Mr. Boyland's office with a signed order for ten computers. He looked up as he unlocked his vehicle. 'Thank you, Sally. I couldn't have done it without you.'

Chapter 11

Pants on Fire won many followers as they played every Friday night at The Fringe and the first Saturday night of each month at the Blue Door in San Mateo. They were playing at least a couple of Tom's songs at every gig. The band was being paid on a regular basis and the other boys often let Tom know how much they appreciated what he did for them.

As they sat around drinking and smoking weed at the end of a night at the Blue Door, Tom spoke.

'Well, fellas, there's good news and bad news. First the good news—I've got us a gig at the upcoming H.P. Sales conference at Lake Tahoe. It's not for a couple of months, so there's no need to get too excited yet. We'll play Thursday, Friday, and Saturday night. Thanks to my excellent negotiating skills, and the fact I'm the VP's son (much sniggering from the others), you are going to be delighted when I tell you what you're going to earn for this little caper. Unfortunately, that's one Friday night we'll have to miss The Fringe, but believe me, it is worth it money-wise.'

The others thumped the table, and there were some catcalls and whistling. Bobby rose to buy more drinks, but Zac stopped him before he could take a step.

'And what's the bad news?'

'I'm taking two weeks off between now and then to go to Australia to catch up with a couple of my friends there; I don't know when I'll get another opportunity. I reckon we're going to get a whole lot busier as time goes by. I'll make it in the middle of the month so we don't miss out on the Blue Door, just a couple of Fridays at The Fringe.'

More thumping on the table and a few boos. Then, when they'd quietened down, he added,

'I'll buy the next round if someone else can supply some weed. I've run out.'

Tom and Sally had fallen into a pattern of having drinks and dinner at the Rooftop Bar once a fortnight and the occasional dinner at the little Italian restaurant near work. She had been to the Fringe twice to watch them play and although some of the guys had joined her at her table between sets, Sally had found her own way home when they finished for the night, as per their agreement.

'Have you said anything to your father about us dating?' Sally asked at dinner one night.

'No,' replied Tom. 'I don't think it's necessary for anyone at work to know we're seeing each other. What do you think?'

'I agree.' replied Sally. 'Nobody else's business. I haven't said anything to anyone except Kara, and she knows how to keep her mouth shut.'

It seemed slightly shady not to tell his father who he was dating, even more so not to tell Gran, but it seemed to be a wiser option until Sally and Tom became an 'item'—or not.

When Tom arrived at band practice at Bobby's place one Thursday night, he seemed to be in a particularly good humour. Harry picked up on his good spirits and put his arm around Tom's shoulder and gave it a squeeze.

'And what is your good mood due to this wonderful evening, young Thomas?' He asked, as he handed a beer to Tom.

'I've had a fantastic week. Sold a few computers, but more importantly, I've written a couple of new songs for us and I reckon they're pretty good. Minor key, a few diminished chords—Harry, please note!—with 'broken heart' lyrics to match, but catchy at the same time.'

Harry loved diminished chords, loved playing them, loved the sound of them. He would often play a bit of soul during a lull in their practice sessions.

'Well, let's get going and play!' said Bobby, picking up his guitar and striking a loud, heavy chord as an introduction to nothing in particular.

All agreed. Both new songs were excellent, and they were keen to play them the following night at the club. Tom didn't mention it had taken half a bottle of vodka and quite a bit of dope for him to turn out the two numbers. But he was secretly pleased with the result.

As Tom planned his upcoming holiday in Australia, he contacted Rooster to let him know he wanted to spend a week in Melbourne to catch up with Paul, and a week in Sydney to spend some time with him. He was delighted at Rooster's enthusiasm to meet up, but when Rooster checked his schedule, his enthusiasm turned to disappointment.

'Ah Man, I've got gigs on the Wednesday and Friday nights of that week.' But then added:

'Hey, why don't I come down to Melbourne during the week before and the three of us can get together for a few days?'

'That would be great. I'm going to stay at the Travelodge at St. Kilda. Why don't you book there as well?'

'Done deal. See you in a month.'

When Tom phoned Paul to let him know dates, and that Rooster was coming down to Melbourne to join them, Paul suggested he take a couple of days off work so they could make the most of their time. Tom made what he thought was a brilliant suggestion:

'Why don't you check into the Travelodge with us for the week? Make it a proper holiday.'

'Sounds like a good idea. I'll do it.'

The two weeks Tom spent in Australia were two of the most pleasant, fun weeks of his life. The three young men dined at some of the best restaurants in Melbourne, drank more alcohol than they should have, and visited a variety of live music venues. Rooster insisted they visit the best jazz club in the city, St. Elmo's, where he knew the guy who ran it. When the manager suggested Rooster play a set with the jazz group, they welcomed him with open arms. Rooster's ability to slot in so easily with musos he'd never even seen before fascinated Tom, but then he realised—the jazz community is like that: comfortable, smooth, a brotherhood type of thing. Rooster's touch was so light, so delicate, his fingers seemed to hardly touch the keys and yet the sounds they made painted a picture of drama, pathos, melody, romance. The audience enjoyed it as much as Tom did. Even Paul was seriously impressed with Rooster's style. The Manager refused to let any of them pay for their drinks for the rest of the evening. None of them remembered getting back to the Travelodge, but they knew it was in the early hours of the morning when they noticed the glow of a rising sun over the Eastern horizon.

Tom even scored an invitation to an office party at the firm of architects where Paul worked. The two partners had won a big contract for an office block in the city and the party was to celebrate a job which would run for at least three years. As Tom told Rooster later:

'Nice Secretary in the office, just Paul's type, and it's not hard to see she's keen.'

All through uni, Paul was reluctant to get involved with girls. It seemed like he was afraid of them. Tom never knew if he was scared he might fall for someone, or if he just didn't understand them. He did date a couple of Tom's cast-offs, but those relationships did not get off the ground. It was only ever one date, two at most.

'So, Paul, what's stopping you from asking her out?' Rooster couldn't understand why a red-blooded guy held back when it came to dating women. He was sure Paul wasn't gay, so what was the problem?

'Yeah, I'll eventually get around to it,' replied Paul, and changed the subject.

Both Tom and Rooster were delighted to be invited to the wedding of Paul and 'the Secretary' a couple of years later, Tom even more so when Paul asked him if he'd be his Best Man.

The enjoyment of the couple of weeks in Australia and the memories of his time with Paul and Rooster stayed with Tom for a long time, even though he was happy enough to get back to his routine at work and the band's regular gigs. Before he knew it, it was time to work on their repertoire for the Sales Conference entertainment at Lake Tahoe. It was five months away, but not only did he have to set out their schedule, he had to prepare for the conference's work sessions during the day as well. One of the major reasons for the annual Sales Conference was to refresh product information for the benefit of the sales reps and to announce the results of the year's sales competitions.

In retrospect, it had been a very successful conference, although Tom was exhausted by the time it had finished. He was almost glad Sally had not been there. She would have been a distraction he didn't need; the three days were busy and required concentration, and the three nights were full-on. He was relieved to get back home and sleep all day Sunday.

Pants on Fire had been an enormous hit with everybody, including the Executive Sales Team. The Sales Director, Ron Boranski, had been so impressed he had booked them to play at his daughter's engagement party in a few months' time. Tom had boldly increased their fee, which the Director accepted, no questions asked.

It wasn't until the following Wednesday night practice session that Tom told the others about the engagement party booking.

'It's not for three months, being held at Mr. Boranski's house—very swish, one of the largest estates in Palo Alto, I believe—and extremely lucrative for us. But then, we're worth every cent they pay us, are we not?'

'Absolutely!' said Bobby.

'You bet,' said Harry.

'We're so good, we should ask for more money,' as only Zac would say.

The engagement party was a formal affair, held in the back garden of the Boranski mansion under an enormous white marquee adorned with thousands of red roses and an enormous crystal chandelier which hung from the centre of the roof. Hundreds and hundreds of twinkling mini- lights decorated every tree in the magnificent garden. The two hundred and fifty guests drank champagne imported from France and served by pretty girls in tiny 'French Maid' uniforms. The food was provided by 'Nothing but The Best,' San Francisco's leading Michelin-starred chef's side business, and served by good-looking young men wearing only black satin shorts, black bow ties, black bovver boots, and white gloves.

But Pants on Fire were the sensation of the evening. The hostess had specifically requested the band members all wear black leather for the gig—pants and vests, worn undone, no shirts. The look and sound created quite an impact when they appeared on the small stage at the front of the specially constructed timber dance floor and began their opening number. And the momentum built from there.

At one point, Tom leaned over to Bobby and whispered,

'If this is the engagement party, can you imagine what the wedding will be like? Think I'll put in a bid for that.'

Bobby replied, laughing: 'The wedding would sure look good on our resume.'

They were inundated with requests during the evening, including several of Tom's own songs, and were pleasantly surprised by the amount of applause and flattering comments from some of the older guests, particularly several of the women. Harry had trouble getting away from one older lady, probably one of the aunts, who asked him more than once, how much he would charge to spend some 'special' time with her.

Towards the end of the evening, during a break, Tom was approached by Yasmin, Mr. Boranski's newly engaged daughter, who was trailing a tall, handsome older man in an expensive-looking tuxedo.

'Tom, I'd like you to meet Reg Levi. Reg asked me to introduce you two.' Then turning to the older man, 'Reg, this is Tom Watson, the front man of Pants on Fire. I'll leave you two to chat while I continue to mingle.' And she quietly slipped away into the crowd.

'Nice to meet you, Reg,' said Tom, extending his hand.

'Good to meet you too, Tom. I guess you've been told many times before you've got quite a unique voice. It really showcases the band's talent and your guitar work.'

'It has been commented on before, yes,' Tom smiled, wondering what was coming next.

'I'm a talent scout and I've been looking for a group as the support act for the Blue Stones for their three-night stint at the Warfield in San Francisco in February next year. Your band is the sound and look I'm after. Would you be interested?'

Tom felt like he was going to faint. Support act for the Blue Stones! Wait until the others hear about this. He tried to remain calm and non-committal, but was sure the older man could hear his heart thumping in his chest. He could feel the sweat break out on his top lip—it was probably glistening in the glow of a thousand tiny lights.

'I'd like to find out a bit more about it before we commit. Perhaps we could meet during the week and discuss it.' Tom could hear his own voice speaking the words, but he couldn't believe he was being so casual about their biggest break. *You idiot!* He thought. *Just say Yes! What is the matter with you?*

But before he shouted YES! Reg was speaking again.

'Do you know the Warfield, the biggest and best theatre in San Francisco? It seats 2,500, plus standing room for another couple of hundred if we do it right. We can talk about the deal and benefits when we meet during the week, if that's OK with you.' He handed his card to Tom and added: 'Give me a ring on my private number and we can set something up.'

Tom could only stare. He couldn't believe it. Thoughts raced through his head: *This guy is trying to sell me on the idea. He obviously doesn't realise we'd play the Warfield for nothing!*

All Tom could say was: 'Sure.' as he graciously accepted Reg's card.

'I look forward to it,' said Reg, as he shook hands with Tom once more and turned and walked away.

I need a chair to sit down and think about what just happened, thought Tom, as he helped himself to another glass of champagne from a sweet young thing as she sashayed past him in her cute little black and white outfit.

'Special band meeting, my place, seven-thirty Monday night. Don't be late.' He barked at the others, as he slipped his guitar strap over his head and stepped up to the mike for the final set of the evening.

Chapter 12

Thursday evening practice sessions were often fun nights. Every couple of weeks, Tom would have a new song for them to try, some better than others. Occasionally, everything fell into place, and they knew they had something special to play the next night at the Fringe.

Tom arrived at Bobby's place early one Thursday evening and the two men were experimenting with various chords and progressions when Harry arrived—looking less than happy. His long face seemed even longer when his brows were furrowed in a frown.

'Why the long face, Man?' asked Tom, casually draping his arm around Harry's shoulders.

'My housemate told me he's being transferred to Iowa next month and now I have to find someone else to take his place.'

'Josh and I have been sharing the house for seven years. You get used to someone over that time. He's a good guy, clean, tidy, and a good cook! He's got a bit of a weed habit, but that doesn't bother me. At least there's always someone to share a joint with.'

'You're in Santa Clara, aren't you? What's the house like?' asked Tom.

Tom had been toying with the idea of moving out on his own for a while. It was convenient living at home. Gran was a superb cook, and he knew she spoiled him, always making sure his clothes were washed and ironed, but he also knew deep down he took advantage of her in that regard. Sooner or later, he needed to make a move. Just last week Jim had commented Tom's drinking had increased quite a bit lately and Tom had reacted angrily. He enjoyed a few drinks, especially when he was writing music. He was glad his father wasn't aware of the amount of weed he smoked at the same time. His Dad didn't understand.

'The house is great. It's a big, rambling place. But the best part about it is it's got a media room which is sound-proofed. I don't use it as a media room, but it's a great place to practice. That's where I keep my keyboards.'

'I'd be interested in having a look at it,' said Tom. 'I've been thinking about moving out of home for a while. Maybe this is the motivation I need.'

'That would be great.' Harry brightened considerably as Tom spoke. 'Come over on the weekend and I'll show you around. Bring your guitar, we could try out the 'Music' room!'

The house was bigger and better than Tom had imagined. He was amazed when Harry told him what he paid to live there, but then explained the house was owned by his father's uncle, who was happy to keep it in the family.

'I'll break it to them at home tomorrow and provided there are no tears and begging me to stay, I'll move in when your current housemate moves out.' said Tom, laughing, but secretly hoping there wouldn't be any ructions about him leaving.

Instead, he was surprised at both Gran's and his dad's reaction when he told them about moving out.

'We thought you'd never go,' said Jim.

'What took you so long to decide to move out into the big wide world? I don't know how you've lived with your grandmother and father for so long,' laughed Gran as she kissed him. 'But always remember, you're more than welcome here anytime for a decent home-cooked meal and a few beers with your dad.'

Tom immediately rang Harry. 'I'm in. Let's celebrate! Meet me at the Hyatt in an hour.'

Tom and Sally had gone public with their relationship as it became more serious, although Tom had been unsure how his father would react when he told him.

'It's none of my business who you date, Tom, but in this instance, I'm really pleased for you. Sally's lovely; not just attractive, but street smart and shrewd. If you've got any sense, you'll pay attention to her.'

Tom was happy with his father's reaction, secretly pleased he didn't press him further on his intentions for the future, even though they'd been seeing each other for over a year now.

He and Sally had a relaxed and comfortable relationship—he believed they were mutually exclusive, and they had never had a cross word—but his father's words itched away at the back of his mind. In those private, deeply buried thoughts that were not to be shared with anyone, Tom did not want the relationship to develop further beyond this point. At this time of his life, in his twenties, doing well at work and even better in the music side of his life, marriage didn't appeal to him. He had other things he wanted to achieve before he settled down with a wife and kids and, although he liked Sally a lot, he didn't think she was 'The One.'

He enjoyed sharing the house with Harry, but loved going home once a week to catch up with Gran and his father. Nobody cooked a roast dinner like Gran!

Gran had always been the shining light in his life, ever encouraging, supportive, loving. His father was the rock on which his life was built, but Gran was his reason for doing what he did, the inspiration for his music. He still missed his mother, thought of her, and had many imaginary conversations with her, often, but Gran had become his mother-figure, his sounding board, his kindred-spirit.

A couple of weeks before the band's big gig at the Warfield, Sally was at The Fringe one Friday night when a regular customer invited the band to a party after the show.

'Sounds good,' said Harry, and turning to Tom: 'Why don't you bring Sally along?'

'Yeah, good idea,' Zac liked Sally. 'She seems like a party girl.'

Sally was delighted to be asked along and followed the others in her car. By the time the five of them eventually arrived at the party, the house was alive with loud music. People were chatting, and eating and drinking, in small clusters, some were dancing. Tom left Sally chatting with Zac and found his way to the kitchen to get them a drink. Fifteen minutes later, when Tom had not returned with her drink, she decided to find out what was keeping him. She wandered from room to room on the ground floor level of the house but couldn't find him. She took the narrow stairs to the next level, but there didn't seem to be anyone up there, although she thought she heard voices coming from one room. Stepping into the doorway, Sally was surprised to see Tom and two other men, one of whom was Bobby from the band, sitting on the couch in the room, leaning over the coffee table.

Sally stopped dead in her tracks. 'Tom! What the hell are you doing?' Sally's shock at seeing Tom about to snort a line of cocaine was echoed in her voice. It was loud and shrill. She clenched her fists, her fingernails biting into her palms, to stop herself lashing out at him.

Undeterred, Tom glanced up. 'It's OK Sally. We're just getting in the party mood. Would you like some?' He picked up the small plastic bag of white powder lying on the table and held it out to her. 'It's good quality.'

Sally looked around the room in disbelief, her staring eyes taking it all in. She knew the guys in the band smoked weed when they sat around and had a few drinks after a gig, but until this moment, she had no idea Tom indulged in cocaine as well.

'Absolutely not,' said Sally through clenched teeth. 'As a matter of fact, I'm leaving. I'm going home. Good night.' And she turned and left the room.

Before she had reached the top landing of the stairs, Tom was beside her, his hand on her arm. 'Come on, Sally. It's OK. It's not that bad, it's just cocaine. It's only for recreational use.'

Sally spun around to face him, her fury obvious by her flaring nostrils and blazing eyes. 'Don't be absurd, Tom. Drugs are drugs.

I thought you were better than this. You probably have no idea where that came from.'

'It came from Bobby's regular dealer. I use the same guy because we know he's reliable for good stuff.'

Sally couldn't believe what she was hearing. 'You mean you've done this before?'

'There's no need to get so upset. Everybody does it,' said Tom, trying to placate her.

'Well, I don't!' hissed Sally. 'And I'm not interested in anyone who does. Goodbye Tom.' Sally hurried down the stairs and pushed her way through the crowd and out the front door.

'Come on, Tom, there's a line waiting for you here,' called Bobby, as Tom looked back over his shoulder into the room. He turned and walked back to the couch and sat down. 'Well, that didn't go well.'

But he continued to roll a dollar bill into a tight tube.

The sound of the ringing phone greeted Sally as she opened her office door the following Monday morning. She rushed to pick up the receiver, sure it was Tom with an abject apology, vowing his fling with cocaine was just that, and promising her that sort of behaviour was merely an experiment—part of his mis-spent youth—and was now behind him. The lack of phone calls from him over the weekend had been disturbing, but she felt confident this was him ringing now.

She smiled as she answered the phone.

'Good morning, Sally Boyd speaking.'

'Oh, Hi Sal, just me,' said Kara quickly. 'Thought I'd see if you'd like to do lunch today?'

The sound of Kara's voice knocked the wind out of Sally's sails, and she replied, flatly,

'Sure. How about The Oak?'

'You OK?' asked Kara.

'Not really. I'll tell you all about it at lunch. Twelve forty-five okay with you?'

'Sure. See you then.' And the two women hung up simultaneously.

Tom thought it would be best to give Sally time over the weekend to calm down after her meltdown on Friday night. At the time, he thought she had a nerve telling him what he can and can't do. He should have known she wouldn't approve of cocaine—she was more of a loner and cocaine was a lifestyle type of thing, something you did with your mates. The camaraderie and unspoken trust were enjoyable, like being part of a tribe, a brotherhood.

On Monday morning, when Tom looked at his schedule for the week, he saw he had two full days on the outskirts of Oakland on Monday and Tuesday. Plus, he'd arranged to stay overnight so he could take his biggest customer in the area to dinner on the Monday night. Oh well, he'd ring Sally Wednesday or Thursday when he was back in the office. She would be well and truly over it by then and would probably be keen to catch up on Friday night.

Only a young man of Tom's naïve sensibilities could have misjudged a situation so badly.

He rang her on Thursday afternoon when he'd completed his paperwork and was about to leave for the day.

A couple of minutes into the conversation, mostly chit-chat about their respective working weeks, Sally took a deep breath and launched into her practised speech:

'Tom, I won't beat around the bush. I expected you to contact me with an apology long before now, but sadly, that didn't happen because you don't think an apology is necessary. In my world, that's wrongdoing compounded by bad manners.

'I am not prepared to continue a relationship with someone who takes drugs. I can now see you prefer them to me, so I won't waste your time any further. I won't be seeing you again.'

By the end of this tirade, Sally's voice had reached fever pitch, her words coming loud and fast. The anger in her voice almost frightened him. It was so unlike her; it was the last thing he was expecting.

'What do you mean—you won't be seeing me again? Sally, you're overreacting. Calm down and look at this from my point of view. So, I enjoy some cocaine occasionally. What's wrong with that? You're not my keeper, Sally. I don't need your permission to live my life the way I want. I'm sorry you disapprove of my recreational habits, but I won't be changing them anytime soon, for you or anyone else.'

'In that case, it's definitely over between us, Tom. Do not ever contact me again, as long as you're using cocaine.' She slammed the phone down. Thankfully, Jim was currently out of the office, and he didn't have to see her burst into tears and run to the Ladies' Room.

Tom stared at the phone in his hand. 'Fine. Fine. If that's the way you want to play it, that's fine with me,' he said to the receiver as he slammed it back on its cradle. He had more important things to think about than a woman—like preparing for a 3-day gig at the Warfield in San Francisco, the most important gig they would ever play!

The midday streets of San Francisco throbbed with shoppers, office workers out for lunch, and couriers on their bikes delivering parcels and paperwork around the city. Harry shouted directions as he studied the city map while Bobby manoeuvred their rental van like an expert. They narrowly missed two lawyer-looking types in double-breasted navy-blue suits carrying expensive looking briefcases who were crossing the street against the traffic. The four young men in the van recoiled in alarm as the van nearly brushed one of the men, but alarm turned to hilarious laughter once the danger had passed.

'Brilliant idea of yours, Zac, to hire this van. It sure is better with all our equipment in the one van rather than each of us having to look after our stuff individually. What a little genius you are!' Tom punched Zac on the arm to show his appreciation.

'Turn right here,' screamed Harry as they were half-way past the entrance to a parking lot Zac had marked on the map as being the closest to the Warfield. In one reflex action, the van miraculously turned into the parking lot and came to a screaming stop in a parking bay.

'We're here!' said Bobby to a round of applause from the other occupants. The four men piled out of the van, emptied its contents of musical instruments and equipment, and wheeled everything to the Warfield.

It was Thursday afternoon and, as requested, they had arrived in time for the practice session for the opening show that evening. The stage area was buzzing with stagehands, musicians, lighting guys, sound experts, and equipment. Tom stared in awe at the speakers on either side of the stage. He had never seen such an enormous bank of speakers, or such a gigantic screen, which seemed to hang in mid-air at the back of the stage. He gazed around at the stage area, then out at the vast auditorium, which disappeared into the blackness. It seemed to go on forever. *Steady-on Boy,* he thought to himself, *easy to get overwhelmed here. It's just another show. Play to the front row. Forget about the other 2,300 people out there. Yeah, right.*

People materialised out of nowhere to help them set up and although it seemed like a madhouse of yelling people, equipment, cords, microphones, and at least four sets of drums and three keyboards, an hour later, the noise dropped and quiet settled over the stage.

A booming voice from somewhere in the wings rang out:

'Tom Watson and Pants on Fire: time to show us what you've got!'

Nervous didn't begin to describe the general feeling which rippled through the four young men. So many of their peers surrounded them on the stage, not the least of which were the guys from the Blue Stones. Tom, Zac, Bobby, and Harry could each feel them judging every note, every cadence, every movement of Pants on Fire. The spontaneous applause which broke out as they finished that first number, unusual at a practice session, set the tone for the rest of the three-day gig. Once they knew they had been accepted into that inner circle of show-stopping talent, they settled into their rhythm and enjoyed every minute of those next three days and nights.

When the practice session had finished, the Stage Manager led them back to the Green Room and pointed out where they would wait, ready to go on, each night, and to where they would return, once their part of the show had finished. A type of holding area, it was a large comfortable room with several sofas and easy chairs placed strategically. A big vending machine, ready to dispense a variety of drinks, stood against one wall next to a table stacked with coffee and tea equipment, and an array of snacks.

'Go now,' the Stage Manager told them, 'Freshen up and be back here by seven-thirty.'

In response to another good idea of Zac's, they had booked into the motel around the corner. Seedy though it was, it was close by and meant they wouldn't have to drive home to Palo Alto each night. It also meant they didn't have to drive to the venue, battling heavy traffic and becoming frustrated and irritable trying to find a parking spot. Instead, they could walk to and from the Warfield.

By seven-forty-five, they were sitting in the Green Room, ready and keyed up, waiting to go on. Nobody spoke. The minutes ticked by and when Tom glanced at his watch and saw it was eight-ten, he began to feel edgy; the show was scheduled to start at eight. At about eight-fifteen, a voice rained down on them from the ceiling: 'Pants on Fire—You're on.' All four men jumped up and ran for the door, bumping into each other in their haste, up the stairs into the wings and onto the stage, into the glare of the blinding lights. They found their positions on stage and, as the screaming and cheering from the audience died down, a hush settled over the auditorium like a warm blanket.

Three seconds into Tom's opening guitar riff of Smells Like Teen Spirit, their cover of the most famous Nirvana song, the audience stood as one and clapped and cheered. At first Tom thought it was just the front row as that was about as far as he could see in the glare, but as the sound swept over the stage like a tsunami, he realised it was the entire auditorium. He could feel Zac smiling even though he couldn't see him.

The discussions about their opening number had continued over several days; when Tom suggested they open with a cover of the most popular song in a generation, only Zac agreed with him. Bobby and Harry didn't think it was a good idea. As Harry said: 'everything after that is going to be second best.'

'Our opening number has got to explode on stage. We only get one go at making an impression and Smells Like Teen Spirit is the biggest thing right now.' Tom was adamant and stood his ground, thankful at least Zac agreed with him. The other two men argued as best they could for as long as they could. It was the reaction of the entire crew at the practice session that afternoon that convinced them Tom and Zac had been right to choose this song to open—and here was the proof. The sound was deafening, but music to their ears.

They followed with one of Tom's original songs, then several covers. They got in three of Tom's originals during the first thirty minutes before taking a break when Tom welcomed the audience and said how pleased they were to be a supporting act at the famous Warfield. The break gave them time to catch their breath and take a sip of whatever was in the glasses which had been placed near their equipment. It wasn't water! Time for another five numbers before they finished and left the stage.

It wasn't until the four of them got back to the Green Room that they discovered how sweat- soaked they were, hair wringing wet. They stripped off wet shirts and changed into the dry T-shirts specially printed for the show—on the front, a picture of a pair of pants on fire, on the back: 'Pants on Fire' at the top, 'at the Warfield' underneath.

'Nice Tees,' remarked one of the Blue Stones through a cloud of cigarette smoke. 'Good show, by the way,' he added. The other Blue Stones looked up from where they were sitting and gave a round of applause.

Bobby took bottles from the vending machine and handed them around as they relaxed on the lounges. Harry produced some weed, and as they lit up, they recounted every minute of the show.

'I've never experienced anything like that before.' Harry had not stopped grinning since he left the stage. 'I want more of that, thanks.'

'It's gonna be hard to go back to the Fringe on Friday night after that,' Zac laughed. 'Don't get me wrong. I mean hard, not impossible.'

'And we've got another two nights of this. Woo Hoo.' Tom took another drag on his toke. *Damn*, he thought to himself, *I wish I'd brought the cocaine with me instead of leaving it in the motel room for later*. But later would come soon enough.

The next night's performance proved to be much the same as their opening night, although all four of the young men were more relaxed and confident. However, Saturday night was the standout show. The audience was fired up which transferred to the performers who gave it their all in that final show. Even the smoke machines performed perfectly and the sale of band merchandise from the Lobby Shop eclipsed their wildest dreams.

The Green Room was crowded with people when the four Pants on Fire members returned after their final performance. The place was buzzing; the Blue Stones were itching to get on stage and when the announcement boomed out from the ceiling speaker that they were 'on,' the atmosphere was electric. Harry and Zac grabbed the seats vacated by the Blue Stones while Bobby and Tom commandeered the vending machine.

'Think I'll have a coffee,' Bobby said as he approached the table full of snacks and hot drinks. Tom retrieved a variety of drinks from the vending machine and returned to the lounge area. The four of them sat and chatted about the show, slowly coming down from the high of their performance. They were quite relaxed by the time the Blue Stones had finished the evening's performance and spilled into the Green Room, flopping down on the remaining sofas. Tom led a round of applause for the Blue Stones, who acknowledged the acclamation by producing a couple of bottles of vodka. One of them gathered up an armful of glasses from the snacks table and handed them around. The members of the two bands sat around drinking vodka and sharing conversations about the show, the music industry, what's hot and what's not at the moment, enjoying the camaraderie, not wanting the evening to end.

Jeff Simpson, the Blue Stones lead singer, sat opposite Tom. As the others all screamed laughing at a joke told by one of the young men, Jeff leaned in and asked Tom,

'Who's your manager?'

Tom replied, 'I'm it.' He grinned ruefully and ran a hand through his tousled hair. 'But lately I've been thinking maybe it's time we started shopping around for a professional.'

'Yeah, Man, it sure is. The record companies won't talk to bands, below their dignity! They only negotiate with managers and their lawyers. You need someone with contacts, someone who's been in the business a while. I'd sign with someone quickly if I were you, you're gonna need them soon. You guys have got a certain sound. I'd say you've got a future in this business.'

'Thanks for the vote of confidence, Jeff. Who do you use?'

'Bryan Castle manages us, and I would absolutely recommend him except he's flat out and not taking on any new clients. If you like, I could ask him if he can recommend anyone else in the business and get back to you.'

'I'd appreciate that, thanks. What's the going rate for a music manager these days?'

'Most of them ask 12% - 15% of your gross. Careful if you get someone who only wants 10%, they've probably taken on too many clients or they're just starting out and haven't got any experience. And don't sign up with anyone who's asking more than 20%. They're ripping you off.'

'Thanks for the tips, Jeff. I'll keep that in mind.'

During the few minutes Jeff and Tom had been talking, reporters and photographers from various newspapers and magazines had descended on the Green Room and before Tom knew what was happening, they were upon him, demanding answers to questions, flashbulbs going off in quick succession.

'Another one of you and the boys against the wall here. These famous posters will make a great backdrop.'

'Where's your next show? Will you be a support act or the main event?'

'How long have you guys been playing together?'

'How about one of Tom on his own? Sit here. Look there. Turn to the right. Face left. With your guitar. Without the guitar.'

As Bobby said, 'All good publicity. Better get used to it.'

Chapter 13

*T*he 1990s was a revolutionary decade for digital technology. Although it was created 20 years before, the World Wide Web became popular and gained unstoppable momentum in the 1990s. Internet-only companies such as Amazon and eBay grew rapidly and by the end of the decade there were about 295 million users on the Internet. Communication technology also continued to develop and by the late 1990s, more than 25% of western countries had mobile cell phone access.

In the area of health and society, the World Health Organisation removed homosexuality from its list of diseases and acceptance of homosexuality in the western world slowly began.

In 1991, what became known as the Gulf War was waged by the US, UK, and coalition forces from 35 nations against Iraq in response to Iraq's invasion and annexation of Kuwait arising from oil pricing and production disputes.

It was during the '90s the media world-wide became a force to be reckoned with, ignoring all in their wake to get 'the next big story.' It is even said that paparazzi were chasing Princess Diana and her friend, Dodi Al-Fayed, when they were killed in a car accident which *inevitably led to their chauffeur-driven car crashing in a tunnel in Paris in 1997.*

United States President, Bill Clinton, was also caught up in a media-frenzied scandal involving inappropriate relations with a White House intern, Monica Lewinsky. He was impeached in December 1998 for perjury under oath but acquitted by the Senate in February 1999.

But it was not all bad:

After being imprisoned for 27 years in South Africa, Nelson Mandela was released in 1990 and was subsequently voted into power in the democratic election of 1994, ending many years of white rule and apartheid in South Africa.

Thanks largely to Mikhail Gorbachev, Germany was reunified following the fall of the Berlin Wall and after integrating the economic structure and provincial governments, focused on modernization of the former communist East.

The United Kingdom handed back sovereignty of Hong Kong to the People's Republic of China on 1 July 1997.

In the entertainment business, the death of the lead singer of Nirvana, Kurt Cobain, at age 27, had a lasting effect on fans all over the world. Female pop icons, the Spice Girls, took the world by storm, becoming the most commercially successful British group since the Beatles. U2, R.E.M, Nirvana, Foo Fighters, Pearl Jam, Red Hot Chili Peppers were a few of the most popular bands of the era.

TV shows, mostly sitcoms, were popular with viewers—The Golden Girls, Frazier, Cheers, Friends. Crime drama and police detective shows such as Law & Order, NYPD Blue, and Homicide eventually took over from the soap-operas.

Harry Potter, the hugely successful book series by J. K. Rowling, was released late in the decade and the series, with only seven major novels, would become the best-selling book series in world history.

Yes, it was an interesting decade to be an ambitious young man in the United States of America.

Tom drove back to Palo Alto on Sunday afternoon to tell Gran and Jim all about the concert. As he tucked into his favourite homemade fruit cake Gran had baked especially for him, she listened earnestly as he told her all about the concert. He omitted the part about getting absolutely wasted on vodka on the Friday night and completely missing Saturday. He didn't know how, but they somehow found themselves sitting in the Green Room at seven-thirty, waiting to go on, having almost sobered up enough to perform. There were certain details Gran didn't need to hear. Little did Tom know Gran understood all about young men and what they got up to. The book club to which she belonged was made up of mothers and grandmothers of young men who were often discussed at length amongst the women, due mainly to the young men's misdemeanours rather than their good deeds.

It was pleasant, sitting there sharing afternoon tea with Gran, just the two of them. Jim was playing golf and wouldn't be home until later in the day, so Tom had Gran all to himself and he made the most of it.

As he stopped to take a breath and a bite of another piece of cake, Tom took a closer look at his beloved grandmother. He hadn't noticed before how white her hair was now, or how her hands were gnarled and bent from the arthritis which had slowly worked itself into her hands and feet, making her movements less smooth than they used to be. But the eyes still sparkled, especially when she was with her grandson, and her mind was sharp and her interest in everything he did and said had never waned. Their special relationship, which had developed in the years after Tom's mother died, had deepened. She reached out her hand and covered his. Her voice crackled slightly as she said: 'I'm happy when you're happy, Tom. It sounds like you're on your way to being very successful. Mr. O'Brien would be so proud.' Then, concerned she may have sounded sentimental, she added,

'But now I must go and get ready. I have to leave in 15 minutes for my book club meeting.'

Later, Tom and Jim sat up at the kitchen counter, the pizza box open between them, the fridge door within easy reach—neither of them having to get off the stool to get more beers. Tom relived the past three days again as he described every detail to his father. Jim was pleased the boys had enjoyed the concert, especially after Tom had put so much work into the preparation and planning. Often, the anticipation of success is far greater than the actual result, but if Tom's genuine delight in the re-telling of the event was anything to go by, it had been a triumph.

When Tom told him of the conversation he'd had with Jeff Simpson about finding a manager, Jim took another piece of pizza and opened his third beer, giving himself time to think of the right words for what he wanted to say:

'I agree it's time you got yourselves a manager. I reckon you've reached the stage where you need professional advice, and possibly guidance, on your future, and that's what a good manager will do for you. Of course, it will come at a cost, but it sounds like you're getting enough work to make that a financially viable investment.'

True to his word, Jeff rang Tom a couple of days later with the name of a music manager Bryan recommended—a woman in Los Angeles. Tom was surprised but contacted the woman, who agreed to meet him in L.A. on Saturday, a meeting which proved to be one of the most important of his career, present and future.

Once all four of the men had arrived at band practice on Thursday evening, Tom filled them in on what a manager would mean for the band. He also explained he had been banking any leftovers after they had all been paid for every gig and, thanks to his money-handling, they had enough put aside to cover a manager for at least a couple of months. They should have a fair idea by then if it was a worthwhile venture.

Three heads nodded in agreement, glad they didn't have to do any of the admin. Tom's handling of the management side of things had worked well up until now, but as Zac said: 'Tom can't go on doing this forever. We want you to know, Tom, we are all grateful for what you've done for the band.'

Tom smiled and said: 'Thanks guys, for the vote of confidence. In that case, you won't mind that I've set up a meeting with Ms. Alice Weinberg in L.A. on Saturday.'

The female name didn't register; they were too busy complaining about having to drive to L.A.

'It's a five-and-a-half-hour drive, Tom! There's no way.' Zac wished he hadn't been so effusive in his praise for Tom. It looked like getting up at five in the morning and driving to L.A. was going to be the trade-off.

'No need to carry on, Zac, our appointment is not until two-thirty, although it's probably a good idea to go straight home after the Fringe on Friday night.'

Huge sighs of relief all round until Harry stopped fiddling at the keyboard and turned to look at Tom, and frowning, said,

'Did you say Ms. Alice someone-or-other?'

'I did indeed,' said Tom. 'She comes highly recommended by the Blue Stones' manager. I didn't know there were female music managers either, but I eventually got used to the idea, as I'm sure you will too. I don't care what gender she is if she's good at her job, so I suggest we all wait and see what transpires on Saturday.'

They arrived at Ms. Weinberg's address at about two-fifteen. After parking in the underground carpark of the dingy five-storey office building, they made their way to the ancient elevator only to find it out of order.

'What is that smell?' asked Bobby, covering his nose with his hand to avoid breathing it in.

'Smells like someone is barbecuing a body over the charcoal residue of burnt car tires,' replied Harry.

'Probably dissipates the higher we go up the stairs,' said Zac, trying to whip up more enthusiasm than he felt.

It was true—the smell did lessen as they made their way up the dirty, rubbish-strewn concrete stairwell to the fifth floor.

All four of them were breathing heavily by the time they arrived at the top floor. Harry bent over and rested his hands on his knees, taking in large gulps of air. At least the smell wasn't so bad up here.

'Just as well we didn't hang around last night, smoking weed and drinking. We never would have made it up those stairs.' Tom grinned, as he knocked on the door of office number five, the one with the hand-written sign attached to the door which said, 'Ms. Alice Weinberg - Do not enter unless you have an appointment!'

'Nice touch,' said Tom, eyeing the sign. He pushed the door open as a gravelly voice called from within, 'Come in, and hurry up or you'll let the smell in. They incinerate the rubbish on Saturday afternoons and my sinuses can't take much more.'

The office smelled of air freshener and cigarettes.

'Ms. Weinberg, I'm Tom Watson and this is Bobby Gardener, Harry Daben, and Zac Robertson. We're Pants on Fire.' Tom made the introductions as he tried not to look around the office. At this stage, he could only see Ms. Weinberg and was worried about what the rest of it was like.

The woman facing them was small but fierce. Her thick dark hair was piled up on top of her head, long bangs sat on the top of her mannish tortoiseshell spectacles, almost hiding the heavy black brows that dipped in a constant frown. Bright red lips highlighted the paleness of her flawless complexion and her crisp white shirt looked expensive, even to someone who knew nothing of such things. The chunky pearl necklace matched the equally chunky pearl earrings, all of which matched her skin colour. It was impossible to judge this woman's age: she could have been 40, or maybe 45, or even 30.

Ms. Weinberg sat behind an old-fashioned battered wooden table that looked like it had lost the fight a long time ago and had completely given itself up to the carved names and Celtic symbols gouged into the top. It was covered in notepads, pieces of paper, a half-empty glass of dirty water, an overflowing ashtray—one of those black Bakelite ones they use in old English pubs—and a soft carpet of dust. The chair she sat on looked like she had brought it in from her no doubt equally old-fashioned dining room. It probably looked wrong in the dining room once it lost one of its arms. No fancy office chair with wheels for Ms.Weinberg!

'How do you do, boys,' said Ms. Weinberg briskly, standing and shaking hands with each of them. 'I'm pleased to meet you. Please sit down.' She indicated they should sit on the four visitors' chairs, which miraculously matched her chair, but with not one arm amongst them—obviously, the rest of the dining suite!

Tom glanced out the window as he sat down, but the blank brick wall of the building next door obliterated any view. It could only have been about six feet away. His dismay must have been obvious from the look on his face as Alice said, 'Don't look so alarmed, Tom. This is not how I live. This is merely where I see prospective clients. And please, call me Alice.'

Tom laughed, embarrassed. 'Actually, it's like something out of a Raymond Chandler novel,' he said, as he took in the rest of the room. It was not until he turned his head and looked behind him that he noticed the posters. Signed pictures of several famous bands were pinned to the wall—Pink Floyd, The Ramones, Guns N' Roses. This setting felt surreal, as if they'd wandered onto the set of an art-house 1940s movie.

Alice got down to business immediately. 'The reason I'm seeing you today is because I owe Bryan Castle a favour. As you probably know, I only do rock bands and I have several big clients. So, what can you offer me?'

What can we offer her? I thought it was the other way around. And I didn't know she only did rock bands! Tom was confused, but kept his thoughts to himself.

Tom glanced at the others. He sensed Zac bristle at the woman's tone then watched in awe as Bobby sat up straighter in the chair and, brushing his hair back with one hand, said in his most lawyer-ly voice, 'Actually, it's what you can offer us.' He leaned forward, holding eye contact with Mrs. Weinberg. 'We're on the cusp of enormous success here and we're looking for someone to manage our fabulous future for us. Do you want to come along for the ride of your life? Because if you don't, we won't waste any more of your time.'

Tom looked at Bobby with a combination of shock and admiration. Zac and Harry sat dumbfounded, looking from Bobby to Tom to Alice and back to Bobby, wondering what the next move was in this game of one-upmanship.

For a couple of silent seconds, time stood still. Then: 'Bryan said you were good. He didn't mention your arrogance, often a good sign in a rock band. The fans love it,' said Alice through a deep, throaty laugh.

'Right. Here's the deal: If I take you on, it will be under a signed contract, renewable every twelve months. You will do exactly what I say, when I say it, and no whining. I, and the entertainment lawyer I use, will negotiate with record companies on your behalf and organise contracts and sundry agreements. I will organise concerts across the country at excellent venues, tours around the country, not necessarily at excellent venues—she paused and smiled at her own little joke—promotions, merchandise, TV interviews, and media events. I will advise you on how to dress, how to behave in public, and how to handle the paparazzi. I will manage your bank account, with your permission, and I will make you a lot of money—if you are as good as they say you are. We're talking millions of dollars if you honour your part of the deal.

'For this, I will take 15% of your gross earnings, paid monthly, thirty days after you receive payment. Do I make myself clear?'

'You absolutely do,' said Tom, wide-eyed. 'Will you put that in writing for us please, Alice?'

'I already have,' she replied, handing Tom a folder containing four copies of written confirmation of her terms.

'Now, why don't I go and make us a nice cup of tea while you boys have a read through that?'

A thought flashed through Tom's mind: *God only knows what the tea is going to taste like!*

Alice disappeared through a door at the back of the office and closed it behind her. Tom handed a copy of the document to each of the others, and they sat quietly and read each page.

'Any comments?' asked Tom when they had finished reading.

'Whatever you think, Tom. You know more about this than we do,' said Harry.

'Agreed,' said Zac.

'I say we go with her,' said Bobby.

'So do I,' said Tom. 'She comes highly recommended. She's been in the business a long time; she's obviously got the right connections. She's fierce—probably eats nails for breakfast. I'd hate to be a record company on the other end of negotiations with her. Plus, I really love this office!'

'I say we sign here and now.'

Right on cue, almost as if she'd been listening, Alice opened the door and walked over to her desk carrying a large wooden tray on which sat five fine bone china cups, saucers, and plates, a matching teapot, milk jug, and sugar bowl, linen napkins, and a plate of iced cupcakes. As she placed the tray carefully on the desk, Alice looked at each of the young men and smiled kindly.

'Well, is this to be a celebration, or are we just going to drink tea?'

Tom replied: 'Alice, you and your eccentric office have won us over. Where do we sign?'

Chapter 14

The following Friday night, as the band was setting up their instruments for the evening performance at the Fringe, Tom glanced around the room. He liked to get an idea of the size of the crowd before they started; it usually doubled by the end of their first set. Tables and chairs were dotted along the raised section, which ran the length of one wall like an old-fashioned nightclub. He was surprised to see this section was already full. He was even more surprised when he saw Alice sitting at one table with three or four young clubbers. She smiled and waved to him in acknowledgement, then rose and made her way to the stage.

'Hi, Alice. This is a surprise,' said Tom. The others stopped what they were doing and welcomed Alice onto the dais.

'Hello, boys,' replied Alice. 'I need to see for myself exactly what it is I'm dealing with here. I'm sharing my table with a group of young clubbers whom I've commandeered to give me their opinions of Pants on Fire. Obviously, they have no idea of why I'm here tonight so let's keep it that way, shall we?'

'Of course. But Alice, you are more than welcome any time.' Tom spoke from the heart. He was genuinely delighted that Alice had taken the time and trouble to travel to San Francisco to see them perform.

'Let's chat again after the show. There are some things I want to discuss with you.'

'Sure,' replied the four men as one, as Alice turned and found her way back to the table, easing herself through the expanding crowd.

During the week, Zac had bought a van the same as the one they hired to drive to Los Angeles. Using one van, and with Zac as their designated driver, made it easier and cheaper for them to travel in the same vehicle to the Fringe and other venues. They all met up at Bobby's place earlier and, in hindsight, it was probably a good thing they had had a few joints and a couple of vodkas. All except Zac—the designated driver. The others were feeling relaxed and confident, not at all phased by the fact tonight's performance was being scrutinised by their manager. However, Tom always enjoyed a few vodkas as a way of winding down when they had finished for the evening, and he knew that probably wouldn't be such a good idea during talks with Alice.

Tonight's show was slow to get going. It felt like the four members of the band were not completely in sync emotionally—maybe it was the weed they smoked before the show, although they had done that before and it had improved their performance. It took about four numbers for the audience to warm up. Fortunately, Bobby's and Harry's girlfriends had come along tonight and were seated at one of the tiny tables in the back. They whooped and applauded enthusiastically after each number, which encouraged the rest of the audience. This seemed to work and by the end of the night, the place was alive with energy, many of the audience singing along with some of the final songs.

As per the standing arrangements with girlfriends, the two women came up onto the stage after the final number to say good night to Bobby and Harry as the men were packing up.

Once the room had cleared, Alice approached them.

'I suggest we sit at my table now everyone has left. We can talk there.' Although she used the word 'suggest,' it was most definitely a directive.

Once seated around the table, Tom couldn't hold back. 'Well, what did you think?'

'I was eventually impressed!' replied Alice. 'You started out like a vase of week-old flowers but by the end of the night you had improved considerably. That's how you need to be for the entirety of every performance.'

You could almost feel the silence.

'The good news is that with my management and chutzpah, you could become the next big thing.' Alice grinned and everyone relaxed.

'But we need to go through certain channels and these things take time.'

She hesitated for an instant before reaching for her cigarettes and lighter, taking her time extracting a cigarette and lighting the tip before exhaling a lungful of smoke.

Tom realised this was all part of her 'performance' and waited patiently for the next part of her 'act,' but Zac drummed his fingers on the table. The others weren't so patient either; Harry tapped his foot in time with an imaginary tune and Bobby stared at the ceiling. Time dragged on; Alice wanted her next statement to have an impact.

'I have made an appointment for myself and the Entertainment Lawyer I use to see the Executive Producer of Red Pony Music in three weeks.'

There was a collective gasp from the four men.

'Red Pony Music!' exclaimed Tom, as he removed his elbows from the table and smoothed his hands over his thighs to quell the excitement he could feel building up in his stomach.

'Did you say Red Pony Music?' said Harry.

Bobby and Zac stared in disbelief, speechless.

The excitement couldn't be completely contained and Tom rushed on, stumbling over his words: 'But they're huge! How did you manage to get an appointment with the Executive Producer?'

'Don't get too excited, Tom. They are also the sharks of the music industry. They feed on the smaller fish. It's only the big and powerful who swim alongside the sharks. We need to get this right from the get-go. That's why I work in conjunction with the best Entertainment Lawyer in the game. Red Pony Music only talks to Suits; they don't waste their time negotiating directly with performers.

'I need to take a demo tape of Pants on Fire to the meeting, and we haven't got long to organise this. I suggest next Tuesday night. I've booked you with one of the best record producers here in San Francisco.

'I also arranged to video your performance tonight. I will look at that tomorrow. I suggest you come to the Hyatt Hotel around eleven am and we'll go over it together.'

Two more directives cloaked as 'suggestions!'

'Of course we'll be there, Alice,' said Tom, looking at the others who, on cue, nodded enthusiastically in agreement.

Alice stubbed her cigarette out in the ashtray. She stood to leave, collecting her handbag and cigarettes from the table.

'Good night, boys. I'll see you tomorrow. Don't be late.'

'Good night, Alice.' in four simultaneous voices.

Alice turned to go but stopped, and, placing one hand on the back of her chair, said,

'Something to remember; weed is one thing—the fans will forgive their favourite band being stoned occasionally, but I suggest you take it easy on the alcohol—they won't tolerate a drunken performance.' And she turned on her heel and strode off into the darkness.

Tom felt as if he'd been reprimanded personally. He was very much aware Alice had looked hard at him when she mentioned the drinking.

Alice had arranged for the video player to be set up in the hotel's Business Suite by the time the boys arrived at eleven am. All four of them were looking forward to seeing the video of their performance from the Fringe. They had never seen themselves perform before, and this would be a novelty. They settled down into the comfortable chairs. The atmosphere in the room crackled with expectation.

The On button was depressed, and the screen sprung into life around the middle of their first number. It might have looked better had the lighting been brighter, but it was watchable, if not a brilliant piece of filming. However, Tom was disappoint-ed—he thought the band looked amateurish. It was not until about halfway through the evening's performance that they lifted their game. During the early part of the video, he glanced sideways at Harry and grimaced. Harry frowned and pulled a face like an upside-down Smiley in response.

The video faded to a halt towards the end of their final number for the night. Alice switched the machine off and turned the lights up.

'I'd like to hear your comments,' she said, looking from one to the other. 'Tom, you go first.'

'You were so right, Alice. We did look like a vase of week-old flowers to start, although I do think we picked up after that first break.'

'And you, Bobby?'

'I agree with Tom; except I thought the finale was great.'

'And what have you got to say Harry?'

'Shit performance. We are so much better than that.'

'Zac?'

'Harry's right. We are usually better than that. But everyone has an off night. We're at the Blue Door in San Mateo tonight. Why don't you come along?'

Alice had already planned to attend the Blue Door that evening, but she was pleased Zac had suggested it, so she let him think it was his idea.

'Good idea, Zac. I will.'

There was a pause in the conversation before Alice spoke again.

'Surprising when you see yourselves as others see you, isn't it? From my point of view, the sound was fantastic, the look – not so much. You really need to loosen up.'

'We're now going to play the video again, and again, and again. We are going to discuss the performance in detail. I'm going to make notes on what's wrong and what's right and you're going to make those changes accordingly.'

'Do I make myself clear?'

'Yes, Alice.' Four voices in unison.

At seven o'clock on Tuesday evening, the four exhausted but excited men stood in the foyer of the music studio. All day Sunday and Monday night, they practised the changes Alice had suggested and their confidence was running high. Tom, Bobby, and Harry had brought their instruments with them, but when Alice told Zac the studio had its own DW drum kit, he didn't bother with his own set. The truth was, he couldn't wait to use the DW. It was the best kit on the market today, but a brand he couldn't afford.

Alice was already there by the time they arrived and introduced them to the producer, Taco. He was a serious-looking man with a full beard, wearing a fireman's uniform and a Greek fisherman's cap. *Probably conservative gear for a record producer*, thought Tom.

Taco showed them into the recording studio without further ado.

It was the first time any of them had been inside a professional music studio and they couldn't help looking around to take it all in. The room was much smaller than they expected, and it was carpeted. Tom leaned over and touched one wall. It was covered, as were all the walls, from wall to wall and up to the ceiling, with a deep pile, hideously patterned carpet. It looked like something you'd see on the floor of a busy pub or nightclub, hard-wearing, and bearing not even a passing glance to any form of decoration. Even the inside of the door was carpeted. The ceiling consisted of sound absorbing acoustic tiles. Several mics on stands, draped with three or four sets of headphones, stood at the front of the room. There was a large window in the wall they were facing, through which they could see the Control Room.

Zac eyed the drum kit up and down. It didn't look much different to his drums, and his disappointment was obvious. Taco smiled.

'You won't want to play anything else once you've played these.'

'Hmmmm,' replied Zac as he settled down on the drum seat and picked up the sticks.

'Do you guys need to warm up?' Taco asked.

'We've been warming up for days,' said Tom, as he looped his guitar strap around his neck. Harry was set to go at his keyboard and played an arpeggio introduction.

'You'll find you sound better if you all wear headphones,' said Taco. 'They prevent one instrument's sound mixing with that of another instrument. They create sound isolation or separation. Also, they allow me to communicate with you from the control room without interfering with the music.'

'Maybe we do need a few minutes to warm up,' said Tom as he fitted his headphones snugly over his ears. 'You're dealing with newbies here. We appreciate your advice.'

Alice smiled as she and Taco disappeared into the Control Room, closing the door behind them.

She spoke into her mike and checked that each musician could hear her through their headphones.

'When you've finished warming up, I want you to start with 'Out into the World.' That's the number I'm going to concentrate on with Red Pony. We'll end up with about five in total, but 'Out into the World' is the best thing you've done, so I'll lead with our longest and strongest.'

Tom was surprised. How did she know 'Out into the World'? They hadn't played that song last week when she was at the Fringe. Tom made a mental note: *Rule Number One: never underestimate Alice.*

It was after one in the morning when they finally finished their recording session. The past few days had caught up with the guys, but Alice seemed to have a fresh burst of energy.

'I am so pleased with these demos, guys,' she said as they piled into the van. 'Now all we need is another video of the new moves we discussed on Saturday, and I'll be ready to blow Red Pony's Producer's mind. I intend to leave them begging for more.'

Chapter 15

'Wooden, she said. We need to loosen up, she said. That's not easy when you're playing a keyboard.' Harry shook his arms and wiggled his fingers, then did a couple of squats and lunges.

'I don't think that's exactly what she meant,' said Tom. 'You saw the video; we looked like store dummies. Relax man, just look like you're enjoying it.'

'I've practiced a few tricks with the sticks,' said Zac. 'Watch this.' And he threw one stick high into the air and caught it without missing a beat. He then threw the other stick in the air from behind his back, catching it easily, again without missing a beat. 'Only took me three hours to get it right! I think Alice wants about eight more like that,' he muttered, as he tried bouncing a stick on the floor but completely missed it as it shot off at a 45-degree angle and hit Harry's keyboard.

Bobby strutted around the music room doing an exaggerated swaggering walk. He leaned back at an acrobatic angle, his left hand holding the neck of the guitar high in the air, his right hand picking the strings which were now in the area of his chest.

'What do you think? Loose enough for you?'

'Looks good,' replied Tom, 'provided you don't trip over anything. Can you see where you're going at that angle?'

'And what about you, Tom? Alice said you should move more.' Zac was reading the sheet of notes Alice had handed out to each of them.

'You know, I always thought I did move, but when I saw the video, I looked like a robot. But don't worry; I've been practising.'

The four of them had agreed to practice on Wednesday and Thursday, to get their act together according to Alice's suggestions. She had arranged for their performance the following Saturday night at the Blue Door to be videoed, and if they met her expectations, that was the one she would take to Red Pony. If not, Alice would not be happy. And nobody wanted to risk that.

But the practice sessions and their live performance on Friday night paid off. Saturday night's show at the Blue Door was fantastic and much appreciated by the audience. They were treated to a standing ovation following their final number and the audience wouldn't let them go until they had played two encores.

Alice rang Tom during the following week to tell him she was pleased with their efforts and couldn't wait to show the demo tape and the latest video to the Red Pony executives.

Following her appointment with Alan Cohen, Record Producer, and Lu Ricci, Head of Sales for Red Pony, Alice phoned Tom to let him know what had transpired.

'Well, they were impressed with the demo and the video, but don't get too carried away; we won't hear back from them for weeks, maybe months. Their Market Research people do a lot of follow-up before they make any decisions.'

What she didn't tell Tom was that the two executives were excited by the demo tape, particularly Tom's voice and the songs he had written.

'This is different to what's out there at the moment,' said Alan, glancing at Lu to see if he agreed. 'And I think we could do something with it.' Lu looked serious but nodded as he added: 'Alan's right. This guy has got a great sound and look. Plus, it sounds like they've been playing together for a while, quite a well-balanced group.'

'We'll run a few test markets and get back to you.'

As part of the negotiations game, Alan and Lu tried not to look too enthusiastic.

At the same time, Alice and her lawyer tried not to look too pleased with how the meeting was progressing.

'They haven't signed with anyone yet,' said the lawyer, 'but we've got a few irons in the fire. Alice is working on a tour across 15 towns and cities within the next few months so of course, it would be ideal to have them signed up before that takes place. A record contract to coincide with a tour would have real impact.'

When the meeting finished a short time later, the four people rose simultaneously and shook hands.

'You know the drill, Alice. We'll be in touch.'

'And of course, we'll let you know if we sign with anyone else before that happens,' replied Alice, smiling like a fox, as she and her lawyer left the office.

A week and a day after their meeting, Alan rang Alice.

'Hi Alice, it's Alan Cohen speaking. We've done our Market research and the results are in. We'd like you to come into the office for a chat.'

'Certainly, Alan. We're seeing Einstein Records Monday of next week. I would prefer to wait until after then to meet up. How about the following Tuesday? Would that suit you?' Alice was looking at the next week in her planner and trying to hide the glee in her voice as she spoke. Monday was empty.

Alan didn't like the sound of that. Einstein Records had poached a couple of their clients recently. 'No, that wouldn't suit. We'd like to see you this week. Can you make it Friday?'

'Let me check.'

Alice turned back to this current week and checked that Friday was blank. 'I've got a few things on Friday but I'm sure I can change them around to suit. I think I could do 10 am. How's that for you, Alan?'

'10 am, Friday, it is,' replied Alan. 'And Alice? Bring your lawyer with you.'

'We look forward to it,' said Alice in her most businesslike tone as she hung up the phone and did a little drum roll on the desk.

Alice Weinberg was the only child of Jewish refugees who fled Germany just before war broke out in Europe and had ended up in the Jewish ghetto of the Lower East Side of Manhattan Island. Mo Weinberg and Ruth Abrams met and married there in 1948 and had settled into a small tenement apartment by the time their daughter Alice was born in 1954.

Growing up in the squalid ghetto, the '50s and '60s taught Alice everything she needed to know to survive hunger, bullying, tough times, and inflexible Jewish parents. Along the way, she developed a cunning and shrewd nature, which she kept disguised as charm and good manners.

A tiny, premature baby, Alice grew into a small woman, but her feistiness and resilience saw her overcome situations that would have crushed a lesser woman. She was a glass-half-full kind of person who saw problems as challenges, who heard 'No' as 'Maybe,' and who didn't believe in taking a backward step.

From an early age, Alice had wanted to be an actress. She managed to land a part, no matter how small, in every school play. The world of show business fascinated her, and she was determined to make it her career. When acting success eluded her in New York, at age 17, she left the family's dismal airless tenement apartment and made her way to sunny California, specifically Los Angeles—the heart of Show Business Land.

Unfortunately, Alice's ego was bigger than her ability as an actress. Within a few months of endless auditions and knock backs, she realised she was a third-rate actress in an unending sea of first- and second-rate actresses. While she tried to find a job that had anything to do with the entertainment business, she waited tables and cleaned other people's houses to keep her head above water. Anything rather than going back to that apartment and her 'I told you so' mother and father in New York.

Alice tried several jobs in the show business industry in L.A. before she discovered she was a natural manager and a successful negotiator. She'd always been organised, which was a talent sadly lacking in the acting community. She was soon arranging auditions, promotions, and publicity for first her flatmates, then their friends, then friends of friends. It wasn't long before Alice had a following among the acting fraternity and she began to charge for her services, moderately in the beginning but gradually raising her commission fee as her booking list grew.

By the late-1970's, Alice was doing well as a manager in the entertainment business and had taken on clients from other professions as well as acting. On her books she had a jazz pianist in downtown L.A., a couple of songwriters, a movie editor, and a cameraman, amongst others. Her big break came in 1979 when she signed the first African American hip-hop group. Nobody else had been interested in them and they approached Alice after a song-writing friend recommended her. There followed a series of events which led to huge success for the group—and for Alice. Their first record was an instant hit, then the first tour Alice organised for them was a sell-out before it even began. Then their lead singer eloped with the biggest female movie star. Serendipity!

Alice had that same feeling about Tom Watson and Pants on Fire.

The meeting began at around 10 o'clock that Friday morning and ran on for the next two hours. The negotiations were arduous, many arguments ensued, and many cups of coffee drunk, but by 12.45, Alan and Lu were wining and dining Alice and her lawyer in L.A.'s most exclusive, and expensive, restaurant.

When the tall, immaculately attired waiter had deftly opened and poured their Krug champagne, Alan held his glass aloft and said,

'A pleasure doing business with you, Alice. You drive a hard bargain, but I think we will all benefit in the long run. This deal feels right.'

'Congratulations, Alice,' said Lu, 'Here's to Tom Watson and Pants on Fire.'

They all gently clinked their glasses before tasting the champagne, which was, of course, superb.

Alice smiled. 'It will be interesting to see where we all are in five years' time.'

'Seriously rich, I predict,' replied Alan.

A waiter glided up to their table. 'Are you ready to order, Sir?' he enquired of Alan. He smiled warmly as he began his well-practiced performance.

'Our speciality is hand-carved American Wagyu Filet Mignon with Foie Gras Sauce made with Grana Padano cheese. It is served with Cremini Mushrooms, Grilled Asparagus, Green Beans Almondine and an Avocado Salad. I can most definitely recommend it.' He beamed as if he was describing his newborn baby son. For a moment, they all thought he was going to produce pictures of the meal from his wallet.

Chapter 16

'Hello, Tom, Alice speaking. I've heard back from Red Pony Music. I think it's time for us to have a serious talk about your future. I suggest you and the band fly down here next Saturday. We'll meet in my office at 11 o'clock sharp; it should only take an hour or two.'

Alice had caught Tom off guard. It was Sunday morning, and he was sitting at the kitchen counter in sweatshirt and track pants, drinking coffee and reading the latest band reviews in the show business paper when the phone rang. He wasn't expecting to hear from Alice so soon. The realisation quickly dawned. This had to be a good sign, and he sat up straight on high alert.

'Sure Alice,' he said, aware she had used the words 'I suggest.' 'I'll arrange for us to come down next Saturday and we'll be in your office at 11 am. You make it sound important, Alice.'

'It is. See you then.' And she was gone.

'Come in, boys,' called Alice when she heard the knock on the door at 11 am sharp the following Saturday morning.

The four young men traipsed into the office and sat down opposite Alice. Tom noticed the table at which they sat had been tidied up—a little. The notes were now in a pile to one side, the ashtray had been emptied, and the glass of dirty water was nowhere to be seen. *Another good sign*, thought Tom.

'How was the flight?' asked Alice, but without waiting for an answer, continued,

'I'd like us to talk about your future. As you know, my lawyer and I met with the Execs from Red Pony Music recently. The good news is we were able to negotiate a record contract with them for Tom Watson and Pants on Fire.'

'What!' exclaimed Bobby.

'That's fantastic!' said Harry and Zac together.

Tom beamed. 'That's great, Alice. But the look on your face tells me there's more to it than meets the eye. What's the catch?'

'Ah, Tom, ever the realist,' replied Alice, smiling. 'There's no catch but the trade-off is you are going to work harder than you've ever worked in your lives. But believe me when I tell you it will be worth it. And of course, this all depends on whether you accept the contract or not. I suggest you accept it, by the way.'

The boys looked at each other. Tom was the first one to laugh, then the others joined in with him. There was that word again 'suggest'—as if they would do anything else.

Alice looked slightly confused by their reaction but continued: 'There's a lot to consider, so I will give this to you in pieces. Let's talk about the reward first. That's always a good place to start.'

'The contract is for three albums within the next five years—all original songs—for which they will advance you two million dollars.'

Zac looked at Tom. 'Did she say two million dollars?'

'Did she?' asked Harry.

'She did indeed,' replied Tom, grinning.

Bobby stared at Alice.

'Hear me out before you get too excited. This money has to cover a lot of expenses. However, there are other income streams as well.'

Alice held up one of her hands, displaying the beautifully manicured blood-red nails, as she counted off the various means from which income would be generated with her other hand.

'The retail sale of merchandise such as records, tee shirts, caps, posters; concert and tour takings; payment from AS-CAP and BMI for air-time worldwide for records played on radio and videos played on MTV; composition royalties for the songwriter; copyright for the recordings which is split with the recording company; and payment for public appearances. There are a few other minor things which bring in some money, but the things I just mentioned are your major income streams.'

Tom felt excited at the thought of becoming a professional musician. He wriggled in his chair and rubbed his hands up and down his thighs as his mind wandered. He could see his dream becoming a reality. He and his father had talked at length about the financial pros and cons of the working life of a musician, and he was aware of the things of which Alice spoke. He was not so aware of the cost and work involved in making it work. The four band members had talked about it briefly from time to time, but once they signed with Alice, they were happy to hand over that side of things to their manager.

By now, Tom and the others were paying close attention to everything Alice had to say. So far, the meeting was going brilliantly.

'And now to the cost of all this.' Alice turned the page of the spiral notebook she had been glancing at as she spoke.

'First of all, there's my 15%. As you know, that comes off the top. This entitles you to my organisational skills, my extensive lists of contacts, and the fact that I will work tirelessly for you.'

Tom noticed that there was no counting on her fingers this time. *Part of her 'act,'* thought Tom, *better to play down the number of ways the money would disappear.*

'As you also know, I use one of the best entertainment lawyers in the business. He doesn't come cheap. I also use the same firm of accountants I have used for many years, and they have never let me down. Also, not cheap. I use a PR firm which is very well-respected in the industry. PR is absolutely necessary as far as the band, and you guys personally, are concerned, so don't think you can get away without it to save money.'

'Concerts and tours generate the most income but cost the most money. Transport, Roadies, accommodation, merchandise, a good sound engineer and lighting person all add up.'

'The cost of making a video for MTV varies depending on how far you want to go creatively, but the rewards are good as far as royalties are concerned. Red Pony Music handles all your audio recordings and produces the CD's although this gives them total control of the finished products. Their A & R people do test-listening and call on radio and TV stations to push your records, which is a vital part of getting your music out there and getting it heard.'

'Are you still with me?' Alice asked. She noticed Zac's eyes glazing over at the thought of all this expenditure. She knew he had a sharp and questioning mind and that he was most likely doing a quick summary of the ins and outs of the money.

'Do you have any questions so far?'

'I do,' said Zac. 'Exactly what do you do for your 15%?' He smiled as he spoke, but his eyes were steely.

The others looked at Zac, embarrassed by his question, even though it was what they wanted to know, had they had the balls to ask.

Alice looked from one to the other before she spoke.

'I make all this happen.'

She leaned forward and rested her elbows on the desk, her two hands touching. She looked earnestly at the young men sitting opposite her and took a deep breath.

'Without me, you guys will continue to play the Fringe every Friday night and the Blue Door once a month until you're old and grey. Now, you may be happy doing that; I know a lot of musos who would be.'

'Or...With me behind you, you can become rich and famous, adored by millions of fans around the world. Tom Watson and Pants on Fire will become a household name. In demand. Masters of your destiny.'

'Turning professional means giving up your day jobs; devoting your lives to living and breathing music; doing as I say, when I say it; reaping the rewards of your hard work and living the good life.'

'It's your choice. You must now decide what kind of future you want for yourselves. I want you to go away and talk about it between yourselves and get back to me Monday morning.'

'Do you have any more questions? Now is the time to ask them.'

The floodgates opened, and the questions flowed over the spillway. Alice fielded questions and answers like a quizmaster in control of an international competition. She had been down this road several times before and it was always stimulating to be involved in discussions such as these with young people keen to sort out their future.

The elderly man seated next to Tom on the plane going home had opened his paperback and was reading even before Tom sat down and fastened his seat belt. Bobby was somewhere in the back and Zac and Harry were in the same row, but across the aisle. Tom was silently pleased to be on his own; it gave him time to think about the consequences of the meeting with Alice. As they levelled out after take-off, he adjusted his seat, put his head back, closed his eyes and let his mind wander.

The thought of turning professional held no fear for him; he had imagined it for so long. Working for H.P. had taught him the value and rewards of hard work, so he was unperturbed by what Alice had said about the work involved in being a successful musician. He made his decision the minute Alice told them about the record contract.

Because Zac was driven more by the dollars than the others, Tom didn't see a problem with him turning professional. Zac would see the rewards as being greater than the effort.

Tom smiled when he thought about Harry as a keyboard player in a famous rock band. Harry's ego would soak up the fan following like a sponge. Harry would be the first in line to sign his autograph on a pretty girl's blouse. He would live for the adrenalin.

Tom was not so sure about Bobby. Bobby had moved in with his girlfriend Janelle about six months ago, and they had been talking about marriage lately. They made a great couple, well-suited to each other and happy together. But a wife and kids and a house and suburban lifestyle did not go hand in hand with that of a guitarist in a rock band. In Tom's opinion, if Bobby tried to combine those two different spheres of his life on a permanent basis, he'd be on a short road to hell. But that was Bobby's decision to make, not Tom's.

As the plane began its descent into San Francisco International Airport, Tom felt a flutter of excitement at the thought of discussing the day's events with Jim and Gran later. Gran had invited him and Harry for dinner tonight, knowing they would want to talk about their day.

The four men had agreed to meet at Bobby's music studio Sunday morning at 11 am to discuss, and finally decide on, Pants on Fire's future.

Chapter 17

'Good morning, Alice. It's Tom Watson speaking. I hope I haven't caught you at a bad time but you did say you wanted our answer on Monday morning.'

It was 7.30am. This was not the type of conversation Tom wanted to have at the office, so he had phoned Alice before he left for work. Harry made fresh coffee for the two of them and placed a cup in front of Tom as he sat down opposite him at the kitchen table so he could be in on the conversation.

'This is a perfect time, Tom,' replied Alice. 'So, what news do you have for me?'

'I have good news and I have bad news. First, the good news.'

Tom cleared his throat and grinned in Harry's direction. He fidgeted, twisting the phone cord around his finger as he began.

'After much soul searching and discussion, Harry, Zac and I have decided to become professional musicians under your mentorship and management.'

'Good choice,' replied Alice calmly, as she silently punched the air with her fist and took a deep breath to quell her excitement. 'And the bad news?'

'Unfortunately for us, but good for him, Bobby has decided to leave the band. As you know, Bobby is a qualified attorney. His father offered him a partnership in his business and Bobby accepted. For Bobby, the band was only ever a hobby and we agreed that he would be mad to turn down the chance of a partnership in such a successful business. He's happy to stay with us until we can find a replacement bass guitarist. I hope we can find someone who fits in as well as Bobby does.'

'That's a shame,' said Alice, 'but as you said, good for Bobby. Unless you've already got someone lined up to replace him, I'll go through my contacts and see if I can come up with a bass guitarist who'll fit your group.'

'That would be great, Alice. I was hoping you might help us find someone.'

'These are exciting times boys. Enjoy them while you can. You've got some demanding work ahead of you. Just remember to slow down and appreciate life occasionally.'

Tom could hear the smile in Alice's voice as she spoke. He winked at Harry as he added,

'Oh, and something else – the three of us have decided to move to L.A.'

'Good move!' exclaimed Alice. 'And one you won't regret. As far as the music scene goes, L.A. is where the action is. Plus, it will make it easier for me to plot your future. There are many things which are better discussed face to face than over the phone.'

'I know you've got a few things to organise, but Tom, you need to start writing stuff for the album soon. The plan is to start recording it in about seven months and you'll want to have at least twenty new songs ready. This is the hard work part I told you about.

'In the meantime, I'll set up bank accounts here in L.A. and transfer money for you to live on. That will be your primary source of income once you've quit your day jobs and are no longer receiving regular income from the Fringe and the Blue Door. I'll also arrange your insurance and plan a calendar for the rest of the year. You've got a tough but exciting year ahead of you but think about where you'll be this time next year.'

It was hard resigning from their day jobs.

Tom had been at H.P. for almost 10 years and the Sales Manager was extremely disappointed when Tom told him he was leaving to move to L.A. to follow a career in music. Although he knew about the band and their regular gigs, he was amazed they had secured a record contract. So amazed, he didn't try to talk him into staying but wished him well for his future career.

It was also hard telling the Fringe and the Blue Door that they were moving to L.A. to pursue professional careers. Both venues had been good to the band over the years but both wished them well with no hard feelings. As Tom told the others at their next band practice: 'Don't worry, there's a line forming on the right of bands who would give anything to play the Fringe or the Blue Door. Our spots won't be vacant for long.'

Finding a place to live in L.A. proved much more difficult. The problem was they lived in San Francisco and were trying to find a place four hundred miles away in a city they didn't know.

Difficult was fast becoming impossible and panic was setting in when Alice rang and saved the day, as she would do many times during the life of the band. A business contact of hers was looking for tenants for a new apartment block he had invested in and she offered to have a look at the apartments on their behalf. Confident that Alice's taste and financial savvy would prevail, they agreed immediately.

Mr. Cohen met Alice in the building's foyer and showed her the apartments. As he explained, every floor was the same floor plan comprising two x two-bedroom and two x one-bedroom units. Wily fox that she was, Alice quickly calculated that she could get a better deal if she took one entire floor than to try to negotiate separate apartments. If one of the guys would take a one-bedroom apartment, the other two could each have a two-bedroom place, which would leave the other small unit where they could store their equipment and practice without bothering near neighbours.

Eli Cohen smiled benignly as he showed Alice around, point-ing out the good points and excellent value of each apartment. He was keen to tell her that several tenants had already moved in and that he felt sure the rest would be taken up quickly. He assured her she would need to decide promptly if she wanted one of these wonderful apartments. Alice made all the right noises and nodded enthusiastically as he rambled on.

Eventually, when she could get a word in, Alice enquired: 'And tell me, Eli, what sort of rental fee are you looking for here?'

She looked suitably shocked when he told her the going rate for each apartment, even though she secretly thought they were almost reasonable rental figures for the area.

Alice turned slowly to face Eli, raised one eyebrow, and smiled sarcastically. Cocking her head slightly to one side, she said: 'Eli, you and I both know, that is daylight robbery.' She paused momentarily for effect before continuing: 'But I'll tell you what I'll do for you. I'll take an entire floor at 50% discount. Oh, and that includes parking for three cars. That's my first and final offer. Let me know by close of business tomorrow if you're interested.' She shook hands with a stunned Eli before adding: 'And now I must run. I have to look at another place over on San Pedro Street while it's still available.'

Alice smiled inwardly as she signed each of the four leases the following morning in Eli Cohen's office, six hours ahead of her deadline. She chuckled when she thought of the added bonus—the block was only a hundred yards or so from her office.

With the men's agreement, Alice furnished the apartments ready for them to move in. Using female logic, she figured because Zac was only a small man, he would be comfortable in the one-bedroom apartment and Harry and Tom could each have a two-bedroom place. She visited every thrift shop within a 20-mile radius—it was amazing what she achieved with little money, good taste, and a head full of ideas.

Alice rang Tom at home one evening before he and Harry headed out for band practice. 'Well, Tom, your places are fully furnished and ready for you guys to move in next Saturday as planned. It will probably take you a couple of days to complete the move, so I've organised for two prospective bass guitarists to meet with you at your place next Wednesday afternoon. I personally know one of them and the other guy comes highly recommended. Let's hope you find one of them a good fit for the band.'

The two men had been waiting for her to phone and confirm that Saturday was a go. Tom felt a tingle of excitement at the thought of moving to L.A. and starting a new way of life. It was really happening.

Alice's news about a replacement for Bobby took a load off his mind. 'Alice, that's great news. I'm also glad you've been able to tee up a couple of bass players for us to check out. I haven't had any luck here, seen a couple of duds but nobody worthwhile. I was beginning to sweat blood, but once again, Alice to the rescue.'

'Alice, we want you to know that we're all looking forward to the move. I reckon we should be fully set up by Monday night at the latest. Why don't you come around and have a welcome drink with us on Tuesday when you've finished work? We've got a little surprise for you.' Tom smiled at Harry, who winked back at him.

'Tell her it'll knock her socks off,' Harry shouted as he closed the dishwasher and switched it on.

'I'd better wear some socks then,' she laughed as she hung up.

Tom had dinner at home with Gran and his father on the Friday before and they talked of little else but his new life in L.A. and the band's hoped-for success. Jim was genuine in his good wishes, even though he was sad to see Tom give up what had been a solid past and even brighter future at H.P. His father was quiet and introspective as Tom hugged him and they shook hands at the front door. As he turned to Gran for a hug, he was shocked to see the tears on her cheeks as she put her arms around him.

'Oh, Tom, we will miss you so.' The words caught in her throat as a sob escaped. 'I wish you everything you wish for yourself. I hope your new life is everything you want it to be. Take great care and remember how much I love you, wherever you are.' She clutched him tightly around the neck and kissed his cheek, sobbing.

As he wrapped his arms around her and kissed her, he was surprised by how thin she had become. He broke away from the hug and held her at arm's length, not wanting this parting memory of her to be about how fragile she felt in his arms. As he wiped away her tears with a tissue he found in his pocket, he said gently,

'Gran, I'm only going four hundred miles. I'll be back from time to time, and remember, you can come and see me anytime you want, can't she Dad?'

Jim smiled and nodded. *Thank God he doesn't know this will probably be the last time we will all be together,* he thought. At that moment, he was glad she had not told Tom of her prognosis.

The three men met up at Tom and Harry's place early on the Saturday morning and finished loading everything into Zac's van and the other two cars. They were on the road by nine on a typical foggy San Francisco morning, which would develop into a sunny, almost-warm day, perfect for the road trip ahead of them.

When they arrived at the apartment block late in the day, they collected their keys from Eli Cohen, who was showing another prospective tenant around the building.

'Let's look at the place for our equipment first,' said Zac, as they entered the elevator. He was keen to unload the van and get their gear set up. That was far more important than hanging clothes in a wardrobe.

He unlocked the door and they spilled into the combined living/kitchen area.

A collective 'Wow!' followed by exclamations of delight and amazement at what Alice had accomplished rendered the air.

Thick grey carpet covered the floor from wall to wall, white acoustic tiles completely lined the ceiling, but it was the walls which drew the most attention. White, pale grey, and navy-blue acoustic tiles arranged in wide diagonal stripes lines all four walls.. Heavy navy-blue drapes hung open at the large double window which looked out onto the street below. Against one wall near the compact kitchen was an Alice 'special'—a battered old table with three matching legs, one odd one, and two drawers of which one was missing a handle. A modern ergonomic office chair nestled under the table within reaching distance of a much used two drawer filing cabinet. Against one wall was a pre-loved old-fashioned leather sofa of indiscriminate colour, and against the opposite wall stood two comfortable looking occasional chairs. Even though the apartment was brand new, it had a lived-in feel to it already which Harry described as 'studio retro.' The men loved it immediately.

'Let's go get our gear and set it up right now,' said Zac. 'I can't wait to find out what we sound like in this recording studio atmosphere.'

'Excellent idea, Zac,' replied Harry as the three of them slammed the door behind them and raced to the elevator.

It required a few trips to the van to lug all their equipment up to the apartment, but they eventually finished messing around with cables and deciding the best places for drums, keyboards, and guitars, etc. Time to discover what the band sounded like in this cloistered room of sound-absorbing acoustic panels and carpet. Without even conferring with each other, they started in on 'Long Cool Woman.' Perfect!

And suddenly, it was midnight.

'We haven't even seen our own places yet,' said Tom, as they finished yet another number. 'We need to get our stuff from downstairs and at least unpack it into our apartments. I guess we forgot to eat. I wonder if there's any diners around here. I'm starving.'

'I noticed an all-night burger joint next door when we drove in,' replied Harry. 'Allow me to take you guys out to dinner before we move in,' he laughed, as he draped his arms around each of their shoulders. They left the building via the front entrance, turned left, and discovered the 'all-night burger joint next door' which would sustain them on many occasions over the coming years.

On Sunday, Tom rang first Paul, then Rooster, in Australia, to give them his new phone number and address and to tell each of them they were more than welcome to stay with him any time they were in California.

'Paul, I know you always stay at some swanky hotel but my door is always open should you ever grow tired of the swankiness. Wait until you see our 'Studio Retro'! You'll wish you played a musical instrument. And you must meet Alice Weinberg, our manager. She is one smart lady and I know you'll like her.'

Paul could hear the excitement in Tom's voice from eight thousand miles away and he smiled as he replied,

'Actually, I'm coming over in three weeks for a meeting with Luke Gardener. Why don't we meet up as soon as the meeting's finished and I'll come and stay with you at your new place. The swankiness, as you call it, is fine, but I'd rather spend some time with you.'

'I can't wait to see your new place and studio,' said Rooster. 'In fact, I'm coming over there sometime in the next six months to play a gig at one of L.A.'s best jazz bars. Of course, I'll stay at your place. Even better if you're there.' He laughed. 'Your place sounds a helluva lot better than the dive I stayed at once before in L.A..'

By five o'clock on Tuesday afternoon, all the hard work of moving in had been done and the three of them were relaxing in 'Studio Retro,' as it was now known, champagne chilling in the fridge. The knock on the door signalled Alice's arrival and Tom rolled off the sofa where he'd been reclining and opened the door.

'Good evening, Alice, and welcome to 'Studio Retro.' With one hand in front of his waist, Tom bowed low and ushered Alice in with a sweep of his other arm. Zac stood inside the kitchen area as Alice entered the room. He held a champagne bottle in one hand, glass in the other. 'Will you join us in a glass of champagne to celebrate the opening of 'Studio Retro'?

'I'd love one, thank you Zac,' said Alice. She looked around the room, smiling with satisfaction. 'I am very pleased to be here. You've done well with your setup, boys,' she said, smiling at them like a mother hen with a new batch of chicks. 'Looks fabulous. I'm expecting big things.'

Zac poured champagne for all of them and when everyone had a glass in hand, Tom held up his other hand to signal an important announcement.

'I'd like to propose a toast. To Alice. Thank you for all you've done for us. We are indeed in your debt.' The three young men raised their glasses. 'To Alice.'

'Thank you, boys. And now it's my turn,' said Alice and raised her glass. 'To Pants on Fire, and your future success – may it be spectacular.'

'Hear, hear,' said Tom, as he raised his glass. Within minutes, all four glasses were empty and Zac busied himself refilling them.

'I hope you've noticed the socks,' said Alice, giggling girlishly as she extended one delicately pointed foot so they could all see her jazzy bright yellow socks, the perfect match for her yellow and black polka dot blouse and black slacks.

'How could we possibly miss them!' laughed Harry.

Tom glanced down at the yellow socks in the shiny black loafers. His eyes slowly travelled up over the beautifully tailored black slacks and the bright blouse to her face. She really was very attractive. Her glistening black hair, previously long, had recently been cut in a short bob, the fringe bangs sitting on the black eyebrows, and as ever, the dark eyes behind the horn-rimmed spectacles missed nothing. He noticed the black and diamond studs in her ears and it occurred to him, once again, that this was an expensively outfitted woman. Like most men, Tom was not much of a judge of a woman's age but as he watched her in conversation with Harry and Zac, he guessed Alice to be five or six years older than he was which would put her at about 37—in her prime, both personally and in business acumen. He recalled her words during that first meeting: 'If I take you on, you will do exactly what I say, when I say it,' and realised that if they followed her advice, Alice would be the key to their success.

'I'm looking forward to my surprise,' said Alice, interrupting Tom's thoughts.

'We'd like you to sit on the sofa,' said Harry.

Alice did as she was told and settled down on the old sofa, crossed her legs, and clutched her champagne in both hands, ready for her surprise.

Tom drew the heavy drapes together and carried one of the kitchen stools into the middle of the room as Zac prepared himself at his drums and Harry sat at the keyboard. Tom perched on the stool, maneuvered the guitar strap over his head and, with one foot on the rung of the stool, rested the instrument on his knee before speaking.

'Alice, I haven't totally slacked these past few weeks. I've written a special number which we've all agreed, we'd like featured on our first album. We want to dedicate the album to you.'

'The number is called 'Alice in the Groove.' We hope you like it.'

Harry played an intro on the keyboard, as Tom struck a chord on the guitar and Zac began on the drums.

Alice listened carefully. It was a beautifully melodic tune in a minor key, sweet and soulful. By the time they were halfway through, Alice knew—because that's what she was good at—that it would be a hit. It was memorable, catchy, and so different from their usual stuff. But most of all, she knew this tune had universal appeal.

It took a minute for her to realise that it was an instrumental piece. But of course, lyrics would have detracted from this melody, rather than enhance it. How clever of Tom.

Alice smiled a tiny smile as her eyes caught Tom's, but she looked away quickly, before the look in his eyes captured her and she knew she wouldn't be able to look away at all.

As they finished playing, Alice placed her champagne glass on the floor, slowly, to give herself time for the unfamiliar rush of emotion to pass. She sat upright and clapped, smiling at the three of them.

'Tom, I'm touched and overwhelmed. I've never had a tune written for me before. And a beautiful tune at that.' She looked away quickly again. *I never should have had that third glass of champagne*, she thought. *It's messing with my mind.*

'I was hoping you'd like it,' replied Tom, as he placed his guitar on the floor against the stool. 'Alice, we love 'Studio Retro' and our apartments, and we thank you from the bottom of our hearts for all the work you've done.'

There was a moment of awkward silence before Zac exclaimed: 'More champagne all round. We need to declare 'Studio Retro' officially open!'

By 7.15, Alice had drunk enough soda water to feel capable of driving home. She said her goodbyes and left the boys jamming in the studio, all three of them more drunk than sober. 'Studio Retro' officially opened and broken in.

Chapter 18

Choosing between the two bass guitarists he interviewed on Wednesday was a problem Tom found difficult to resolve.

The first one arrived 10 minutes early. Alex Martinez was a neat and tidy, good-looking young man. They talked for a while and Tom explained the band's position and why they were now looking for a bass player. Alex was keen and likeable. He wore tight black jeans tucked into black and silver studded boots and a spotless white shirt; the fringe of his long black hair fell over one half of his face, giving him a rakish air. He smiled often, his dark brown eyes twinkled and creased at the corners as he spoke. He was Latino, born in Mexico, but a long-time resident of L.A..

When Tom asked him to demonstrate his playing ability, Alex proudly unpacked an Epiphone Thunderbird Vintage Pro bass guitar from its case. This was a serious bass player—the Epiphone was an exceptional, quality instrument, and expensive—but unfortunately, Alex had not mastered the art of playing an instrument as finely crafted as this one. His pleasant nature and handsome look were far more impressive than his playing ability, which, although competent enough, lacked personality, unlike Alex himself.

They chatted for a half-hour or more, and Tom could tell that Alex would fit in with the others well. *Nice guy,* he thought. *But…*

An hour later, when Tom opened the door to Danny Toland, who had arrived 20 minutes late for the interview, the air crackled between them. When Danny sauntered in and made himself at home in Studio Retro, it was as if an electrical storm had entered the room.

'No need to see anyone else. I'm your man, Guv'nor,' said a cocky, confident Danny as he sat on the sofa, took a comb out of the pocket of his jacket, and combed his wind-blown, long, blonde curls. 'Nice place you've got here,' he added, as he glanced around the room and took everything in. He seemed completely ignorant of the fact that he was late, and impertinent.

'Oh, are you?' replied Tom, as he deftly hid his annoyance at this cheeky upstart with the Liverpool accent. Tom swung a kitchen stool into the middle of the room. 'How about you play something and show me why we should take you on.' *Alex is looking better by the minute,* thought Tom, as he watched Danny flip open the battered guitar case and produce an equally battered bass, a no-name brand of unknown age and history. *The bass looks like it had endured a long, hard journey from Liverpool,* thought Tom. *This guy makes Alex look genius.*

Until Danny started to play.

It was magic. Alive. The instrument took on a life of its own. The musician and instrument were as one, each enhanced the other. Danny assumed a different persona when he played. He even looked different; eyes closed, relaxed, confident of his ability to make the instrument sing. Tom felt this guy would be at home playing in a 100-piece symphony orchestra, would probably be the lead instrument. The bass was perfectly tuned, and the music Danny made flowed and harmonised so beautifully his bass playing could have been a stand-alone feature in any band.

'So, whaddya reckon?' said Danny as he put the bass down in its case. 'I can start any time. When's your next practice session? I'll be there.'

Tom didn't know whether to laugh or cry. This guy was so pushy, so brazen, but he certainly knew how to handle that bass.

'Take me on. You'll not regret it.'

Danny didn't ask any questions of Tom, didn't want to know anything about the band, just wanted the job. And Tom was reluctant to ask much of Danny, concerned he wouldn't be able to stop him if he got started on his life story. The thing was: there was absolutely no question about his musical ability, but could they work with him?

'I'll get back to you within the next few days,' said Tom as he opened the door for Danny and ushered him out.

Danny turned to shake hands with Tom. 'Don't leave it too long. As you can imagine, I'm in demand.' He winked as he raised his arm in mock salute before turning and sauntering down the hall to the elevators without a backward glance.

Hence the dilemma Tom now found himself in. Alex would be a good man to work with—except for his playing ability. Danny's musical ability was beyond reproach, but could they stand his audacity?

Time to talk to Alice!

'Hi Alice, Tom here. I've seen the two bass players and I'd like to discuss them with you if you've got the time. I can come to your office, or you could come here and I'll make you a coffee. I've even got left-over donuts from lunch. Whichever suits you.'

Alice was about to agree to Tom's suggestion to meet up in his apartment when a little voice in her head whispered: *a one-on-one meeting in Tom's apartment? Sounds innocent enough but—don't do it.*

Before she had time to change her mind, Alice said,

'Why don't you come here in about half an hour. I'll make you a cup of tea and we can have a chat.'

Tom was hoping to avoid a cup of Alice's tea; he much preferred his coffee, and he thought the prospect of donuts would do the trick. However, he agreed to her suggestion and hung up.

Thirty minutes later, Tom sat in Alice's office, a cup of her tea on the desk in front of him. For the next half an hour, he related the tale of the two bass players in detail.

'Alice, I regard you as my mentor and although I don't want you to decide for me, I would like your advice.'

'This is the way I see it, Tom,' said Alice, as she drained what was left of her second cup of tea before she placed the cup and saucer on the desk and sat back in her chair. She adjusted her spectacles as she sought the right words, which would convince him without sounding like a directive.

'The first guy sounds like he would sit nicely in your comfort zone, and that's fine. I think the second guy may have come on a bit strong to cover his insecurities—which disappear when he plays.'

Alice leaned forward in her chair and rested her arms on the desk before continuing.

'I would not compromise the integrity of the band just to feel comfortable. Don't let minor personality clashes get in the way of what you want to achieve. We all have to deal with irksome people occasionally. That's life.'

On his walk back to his apartment building, Tom considered what Alice had said and how she had said it. He would ring Alex when he got home and let him know he hadn't got the gig.

The boys fell into a routine of practicing at least three afternoons a week in Studio Retro. Because Tom had explained what Danny was like to Zac and Harry, they were prepared for his cheekiness and his weird accent and although he was not particularly likeable, at least they could appreciate his musical ability. Although he was quite obnoxious at first, he eventually settled down when he saw that this was a permanent gig and he didn't have to constantly prove himself. Zac discovered the best way to deal with Danny was to tell him to 'just shut up and play!'

On the days they weren't practicing, Tom would go to Studio Retro and endeavour to write songs for the album. He was keenly aware of the pressure on him to come up with 18 or 20 new songs within the next four to five months. He struggled to produce anything during that first week and blamed the new surroundings.

Tom was usually comfortable writing and found it an enjoyable experience. He could sit at the keyboard for a few hours and turn out the basis of a melody and even some lyrics. Of course, it needed refinement, but within a week, he'd have a dozen bits and pieces, which he would eventually whittle down to a shiny new melody and lyrics. Occasionally, the process would run into a few weeks, but conversely, the whole thing was sometimes completed within five or six days. So why was he having trouble this time?

By the end of the second week, a panicky feeling was manifesting itself in the pit of his belly that even several vodkas didn't alleviate.

It was during a chance conversation in the burger joint next door late one night that he connected with a new dealer. Within a day or two, he was set up with a stash of weed, white powder, and a good stock of vodka in the bar fridge. With the door of Studio Retro securely locked, and totally relaxed, he felt able to write freely and more productively.

He had written five new songs when, three weeks later, Alice called a meeting for Tom and the band in her office. 9 am on a Monday morning was not easy to organise for Tom, Zac, and Harry, but they managed it. Alice made them tea, and they chatted easily together before Danny arrived 20 minutes late. Tom was quietly furious, but politely introduced him to Alice.

'Pleased to meet you, Danny,' said Alice, as she shook hands with him. 'Can I pour you a cup of tea?'

'Yeah, pleased to meet you too,' replied Danny. 'And tea would be lovely, thanks.' With a wicked smile, he winked at her, confident of his charm on older women.

Alice poured a cup of tea and handed it to Danny, smiling graciously.

'Now, Danny, there's something you should know.' She said gently.

Although Danny was blissfully unaware, the others noticed her frown deepen and the glint in her eyes turn steely. The smile disappeared and her face took on a fierce, stony look. Her stare concentrated on Danny. She took a deep breath and said slowly and deliberately,

'This is the first and last time you will ever be late for a meeting with me. I will not tolerate it a second time. Do I make myself clear?'

Danny looked taken aback and, to his credit, instantly remorseful. He glanced at the others in shock before looking at Alice and replying softly,

'Sure. Of course. Sorry.'

The smile quickly returned, and the atmosphere lifted as Alice said: 'Now boys, the reason for the meeting: I am in the process of organising a tour of the West Coast to coincide with the release of your album later this year. It is going to be big. You will be the headliners and I'm currently looking at support acts for the concerts. We're going to need another van, maybe two, for roadies, sound and lighting people, and backup singers and musicians.'

The four young men looked at each other in amazement, which quickly turned to delight as they realised—this is the big time!

'Wow, you don't gather any moss, do you Alice?' said Harry.

'No, a Rolling Stone I am not!' replied Alice, laughing at her own joke.

'Here is a rough calendar of events for the tour,' she said as she handed typed sheets to each of them. 'I'll issue more details as they are confirmed. As you can see, it's going to be quite arduous but this is where the bulk of your income will come from. As they say—no pain, no gain—and believe me, if we do it right, it will be worth it.'

'Before the tour, I'll organise a few photo sessions and some media interviews so keep yourselves nice.'

'So, this is what is required of you: Tom, I need those songs, and boys, I need you to have them 'practice perfect' by the time we record, which is scheduled for approx. five months from now.

'I would suggest you practice them until you are sick of them. And then practice them some more. I do not want to waste time and money on recording them over and over and over to get it right. I want each one right in one take if possible.'

Tom smiled inwardly at the mention of the word 'suggest' and thought to himself: *do exactly what I say, when I say it.*

Alice continued: 'I'll keep it simple. My job is to organise everything for the tour. Your job is to come up with twenty songs which you can play in your sleep, within our time frame. Now go and do it.'

She stood and began collecting their cups and saucers, a sign that the meeting was over and they should leave.

'Thank you, Alice. We know exactly what is required and we'll do it,' said Tom, looking at the others as he spoke. All nodded in agreement as they stood and prepared to leave. He thought Danny looked a bit shell-shocked. The thought made him feel good.

At least two out of every three practice sessions, Danny would arrive late. Zac worried about what he would be like when they were on tour—what if he was late when they were supposed to go on? What if he arrived late to media interviews? However, his performance was always so flawless, they forgave him for his transgressions. Whenever Tom handed around a new tune in rough form, scribbled on notepaper, Danny could play it exactly as Tom imagined. He could also help the others understand complicated renditions of certain songs, his knowledge of chords and chord progressions beyond anything they had encountered.

But the most amazing thing about Danny was that he had never had a music lesson. He had picked up a guitar at age 12 and had plotted his future career within the next few hours. Tom believed his natural ability was such that it wouldn't have mattered what type of guitar or bass he played—old or new, cheap or expensive—Danny could make it sing.

Practice sessions may have been going well, but Tom struggled with having to write so many new songs on a deadline. Many nights he would work late into the night, sometimes not closing Studio Retro's door behind him until the early hours. He knew he was drinking more vodka than was wise. However, he also believed that the combination of weed and coke was helping keep the demons of creativity alive and well in his system. Besides, he could always stop when he'd completed his part of the job Alice had set out for them. He would often sleep a drugged sleep only to wake a few hours later, feeling slightly woozy until that first cup of coffee kicked in and brought him alive once again.

Late one night, he bumped into Bo, the dealer, in the burger joint. Tom indicated with a slight nod of his head that he would like to speak with him outside. As they stepped out into the dark, damp evening air, Bo pulled his jacket collar up around his chin and offered Tom a cigarette before lighting up one himself.

'So, how's it going, Man?' asked Bo. 'You finish those songs yet? Need a bit more 'help'?'

'As a matter of fact, I do,' replied Tom. 'I could really use some Speed. Can you get me some?'

'Sure. I'll have it here tomorrow night, around this time. It doesn't come cheap, but I'm sure you already know that. Meet me here, same time tomorrow night.' And he turned and walked over to a late model sedan, knocked twice on the bonnet before opening the passenger door and climbing in. As the car pulled silently away from the curb, Tom wondered who was driving. It seemed Bo had a partner in crime.

It was a few days later that Tom received a phone call he never wanted to hear.

'Hello Tom. It's your dad here.' Jim didn't sound the same as usual, and he never rang Tom this late in the evening. Tom was in the burger joint getting a quick bite before going back upstairs to Studio Retro for a long writing session. Fortunately, he had remembered to pick up his phone on the way out the door or he would have missed Jim's call.

'Dad! Hi,' replied Tom. 'How's things?'

'Not good, I'm afraid. Gran has had a stroke and she's not doing well. Tom, she's asking for you. Can you get away for a few days? The doctors don't think she will last long.'

Tom felt sick. He jumped off the stool at the bar and raced outside, where the phone signal was stronger. Standing on the sidewalk, gasping for air, he leaned against a post, running his free hand through his hair. He was aware of sweating profusely. Even as the chill of the night air wafted around his face, he could feel droplets of sweat forming on his forehead.

'Where is she? What happened?'

'She developed a severe headache very quickly a couple of hours ago and couldn't speak properly, so I rang for an ambulance immediately. They got to the house within about fifteen minutes and took her to Stanford Hospital. By then, her headache was quite bad. I'm here with her now. How quickly can you get here?'

'If I left now and drove, I reckon I could be at the hospital within about six hours. I'd rather do that than wait to find a flight tomorrow. Will you please stay with her until I arrive?'

'Of course, I'll stay with her for as long as necessary. She's in Room 24 on the fifth floor of the hospital. Promise me you'll drive carefully and concentrate. It won't be an easy drive.'

'Don't worry about me, Dad. Tell Gran I'm on my way and I'll see her soon.'

Back in his apartment, Tom threw a few things in an overnight bag and was down in the underground parking area quicker than he would have thought possible. He reversed out of his parking place and roared up the ramp to the street. Within minutes he was on the road out of town.

Strange how things work out sometimes. This afternoon's practice session started later than usual and Zac had called it quits and gone home at about eight o'clock. He had a heavy head cold and was feeling miserable. Danny and Harry left soon after to try a new club downtown, which was when Tom decided he was hungry. These combined factors meant that none of the men had had anything to drink, nor any drugs of any kind. Ordinarily by now, Tom would have enjoyed a few vodkas and probably some weed, or even something stronger, and would have been in no state to drive. And yet, tonight, of all nights, here he was starting out on a five- or six-hour drive to San Francisco, stone cold sober.

It was better driving through the night, much less traffic to slow him down. It was still dark when he pulled into the parking lot of the hospital. He raced past the reception area and into an elevator, pressing the fifth-floor button. Why was this elevator so slow? The minute the doors opened, he ran down the corridor and around the corner looking for Room 24.

Why was Dad sitting on a chair outside the room? Why wasn't he in with Gran, being with her when she needed him? As he approached, Jim rose and Tom noticed his father looked small and old.

The two men embraced as Tom asked in a small voice,

'What are you doing out here? How is she?'

'She's gone, Tom. She passed away about half an hour ago,' said Jim in a flat voice. His body seemed to shrink further in Tom's arms with each word he spoke, as if saying the words confirmed irrevocably that it was indeed true.

Tom felt the breath go out of his body, as if something had broken inside. *That must be my heart*, he thought, as tears escaped from his eyes and slid down his face.

He broke from his father's embrace and slumped into one of the plastic chairs outside the room. He reached up and took hold of his father's hand, coaxing him into the chair alongside his.

'Dad, I am so shocked. I only spoke to her last week. She seemed fine.' He was weeping openly now, unashamedly.

'Tom, Gran has been unwell for quite some time. She was diagnosed with inoperable cancer not long before you left for L.A. but she wouldn't let me tell you, made me promise. Didn't want to spoil your excitement, didn't want to put a dampener on your move into the big time.'

Jim stopped momentarily and wiped his eyes with a hanky before he took a big breath and covered Tom's hand with his own as he continued,

'You know what she was like. You were the most important thing in her world. She would have done anything for you, which included protecting you from bad news. But you mustn't think badly of her, that's the way she wanted it.'

'And I don't think she'd be happy to know that the two of us are sitting here, crying, so I think we should both stop now,' added Jim, smiling weakly.

'I can't,' said Tom, wiping the tears from his eyes and smothering a sob. 'I can't believe she's gone. I am so sorry I didn't get here in time.'

'She was on heavy medication for the pain at the end. I doubt she would have known you were here. Would you like to see her, Tom? I asked the nursing staff to leave everything until you arrived.'

'Yes, I would,' replied Tom as he opened the door and entered the room on his own.

Jim waited outside to give Tom some time alone with Gran to say his goodbyes.

A short time later, when Tom came back out into the corridor, Jim stood and said gently,

'Come on, let's go home and I'll ring Lola. I rang her while we were waiting for the ambulance, so she'll be waiting for our call.'

The two men walked quietly from the hospital and drove home to the empty house.

The funeral was held four days later.

Lola had arrived from Arizona a few days before, as had Paul, who had flown over from Australia. Zac, Harry, and Danny had driven overnight from L.A.. Alice had flown in early that morning and gone straight to Jim's house. Although she had contacted Tom as soon as she had heard about Gran's passing, she wanted to express her condolences again to him privately, rather than with all the others at the funeral.

Tom opened the door immediately when she knocked, and she wrapped him in her arms as they embraced.

'Oh, Tom, I'm so sorry. How are you holding up?' Her arms tightly around his neck, she whispered: 'This will be a tough day for you but remember I'm here for you.' Then added quickly: 'We're all here for you.'

He put his mouth down to her ear and whispered: 'Alice. I'm so glad you're here.'

Their embrace lasted longer than it should have. Alice's heart was racing and she could have stood there in Tom's embrace for-ever, but she broke away as Jim walked up the hall towards them.

And their private moment was gone, as if melted in the sunlight in which they were standing.

Tom turned. 'Alice, this is my father, Jim.'

'How do you do, Jim. I'm sorry we're not meeting under happier circumstances. I'm so sorry for your loss.'

'Thank you, Alice. I'm pleased to meet you. Come in.' Jim replied, taking Alice's extended hand.'

'Come and I'll introduce you to my Aunt Lola,' said Tom as he led Alice into the kitchen where Lola was making fresh coffee.

The four of them chatted quietly over coffee, mostly about Gran and their family dynamics, how Gran was the glue which had held the little family together since Tom's mother's death.

Tom felt considerably better. His spirits lifted as he opened the cab door for Alice half an hour later.

'Thank you so much for coming here this morning, before the funeral, Alice. It meant a great deal to me.' Tom squeezed Alice's hand before closing the cab door. He waved goodbye as the cab pulled away.

The ceremony later that day, was perfect. Gran would have loved it. What could have been a sad and difficult day for Tom was made more bearable by the presence and support of his friends.

The gathering at Jim's house following the ceremony was full of warmth and love, and Tom again realised the true value of friends and family.

Between bouts of writing, and practice sessions, Alice had secured a few gigs for the band in and around L.A.. It was good to be in front of a live audience again and the boys enjoyed sitting around having a few smokes and drinks when the audience had dispersed for the night and the venues were in darkness. Zac and Harry noticed that whenever they ordered drinks, usually beer or bourbon, Tom would have a double, always vodka. And yet they had never seen him drunk. Whereas Danny didn't drink alcohol—unusual for a musician nowadays. He was happy to sit with the guys and chat and smoke the occasional joint, but he made it clear from the beginning not to order a drink for him.

The weeks grew into months until suddenly, Alice notified them to be at Red Pony's Recording Studios in two weeks, on the Wednesday at 11 am, with their instruments and twenty original songs. Oh, and don't be late!

When the four of them arrived at the Studio, Alice introduced them to Alan Cohen, the head producer, a few of the other producers, and the sound engineers and editors.

'Nice to meet you,' said Alan, as he shook hands with the four young men. 'I'm a bit more experimental than the other producers here, but I think we'll play it straight with your tracks to begin with; it's not a good idea to play around too much with your first album. Lu and I believe you've got a star quality about you and your sound, so let's concentrate on getting that sound right.'

The recording session went brilliantly. The hours of practice really paid off for the band, and the record producers and executives of Red Pony were seriously impressed. By the end of the fourth day, they had bedded down the instrumental base of twelve tracks. The recordings went so smoothly the producers didn't need any more—every track was usable. *Great,* thought Tom, *there's eight already done for the second album.*

Then began the vocals, including the backing vocals, and the overdubs. Alan introduced them to the three female backup singers and the extra studio musicians. The group melded well over the next few days as the recordings were finalised and polished. This left the mixing and mastering. These jobs took the most time to complete and were the most expensive part of the entire operation.

It was the first time the four young men had been involved in the detail of making an album and studied every action, asking questions and soaking up information about what exactly is involved in making a record, or a Compact Disc.

At one stage, Alan asked the boys if they had any ideas for the album's name. A few names were thrown around, but nothing stood out. It was Alice who made the suggestion which would prove to be genius in hindsight.

'There's no doubt in my mind that 'Out into the World' is the best song on the album,' she said. 'And I think Alan will agree with me.' She looked over at Alan who replied: 'You are so right Alice. It stands out. Plus, it would make a great name for the album. It's a good play on words, this being your first album.'

Tom felt himself turn pink with self-conscious embarrassment as the others turned to him and clapped. Who would have thought that the little tune he had written for the end-of-school dance would be the best thing on their debut album?

The others nodded in agreement. It was a good name for their first album. Done deal!

The entire record-making process took about three months, during which Alice had arranged several photoshoots for the CD cover and notes, and promotional material for the coming tour.

Excitement was building, no more so than when Alice handed out the completed schedule and details for the tour.

'Alice, this is amazing stuff,' said Tom, in awe. 'I cannot imagine the work involved in organising this. And I love the name of the tour: the 'Out into the World' Tour. I can't believe it's really happening. It's all coming together in the best possible way.'

'Bloody hell,' said Danny. 'I've never seen anything so detailed.' Danny shook his head in genuine wonder as he read the schedule. 'I didn't realise the tour would take a month to complete but I can now understand why. Tom's right, Alice, this is amazing.'

'Wow, Seattle to San Diego – that's more than 1200 miles, isn't it?' said Zac. 'I hope you guys are going to share the driving.'

'Actually, Zac, that's going to be at least 2,500 miles by the time we drive there and back to base, here in L.A..' Added Harry.

'It's not as bad as it seems,' said Alice, seeing the look of alarm on Zac's face. 'The longest leg is about a hundred miles. All the other legs are less. And the roadies will set up and take down, so really, all you have to do is perform. And fight off the groupies. Oh, and do a few radio and TV interviews along the way. Oh, and drive a bit.'

'You certainly have a way with words, Darlin',' said Danny. 'You make it sound like a month-long picnic.' He put his arm around her shoulders and gave her a squeeze. Tom stared in horror; nobody got personal like that with Alice; theirs was a strictly business partnership. He glanced at the others and saw the same look of surprise on the faces of Zac and Harry as they waited for Alice to recoil. Instead, she elbowed Danny in the ribs and laughed.

Everyone relaxed, and they began to discuss the cities and towns they would play.

Chapter 19

No matter how you looked at it, the 'Out into the World' tour was a triumph. It was grueling, exhausting work, but the success? Unquestionable.

In the lead-up to the tour, Alice called in a favour from an Indie film director she knew from her early days in Hollywood to make a 30 second trailer featuring the boys in action—talking, playing, just being themselves—a sneak preview of their show. It was the most challenging of the pre-tour work. So many takes, they did one scene about eight times. By the third day, tempers were frayed and appearing to have fun when the cameras were rolling became almost impossible.

The trailer was to be shown on the major TV stations in each town they were playing. Alice had arranged for it to be run every night in prime time the week before their scheduled concert. The investment paid off handsomely. Every concert sold out before they arrived.

The album had been released to retailers, radio stations, and DJs across America the week before the band's first concert—headliners at the Warfield in San Francisco. Record stores sold out the day after the concerts and re-orders flowed into Red Pony distribution centres. The Sales team from Red Pony made sure that every store up and down the West Coast had enough stock of the album to cope with the predicted demand once the tour got going.

Even though Alice had tutored them in the art of the interview, the four young men's first interview, on KEXP in Seattle, was amateurish. Despite their efforts to appear professional, the interview turned out to be hilarious, the two on-air radio jocks dissolving into uncontrollable, but good-natured, laughter. This set the tone for all interviews which followed, in every city they played. The members of Pants on Fire became popular and well-liked for their self-deprecating good humour and easy manner, and the interviews won them many fans.

The number of groupies waiting for them after each show grew with every passing day, girls who were happy to satisfy the band's every need just to spend a few hours with a 'rock star'. And the boys made the most of this 'admiration society' who they regarded as simply there for their convenience, no strings attached. Of course, along with the girls, there was never any shortage of 'soft' drugs and unlimited alcohol. What Danny shunned in the way of alcohol, he made up for in women. The boys noticed that he often left the parties being held in one of the boys' rooms early to, as he said: 'Go back to my room to get a decent night's sleep. Ha Ha.'

It wasn't until mid-way through the fourth week of the tour that Harry made a startling discovery. He left the party in Tom's room sooner than the others, feeling woozy from too much booze and weed. As he unlocked his door and entered the room, he turned to gently close the door behind him, and heard a noise outside. He pulled the curtain aside an inch or two and peered out of his motel room window—and saw Alice leaving Danny's room, quietly closing the door behind her. He recoiled in horror before a wide grin spread across his face. 'The little devil,' he whispered to himself, not sure if he was referring to Danny or Alice.

Alice, who was travelling with the boys, couldn't hide her delight with the way things were going. The only real drama happened in Escondido, a town of 150,000 people, forty miles northeast of the Mexican border. Fifteen minutes into the show, the venue was thrown into darkness when lightning struck the building during a thunderstorm. The band carried a generator with them on tour and the Roadies could install it for their amps and mics in a matter of minutes. Fortunately, the stage manager and his staff had lived through many blackouts and were well prepared for such emergencies. They quickly set up hundreds of battery-operated candles on the stage and dotted around the venue. The stage took on the appearance of a fairyland and the audience went wild when Tom made light of the incident and led the band in an impromptu performance of 'Together in Electric Dreams.'

Thanks to Alice's forward planning, their promo merchandise had been delivered directly to each venue before the tour began, so they wouldn't have to transport it with them. But it had flown off the shelves, and one month later, there was virtually no stock left.

At the end of the third week, Lu Ricci, Head of Sales for Red Pony, contacted Alice with news which made all the hard work worth it—'Out into the World' the single, had reached No. 18 on the Billboard Top 100.

Alice called the boys together to make an announcement. She looked serious.

'So, Tom Watson and Pants on Fire: you know how you complained about doing that eighth take when we were making the trailer video? You know how you whined about that crummy out-of-town motel we had to stay in in Portland when they didn't have our booking at the Hilton? You know how you all complained about Danny's driving? Well, all credit to you, guys. You did suck it up.'

A wide grin slowly spread across Alice's face as she continued, her voice growing louder and more excited with each phrase:

'Now, just to show you it was all worth it, 'Out into the World' today reached No. 18 on the Billboard Top 100. Congratulations boys, you're on your way.'

This was it. This was the moment they realised all things were possible.

The other three were yelling and shouting, slapping each other on the back in their exuberance at the good news. Tom stood quietly aside and smiled as he caught Alice looking at him. He held her gaze for a moment as if to say, 'Thank you for all you did to bring us to this point.' She returned his look and gave a small nod of her head in acknowledgement of the part he had played in their success. Their shared gaze lasted longer than either of them realised, and Tom sensed Alice felt uncomfortable. Or was it embarrassed? He immediately turned and joined the others in their celebrations.

Zac, Harry, and Tom had been playing together as a band for 10 years, so they weren't exactly an overnight sensation. Although Danny was a latecomer to the group, he had proved he could work as hard as the rest of them. And Tom was the tie that bound them all together. They wouldn't even be standing here in this situation had it not been for Tom.

'Come on,' said Harry. 'Let's go and open some champagne or something.'

'Yeah. The first of many,' replied Tom.

Once the tour was behind them and they had settled back into the daily grind, Alice decided to throw a party for the boys, and invite music industry executives, the media, venue operators, and her contacts in the movie industry. Ostensibly it was to celebrate the success of the tour and their debut album, but it was also part of Alice's overall marketing and promotion strategy for Tom Watson and Pants on Fire, which would pay dividends down the line.

The following month, Alice summoned the boys to her office one Tuesday morning at 10 am. As Tom told them the day before: 'Don't forget there's a meeting at Alice's office tomorrow morning at 10. You know what that means—morning tea and probably cakes, so make sure you guys have a light breakfast. And Danny, don't be late!'

As per Tom's forecast, they arrived as Alice was preparing tea, but instead of iced cupcakes, today's repast consisted of a delicate jam sponge, so perfect it looked like a picture in an English recipe book. If Danny's 'oohs and ah's' were anything to go by when he spied the cake, one would think it had been made especially for him.

Tom particularly noticed what Alice wore today. The pearl necklace and earrings offset the severe black business suit, and her shiny black high heels highlighted her shapely legs in their sheer black stockings. He also noticed that she was wearing new bright red glasses. Alice meant business today.

Once everyone had a cup of tea and a piece of the cake, Alice began,

'Well boys, I wanted to bring you up to date with our cash flow position. By this time next week, we will have recouped the total cost of the tour, which was just over one point six million dollars.'

Zac gasped and cake crumbs exploded out of his mouth. He almost dropped the plate, but instead, placed it on the desk in front of him.

'Do you mean to tell us the tour cost one point six million dollars? I can't believe it could have cost that much.'

'Then it's just as well you're not running the business side of things, isn't it?' replied Alice. Tom covered his mouth with his hand to hide his smile; Danny wasn't quite so discreet and laughed. Alice took a sip of her tea. 'Allow me to continue.'

'By this time next month'—she paused to emphasise the time frame—'we should have roughly nine million dollars back from takings. The sale of merchandise and records on tour will have brought in another two point one million dollars by the end of this month. I have not yet begun to calculate royalty payments but I know it's going to be quite a reasonable sum.'

'Are you telling us that we're rich, Alice?' asked Harry, laughing.

'Well, you're not poor,' replied Alice, 'but remember, you all worked extremely hard preparing for this tour, and although I noticed you all had fun whilst you were away, the tour itself was hard work, was it not?'

'It was indeed,' said Tom.

An air of bonhomie had descended over the office like a fluffy cloud. There were smiles all round, and the boys laughed and chatted amongst themselves as Alice poured more tea for everyone. *Even the tea tastes good this morning*, thought Tom.

'Now, the second thing is...' Alice paused for effect.

'I suggest you do another tour in about 12 months' time—thirty cities and towns across America—which will take roughly four months, maybe a bit longer, but which should make about thirty million dollars profit.'

Giggles and guffaws rebounded around the room.

'Thirty million dollars?' Once again, Zac didn't comprehend very well.

'That is what I said, Zac.'

'Would we need another album to release in tandem with that tour?' asked Tom.

'That would be great but think twice before committing to that. It's a big ask.'

'The four of us have a lot to talk about Alice. Can we come back to you with our thoughts in a few days' time?' Tom looked apprehensive, hoping he didn't sound too negative.

'Of course,' replied Alice. She looked at the four of them, one at a time, and smiled. 'You four young men are in your prime as far as your careers are concerned. You're approaching your peak and if you do it right, that peak can last for quite a few years. Don't underestimate your ability to accomplish great things. And remember, I am here to help you do just that.'

'The other thing I wanted to tell you about is that I'd like to throw a party for you in a couple of weeks. It will be at my place on a Saturday afternoon and evening, for around ninety to a hundred people. Music industry bosses, media people, movie people, that sort of thing, but you'll be the stars of the party. Think you can manage that?'

'Wow, can you get a hundred people in your place?' asked Zac in amazement.

'Don't you worry about that, Zac. Just get yourself there and I'll take care of everything else. I'll send you all an official invite showing time, date, how to get there, etc.'

'That sounds fantastic, Alice,' said Harry. 'We'll be there with bells on. We love a party.' He looked at the others and winked.

'And now for the best news of all,' said Alice, grinning from ear to ear. 'I've been contacted by Oprah Winfrey's people. Oprah wants you on her show. It doesn't get much bigger than that.'

'Wait until Mom hears about that!' said Zac proudly, and clapped his hands in glee.

The five of them continued to discuss Alice's words and the feeling of success permeated the room until the dingy little office took on the aura of a palace.

'You got anything stronger than tea?' asked Tom.

Until the invite arrived, Tom had no idea where Alice lived. He'd never really thought about it. When he read she lived on Strathmore Drive, Los Angeles, he was no wiser. None of them knew L.A. that well and had never heard of Strathmore Drive. However, attached to the invite was a handwritten note from Alice saying she had arranged for a limo to pick them up and bring them to the party. She also suggested they get Danny to their place so the limo could bring the four of them together.

So much more civilised than driving or taking a cab, thought Tom, smiling to himself.

Come the afternoon of the party, the boys dressed as if they were doing a concert. Tom wore his black T-shirt and jeans, black leather vest, and silver studded black cowboy boots. He had even washed his hair, better to show off the handmade silver earrings he'd picked up in Seattle.

He noticed Zac was wearing a spectacularly colourful Gucci shirt tucked into classy white slacks, and Gucci loafers. At first glance, Harry looked like he was going to church in a navy-blue suit over a white t-shirt, but his bright red sneakers crushed that idea quickly. When Danny arrived—on time—he looked like he had just gotten out of bed; his matching shirt and slacks were made of red, white, and blue fabric with stars and stripes to remind everyone that he was an American now. Except they looked like pyjamas.

The boys were in party mode.

The atmosphere in the limo was full of fun and good humour. Tom opened the bottle of champagne nestled in the ice bucket in the limo and poured drinks for the four of them.

'Here's to us,' said Danny as he raised his glass. 'Cheers, mates.'

'Yes, here's to a good party,' replied Tom, and they clinked glasses and downed the first glass.

The road wound up into the hills and became gradually steeper, with more bends and corners.

'Um, this area's a bit posh, isn't it?' said Harry. He was looking out the car window as they passed beautifully manicured lawns and gardens and large executive-looking homes set back from the road.

'It certainly is,' replied Tom. 'I've never been up in the hills before.'

'Nearly there,' said their driver as they turned right onto a wide driveway and through big, fancy iron gates. A valet directed them up the concrete drive lined with Mediterranean cypress trees. The car finally came to a stop in front of a magnificent Spanish-style white stuccoed mansion overlooking L.A.

The four young men climbed out of the car, drinks in hand, and took in the view, wondering where they were, slightly confused by this turn of events. If there was ever any doubt in their minds that Alice was an extremely clever and successful manager, it disappeared like mist in the sun at that moment. Each of them silently pledged to follow Alice's 'suggestions' unquestionably in future.

'Welcome to my home,' said Alice, as she glided down the front steps. 'Great timing.'

The four of them turned as one and smiled at the vision before them.

She wore a long white jewelled kaftan, its centre thigh-high split revealing slim, tanned legs accentuated by the flat barely-there sandals on her tiny feet. Her shiny black hair moved in the breeze, displaying large diamond studs in her ears. She positively glowed with confidence, fully aware of the image she conveyed in this splendid setting. She looked like something on the cover of Vogue—a picture of sartorial elegance. Expensive sartorial elegance!

'Wow, Alice, this is some place you got here!' said Zac, in some sort of weird accent to cover his amazement. The others were speechless.

Alice smiled graciously. 'Well, don't you all look like rock stars! Come on through. I'll introduce you to some of the other guests. You can leave your glasses with the limo driver; we'll get you fresh ones along the way.'

She led them up the steps and through the house, which oozed good taste and money. The modern leather furniture sat lightly on the exquisite Aubusson rugs which were specifically placed to compliment the Spanish terra-cotta tiled floor. The faint fragrance of gardenia wafted through the rooms from the softly burning candles scattered around, enhancing the feeling of elegance and sophistication.

Zac trailed behind the others, unable to drag his eyes away from the art on the walls. He made a mental note to come back and spend more time with them later.

They emerged into the afternoon sunlight and onto the stone terrace overlooking a turquoise pool. A few dozen people stood in groups around the pool, chatting and sipping cocktails as a waiter carrying a tray of drinks offered refills.

Tom recognised Alan from Red Pony and raised his hand in acknowledgement. Another man in the crowd waved and Harry remembered him as the guy who ran the Warfield Theatre in San Francisco.

A hush descended on the crowd as Alice raised her hand for silence.

'Everybody, I'd like to introduce you to Tom Watson and Pants on Fire – the next big thing!'

There was a round of applause, and Alice took the boys around and introduced them individually to many of the other guests. As the sound of music drifted on the breeze, another waiter glided by offering hot and cold snacks, and the party was underway. Over the next hour, another five or six dozen people arrived and circulated, and the noise level rose significantly.

Later, as the red ball of the setting sun slid towards the horizon of Los Angeles, Tom stood alone on the terraced lawn absorbed in the grandeur of sunset over L.A. In the stillness of the approaching evening, he felt the presence of another person and turned to see Alice standing beside him, her signature perfume faded but still present, her eyes shining with pleasure at the sight of him.

'I thought I might find you here,' she said. 'I brought two glasses of champagne with me in case you didn't have one. Here, let's drink to our shared success.'

They sipped their champagne in silence for a few minutes, then Tom spoke, his soft voice tinged with awe and admiration.

'Alice, this is a magnificent house and grounds, not to mention the view. You must have worked very hard for it.'

Alice smiled. 'Do you remember that first time you came to my office? When I saw the look of distaste on your face, I said to you: don't worry Tom, I don't live like this!'

They both laughed at the memory.

'It's true Tom, I did the hard yards, put in some long hours over the years, took some risks. But I've had a lot of luck too. I got lucky the day I took on Pants on Fire, and I've got a feeling we're going to get luckier.'

She turned and sat on the low stone wall. As she crossed her legs, the split in the front of her kaftan fell open, revealing a hint of a lace thong at the top of a honey-coloured thigh. She made no attempt to adjust it, secretly delighting in Tom's reaction. He couldn't tear his eyes away from the top of the split. The thought of what was hidden there created erotic images in his mind, as did the subtle message implied by the way she was sitting. He sat down next to her, all pretence of why they were here, alone, together, gone.

Tom softly traced the outside of her exposed thigh with his fingers and was about to speak when, out of the almost dark, a waiter approached, breathless. 'Ms. Weinberg, I'm so glad I found you. Mr. Ricci is leaving now and would like to speak to you before he goes.'

'Of course,' said Alice, as she slowly stood up. 'Tell him I'm coming.' And then, turning to face Tom: 'I must get back to the guests, Tom. Thank you for a few lovely moments of quiet.' And she was gone.

Tom continued to sit on the wall, thinking, before he rose and walked back into the now noisy throng. The music was pumping, and the alcohol was flowing. The moment with Alice was gone. He might as well have another drink.

He circulated and chatted with several people, important people, influential people, amazed to find himself in this place at this time. Alice had spoken of luck, and Tom thought about how lucky he had been. Yes, he had worked hard, practiced hard, wheeled and dealed to get here, but when he thought more deeply about it, there had been a lot of luck involved. His life had been a string of small successes, one after the other, starting right back at age nine, when Gran had given him that guitar. A lot of good things had come his way; he had travelled through life with an open mind and a positive outlook, and money in the bank and nights like this were the reward.

He eased himself away from the crowd and wandered down another lawn area where he stumbled across Zac and Harry smoking a joint.

'Want one?' said Zac, passing him a fancy Gucci leather pouch.

'Good idea,' replied Tom, and the three of them sat on the grass and quietly got stoned.

A while later, Tom stood and announced that he needed to visit the 'john.' 'Don't go away boys. I'll be back. Don't use up all that stuff before I return.' And chuckling to himself, he made his way into the house.

As he walked out of the bathroom and along a small corridor, something caught his eye twenty or thirty feet away on the wide balustraded staircase which led up to the bedrooms. He stepped into the shadows, not wanting to be seen, and looked more closely. He could hardly believe what he saw. Danny was leading Alice upstairs by the hand. They were whispering and giggling. Tom's breath caught in his throat as his mind raced ahead. *He was leading her by the hand because he knew the way. He'd been here before.*

He found his way back to the boys and flopped down on the lawn. He grabbed the joint from between Zac's fingers and took a long drag on it. Undeterred, Zac lit another one for himself. After three or four more drags, Tom said,

'I think Danny and Alice might be a thing.'

'I'm sure they are,' said Harry. 'I reckon they have been for a while.'

'Cheeky types like Danny always get the girl.' added Zac despondently. It didn't occur to him to query what Harry said. Today had been such a weird day, full of eye-opening discoveries, not the least of which was Alice's fabulous house and its array of interesting art.

And the three of them laughed and laughed, high as kites.

Chapter 20

*In the decade which began in the year 2000, several things hap-
pened which affected the entire world.*

*When programmers wrote the first complex computer programs
in the 1960s, they used a two-digit code for the year, omitting the
'19.' As the year 2000 approached, many believed that the systems
would not interpret the '00' correctly, therefore causing a major
world-wide glitch affecting everything from banking to air travel.
Before the turn of the century, governments around the world worked
to overcome predicted major difficulties, at a total cost of approx.
$US300 billion, which ultimately averted disaster.*

*The bombing of the World Trade Centre in New York City on
September 11, 2001, had serious repercussions around the world.
It was part of a series of four coordinated suicide terrorist attacks
across America carried out by the militant Islamic extremist net-
work al-Qaeda, led by Osama bin Laden. The attacks killed 3,000
people and injured over 25,000, and caused at least $10 billion in
infrastructure and property damage. The United States responded
by launching the War on Terror and invading Afghanistan.*

*The most significant loss of life because of a natural disaster oc-
curred in 2004 when an earthquake in the Indian Ocean caused*

enormous tsunami waves to crash into the coastal areas of several Southeast Asian Island countries, killing around 230,000 people and displacing well over a million others.

In 2005, Hurricane Katrina made landfall in Mississippi, devastating the city of New Orleans and nearby coastal areas. Katrina was recognised as the costliest natural disaster in the United States at the time, causing a record $108 billion in property damage and over 1,200 deaths.

The Black Saturday bushfires occurred in Victoria, Australia over three weeks in February and March 2009 during extreme bushfire-weather conditions, killing 173 people, injuring over 500, and leaving around 7,500 homeless.

A crisis in housing and credit in the United States in late 2007, known as the subprime mortgage crisis, led to the bankruptcy of major banks and other financial institutions in the US. By 2008, the crisis had sparked a global recession which became known as the GFC—the Global Financial Crisis—severely affecting the rest of the world for years to come.

On a lighter note:

Social media and media sharing took off and changed the way we communicate and obtain information. In 2004, Facebook was launched, followed by YouTube in 2005, Twitter in 2006, and Google Chrome in 2008. Email surpassed snail mail as the preferred method of correspondence, world-wide.

Barack Obama was sworn in as the 44th President of the United States in 2009, becoming the nation's first African American president, and the country rejoiced.

The iPod became a hit as a digital music player in the 2000s. The iPhone was released in 2007 and was the first smartphone to utilise a touch screen and a home button.

Digital cameras became widely popular due to rapid decreases in size and cost while photo resolution steadily increased, and by 2003, digital cameras outsold film cameras.

In the Entertainment industry:

The television series Friends became the most watched TV show of the decade. Its final episode aired in May 2004 with over 52 million viewers in the United States.

American television in the 2000s saw a sharp increase in the popularity of reality television, with many competition shows such as American Idol, Dancing with the Stars, Survivor, and The Apprentice attracting large audiences.

It was during this decade that Tom Watson became a rich and famous Rock Star. It was also during this decade that Tom Watson accelerated his descent into a life of addiction as he became dependent on drugs and alcohol.

Alice's suggestion for the band's tour across the United States required more time and work to organise than even she expected. It was moved back several times to coordinate the 35 towns and cities that were scheduled on the tour and was eventually set for December 2001.

Things changed again after the United States went into shock on September 11, 2001, when several suicide terrorist attacks rocked the country and the world. The first plane, which had been hijacked by the terrorists, ploughed into the North Tower of the World Trade Centre in New York City around nine o'clock on the morning of September 11. Because several people immediately began filming the unfolding disaster, the explosion which happened when the second hijacked plane crashed into the South Tower seventeen minutes later, was watched by millions of people around the world as it happened. It took America and Americans many months before they could begin to come to terms with what had happened to them.

It was not the time for a rock band to tour America.

Alice set up a meeting with the band in her office a couple of months later. The terrorist attacks, which became known as "9/11", were the major topic of conversation for the first hour or so. The five of them drank tea and talked about things they had each heard and seen involving the attacks and how it had affected them and people they knew. Everyone had a story to tell.

Eventually, there was a break in the conversation and Alice took the opportunity to talk business.

'The country's in a mess at the moment,' said Alice. 'I'm sure you and your music would cheer up a lot of people, but it's too difficult to organise transportation and accommodation right now and probably will be for a while yet. I'm going to plan on the tour going ahead in May next year.'

'One good thing about the postponement is that we should be able to organise your second album by then. I suggest we work it so that the album is released to coincide with the tour.'

All nodded in agreement, thankful to leave behind the subject of "9/11".

'I've got the eight songs that were left over from the first album and I've done another four since,' said Tom. 'I'd like to write another four or five as well so we've got a good range to choose from. Also, Alice, I don't know if you are aware of it,' but Harry and I have been singing a few things together at some of our recent gigs. We sound pretty good. Harry harmonises well.' Tom glanced at Harry and smiled. 'I'd like to do a couple of them on the record.'

Harry beamed.

'Great idea,' replied Alice, as she scribbled in her notebook. 'I'll speak to Red Pony and see if they'll agree to record in, say, January.'

She raised her head when she finished writing and looked at Tom. 'Tom, I notice you're getting quite a bit of publicity lately. Great pic of you leaving the Viper Room with a girl on each arm.' She smiled at him as she spoke. As quickly as it appeared, the smile vanished as she continued: 'but the one of you, drunk and slumped in some woman's lap in a corner at Vinyl was not. That's the second time I've seen a photo of you like that. If you're bent on getting high, don't get photographed doing it. Do I make myself clear?'

'I'm getting sick and tired of the press following me around,' said Tom defensively. 'I'm beginning to feel like public property.'

'I'm afraid that comes with the money and the fame, Tom. The trick is not to let the fame become notoriety.'

'OK. OK. I get it,' said Tom petulantly, throwing his hands in the air.

'Yeah, why do you think I don't drink?' said Danny. 'At least, I don't have to think about what I'm going to look like in the papers tomorrow morning if the paparazzi catch up with me.'

'Good point, Danny,' said Alice as she smiled sweetly at him. Harry kicked Zac under the desk and the two of them exchanged knowing looks.

'So,' said Alice, 'I know you've got a few gigs locally coming up but we've also got the album to organise. Plus, I'll need a couple of videos for the pre-booking phase of the tour. You've got a lot of work to do before next May. You're going to be busy, busy, busy.'

'Busy?' replied Zac. 'I still haven't completely settled into my new house in Malibu yet. I've still got stuff in boxes all over the place and I moved in three months ago.'

'Yes, well if it weren't such a mega mansion with millions of rooms, you would have completed the move by now,' said Harry, laughing good-naturedly at Zac. 'How many rooms did you say you had for your drums?'

'You're saying that 'cause you're jealous. Your apartment might have a fabulous view over L.A. but you've got to admit, it's not very big.'

'How come you're still in your apartment?' Danny enquired of Tom, 'when we've all moved up in the world?'

'Oh, I'm waiting until I can afford something like Alice's place. Now that's something to aspire to.' Tom looked at Alice and winked.

'Now boys, enough of the 'house' jibes.' Alice brought the meeting back to business as she stood and collected the tea things. 'You've all got your schedule of work for the next four months so off you go and get your act together.'

The four men stood and were moving their chairs back to their original positions against the wall when Alice said,

'Tom, will you please stay behind? I'd like to have a talk with you.'

Tom instantly felt uneasy. A one-on-one with Alice was unusual. He was annoyed with himself that she could make him feel like a naughty schoolboy with that one phrase. 'I'd like to have a talk with you!' A phrase to make you quake in your boots. He had an uncomfortable feeling in the pit of his stomach.

'Sure,' he replied as casually as he could. And to the others, as they sauntered out the door: 'See you guys at practice tonight.'

'Sit down,' said Alice when the door had closed and they were alone.

He sat down. He knew what was coming from the steely look on her face and the frown.

'Tom, I'm worried about your drinking and the drugs. I meant what I said about photos in the papers and magazines of you drunk. If you're going to get drunk, do it privately, not in some downtown club. If you get caught and end up in front of a magistrate, there's only so much I can do. You're sailing very close to the wind here Tom.'

'Alice, Alice, Alice,' said Tom, placing his hands on the desk in front of him and leaning forward conspiratorially. 'It's no big deal. I can stop any time I like. You know I've always enjoyed my vodka and the drugs are only recreational. I can stop anytime I want, but why should I? I'm not hurting anyone and it's not like I can't afford it.'

'Tom, if you're not hooked already, you soon will be. You've got the world at your feet. Don't put what you've achieved at risk by being stupid and careless.

He had to get out of here. He didn't like the way this conversation was going. *She's not my mother*, he thought to himself.

He stood and proceeded to move towards the door. 'There is absolutely no need to worry about me, Alice. I'll ease back if it makes you feel better.'

'Yes, please Tom. It would make me feel better. I've worked too hard for you to fuck things up at this stage. Now go and get back to work. We'll need those four or five new songs within the next two months.'

She walked around the desk to the door and opened it for him.

He had to squeeze past her to get through the doorway and as he did so, he bent down and, taking his time, placed a lingering kiss on her cheek. Not a peck, a meaningful kiss. He leaned in a fraction closer and whispered in her ear,

'Don't worry, Alice. I would never do anything that would hurt you.'

And left the office.

Alice closed the door quietly behind him. She leaned back against the door and placed her hand on the part of her cheek where his lips had been as she closed her eyes and thought *I'd forgive him anything if he would do that again.*

But it was Tom the celebrity photographers wanted. His good looks and swagger attracted the ladies, and that combination always made for a good photo. Tom was rarely seen without at least one pretty young woman on his arm.

He had recently spent a night at 'the Ranch,' an out-of-the-way club downtown. Situated in a back alley behind an old broken-down door with no handle, it was hard to get into unless you were someone famous. Tom's dealer, Bo, had introduced him to it. Drugs of every variety were readily available at the club and Tom had tried quite a few different types, most of which he enjoyed immensely and wanted to try again. It was easy to be cavalier about these things when money was no object.

At this stage, the club kept the paparazzi out but could do nothing about the group that formed outside in the alley, waiting to see who would leave, and if they could get a pic that was worth good money to one of the newspapers or magazines.

Tom heeded what Alice had said and was more careful about with whom and where he was seen when he was out and about. He eased off the drinks in the clubs and always made sure he had plenty of alcohol at home. Whenever and wherever he obtained any drugs, he made sure he didn't use them in too public a place. If he was with a group of people he knew in a club, he would often ask them back to his place, which was one reason he hadn't bought a big, fancy house like the others had. None of the paparazzi or journos took any notice of the ordinary-looking apartment block on an insignificant street in L.A..

Over time, his circle of these 'friends' grew and soon he had quite a following. Deep down, he knew they were hangers-on more than friends but as he didn't have any other friends in L.A. aside from Zac, Harry, and Danny, he was happy enough for them to hang around.

Cutting down on both the drinking and the drugs had helped him to write melody and lyrics for another five songs by the beginning of January. He was particularly pleased with one song which he called Absolute Power Over Me. It had a great guitar intro and a strong, pumping rhythm which ran through the entire song. Tom wanted it as the first track on the album. He also thought it was a good title for both the album and the tour. The Absolute Power Tour had a good ring to it.

The making of the album at Red Pony studios went well, and the producers were excited with it by the time recording was complete. It contained three instrumental numbers, including one which Tom called Alice's Lovers. It had a heavy rock sound and a fabulous drum solo in the middle. Everyone loved it. Everyone except Alice, who was alarmed when she heard what Tom had named the track.

'Exactly what are you inferring with that title, Tom?' asked Alice, looking ever so slightly embarrassed. 'It's very suggestive.' She removed her glasses with the urgency of someone about to deliver a Supreme Court ruling and furiously wiped them clean, as if clearer lenses might somehow change reality. 'I love the number but you must change the title.' Although she was flattered to have another song named after her, the title was very cheeky.

Tom, ever the gentleman, placed his hand over his heart and bowed theatrically. 'Okay, okay. In deference to you, dear Alice, I'll change the title.' He paused for effect, and, tilting his head slightly to one side, and with a serious face, added: 'Just to show you I'm able to compromise, I'll drop the 's'.' He cupped his hands around his mouth like an old-town crier and, with a wide grin, declared: 'This track will henceforth be known as Alice's Lover.'

The studio erupted in cheers and laughter. Alice shook her head and muttered under her breath: 'marginally worse,' but she realised she'd lost that argument and laughed along with them.

***

The Absolute Power Tour was an amazing success interspersed with moments of high drama. The 35 cities and towns included some places Tom had never heard of, as well as some of the major cities of America. The four concerts in Chicago were exhilarating thanks to an extremely receptive audience. Their popularity there was boosted further when Alice told the band that Absolute Power Over Me had entered the Billboard 100 at No. 38. Alice looked slightly demure as she announced that Alice's Lover had hit No. 57 the first week in.

Tom announced this news at the following night's concert to thunderous applause and much foot stamping.

By the time they reached Boston three days later, news of the two tracks' success had already reached the city. Although they only did three concerts in Boston, they could have easily done another five, such was the demand for tickets.

But the five nights at Madison Square Garden in New York drew the biggest crowds. The first time the band heard 20,000 people screaming for more, they were temporarily overwhelmed and had to wait for the noise to quieten down before they could go on. But by the fourth night at the venue, the sound was merely exhilarating, even expected.

Alice had booked them at The Peninsular in New York to celebrate the half-way mark of the tour. She felt they needed to enjoy a little luxury at this point. The tour so far had been exhausting, and they were only halfway through it. Around midday on the day after their last concert in New York, the boys met up in a private dining room of the Peninsular for a late breakfast. They were joined by two of their backup singers, one of whom had woken up in Tom's bed an hour ago, their sound engineer, and the manager and stage manager of Madison Square Garden. It was a subdued group who ordered breakfast and lots of coffee and were slumped around the table in varying degrees of hangover when Alice entered the room.

'Alice, you're looking particularly fetching this morning,' said Harry, as he raised his head from the table where it had been resting on his arms and opened his tired eyes. Alice walked over to the chair at the head of the table and sat down.

'Ditto,' added Tom as he removed his sunglasses and put them on the table. He quickly retrieved them and put them on again as the glare from the white tablecloth pierced his eyes. *God, I could do with a drink. And a sleep.* Thought Tom. *I suppose she'd have a fit if I ordered a vodka for breakfast.* That last night at Madison Square Garden had been a big one. The after-party in the Green Room had been wild. He remembered having a good time, but couldn't remember how he got back to his hotel room and was surprised when he woke to find Jody in his bed. It crossed his mind that the Madison Square Garden's manager and stage manager had showed up this morning to make sure they were all still alive.

When he concentrated and really looked at her, Tom could see that Alice did indeed look good. She was wearing a sexy floral sundress and white strappy high-heeled sandals and had obviously gone to a lot of trouble with her hair and make-up. *Actually*, he thought to himself, *she looks fabulous.*

Alice picked up a spoon from the table and tapped it against one of the glasses. She looked so serious that everyone scrambled to sit up straight and silence fell over the room.

'I've got something to say, and I'm not quite sure how to say it.' She began.

Christ. What's happened? Thought Tom. *Something terrible by the look on her face.*

'Well just bloody say it, will you,' said Zac. 'I feel bad enough as it is. And you look like somebody's dog died.'

'Right. I won't mince my words,' said Alice, as she touched the pearls around her throat as if re-assuring herself that everything was going to be alright.

She stood up and pushed her chair back.

'I just got Billboard 100's list for this week. Absolute Power Over Me just hit Number One and Alice's Lover rocketed up to Number Two.'

She flopped back down onto her chair and started to laugh. Mayhem broke out in the room and suddenly all hangovers and feelings of serious sleep deprivation were forgotten as people began hugging and congratulating each other.

Tom moved to where Alice was sitting and knelt on the floor beside her chair. He threw his arms around her and kissed her soundly on the cheek. She looked into his eyes, and taking his face in her hands, said to him: 'I wouldn't have believed this could have happened so soon. But it has. All our hard work. This tour has nearly killed me, but it's worth it for a Number One record.'

Harry yelled at the top of his voice in the direction of where the waiter was last seen: 'Champagne. Lots of Champagne. Needed here. Right now!'

Prior to New York, there were a few moments of minor drama. On four or five occasions, Tom, or even some of the other band members, had too much to drink after a show and had slept all day the following day. Three times Alice had to wake Tom and make him stand under a cold shower to bring him to a point where he could get to the theatre in enough time to prepare for a show.

However, the first serious incident occurred in Philadelphia.

The entourage left New York early in the morning following two days of R & R, refreshed and ready to party at the next stop, Philadelphia. The caravan of trailers full of equipment and crew trundled into Philly around midday and after checking into their hotel and grabbing a bite to eat, Tom and Harry left the others to try out some bars in the downtown area. They timed it so that they would be back at the hotel by 5.30. The limo would pick them up at the hotel at around seven o'clock. Showtime that night was eight o'clock.

They chose dingy, out-of-the-way places to avoid being recognised. This worked for most of the afternoon until a woman from a nearby office building approached Harry for his autograph, mistaking him for the lead singer from another band. He scribbled an unreadable signature, and they heard her excitedly muttering 'I can't believe I got his autograph' as she walked away.

Sitting in a back booth in the third bar of the afternoon, Harry made an announcement as he placed his fifth empty glass on the table:

'It's nearly four o'clock. Think I'll call it quits and go back to the hotel. I could do with a nap before we do the show tonight.'

'Sure,' replied Tom. 'I'm going to have one more here before I head back. See you in the foyer around seven.'

But by 7.15, as the others stood around in the foyer while Alice checked everywhere in the hotel, there was still no sign of Tom. Alice had a quiet word with Harry. 'I'll send the others to the venue and you and I will get a cab to the last place you and Tom were drinking this afternoon.'

'Good idea,' replied Harry. 'It's not far from here.'

They pulled up to the Bar and Alice hurried inside as Harry told the cab driver to wait. Once inside, they found Tom draped over the table in the booth, empty vodka glass in hand, very inebriated.

'Come on,' said Alice to Harry, as she grabbed Tom's left arm and heaved him to his feet. 'Help me get him into the cab and we'll go straight to the venue and try and get him sobered up.' Harry thought he noticed a tinge of panic in Alice's voice—but he had mistaken panic for anger.

Alice grabbed a bottle of water from the barman as they left and insisted Tom drink as much of it as possible while they were in the cab. With his head out the open window of the cab gulping in as much air as he could, he had almost finished the bottle by the time they got him into the Green Room around seven forty-five.

Alice occasionally thought about how things would pan out if it ever transpired that Tom was maybe too sick, or had an accident, and was unable to perform. The insurance Alice had taken out to cover that sort of incident didn't cover being too drunk to go on. She made up her mind to get Tom on stage—whatever it took.

Coffee. Strong black coffee. And more water. And a face dunk in a bowl of ice water.

Eight o'clock came and went. At 8.15, Alice sent the others on ahead to play some sort of long intro to the show, to keep the audience happy. At this stage, the audience was not bothered, but Alice knew they couldn't keep them waiting too much longer. By 8.30, Tom was not so obviously drunk and insisted he was ready to go on.

'Tom, you are going to have to really charm the audience when you get out there. They've waited long enough and they're getting restless,' said Alice in her most appealing voice. 'Can you do that for me?'

'Alice, don't worry about me. I'm fine. I'm at my best when the pressure's on.' His speech was hardly affected and he smiled so sweetly at her, she almost believed him.

Contrary to her worst fears, Tom put on a fabulous show. He was relaxed and amusing, and the audience loved him. They seemed to think it was charming and funny that he was slightly tipsy and the reviews in the papers the following day were glowing.

The next two months of the tour went like clockwork, which was amazing considering the amount of alcohol and drugs which were consumed by Tom Watson and Pants on Fire, and their entourage as they played many small, and some large, towns across the country.

Until they reached Las Vegas.

By then, the band, backup singers, extra musicians, the tech crew, even the roadies, were sick of touring. Sick of living out of suitcases, sick of putting up and taking down, and sick of performing. Tempers were frayed; nobody was happy anymore. All the excitement of adoring audiences, record-breaking sales of merchandise, fun TV and radio interviews across the country, had palled. Even Alice was struggling to hold it all together.

But Las Vegas was important. They were booked to play five nights at Caesar's Palace before an audience of approx. 4,000 people a night. It was to be a fabulous production with a spectacular stage setting and special sound and lighting. The revenue from this venue, including sales of merchandise, was forecast to be around ten million dollars. Nothing must go wrong......

And nothing did go wrong. It was bigger and more successful than Alice had dared hope, and she had cemented some excellent contacts with the casino management team which would pay dividends in the future.

But it was late the following morning when they were due to leave the hotel for the airport that all hell broke loose.

When Tom didn't show up for the limo to take them to the airport, Alice sent the others on their way to catch the plane to L.A. while she and Harry searched the hotel. They found Tom passed out in his room, his system unable to cope with the amount of alcohol and pills he had imbibed whilst partying long into the previous night. The only good thing about the incident was that at least he had made it back to his room. He was fully clothed, flat out on his back on the bed, the young lady next to him in the same state. Alice phoned the Hotel Manager and he and the resident doctor were there within minutes. The Doctor brought the unconscious couple around and the Manager arranged for Security to move the woman to another room to recover and leave the hotel as quickly as possible.

'What do I have to do to keep any of this out of the papers?' Alice asked the hotel manager.

'I'll send you a bill,' replied the manager curtly. 'Make sure you pay it pronto! The media here don't let up if they get a whiff of drama with any of the entertainers.'

Several phone calls later, and after much negotiation, Alice, Tom, and Harry left the hotel for the airport where the private jet Alice had organised was waiting to take them to L.A.

Two weeks later, the five final concerts of the tour were held at the Hollywood Bowl in L.A. to capacity audiences of 18,000 people a night. They were the high point of the tour and cemented Tom Watson and Pants on Fire as the Number One biggest selling and performing group in the United States.

The tour lasted seven months and ticket sales alone were well over one hundred and twenty million dollars. The Absolute Power album sat at Number One for twelve weeks in a row, and the royalties were huge.

Chapter 21

Tom and the boys were riding the crest of a wave. In the eyes of the public, they could do no wrong. Even when Tom appeared in the papers for doing something improper, like being photographed canoodling with another man's wife, or being booked for speeding, they forgave him. TV, newspapers, and magazines couldn't get enough of him: Tom Watson, sex symbol, handsome, exceptionally talented musician, funny, self-deprecating, photogenic, all-round good guy—and sometimes bad-boy. Hosts of TV talk shows waited in line to sign Tom as a guest on their shows. They knew ratings would soar whenever Tom was on.

It was Ellen who first referred to it as his 'Golden Glow,' that warm and fuzzy aura which seemed to surround Tom, and the name was picked up by other TV hosts, and industry papers, radio, and magazines. But although he appreciated the benefits of all the flattering adjectives, at heart, Tom was a realist. Deep down, he was self-aware enough to know his world was full of hangers-on and so-called friends who were just there to bathe in his reflected glory.

Occasionally, when he'd had a few more vodkas than usual, his mind would wander back to the days of playing at the Fringe near Stanford University in Palo Alto and he'd remember what fun they had in their struggle to make a name for themselves—practicing in Bobby's music room, experimenting with an arrangement of the latest song Tom had written, laughing at one of Zac's lame jokes.

And then other times his mind would return to the night in some downtown club he couldn't remember the name of, when he was sitting with a group of 'friends,' snorting cocaine, and drinking, when a thought had entered his head and hit him hard: *what the hell am I doing in this place, with these people I hardly know and like even less?* He had stared, unseeing, into the darkness of the room, thinking dark thoughts. But someone had brought another drink back to the table for him and the thoughts disappeared into the back recess of his mind, only to flicker and burn again when he least expected it.

He enjoyed the time he spent with Zac, Harry, and Danny, but they were more like work colleagues than friends. Music was the common thread that tied them together. Would they be friends without that shared love of music? Probably not.

Over time, Tom came to value his friendship with Paul and Rooster on a deeper level. He frequently phoned each of them in Australia and often caught up with Paul when he visited the States on business, four or five times a year. Paul was a down-to-earth, uncomplicated man who knew and understood his place in the world. The fact that he was now a millionaire computer genius was incidental, and he had not changed since they first met at university in Melbourne all those years ago.

It was a sign of his profound regard for Paul that Tom had never sold the Porsche Paul had given him many years ago. It had been Paul's way of thanking Tom for setting up the meeting with Luke Gardener, who subsequently bought Paul's Architectural computer program, which made Gardener even richer and more successful. Paul made millions of dollars on the deal, which set him up for a life of comfort and success.

Paul was a good listener, always succinct and straightforward with his replies whenever Tom wanted his opinion on something, a rare commodity in today's world when everyone had their own agenda. Everyone except Paul, who was an unusual man and a true friend.

Although Tom and Rooster shared a love of music which had kept them grounded as friends all these years, their friendship went deeper than that. They both had the same values, the same view of the world. Rooster occasionally visited America for jazz festivals, and Tom looked forward to meeting up with him whenever the opportunity arose.

Tom was rarely seen in public without a beautiful woman on his arm, often a celebrity, sometimes a supporting musician from one of their performances, occasionally a groupie whose name he didn't even know. Settling down with one person was not something Tom thought about. He enjoyed his own company and had never been moved enough to want to share it with anyone else.

If there was no one else around at the time and he felt like some female company, there was always Alice. Her position of manager of the band had evolved into that of a friend to Tom. A casual friend, a friend who did not share his fondness for alcohol or drugs, but a friend none-the-less. Good old Alice.

It was Alice who had pulled strings and got him out of the shit when he was charged with DUI as he left a downtown club. And it was Alice who had slipped a plump envelope to the magistrate when Tom had been charged with drug possession after he'd been picked up exchanging money for drugs in a back street in L.A. His regular dealer was in a jail cell somewhere awaiting arraignment and Tom was desperate; he'd stupidly contacted a second-grade dealer who was also a police informant. But once again, Alice to the rescue.

Each time, he promised Alice he wouldn't do it again.

But he always did.

As Tom's star had risen, so his wealth had increased.

When he decided he needed something larger than his original apartment in L.A., it was Alice who had helped him find a trophy home in Beverly Hills. Alice had looked at four or five houses before she found one she thought would suit Tom. It was a characteristic Californian Mediterranean house, built in 1931 on an acre of ground overlooking L.A., complete with CCTV at the handmade wrought-iron front gates. The gardens had always been professionally looked after and the prolific purple bougainvillea which clung to the white stucco walls at the front of the house had been planted when the house was new, as were the gnarled olive trees which lined the perfectly paved drive. But it was the music room and home theatre that had been added onto the back of the house in recent years which sealed the deal for Tom. The previous owner had been a music composer/songwriter for the movies with a knack for designing the perfect music studio.

Tom loved the house the moment he saw it and bought it immediately. The Porsche looked good in the garage, and so did the Bentley Tom bought on a whim to celebrate owning his first home.

He was a rich and famous rock star now. He could do anything he liked and get away with it.

The dynamics of the band changed over the next few years as the boys matured. For a couple of them, the wild life of a rock star evolved into the lifestyle of a family man with family responsibilities.

Zac met and married a 5'11' supermodel who featured in one of their music videos. The band was no longer the number one priority in his life. Cassandra was a beautiful, successful, in-demand model with legs that went on forever, and Zac was smitten from the moment they were introduced. They both had that ridiculous sense of humour—she even laughed at his jokes—and they both loved the social life and being in the spotlight. When Zac fell in love, he fell hard. He adored being married to Cassandra even though she literally towered over him, and he would have left the band tomorrow had she asked him. Fortunately, she didn't, and their life of married bliss blossomed as they became one of showbusiness's 'power couples.' They were constantly in the social pages of every newspaper in the country and never missed a 'red carpet' occasion.

Around the same time as Zac's wedding, Harry's girlfriend of four years, Maddie, moved in with him on a permanent basis when they discovered she was pregnant. They were deliriously happy with the news and spent weeks looking for a suitable house for their future family. His apartment with the fabulous view of L.A. gave way to a 'home in the Hills' and Harry was no longer seen at any of the clubs or nightspots in L.A.. He preferred to spend time at home helping Maddie decorate the nursery. When baby Joey came along, Harry's world was complete. He and Tom wrote a song to commemorate the occasion and added it to the list for their next album.

Danny's fling with Alice had been short-lived: it had ended amicably, with no hint of animosity between them. Thereafter, Danny drifted from one relationship to another, happy enough in his large, if untidy, penthouse apartment. He'd honed his arrogance to an art form, and the ladies loved him for it. He was rarely alone but wasn't concerned when he was. As long as Danny had his battered old guitar beside him, he was satisfied. Any attractive woman in his life was a bonus.

Tom scrambled out of bed as he woke and saw the time was nearly 9.15 on the Tuesday morning Alice had scheduled a meeting at her office at ten o'clock. He felt nauseous and headachy. In other words—hungover.

Christ, I wish I hadn't stayed for that extra drink last night. Shit! Only three hours' sleep! thought Tom, as he glanced at the clock again, by which time it was 9.20. *I can't be late again. I don't want another one of her lectures on the benefits of time management.* He flew into the shower and immediately felt worse as the full force of the cold water hit him. After the fastest shower ever, he threw on some clothes before he'd even finished drying off. Thirty minutes later, he parked his car in the underground garage and took the elevator to the top floor. He stopped outside Alice's office and glanced down at himself to make sure he looked OK for the meeting. Damn! His left shoe was different to his right shoe but at least his socks matched, and his shirt was clean and tucked into his jeans.

He ran his fingers through his hair and, satisfied he looked almost presentable, tapped on her office door. On the stroke of ten, he entered the office. The others were already there.

'Good morning, Tom. Cup of tea?'

'That would be wonderful, thank you, Alice,' replied Tom, hoping it wouldn't cause him to throw-up.

He glanced at the others. Zac had had his hair bleached, thanks to Cassandra; Harry looked like he hadn't slept in years; and Danny was beaming. *What a crew*, thought Tom. Alice, of course, looked her best business-like self, complete with pearls and new tortoiseshell glasses.

He took a sip of tea and, miraculously, felt better.

Once Alice had made sure everyone had tea and cakes, she sat up straight and started her speech:

'Time for another album,' she said, as she adjusted her glasses. 'Red Pony are getting restless. The videos you've been doing for MTV have been great and they've certainly kept your name in front of the public, but they are only singles, and singles don't produce enough revenue, particularly in relation to what they cost to make. There's nothing like an album to kick things along. Tom, what have you got in the way of new material?'

Tom snapped out of his 'asleep-while-seemingly-awake' mood and replied like he was a robot on speed,

'I've got seven new numbers, plus the one Harry and I wrote for little Joey called 'Dreamland.' You are going to love it, Alice. It's sweet, and melancholy, and melodic with a great hook—a type of lullaby.'

'Also,' he paused as he took a breath.

'Also,' he began again, 'You know how the music video of 'Bohemian Rhapsody' went for nearly seven minutes, and you know how 'Thriller' lasted thirteen minutes, well, I've written something along those lines which lasts for about eleven minutes—which is as long as three separate tracks. It's called 'Midnight in the Garden of Sorrows.

'Alice, it's fabulous. Best thing I've ever done. Sort of a cross between Eleanor Rigby and American Pie. I've just got to finish off the middle section.'

Then, quickly, before anyone had a chance to speak: 'Also, I reckon Midnight in the Garden is a good name for the next album.'

Stunned silence. Four pairs of eyes stared at him.

'When did you do that?' asked Harry.

'When are we going to hear it?' said Zac.

'Is it really that good?' added Danny.

Alice smiled. Why did she always feel a tiny bit responsible when Tom did something exceptional?

'Midnight in the Garden of Sorrows' *was* that good. And by the time the new album was completed and ready for release six months later, it was the best thing Tom Watson and Pants on Fire had produced so far.

The album sold 2.5 million copies in the first week.

The boys' individual wealth doubled in the next month.

Zac and Cassandra bought a holiday home in the Bahamas.

Harry and Maddie set up a trust fund for baby Joey.

Danny bought a new bass guitar.

And Tom bought a good supply of the newest designer drugs, some rare handmade Russian vodka which was only available on the black market, and the most expensive call girl in Los Angeles.

Alice counted her money and increased the size of her investment portfolio.

Chapter 22

Over the next few years, things changed for Tom and the band. The crest of the wave they had been riding began to flatten. They were usurped in the number one place in pop lovers' hearts by a hot young woman from Florida with a fascinatingly wide vocal range. It was only ego, and the fear of having too much time available and not enough meaningful pursuits to fill it, that kept them from mentioning the word 'retirement.'

Money was no longer an issue; it was more a question of how long they would continue to be hero-worshipped by their adoring fans? Would people in the street continue to recognise and gush over them? Would people continue to clamour for photos and autographs whenever they appeared in public? How long would it take for them to fade from the collective memory of their current fans?

Alice knew that the business she had nurtured and worked so hard for had perhaps reached its zenith and would soon begin its natural trajectory downwards.

Unless she did something to maintain the status quo.

Another tour! She felt that any suggestion of another tour would not be welcomed. She needed to plan the best way to achieve agreement from all concerned.

She spent the next few days planning and budgeting a 'grand tour' then called a meeting.

As the boys trouped into her office one by one, Alice couldn't help noticing that Tom looked as though he hadn't slept in a while, and he seemed to have lost weight. Although she knew that his questionable lifestyle was the reason for his appearance, she still felt that rush of blood, that tingle in the pit of her stomach, whenever he appeared. Zac looked like a fashionista in cargo pants and a $300 designer t-shirt, Cassandra made sure of that, and Danny looked like he'd just gotten out of bed. Only Harry seemed truly happy to be there. *And why wouldn't he?* Alice thought to herself, *with a three-year-old with too much energy, and a new baby keeping him and Maddie up most nights, he'd be glad of any reason to get out of the house for a while.*

As Alice poured the tea, she looked at Tom and enquired,

'Tom, how did that interview go with the journo from the magazine last week?'

'Christ, those things are dreadful,' replied Tom. 'They ask the most inane questions. Do me a favour and don't agree to any more for at least six months. That'll give me a chance to think up some stupid answers for their stupid questions. The paparazzi are bad enough, chasing us all over town. They were at my front gate the other day, snapping away as I drove out. They are driving me mad and they're rude as hell. Absolutely no regard for your privacy. And I am so sick of hearing the expression 'Golden Glow.' I am beginning to really hate the media.'

'As I've said before, Tom. It's all part of the job. You like the fame and fortune but not what it takes to obtain it. Suck it up, Buttercup.'

Alice had seen a proof of the article from last week's interview. The pics were gorgeous but the text was awful. Tom was right. Most of the questions were downright silly.

'Anyway,' she added. 'They sent the proof of the article to me, and I made a few changes, reduced some of the text and enlarged the pics. Overall, it looks quite good now. It's just as well you're so photogenic.' Alice smiled and winked at him.

Danny put one hand on his hip and gave a low whistle in Tom's direction. Had it been directed at a woman, she would have slapped his face.

'Ooh, Tom. You're so sexy,' mocked Zac in a 'little girl voice'. 'Can I have your autograph?'

Tom couldn't help laughing.

Once tea and cookies had been dispensed, Alice began the meeting in earnest.

'As you know, Pants on Fire has been displaced as America's idols by the 'Mouth from the South' and unless we do something noticeable, your slide will continue until you become has-beens in the music industry, no longer relevant. We've all seen that happen to entertainers over the years.'

'You guys are at the point where you need to decide: do you want to continue to stay on top for a few more years, or are you happy to inevitably fade from sight?'

'So, what are your thoughts, Alice?' asked Tom. This situation had crossed his mind on more than one occasion recently.

'It's been a few years since your last album, and I know you do lots of gigs on the West Coast, but we need to come up with something now which will keep your name in the forefront of the music scene, if you want to stay on top of your game.'

'You're all in your forties now, too early to retire completely, still enough energy to go on for a few more years. I think it's time for an album and I'd suggest another tour.'

Alice put her hands in the air to hush the moans and groans and mutterings from the four men.

'Let me finish, please.' She hesitated before continuing her practiced speech.

'I'm talking about a world tour —the UK, Europe, Australia, Japan, spread out over two years. It would certainly boost sales in those countries as well as at home, which would keep you going for quite a few more years.'

It was quiet in the room for a couple of minutes. You could almost hear the four minds ticking over.

'Any questions?' asked Alice, knowing there would be.

Danny was the first to speak. 'When do you think this tour should happen?'

Alice replied: 'It would take me at least 12 months to organise it so I'm thinking probably the year after next.'

'So, you're saying we would have to release another album to tie in with a tour.' said Tom.

'Ideally, yes.'

Before they could say another word, Alice continued,

'Let me explain a few things which may convince you that it's not such a bad idea.'

Alice had made some notes prior to the meeting. She shuffled through the papers on her desk until she found the one she wanted, glanced over it, and began:

'We can comfortably afford to do this tour in style. By that, I mean you would stay at the best hotels. I suggest hiring a large jet and crew to fly us wherever possible, chauffeur-driven limos for shorter distances. By having our own plane at our disposal, we could fly family and friends back and forth from the States if they weren't able to accompany you on the tour. I would also suggest doing the tour over two legs. The UK and Europe could be one leg, and then a few months later, South Africa, Australia, the Philippines, and maybe Japan.'

Like a good detective story, Alice released information at a calculated pace.

'Based on my rough calculations, I'm thinking about 40 concerts in 21 cities over about three months on the first leg and two months on the second leg.'

'I don't think I could stand it,' said Zac, as he lifted his right foot in its expensive trainer and rested it on his left knee. 'That last one was too long and too hard.'

'I agree.' added Harry.

'It's tempting,' said Danny. 'But no thanks.'

'I'll make a deal with you, Alice,' said Tom. He looked hard at the other three men, then back at Alice. 'I'll agree to the album and the tour, but they will be the last ones I do. I'm getting sick of this treadmill we're on and I'd like to get off. I've had enough.'

'Me too,' said Zac. 'I reckon I can just about last that long.' Harry nodded agreement. Danny glanced at Tom with a quizzical look on his face, surprised that Tom felt that way.

'Oh, and one other thing,' added Alice, who had been saving the kicker for last.

'I estimate the gross ticket sales to be around three hundred million dollars.' She took a breath to let that sink in. 'Don't get too carried away, expenses would be huge – but then, so would royalties long-term.'

'That's a lot of money, Alice,' said Danny, who had a genius for taking the bait. 'You sure know how to turn the screws.'

'You certainly do, Alice.' said Tom, looking at the others. 'Are we agreed that we do the album and the tour and then that's it?'

'Agreed,' said three voices in unison, as Zac extended his arm, palm down, to the others. Harry reached out and placed his hand on top of Zac's and Danny and Tom added theirs.

'All for One, and One for All.' And they laughed, as Alice concealed a wicked smile. She loved it when she won.

'I think that's a reasonable deal. I'll get started on my part of it, and you guys get started on material for the album.'

But at the back of her mind, Alice hoped with all her heart that Tom would still be capable of doing a 40-concert tour the year after next. He seemed to be handling his drug habit OK, but Alice was seriously concerned about his alcohol addiction. She knew from previous clients of hers that alcohol was often the more difficult to quit if you decided to stop. Even though Tom denied he had a problem, she knew that one day he would come to the realisation he had become an alcoholic and it was slowly ruining his life.

As Alice toiled away organising the tour, Tom wrote furiously. He had to write 12 fresh new songs for the album to tie in with the upcoming tour, and he wanted them to be exceptional. He took it as a personal challenge to come up with something special. He knew it would take a great deal of concentration and many late nights/early mornings to make it happen, but he would make sure it would be worth it. Fortunately, he had a good supply of uppers and alcohol to back him up.

He wrote like a man possessed. He called the first one 'Champagne for Breakfast.' It was a punchy instrumental piece and required many key changes to fit the varying rhythms and cadences. Usually, these changes in key and rhythm made a number memorable. He couldn't get it exactly right, so he put it to one side, hoping that when he returned to it later, something wonderful would happen. And it did.

A few months later, Paul called during a business trip to the States and as the two friends shared a beer at Tom's house and caught up on each other's lives, Tom played it for Paul and asked for his opinion.

'Tell me what you think of this,' said Tom, as he sat down at the baby grand piano in the living area. 'I've finished all 12 numbers for the album but to me, this one is different to the others. The thing is: is it too different?'

He played it through to the end, then spun around on the piano stool and faced Paul on the sofa.

'Well? Honest opinion.'

Paul clapped enthusiastically. 'It's great. Probably sell a million copies,' said Paul. 'I'd buy it.'

High praise indeed from Paul. The only time Tom had ever seen him excited was during their holiday to Arizona many years ago, when they stayed with Tom's Aunt Lola. She had taken the two of them along with her when she had to make a delivery to Taliesin West, Frank Lloyd Wright's wonderful winter home, in Scottsdale, Arizona. Paul had become so entranced by Taliesin West that he changed his life's course, then and there, from maths and computer coding to Architectural Design programming. He then combined his love of computer science with a degree in architecture and become very successful and very rich.

'Thanks. Your opinion means a lot to me.' He sat back down in his big leather armchair next to the sofa and opened another beer.

Paul looked thoughtful for a full minute. He often liked to think about what he was going to say before he spoke, and Tom found it was a good idea to sit in the silence and let him think.

'I'm here in the States to present a proposition to Luke Gardener about our brand. I want to incorporate backing music into our architectural design programs and videos and all our advertising of the product, worldwide. You know, make our brand synonymous with a certain song or catchy tune.'

'What do you think about me using 'Champagne for Breakfast' as our signature brand tune? I don't mean instead of on your album, I mean as well as on your album. We could both benefit. Between you and me, we've sold 5.6 million copies of the program so far this year. Our budgeted sales forecast for the next twelve months is 8.2 million. That would be a lot of 'Champagne for Breakfast' being played in offices all over the world. We've also increased our TV advertising schedule dramatically, particularly in Europe, so the song would get good exposure.'

'Are you serious? That is a fantastic idea.'

Tom laughed as he leaned over and extended his hand to Paul. 'Let's do it.'

'Done deal,' replied Paul, shaking Tom's hand. They both knew it only needed a handshake to seal their agreement.

'Here's to 'Champagne for Breakfast.' It's a pleasure doing business with you, Paul.'

And the two men clinked glasses and drank to their shared success.

Chapter 23

Throughout the decade that began in 2010 there were many events to celebrate, but also several disasters rocked the world. With much fanfare and celebrations all over England, the wedding of Prince William and Catherine Middleton took place on Friday, April 29, 2011 at Westminster Abbey in London, England. The ceremony was viewed live by tens of millions around the world, including 72 million live streams on YouTube.

Seven years later, in May 2018, American actress Meghan Markle married Prince Harry, and they became the Duke and Duchess of Sussex. Their marriage made Meghan Markle the first mixed-race person to marry into the UK royal family.

The UK had its first Conservative leader in 13 years, and its youngest prime minister since 1812, when David Cameron became Prime Minister of Britain following the general election in May 2010. In 2016, he called for a referendum on whether Britain should leave the EU. The referendum resulted in 52% of Britain voting to leave the EU in a move that would become known as Brexit. David Cameron had backed Britain staying in the EU and he subsequently resigned as PM and was replaced by Theresa May.

The entire western world was shocked when Donald Trump was elected the 45th President of the United States on November 6, 2016.

In April 2010, 20 countries and as many as 10 million air travellers were disrupted and Europe's airspace was closed for six days when Iceland's Eyjafjallajökull volcano, which had lain dormant for years, erupted and spewed volcanic ash 10 kilometres into the atmosphere.

A magnitude seven earthquake rocked Haiti in January 2010, killing 220,000 people.

The South African anti-apartheid revolutionary, Nelson Mandela, died in December 2013, aged 95, and the world mourned a truly great man.

The Sunni jihadist group drove Iraqi government forces out of key cities in the country in 2014 and shocked the world with horrific images of executions. The group, which was known as ISIS, took responsibility for many terrorist attacks around the world in subsequent years.

2014 was a disastrous year for Malaysia Airlines. Described as being one of the biggest aviation mysteries in history, Malaysia Airlines plane MH 370, with 239 passengers and crew on board, completely vanished on 8 March 2014 after the scheduled flight left Kuala Lumpur destined for Beijing. Neither the plane nor its passengers and crew have ever been found.

Four months later, another Malaysian plane, MH 17, was shot down while flying over eastern Ukraine, killing all 283 passengers and 15 crew.

During this decade the environment became important to the man in the street. Drastic measures were taken to reduce waste. In an effort to clean up the ocean, plastic straws and single-use plastic bags were banned in several countries in the western world, including many states of America.

Solar panels were installed on the roofs of more and more buildings and the sales of electric cars increased dramatically.

Smartphones became the norm for most people, an essential part of everyday life. The smartphone became your camera, your photo album, your MP3 player, your wallet, your credit card, your flashlight, your map.

The rise of Twitter had a surprising effect on politics in the 2010s. In America, the 2012 and 2016 elections had an enormous impact on the platform. It turned out to be a useful political tool—and a divisive one. Donald Trump used Twitter very successfully during his campaign for president.

In the entertainment world, millions of people around the world were saddened by the death of the popular actor and comedian, Robin Williams, who died by suicide in August 2014.

Hip-hop and Rhythm and Blues dethroned rock as the most popular music genre in America in the 2010s for the first time. Hip-hop alone accounted for 25% of music consumption.

It was a decade of ups and downs for the world. And for Tom Watson.

Tom stirred from an alcohol-induced stupor and rolled over onto his side. With the help of his thumb and forefinger, he pried open first one eye, then the other. His vision was hazy and his head felt like it was on the verge of exploding. *At least I seem to be in my own bed*, he thought. He gazed at the clock and thought it read five past five. *That can't be right. I didn't get home until after seven this morning.* Then it dawned—it must be five after five in the afternoon.

He groaned loudly as the fog in his head began to lift and he remembered he was supposed to be at the studio at eleven o'clock this morning for a final practice session before the start of the tour next week. *Well, too late to do anything about that now. I'll have to wing it.* But the thought made him flinch as he envisaged the tongue-lashing he'd get from the others.

He sat up and swung his legs over the side of the bed, ignoring the banging on the front door. It was getting louder and more demanding. Whoever it was, was not giving up and going away.

'Alright, alright. I'm coming,' he yelled as he staggered to the chair and dug around in the discarded clothes until he found a pair of jeans. He pulled the jeans on and did the zipper up as he headed towards the front door. He yanked it open and Harry pushed past him, obviously angry.

'Where the hell have you been? You missed practice—again!' Harry was speaking loudly. 'You look like you just woke up.'

'There's no need to shout,' said Tom, rubbing the back of his head where it hurt the most. 'Sorry I didn't make it, but I don't actually need to practice. I know exactly what I'm supposed to do and when. I'm going to make a coffee. D'you want one?'

'Not a bad idea,' replied Harry. He followed Tom into the kitchen and hoisted himself up onto one of the stools at the kitchen island. Harry watched Tom prepare the coffee at the other counter where he stood with his back to him and was shocked to see Tom surreptitiously add a good dash of brandy to his coffee.

He handed a steaming cup to Harry and sipped his own.

'Do you always add brandy to your first coffee of the day?' said Harry in amazement.

'None of your business,' grumbled Tom. 'You're not my mother!'

Then, in a more conciliatory tone: 'Are you all set to leave on Sunday?'

'We all are. How about you?'

'Oh, don't worry about me, Harry. I'm fine. I'm packed and ready to leave.'

Harry suddenly felt sorry for his friend. How could he have come to this? He looked a mess; his eyes were sunken into their sockets and he hadn't shaved for days. His hair was lank and greasy looking and his jeans hung on his hips as if they were two sizes too big for him.

In a quiet voice, Harry said: 'Alice rang at practice this afternoon. We covered for you so she doesn't know you weren't there. You need to get your act together, Tom. You're drinking far too much and you're putting the band and the tour at risk. Look, you need to stay sober for the length of the tour. Don't do anything stupid. When the tour is over you can do anything you want, but please, do the right thing and don't hit the booze so hard during the next few months.'

'No problem Harry. I'll do that for you.' Then in a lighter tone: 'Now buzz off, so I can have a shower and freshen up. I'm meeting some guys at the Viper Room later.'

Harry sighed in exasperation as he let himself out the front door.

The 'Champagne for Breakfast Tour' got off to a good start. Everyone assembled at the airport on Sunday with plenty of time to spare. The jet Alice had hired was roomy and comfortable. Champagne was served before take-off and continued until the hostess set out a wonderful lunch about an hour into the flight. The flight was uneventful and by the time they had arrived in England, passed through customs, and took the limo to their hotel, Tom and the band were feeling chilled and ready to entertain the fans.

The UK was a sell-out. At their concerts in Glasgow, Edinburgh, Manchester, Liverpool, and London, they had performed in front of more than half a million people in a matter of three weeks. Similarly, the Amsterdam, Prague, Munich, Milan, and Rome concerts were more successful than even Alice had predicted. Another half a million tickets were bought in these cities.

Paul's architectural program and videos had been advertised on TV across Europe and the UK regularly over the past year and had become a recognised brand. The brand's slogan: 'Champagne architecture on a cereal budget' had become common parlance linked to the record and Pants on Fire audiences loved it when the band played 'Champagne for Breakfast.' The audiences chanted the slogan whenever they played the intro.

True to his word, Tom was on his best behaviour. He and several members of the band and crew had shared a few uppers before some shows to get in the mood and had enjoyed drinks after each show during their wind-down time. However, none of them had become seriously intoxicated or ridiculously high. Tom had also won more and more fans with every concert. Sales of merchandise had outstripped all previous concerts across the US and by the time they had finished in Italy, there was not much stock left. Alice had to place an urgent order for more CDs, t-shirts, and posters to be urgently delivered to Berlin.

The concerts in Berlin were an enormous success, more so than those in Britain. Many of the concert goers had attended two or three concerts, some of the hard-core fans waited at the stage door for Tom and the band to leave so they could speak to them and get autographs. Tom struck up a conversation with a group of the regulars who were keen to tell him all about the notorious nightclub in Berlin, the Berlina. On the Saturday night after their last show, young Klaus and two of his friends, who had been at the stage door the previous evening, cornered Tom:

'Tom, you must visit the Berlina. It's only open on weekends, from midnight on Saturday until six o'clock Monday. The techno music starts on Saturday night and doesn't stop til Monday morning. You'd love it.'

One of his friends, his eyes big as dinner plates, went on: 'It's not like anything you've ever seen. We can't show you photos because there's a 'no photos' policy, but one friend of ours, Peiter, from London, flew in last Saturday evening and went directly to Berlina. The only time he left was to return to the airport for his flight home on Monday morning.'

Klaus butted in: 'Tom, Tom, you should come with us. We're going on there now. It's very difficult to get in but you're famous, they will probably let you in.'

Thanks to the several vodkas Tom had enjoyed in the Green Room after the show, he was feeling extremely relaxed and it seemed easier to go with them than to resist. And why not? That Saturday night's concert was the last one in Berlin and they weren't due in Barcelona for the next concert for three days. Why shouldn't he have some fun with these young people?

The taxi deposited them outside what looked like a huge derelict building, which Tom later discovered was previously a power plant. The line of people waiting to get into the club was a couple of hundred yards long and he could see that many were being turned away—it was true, the Berlina was notoriously difficult to get into—but as his new German friends had predicted, Tom was recognised as a celebrity and the four of them were ushered past the line of waiting patrons and into the club.

The loud metronomic thumping bass of techno music, which would play non-stop for 36 hours, assaulted Tom's ears immediately. Past the cloakroom, up the shuddering steel staircase, the only lights were lasers. Glass windows spanned the 18 metres from ceiling to floor, the hundreds-strong dance floor simmered and bubbled like a pot on a stove. He soon became separated from his friends, and although the heat from the dancefloor enveloped him, he was content to meander through this weird and wonderful place alone.

He passed a long bar with leather stools similar to what you'd expect in a five-star hotel. Next to the bar, a canvas and rope swing looked large enough to hold 10 people. Up the adjacent metal staircase, an ice cream parlour was conveniently serving gelato and fruit smoothies.

Secluded booths lined two walls and Tom wandered along, staring in wonder at what he was witnessing. He saw small groups doing drugs, other groups of men and women openly having sex.

Leather appeared to be the choice of many, as were studded collars, jumpsuits, tight pants, the occasional strap, or rope. *Klaus was right*, thought Tom. *I have never seen anything like this.*

As he stumbled past a booth, a young woman called out to him in a heavy German accent,

'Tom! Tom Watson! We saw your show last night. Come join us.' She tugged at his sleeve and beckoned him into the booth to sit with them. He noticed her friend was smoking a joint, and the smell wafted around him and seemed to soften the loud music. Tom slid into the booth and sat down next to her.

'Welcome to Berlina,' she said in her heavy accent. 'Have you been here before?'

'No. It's amazing,' replied Tom.

The woman said her name was Deit and introduced her friend as Wolfgang. She was dressed in a skin-tight strapless black leather mini dress and wore thigh high black high-heeled boots, a silver studded choker around her throat to which a silver chain was attached; the other end was pierced through her right ear. She wore her jet-black hair shaved at the back, long at the front covering one half of her face, almost hiding her black-rimmed, strange pale blue eyes. She smelled of sex.

She placed her hand, with its long, black painted nails, on Tom's leg above the knee and stroked his thigh as she began, in her husky, heavily accented Germanic voice: 'The Berlina is a most interesting place. It began in 1998 as a gay club and vas instantly famous for its hedonistic atmosphere where anything and everything vas allowed, but now both men and women are welcome, nobody is judged. Now, the area in the basement is reserved exclusively for gay men.'

Wolfgang leaned across Diet and offered Tom a joint. 'I have something stronger if you would prefer,' he said in perfect German-accented English, and Tom instantly felt he was among friends.

He stayed with Wolfgang and Deit for half an hour or so and snorted a few lines of cocaine with them as they told him more about the club. When he said goodbye to his newfound friends, he wandered back to the bar and ordered a drink.

Several hours later, Tom began to feel strange. He knew he'd probably had more drinks than he should have and had shared a few joints with some people he'd met on the dancefloor. He had also swallowed some pills which he believed to be Ecstasy, but he'd had them many times before and they had not affected him in this way. His mouth was dry, and he was getting a headache, but it was the dizziness and weird vision that was bothering him. He looked around and couldn't exactly recall where he was, but it looked like it might be a club. The music was loud and throbbing and felt like it was inside his head.

He put his hand to his head to try and regain his equilibrium. It was then he realised how much he was sweating. It was so hot in here: he had to get out, but his legs felt like lead. He glanced down at his arms and was alarmed to find he couldn't see his hands; his arms tapered off into nothingness. The floor beneath his feet felt like water, moving and swishing about, and he felt panic rising in his gut. He looked up and saw strange creatures swooping down from the ceiling, reaching for him with claw-like talons and huge teeth. He tried to scream, but no sound came out and panic overwhelmed him.

Suddenly, someone grabbed hold of him from behind and guided him to a booth. 'Sit down here, I'll get you some water, you don't look very well.' But as Tom tried to sit down, he felt like the room went dark and his head swam uncontrollably. Bright gaudy images flashed before his eyes, and he felt violently sick. He thought he heard somebody scream and he felt himself fall forward as the floor rose up to smash him in the face.

Then the entire world went black, and silent.

Tom slowly opened one eye but the glaring brightness hurt his head. He seemed to be lying down. He imagined he saw Alice nearby, but she was blurry, so he closed his eye and drifted back into his silent world.

A while later, he opened both eyes and this time, he could see Alice more clearly. She was sitting on a chair next to his bed. He felt a little better, not so nauseous, but very weak.

'Hello, Alice. What are you doing here?' he looked around and saw that he was in a hospital bed.

'I've never been so glad to see anyone wake up before,' said Alice. 'Welcome back.' She smiled and took hold of his hand, rubbing it gently.

'Do you remember what happened to you? Do you know where you were when you passed out?' Alice looked more caring than worried, and Tom presumed everything was OK.

'I think I was in a club. I'd been there for an hour or two, but I don't remember exactly what happened.' In his mind, he tried to recall exactly where he had been and what he'd done, but the memory wouldn't come. The harder he tried to remember, the more his mind felt like a black hole.

'Well, you're in the hospital now,' said Alice. 'You've been in a medically induced coma. The doctors thought you wouldn't make it at one point but you defied the natural order of things and it looks like you'll live.' Once again Alice smiled, but it was a false smile and Tom thought she looked like she was angry inside.

'You were there for a lot longer than an hour or two, Tom. The doctors think you had too much alcohol and some mind-altering drugs, a dangerous combination. You collapsed at the club. Fortunately, someone had the sense to get you into an ambulance quickly or you would have died.'

Tom tried not to show how shocked he was at this last remark.

'How long have I been here?' he asked, trying to hide the alarm he felt.

'Eight days,' replied Alice. She paused to let that sink in, knowing he had no idea of what had happened to him or how long he'd been in hospital. She also knew the consequences of too much alcohol and some questionable heavy drugs were serious.

'Eight days! Have you been here all that time? Oh, Alice, I am so sorry.' Sitting up was difficult with the IV in his arm and the oxygen tubes in his nose, but he dragged himself up from a prone position. His remorse was genuine.

The doctors had roused him from the induced coma earlier that day, confident that his body was on the mend. They had told her he would be weak and probably a bit confused for a few hours, but other than that, he should continue to improve.

Alice breathed a sigh of sadness. 'This is the last time, Tom. I am tired of picking up the pieces of your overindulgence in drugs and drink.' Before he had time to say another word, she added: 'I won't be doing this again. Do you understand what I'm saying?'

'Yes Alice,' he replied meekly.

She shook off the feeling of melancholy and in her most businesslike voice, said: 'We had to cancel the remainder of the tour. The others have all returned home to the States. You're not very popular right now.'

His mind was racing, trying to decipher the implications of her words. The truth of what she had said was becoming clearer. He was deeply shocked that the rest of the tour had been cancelled. That was going to cost the band, and Alice, a great deal of money. No wonder he was out of favour with the crew.

'You're going to be here for a while yet. I'll come back tomorrow and see how you are.' Alice picked up her jacket and bag and as she turned to leave, added: 'We need to have a long talk when we get home, Tom. It's time to get real about your situation.'

As Alice reached the hospital room door, she turned and said: 'Your father has been here every day too. He's waiting to see you now.'

A surging wave of shame washed over Tom when he saw his father. Jim seemed to have shrunk. He looked so much older than the last time Tom had seen him, obviously worn down by the worry of his son's reckless lifestyle.

'It's good to see you awake at last,' said Jim as he leaned in and hugged Tom. 'How are you feeling?'

Tears filled his eyes and words choked in his throat as Tom clung to his father. When he felt he could speak, he laid back in the bed and murmured: 'Dad, I am so sorry I've caused this horrible disruption to your life of retirement. When did you arrive?'

'The minute Alice rang me to tell me what had happened, I got on a plane. I've been sitting with you each day, waiting for you to wake up, as I knew you would.' He smiled for the first time in several days.

'It was touch and go there for a while but you look a lot better since you've woken up. Looks like you'll be here for a few more days yet. Alice suggested I stay until you're released from hospital and she'll arrange for the three of us to go home together.'

The Doctor eventually signed Tom's release from the hospital seven days later when he was satisfied that Tom was well enough to travel, that his body had recovered sufficiently from the trauma of sepsis, exacerbated by alcohol abuse. During his final examination, the doctor had explained that if Tom wanted to enjoy a long and healthy life, he would need to stop drinking alcohol and doing drugs. If he continued along the same path he had been on for years, he would probably only last another three or four years at most.

'It's up to you, Tom. If you want to die young, that's your business. But if you would like to live a full and worthwhile life for quite a few more years yet, you've got to stop drinking now.'

'But I don't drink that much,' said Tom, as much to convince himself as the doctor. 'I've rarely been drunk. I have a couple of vodkas to relax after a show. And I find it helps me write my music.'

'I'm just telling you the facts, Tom. As I said before, it's up to you.'

The following day, Alice, Jim, and Tom flew back to L.A..

Tom couldn't get his mind around the fact that the doctor had told him he had to stop drinking. *That can't be right*, he thought. *I'm not a drunk!*

But Alice noticed he didn't have a drink on the plane during the twelve-and-a-half-hour journey.

They landed at LAX and exited through a concealed tunnel used by dignitaries, royalty, rock stars, etc. to avoid the press. The waiting limo took them back to Tom's place, where Alice left him to unpack and settle in. She told him she would return in two hours to check in on him.

Later that day, as they sat drinking coffee in the comfortable living room, Alice filled Tom in on the things that had happened whilst he had been in hospital. She told him how she had managed to keep the news of what had happened to him out of the papers. She said the upside of the whole incident was that it had happened in Germany where he wasn't quite the rock star he was in America and that with a bit of luck he hadn't become the hottest topic of entertainment industry gossip here in the States.

'I really appreciate the way you handled it, Alice,' said Tom as he refilled their coffee cups. 'I owe you big time.'

Concerned that Tom may have underestimated the seriousness of his misdemeanours, Alice had saved the most devastating news for when it would have the most impact.

'You should also know that the band wanted to break up and go their separate ways. Although they're all fond of you Tom, Harry, Zac, and Danny don't want to be involved with you anymore. The cancellation of the remainder of this tour, and the Asia/Pacific tour, cost them a huge amount of income. They've had enough of your drinking and drugs.'

'However, I convinced them to stay together as long as they are happy to continue to perform. I suggested they announce that Tom Watson has decided to take a break from music for a while and that we find a lead guitar singer to replace you. That way they can continue as Pants on Fire and maintain the value of the brand which has taken years to establish.'

Tom was rocked by this information and opened his mouth to say something, but Alice stopped him.

'I haven't finished,' she said loudly. Tom had never seen her look so fierce; her black glasses accentuated her frown. Alice was very angry. Very angry indeed.

'Tom, your drinking and drug habit has cost you your band, and your career. Your fame will roll on for a long while yet, and your fortune has been invested wisely and will continue to grow even if you never work again.'

'Your only way out of this mess is to go into rehab and get clean. I am no longer interested in representing you unless you do something positive about your addiction.'

She stopped for a breath. Then once again, in the loud, angry voice:

'Look at you! You've lost weight, you look dreadful. The reason for your hospitalisation was the last straw for me. I'm happy to help you find the best rehab available and to support you through your rehabilitation but unless you'll agree to that, I'm out of here.'

Alice's searing words shattered Tom. He was speechless, unable to know what to say to convince her he was OK. He could feel himself shaking inside, but clenched his fists, breathed in deeply, and mustered all his willpower not to sob.

But deep down, he knew he was not OK. The urge to find a glass and the vodka bottle was almost impossible to suppress.

'Alice, I'll think about it.' He leaned forward and put his head in his hands as he thought about some of the awful things he'd heard about rehab.

As Alice stood up and moved towards the front door, she said: 'I'll get back to you in a couple of days when you've had more time to think it through. But remember Tom, I meant every word I said.' And she closed the door quietly behind her.

Less than two hours later, the sound of the doorbell made Tom's heart leap with joy. Thoughts went through his mind as he opened the door. *She's back sooner than I thought. Obviously changed her mind, wants to talk about another recording session, a tour, rehearsals.*

But instead of Alice, Tom opened the door to Paul. Tom was thrilled to see him and they greeted each other with a warm hug before Tom led the way into the kitchen, where he had made a fresh pot of coffee. Between several 'Great to see you's', and 'How are you's' he poured two coffees and took them into the living area and settled down for what Tom thought was going to be a long chat.

But instead of a chat, Paul put his cup on the coffee table and stood up. A shadow passed over his face. All the warmth and affection of a few moments ago was gone, replaced by a look of steely focus. Tom had never seen that look on Paul's face before. It took him a couple of seconds to register that it was anger. He had never seen Paul angry.

He began in a quiet voice, speaking slowly and distinctly: 'Alice told me about what's happened to the band, and to you.' He took a step sideways and turned slightly to face Tom full on, placed his hands on his hips and began, 'What the hell do you think you're doing Tom? You've got so much to offer, so much talent, but instead of using it to help make the world a better place, you've become a drunken bum.'

By now, Paul was pacing, his voice becoming louder and more hostile with each word until he was virtually yelling at him.

'Wake up, Tom. You're flushing your life down the toilet. You need to get yourself into rehab immediately.'

Tom sat in stunned silence for a minute, staring up at him, unable to move, hardly able to breathe. He eventually found his voice, a soft voice, a sad voice. 'I thought we were friends. I always thought you supported me,' he said, shaking his head in bewilderment.

Paul's anger faded and morphed into a type of desperate exasperation. 'I am your friend, Tom. We've been friends for many years and I've always looked up to you. I've always envied your talent, your ability to engage with people, your self-confidence, your charm. But not anymore. I've had enough of watching you slowly kill yourself.'

'I've never issued anyone an ultimatum before but here's one tailored specially for you: unless you get clean and stay clean and get off the booze, I won't continue this friendship. Enough is enough.'

Paul turned and left the house, slamming the front door on his way out.

In all the years they had known each other, Tom had never heard his friend raise his voice before. Paul was the most even-tempered person he had ever known. During all the years they had known each other, Tom had never seen him angry.

Tom sat on the sofa for a long time, his head in his hands, unable to move, thinking through what the two people who were closest to him, his dearest friends, had said to him. He replayed those conversations over and over in his head, full of indignation.

How dare they chastise me like a child! What right do they have to criticise me so harshly? They haven't walked in my shoes; they have no idea of the pressures I live with.

His mind was full of replies he wished he'd made, retorts that would have explained his position better, and made them understand how he felt.

Indignation turned into denial.

They make me out to be so much worse than I am. Just because I was in the hospital, you'd think the world was ending.

Denial turned into self-pity:

How has it come to this? I've tried to cut down on the Vodka, and the drugs, but they don't understand how difficult it is for someone who's as creative and sensitive as I am.

It took a couple of hours and many cups of coffee, but finally, the realisation dawned and a sobering voice in his head asked: *could Alice and Paul be right?* Maybe this was his 'dark night of the soul,' his inner void.

He walked over to the hand-carved African blackwood liquor cabinet, opened the glass door, took out a bottle of vodka, and gently closed the door. He turned the bottle over in his hands and examined the contents, then turned and walked through to the kitchen. He was sweating profusely, and the bottle felt slippery in his hands. His fingers shook as he unscrewed the lid and, taking a deep breath, he emptied the contents down the sink. He stood staring at the glistening clear liquid, mesmerised by the fluid motion, as it flowed out of his life, and into eternity,

He ceremoniously dropped the empty bottle into the kitchen trash can with a loud crash and slowly walked back into the living area.

Tom picked up the phone and dialled Alice's number. She answered on the second ring and heard Tom say in a soft and sorry voice,

'You're right, Alice. I need help.'

Alice could hear the pain and the shame in the voice on the other end of the line as he continued,

'Which rehab do you reckon is the best for me, and can you please come and stay with me and keep me on the straight and narrow until I can get in?'

And so began a cascade of unintended consequences.

Chapter 24

They shared the driving from L.A. to Scottsdale, Arizona. Alice had driven for an hour since their last stop for a bite to eat at Wintersburg so Tom could enjoy his memories of the area. He sat silent and deep in thought in the passenger seat of Alice's comfortable convertible as it glided along the smooth desert highway. He recalled some of the wonderful holidays he'd spent in Scottsdale with his Aunt Lola, especially the time he and Paul had stayed with Lola to celebrate passing their final university exams. Some memories were blurry; although he tried to remember how long they had stayed with Lola, that time-frame wasn't there. Sadly, Lola had passed away a few years ago, but he couldn't recall exactly when that had happened either. He decided to only concentrate on the happy times they had shared as the miles ticked over.

At last, Alice turned into the driveway of a remote desert building in a typical Arizona setting surrounded by magnificent cactus and rock formations. She cut the engine under the porte cochere at the entrance to the building and Tom climbed out of the car and stretched his arms and legs.

'So, this is home for the next couple of weeks,' he said, looking around as he lifted his guitar and small bag out of the trunk. 'I still don't know how you got me in here so quickly. You must have pulled strings, as usual,' he smiled.

Little did he know Alice had booked him into The Hermitage rehabilitation facility in Scottsdale the day Tom had been admitted to hospital in Germany, nearly three weeks ago. That same day, she had spoken to Paul in Australia and together they had set up their plan of attack for when Tom returned home to L.A.. They had also agreed that if the plan didn't work, they would both walk away and leave Tom to his life of dependancy and addiction, knowing that they had done all that they could do to help him.

Together, Alice and Tom entered the building and were greeted at the reception desk by a middle-aged, motherly-looking woman with short grey hair and a welcoming smile.

'Hello,' she said in a quiet voice so as not to disturb the peaceful atmosphere. 'My name is Maureen. You must be Tom Watson. And you're Ms. Weinberg.' She looked at Alice and smiled a knowing smile, recalling the phone conversation she had had with Alice the day before.

'Welcome to The Hermitage, Tom. I'll show you to your room in a moment, but first, I'll fill you in on a few rules we follow here. Firstly, we only use these cell phones for phone calls.' She handed Tom a small cell phone. 'If you'll give me your phone, we'll swap it for this one.'

She was so gracious and charming Tom handed over his phone and pocketed the replacement before he realised what he was doing.

Maureen handed Tom's phone to Alice, saying: 'I'm sure Alice can take care of your cell for you whilst you're here.'

'I'll ask you to leave your luggage and your guitar here. They'll be brought to your room and unpacked by us. It is imperative that your room and personal effects are clean.' She smiled so sweetly at him; how could he object?

'Secondly, you are responsible for your room which must be kept neat and tidy. You will be required to make your bed each day.' To soften this seemingly outrageous directive, she went on without taking a breath: 'The food here is wonderful,' she beamed, 'and you will be expected to attend all meals at the set times.'

'Thirdly, you have been allocated a one-on-one councillor. Your councillor is an ex-addict so he knows all too well what it takes to get clean. I'll introduce you to him in a moment. You will also be required to attend group meetings.'

She continued: 'Alice and any other friends and family can visit you any time they wish, they just need to let us know in advance.'

'Now, if you'll both follow me, I'll show you around.'

The atmosphere inside the building was cool and peaceful. Maureen was unhurried as she led them down a corridor of deep terra cotta-coloured stuccoed walls on which were displayed several framed paintings. Alice noticed that some had small cards attached to them containing notes of gratitude and thanks from grateful residents whose lives had been turned around at The Hermitage. A Mexican patterned carpet runner sat softly on the stone tiled floor, concealing the wear and tear of many footsteps the corridor had endured over the hundred or so years this building had stood here in the Arizona desert.

Several doors led into rooms which Maureen explained were offices and counselling rooms. At the end of the corridor, the glass door automatically opened as they approached, and they walked through the open doorway and stepped out into the heat of the day onto a grassed area surrounding a small swimming pool. Two women sat on side-by-side sun lounges deep in conversation. They glanced up at the visitors and smiled acknowledgement but immediately went back to their discussion.

Although they hadn't discussed the cost, Tom had somehow got the idea from Alice that The Hermitage was extremely expensive. He had presumed this when Alice explained that the staff ratio was two staff for every resident and that it produced excellent outcomes for sufferers of addiction. And yet, it certainly didn't look expensive. Not glamorous at all. Sort of homely and well-worn. A bit like Maureen.

Once back inside, at the end of the long hallway, Maureen led them to the last door, which was open and displayed a small room with a single bed bathed in a shaft of sunlight which streamed in through a high window. She stopped and stepped back to allow Alice and Tom to enter the room.

'This is your room, Tom. The residents' rooms here are all the same and as you can see, fairly basic.' *Fairly basic*, thought Tom, looking around at the lack of decoration. *My God, it looks like a monk's cell!*

Tom was standing behind Maureen. He glanced at Alice and made a childish face of disapproval, but Alice ignored his grimace and said,

'It looks like your luggage has already been unpacked, Tom. Isn't that wonderful service?' Alice smiled benignly at Maureen.

'Now let's find Ivan and introduce you,' said Maureen, ushering them out of the room.

In a small office tucked behind the reception area sat a huge man in a T-shirt and jeans, his smiley round face half hidden by a bushy black beard. But even the lustrous beard couldn't detract from the twinkling brown eyes that sparkled with fun amongst the deep laughter lines, the result of a perpetual state of cheerfulness and years of laughter.

He stood as Maureen led Tom and Alice into the room.

'Ivan, this is Tom Watson, who's here for a few weeks. Tom will be your patient for however long he's here.'

'Tom, this is Ivan. He's the best ex-drug addict, ex-alcoholic, ex-bikie gang member in the country.'

Maureen looked at Ivan adoringly as she introduced them. Ivan was even bigger and more intimidating when he stood to shake hands with Tom.

'And this is Tom's friend, Alice.'

Ivan blushed as he extended his hand to Alice. Tom thought Alice looked a bit stunned as she took the large and powerful hand in her own. *Almost coy*, he thought. *That's not like her. She's usually more assertive than that.*

Ivan dragged his eyes away from Alice and looked at Tom. 'Don't you worry about a thing, Tom. We'll look after you,' he said, in a surprisingly cultured voice. And looking back at Alice, added: 'Maureen, did you explain to Alice that she can visit any time she likes?'

'Of course,' replied Maureen, smiling broadly. 'Now, come with me, Alice. You and I can finish up the paperwork while these two get acquainted.'

Sweat was beginning to trickle down Tom's back, and he noticed his hands were shaking as he sat down opposite Ivan in the small office. It was cool in the room, so why was he sweating? His hands shook and his mouth was dry. He needed a drink!

'Welcome to The Hermitage, Tom, and to the first day of the rest of your life.' Ivan's eyes twinkled. He loved welcoming a new recruit, someone who had reached the stage where they were pre-pared to try anything to stop the rot. And this one had all the hallmarks of a dedicated alcoholic.

Ivan loved a challenge.

'Feel like a drink?' said Ivan conspiratorially.

'I sure as hell do,' replied Tom with a big grin on his face. He sat up straighter in the chair. *Well, this was a good start*. He thought.

'So do I,' said Ivan, all fun and twinkle gone from his eyes. 'Every. Day.'

'Not going to happen.' Pause. 'For either of us.' Pause. 'Ever again.'

Tom's joyful expectation instantly disappeared down a black hole. He was left wondering if he would ever feel any sort of heart-fluttering anticipation again.

'But it's not all bad. With our help, you'll learn to live with it. I've been in your position, been where you are now. Ended up in the hospital from an overdose. But you've got one enormous ad-vantage, although I'll bet it didn't seem like it at the time. They put you into an induced coma. That helped your body through what would have been an almost unbearable withdrawal, and you didn't even know about it. I know you're still suffering but nothing like what you would be going through right now if you'd been left to your own devices.'

'I notice your shaking hands and sweats but you can get through that. Your body can stand that. It's the psychological process which takes time. But believe me, it will be worth it in the long run.'

'You and I are going to start work on your rehabilitation at eight-thirty tomorrow morning. Right after breakfast. Right here.'

'It's nearly dinnertime. Why don't you go and freshen up and get ready for dinner in the dining room? It's a fabulous seafood spread tonight. You picked the right night to check in.' He smiled and his big, friendly, weather-beaten face radiated kindness and understanding.

He stood up, signalling for Tom to leave and as the two shook hands again, added,

'I look forward to getting together with you tomorrow morning.'

Ivan was right—the food was excellent. Unfortunately, that was the only good thing about the place. Those first few weeks were the toughest Tom had ever experienced in his life.

From making his bed every morning, which he thought was childish and petty, to the damn bells which rang every hour on the hour to signal the start or finish of a session, a group meeting, or a meal break. He hated every irritating thing about the place.

Ivan was right about another thing—Tom wanted a drink, every day. His spirits plunged even deeper when another resident told him: 'Give it up, Buddy, there's no alcohol within twenty miles of The Hermitage so try and think about something else.'

If Ivan had really been through this, he should have understood how much Tom wanted just one vodka with dinner. He should know how Tom had trouble sleeping. What was wrong with having one little pill to help him sleep? He'd feel so much more human if he could get a good night's sleep. But Ivan, likeable though he was, was nothing more than a jailer. With questions. So many questions.

He always seemed to end up angry after a session with Ivan. Why did he have to bring up all that stuff about Tom's mother's death? Why did he have to keep telling Tom what a charmed life he'd had, how lucky he was? When were these sessions going to produce some sort of result? He thought he'd have magically gotten over his addiction by now. Wasn't that how it worked? You came to these places, you put in the work, answered their damn questions, and Voila, you were 'cured' and could go home and get back to where you were in your life before this stupid interruption.

But that was not how it worked.

He didn't let on to Ivan, but by the end of the third week, he found himself almost enjoying making his bed. He timed himself each morning and could do it in less than two minutes now. And the last couple of nights, he'd put his guitar away in its case rather than leave it standing up against the side of the wardrobe. He hadn't even noticed some of the bells recently, and last night, he had slept the entire night through.

He still didn't quite understand what he was doing here though. He had only attended two group therapy sessions so far and was surprised at the serious problems experienced by some of the others at The Hermitage. Most of them seemed like real addicts, whereas Tom just 'liked a drink' and something to make the day brighter and easier to write music.

One woman in group therapy, Jenny, was addicted to sleeping pills and because of her addiction, had stolen prescription pads and forged doctors' signatures to get supplies. Rather than send her to jail, the judge had sentenced her to rehab. She had screamed and cried her way through the group sessions so far due to sleep deprivation. When she wasn't crying or yelling, she was making sarcastic comments about or to the others. Jenny was one angry, and possibly scared, woman.

Another older man, Harry, was a gambling addict. His habit had cost him everything—his job, his wife and kids, his house. Tom thought he was probably here because he had nowhere else to go, but if he had gambled everything away, how come he had the money for rehab? Wow, that guy had serious problems. *Not like me*, thought Tom.

So, why did he let Ivan talk him into extending his stay for another three weeks? How did he fall for that?

On the second day of the fourth week, Alice came to visit. The joy on Tom's face when he saw her standing in reception warmed Alice's heart—almost as much as when Ivan stepped out of his office and smiled his cheekiest smile at her. She noticed when she shook hands with him he looked right into her eyes and their hands remained linked for a moment or two longer than was necessary.

'I am glad to see you, Alice. I'm sure you'll be a big help in group therapy this morning,' said Ivan as Tom approached.

'Alice!' said Tom in genuine delight. 'Am I glad to see you. How are you? How are things out in the real world?' He hugged her so hard she had to catch her breath when he finally let go.

'Tom, it's wonderful to see you. You look so much better than the last time I saw you. Ivan has invited me to sit in on the group therapy session today which I believe is due to start shortly.'

Tom looked apprehensive as he glanced from Alice to Ivan, not sure if this was a good idea.

'It's OK, Tom. We encourage family members or friends to sit in on group therapy occasionally. It helps us get a clearer picture of the resident.'

A bell rang at that moment and Tom led Alice down to the group therapy room where five of the other residents were already seated and chatting amongst themselves. Another four arrived in the next couple of minutes and Ivan introduced Alice and sat down and opened the session.

Until this meeting, Tom had merely been an observer, not really interacting much with the others. They all seemed to have such major problems that he was fascinated listening to them share their lives and addiction troubles. So, he was surprised when Ivan said,

'Tom, would you like to tell us all why you're here.'

There was a moment's silence as Tom gathered his thoughts. He felt flummoxed. He wasn't expecting this with Alice here. He self-consciously rubbed the back of his neck with his hand to stall for time as he tried to find the words to put his situation in a good light.

'Well, as you all know, I'm an entertainer. Alice here is my manager and friend, and I'm here to keep Alice, and my closest and oldest friend, Paul, happy. I personally don't think my situation warrants being here, but they insisted I do something positive about my drinking.'

'And what about your drug habit, Tom? Tell us about that.'

'Of course, I've done a variety of drugs. I'm in show business for God's sake. It's normal. And sure, I drink regularly, but it's not that much, really. Some things I've heard here have shocked me. My 'addiction,' as you call it, is very low-level compared to some of the others.'

'How much would you estimate you've been drinking regularly, Tom?' asked Ivan pleasantly.

'Well, I usually have a few vodkas after a show or practice session and maybe a couple of pills or joints. And I like a bit of a hit when I'm writing music.'

A few of the others sat up and began to take notice. They knew he was sort of famous; they had all heard of Pants on Fire, but addicts were so centred on themselves and their addiction they paid little attention to what the rest of the world was doing.

Ivan nodded, then looked directly at Alice.

'And Alice, would you agree with that? In your opinion, is that the true extent of Tom's drinking?'

A few more residents stopped swinging their legs and sat still in anticipation. Johnno had been staring at the ceiling for the past few minutes, but now he brought his head down and looked around at the others as if something momentous was about to happen. All eyes were on Alice. Jenny crossed her arms over her chest and smiled smugly as she whispered to Charles, who was sitting on her right: 'This is going to get interesting. She's about to unload on him and he doesn't even know it.'

Tom suddenly felt uncomfortable as Alice turned on her chair and leaned down to take a small notebook from her handbag. When Ivan rang her to talk about her attending one of the group therapy sessions, he had explained what usually happens when a friend or family member tells the truth about the addict.

'I won't pretend it will be pleasant, Alice. An addict will do anything to protect their addiction. Tom will accuse you of overreacting, exaggerating his addiction. He'll try to make you feel guilty for putting him in here. It will be all your fault.'

'Oh, Ivan. I'm not easily intimidated by Tom, or anyone else. I'm prepared to do whatever it takes to get him clean. Don't worry, I'll come prepared with irrefutable evidence.'

She flipped through a couple of pages until she found the one she wanted, and began,

'Tom is fooling himself, and all of you.' She looked around at the others as she spoke. 'As you all know, I'm his manager, and as such, I handle his money, pay all his bills. That includes his liquor bills.' She glanced down at the notebook and continued,

'I only extracted the past year's figures but the situation hasn't changed much for a few years now. Over the past year alone, Tom purchased a carton of vodka every couple of weeks. Plus, approximately four cartons of a mix of red and white wine per month. This doesn't include what he drinks when he's out, say after a show, or a practice session in the studio, which is paid for by his record company.'

There was a small collective intake of breath before Jenny exclaimed with a sarcastic grin: 'Gee, Tom, you really like a drink, don't you!'

'Shut up, Jenny,' snapped Tom, and then, glaring at Alice: 'You're making that up, Alice. Nobody would drink that much liquor.'

Alice reached down into her bag and produced a large, clear plastic, zip-lock bag full of credit card receipts and bank statements, which she handed to Tom. 'Would you like me to hand these around Tom so that everyone knows the facts?'

Tom looked down at the bag and threw it on the floor like a petulant child. His anger rising, he snarled at Alice: 'It's my money. I can spend it on what I like. I merely pay you to handle the bills and investments. What I do with it is really none of your business, Alice.'

Alice placed her hand on Tom's thigh and, looking him in the eye, said in a soft but firm voice,

'It's not actually about the money, Tom.'

She looked back down at the notebook and turned the page, took a breath, and steeled herself for the shitstorm she knew would follow what she said next.

'Then there's his drug dealer. Tom usually pays him cash—to the tune of about five thousand dollars a week. That's roughly a quarter of a million dollars a year, but it's probably quite a bit more when he's on tour.'

This time, everyone had something to say, and most of it at the same time.

'A quarter of a million dollars in a year!!! Dear God, how could anyone spend that much money on crack?'

'Five thousand dollars a week! Every week! That's like four new cars a year!'

For once, Jenny sat in stunned silence.

'I don't believe that for a minute,' shouted Tom, turning on Alice. 'You're lying.'

Alice picked up the plastic bag from the floor and opened it, pulled out the bank statements at the back of the credit card slips and handed them to Tom.

'The bank statements don't lie, Tom. What else did you do with the five thousand dollars a week you took out of the bank in cash?'

Silence. The air was thick with anticipation, as if all the energy in the room had been sucked out of it. It felt devoid of oxygen. Nobody dared breathe. Even Ivan held his breath.

'Why didn't you tell me, Alice?' he spat the words out at her, as if all this was her fault. His face had taken on the look of a crazed person, with bulging eyes full of hatred for the person who was making these wild accusations, a vein at his temple visibly throbbing as he spoke in a guttural, other-worldly inflection, 'Why didn't you stop me?'

'I'm trying to stop you now, Tom,' she said slowly in a voice filled with great caring.

Shame swamped Tom as he glimpsed the reality of his situation through a chink in the solid wall of his refusal to acknowledge the extent of his addiction. The pain in his chest threatened to overwhelm him and he shuddered as he leant forward and put his head in his hands and sobbed. He felt Alice's hand on his back, gently rubbing in small circles as you would to soothe a baby, felt the compassion in the warmth of her hand.

The others were silent, stunned by Alice's disclosures and her courage to be so honest about the cost of Tom's addiction.

Ivan stood and said in the most professional voice he could manage under the circumstances, 'I think we'll call this meeting done. Thanks, everyone. See you all here tomorrow afternoon.'

And as the others shuffled quietly out of the room, muttering to each other, Ivan sat down next to Tom and said: 'This is probably a good time for you and me to have a one-on-one session, Tom. I'll ask Maureen to take care of Alice for the next hour or so.' And he smiled his sweetest smile at Alice, who nodded in agreement. Ivan was the boss here, and she was more than happy to go along with whatever he suggested.

That morning's meeting was a turning point for Tom.

The one-on-one session with Ivan that followed the group meeting was significant. It was the first time Tom was truly honest with Ivan, the first time he allowed himself to be vulnerable, and the first time Ivan believed Tom could beat his addiction.

By the end of the second month, Tom was sleeping well and felt sharper and more alert than he had in a long time. Even his ability to concentrate had returned. The fatigue, the cravings, and the insomnia that had wracked his body throughout that first couple of weeks of his withdrawal, had waned considerably.

During one of their one-on-one sessions, the conversation developed into a meaningful and profound discussion on life after addiction, and Tom decided he wanted to extend his stay at The Hermitage for another six weeks.

Ivan stared out of the office window for a minute while he chose his words carefully before he turned to Tom and spoke slowly and decisively:

'We need to be careful that you don't become dependent on me and this environment to sustain your abstinence from drugs and alcohol. This has become your comfort zone and you feel powerful and in control here.'

'However, I've watched your progress over the past eight weeks and since you now understand how and why you are here, I think you would handle another few weeks well. But I also think four weeks is all you need.'

'I'm comfortable with that,' replied Tom.

The group meetings occurred three times a week. After the meeting which Alice attended, and the humiliation of being forced to acknowledge the depth of his addiction, and his growing confidence in his ability to beat it, Tom began to participate in the meetings. He was fascinated by the other attendees, their personalities, their addictions, and how they responded to criticism and compliments—how some of them beat their addiction while others gave up and left The Hermitage in no better condition than when they entered.

But the biggest benefit of the group meetings occurred when friends or family members of some of the residents joined them. When the truth was revealed in front of other people, he was amazed at the lies and cover-ups some of them had used to hide their addiction from those closest to them.

He was shocked when he realised he had done the same.

When he first checked in, Tom played his guitar quietly in his room each evening before lights out. Several weeks later, Jenny confronted him at breakfast one morning.

'Hi there, young Tom,' she said as she helped herself to black coffee, which was all she ever seemed to have for breakfast. 'Was that you playing your guitar last night before Lights Out?'

'It was indeed,' replied Tom.

'It was wonderful. Why don't you play for us after dinner tonight?'

'The guitar sounds a bit thin without the backing of the band, but OK, I'll bring it with me and you can tell me what you think.'

When dinner was finished, seven of the residents, including Tom, moved into the living area where they sometimes watched TV. Jenny smacked Charles' hand away as he turned on the TV. 'No, we're not watching TV tonight, Charles. Tom is going to play his guitar for us.' Charles sulkily dragged his chair into the furthest corner of the room, as far away from the others as possible.

Tom pulled one of the straight-backed dining chairs over and sat and tuned the guitar for a few minutes as the others made themselves comfortable on the sofas and occasional chairs. As he began to play, Jenny interrupted him: 'No, not that one, play the tune you were playing last night. It was much softer than that.'

In the weeks that Tom had been playing his guitar in his room each evening, he had changed his repertoire to suit a single guitar and developed a style more akin to a jazz arrangement—less rock and more of a blues quality. Because it was not the sound that had made him famous, he was reluctant to play this style for other people, but then he thought, *what the hell!* And began to play.

There was a quiet but enthusiastic round of applause when he finished the first tune. Nobody noticed Charles stand up and drag his chair closer in near the others.

'More like that, Tom. That is so much more 'easy listening' than that hard rock stuff Pants on Fire plays,' Jenny smiled coyly. A young man who only arrived at The Hermitage yesterday, and who had barely said a word to anyone, spoke up.

'That is beautiful, Tom. I've been to some of your live concerts but that is so different, it really is beautiful.' He blushed deep red with embarrassment as everyone stared at him. When they all nodded in agreement, he grinned and quickly sat down.

And so, it became part of the evening routine after dinner that everyone would wander into the living area, take a seat, and listen to Tom play for a couple of hours. Some of the staff joined them and even Ivan had become a regular member of the audience. Tom's playing evolved into a smooth, intimate type of rhythm and blues and he enjoyed developing more complicated chords and finger work. At the end of the first week of nightly concerts, he spent all day Saturday writing a new song especially for his nightly audience. The following evening, about 20 minutes before Lights Out, he made an announcement:

'I wrote this next song on the weekend for you guys to show how much I appreciate your encouragement over the past couple of months. It's called 'Desert Holiday with Friends'. I might even record it when I get out,' he added, grinning.

There were a few giggles as some of them got the subtle meaning in the title, but when Tom played, a hush descended on the room and everyone listened in rapt silence. As Tom finished playing, Charles stood and began clapping loudly and enthusiastically, and was soon joined by everyone else in the room. The applause went on for several minutes, and Tom stood and acknowledged their genuine appreciation.

He had merely made the remark about recording the song for something to say, but as he made his way back to his room that evening, he repeated the throwaway line a couple of times in his head.

He hadn't expected the song to be so warmly received; maybe his career was taking a turn to the right.

Chapter 25

Mid-afternoon of the second day Tom had been back in his own home, there was a knock at the front door. *A visitor*, thought Tom, suddenly gripped by apprehension. *Nobody even knows I'm back home. God, I hope they don't want a drink.* He smiled as he thought of how he and Alice had spent yesterday emptying the liquor cabinet and the fridges of every bottle of alcohol in his possession. He had given the good stuff to Alice and poured the rest down the sink, so pleased with his efforts that they celebrated with a cup of English Breakfast Tea and some of Alice's cupcakes. Alice considered getting rid of all the alcohol in Tom's house before he got home, but changed her mind when she realised he would forever be confronted with alcohol and that it was something he needed to do himself.

When he opened the front door, he was delighted to see his father standing there with a huge grin on his face and a bunch of flowers in his hands.

'Welcome home, Tom,' said Jim, as he handed the flowers awkwardly to Tom. 'I've never been so happy to see anyone in my life as I am to see you, right here, right now. You look great.'

Tom suddenly felt overcome with emotion and warmly embraced his dad with one arm whilst managing to hold the flowers at arm's length with the other hand. He hoped his father wouldn't notice the way Tom's eyes glistened when he stepped back and said,

'You can't imagine how glad I am to see you, Dad. Come in. Come in. And you can't possibly imagine how good it is to feel clean again. I haven't felt this fit and well for many years. Let me make you a coffee.'

Jim examined Tom closely as he prepared the coffee. His eyes were clear and bright, his face smooth and slightly tanned, his shiny black hair pulled back in a neat ponytail. In a plain white T-shirt and beautifully tailored black slacks and loafers, he looked like a model for an expensive European clothes brand.

The two men sat opposite each other at the kitchen counter and Tom relayed his 'desert holiday' at The Hermitage.

'Those first couple of weeks were tough but thanks to my councillor, 'Ivan the Terrible',' laughed Tom, 'I began to see the light. I can honestly say I feel like a new person. Even my music has changed.'

Jim couldn't help but notice Tom's new confidence and candour. He seemed so much more relaxed, and the few extra pounds he had gained really suited him.

Tom continued: 'I haven't seen any of the band since Germany and the funny thing is, I don't miss them. This feels like the start of a new life for me; I don't need any part of the old one.'

Tom was thrilled when Jim asked him if it was OK if he stayed overnight. The two men chatted for hours before Tom suggested they order some takeout. They were both exhausted by midnight and decided it was time to call it a night. As Jim climbed the stairs to the guest bedroom, he felt warm and fuzzy after the most enjoyable several hours he had spent in the past twenty years.

Alice checked up on Tom every day to make sure he hadn't slipped back into any of his old ways. She usually found him writing music. About once a week, they would go out for lunch. Alice loved the way Tom didn't think twice when asked if he'd like something to drink. His automatic answer was always the same: 'Just water for me, thank you.'

During the third week, they had lunch at The Cabana Café in the Beverly Hills Hotel. They chose one of the comfortable, green-striped banquettes in a corner of the restaurant and Alice ordered a Caesar Salad with grilled shrimp, and Tom, a McCarthy Salad. Once they had ordered, Alice couldn't contain herself any longer. She placed her glass on the table and put her hand over Tom's as she asked,

'When are you going to tell me about what you're writing and why? I've got the feeling something's changed.'

'Funny you should say that Alice.' Tom felt a tiny tingle of excitement creep up through his chest as he looked into Alice's face and a slow smile spread across his face. 'I didn't want to say anything until I had enough material for an album but seeing as your antenna is working overtime, I'll fill you in on what's been going on in my head for a few months now.'

'A couple of the other 'inmates' at The Hermitage asked me to play the guitar after dinner one night. As you would know, after being used to playing loud rock guitar with a band, one guitar sounds very different, so I modified my style. Turns out, I play pretty good rhythm and blues, even some cool jazz.' By now, his words were tripping over each other as if he couldn't get them out quickly enough. 'I wrote one song while I was there and I've written another six since I've been home. My head is a lot clearer now and I seem to concentrate more on what I'm writing. I can put stuff down on paper more quickly. One song fell into place, from start to finish, music and lyrics, in just over three hours.' By now he was almost breathless with anticipation of what Alice might think of this revelation, so he stopped talking and forced himself to slow down as he told her about 'Desert Holiday with Friends'.

Alice sat quietly and fiddled with her knife as she listened to Tom, not sure how to respond to this turn of events. Only this morning, she had put together some salient points about how they could find some new band members, a new name for the band, a new album, promo videos, all the stuff necessary to re-launch Tom Watson, Rock Star. But as she listened, she caught some of his excitement as he recounted the story of how he wrote 'Desert Holiday with Friends' at The Hermitage and the grand reception it had received there.

Before she had a chance to reply, Tom grabbed both of her hands in his and, speaking quickly and earnestly, said,

'Alice, I want to change the direction of my career, and I want you to help me do it. I want to release an album of R & B/Jazz numbers. I'm over the 'rock star' thing, I reckon I'm ready to work on my own as a single performer. What do you think?'

Alice didn't know what to think. She had not seen this coming. Whilst she had continued to manage Pants on Fire and their new lead guitarist, she had been wondering how she was going to manage and promote two rock bands simultaneously, especially as they would ultimately compete with each other.

'Tom, I'll be honest with you. I don't know what to think. This is a surprise. I'd like to hear some of the new stuff you've written before I make any decisions that will affect both our futures.'

'Great. Come on, let's do that now,' he made a move to stand up. She pulled him back down as the waiter arrived with their salads.

'No. Let's have lunch first. I'm starving.'

Initially, Alice was not totally convinced that Tom's planned career change was a good idea. However, when she heard the songs he had written in his new style, she changed her mind. These songs suited his new lifestyle and more mellow frame of mind and she figured because his name was so well known by the album-buying public, anything by Tom Watson would probably sell well.

Within six months, the album was recorded and ready for release. Alice planned a top-quality promotional music video and organised several media interviews for Tom across America to coincide with the album's release. One such interview was with the well-respected and popular entertainment reporter from the Seattle Times, Eddie Gleeson.

The week before the scheduled interview, the Times contacted Alice to advise that Eddie had been involved in a traffic accident and had been admitted to hospital, but was expected to be released in a few days.

The flight from L.A. to Seattle was uneventful, and Tom and Alice arrived at the Four Seasons Hotel in plenty of time for Tom's

11.30 interview. They were enjoying a coffee in the Lobby Lounge whilst waiting for Eddie Gleeson and his photographer to arrive when Alice's phone rang. Tom could tell from the look on her face as she spoke to the caller that it was not good news.

'Well, that was not good news,' said Alice, mirroring Tom's thoughts. 'That was the Times. Unfortunately, Eddie has been re-admitted to hospital this morning so they're sending their business reporter in his place. In my experience, any reporter who covers Business hasn't got a clue about music.'

When Alice was annoyed, it showed, but she also got over it quickly.

'Anyway, he'll be here in about 15 minutes. We've got time for another coffee.'

Exactly 15 minutes later, a young woman, her short blonde hair styled in the latest pixie cut, and wearing white sneakers, faded blue jeans and a navy and white striped man's business shirt, placed her small carry bag on the floor next to Alice's chair and extended her hand.

'Ms. Weinberg? How do you do. I'm Callie Williams from the Seattle Times. I'm so sorry Eddie is unable to do the interview this morning. The paper has asked me to fill in for him. I hope you don't mind.'

Her business-like manner momentarily disarmed Alice, but she recovered quickly and stood and shook hands with Callie.

'Hello, Callie,' said Alice, ignoring the apology. Alice turned to Tom as he stood up. 'This is Tom Watson.'

'Callie, is it?' said Tom, shaking hands with her while mentally trying to calibrate how anyone who looked so cute could report on business for a major newspaper.

'I'm pleased to meet you, Tom.' As she smiled at him, her one-thousand-watt smile lit up the entire lobby of the hotel like a bonfire. The smile did it. And the strong, warm hand in his. That was the moment he knew. Knew he'd tell her anything she wanted to know. Anything.

In the elevator, as they proceeded to Suite 1204, where the interview was to take place, Alice, still not quite on top of the situation, couldn't help enquiring: 'Will your photographer be joining us?'

'Oh, I do all my own photography, Ms. Weinberg. I've also set up a camera in the suite to video the interview. I'll send you a copy of the video and my finished article so you'll be able to vet everything before it goes to press. I've found this is the best way to keep everyone happy.'

'Excellent idea,' was all Alice could say and smiled a half-smile. 'And please call me Alice.'

Callie opened the door to 1204 and led them into a spacious, light-filled room decorated in typical 5-star hotel style. A gracious white rattan sofa and two matching occasional chairs were upholstered in a classic blue and white fabric to complement the dark blue drapes. An arrangement of yellow flowers and a marble table lamp with a navy shade sat atop an antique French provincial desk. A video camera was set up on a tripod facing the sofa and two photographer's lamps on stands stood waiting to further illuminate the subject to be photographed.

'Might I suggest you relax in the adjoining room, Alice?' said Callie as she extracted a small camera from her bag and placed it on the glass coffee table in front of the sofa. 'Is that OK with you, Tom?'

'Of course.'

'I'll give you a call if I need your input on anything, Alice,' Tom said as he gently pushed a nonplussed Alice through the door to the other room.

An hour and a half later, Tom popped his head around the door of the adjoining room to let a slightly anxious Alice know that the interview was finished.

Alice wondered if Callie knew what she was doing. During most interviews, Tom needed to ask Alice to clarify something or to supply a fuller answer to a question about a part of their business he was unfamiliar with. But there had been no such interruption during the last hour and a half, just the muffled sound of Callie and Tom's voices in the next room, their occasional laughter, and sometimes silence.

'I'd love to take you both to lunch,' said Callie as she walked them to the door of the suite. 'But unfortunately, I've got an interview with Bill Gates in half an hour which I couldn't re-schedule. I'm sure Eddie will make it up to you next time.' And she quietly closed the door behind them as they stepped into the hallway.

In the elevator: 'First time I've ever been passed over for Bill Gates,' said Alice, sardonically.

No more was said until the waiter showed them to a quiet table in the corner of the hotel restaurant. Following a melodramatic flourish of the stiff white linen napkins as he placed one on each of their laps, he produced detailed and elaborate menus for their selection. He was about to elaborate on the "Lunch Specials" when Alice waved him away with a ladylike gesture as she turned to Tom and asked:

'So, how did it go? Did she know anything at all about the music industry?' Alice being her best sceptical self.

'Best interview ever! She was amazing,' replied Tom, smiling broadly as his mind replayed bits of the past hour and a half.

'Well, I'll give you my opinion when I see the copy and the video. We won't accept it if it's not up to scratch.'

When Alice opened her email two days later, she was surprised to see one from Callie. *Boy, this must be one rough copy if she's done it already,* thought Alice as she opened the email. She glanced over the standard 'nice to meet you and Tom, etc. etc. Attached please find etc. etc.' email and opened the attachments.

What Alice read stayed in her mind for days. It was the most in-depth interview she had ever read. The full-page article was insightful, interesting, and in parts, intimate. Alongside it were nine pics of Tom, all in black and white—smiling, laughing, thoughtful, in conversation, standing, lounging, in shadow and in light. So much depth in the photos, some so intimate, some raw, some quirky. Alice was more impressed than she cared to let on. This woman knew how to draw her subject out and how to show him in the best light. Even Alice wanted to know about the person featured in this interview, and as a reader, she couldn't wait to buy his album.

Callie's research was comprehensive and relevant. She knew exactly the right questions to ask, and the questions to leave out. And this judgement was made before Alice watched the video.

The video was raw, but it could have been entered into the Sundance Film Festival and would probably have won. It was grainy and occasionally skewed, but the sound was near perfect, and anyone watching it couldn't help falling in love with Tom. Their conversation, the laughter, and the occasional bashfulness made him seem so human, but his superstar quality was very much on display.

For a few minutes towards the end of the video, Callie had come and sat next to Tom on the sofa. Alice had to look away for a moment when she saw the way Tom had looked at her. There was no denying they were magic together. *I'd like some of that*, thought Alice enviously.

When the video finished, Alice sat very still for several minutes and thought about it. She thought about what she could do with it, playing parts of it over and over in her head. She picked up the phone and called Tom.

'Hello Tom, any chance you could pop into my office? I've received a rough copy of the article by Callie, and I think we should look at it together. I won't make any changes without your approval.'

'Wow, that was quick,' replied Tom. 'What do you think?'

'I'll reserve judgment until you've read it.'

'I'll be over later today.'

But Tom couldn't wait that long to see it. He was in Alice's office within 15 minutes.

Alice handed him a print-out of the article and suggested she make them tea while he read it.

He was still reading it when she brought the tea in and put his cup down in front of him. He glanced up at her.

'I told you it was a great interview. It was as if she had known me for years. She knew stuff about me I hardly knew myself. She must be a Master of Research. Even I'd buy the album after reading this.' He laughed.

As he placed his cup back on the saucer on the desk when he had finished reading, he noticed the stack of black-and-white photos. He looked at Alice and raised his eyebrows as if to say, 'Can I have a look through these?' She nodded enthusiastically and he went through them, studying each one before moving on to the next.

'Alice, these are great photos. Can I get copies?'

'They are good, aren't they? Callie wants us to choose four for the article. Personally, I think that one of you lounging back on the sofa, in that lovely moody shadow, would be great for the cover of the album. I'm sure Callie would let us use it, for a fee.'

'But you ain't seen nothin' yet,' she added, grinning from ear to ear.

She loved this part of the business, when she came across someone who knew what they were doing, who was professional and smart, someone who just got it. Someone who didn't need an eleventy-thousand-word explanation of what you were trying to achieve. Someone with good judgement and even better instincts.

'Wait until you see the video of the interview.'

She turned the laptop around to face Tom and walked around the desk to sit beside him so they could both watch it together, and hit Play.

For an hour and a half, neither Tom nor Alice moved.

Tom spoke first.

'I told you it was the best interview I've ever done.'

Alice smiled. 'I agree. I'm going to talk to Callie about using it. I think 60 Minutes might be interested in showing it as a Special, perhaps the week before the album is released. I know one of the producers there who owes me a favour. In this business, it's not what you know, it's who you know. Plus, it would only need some editing instead of two weeks' work and a big financial input on their part.'

'Why don't I go up to Seattle and talk to her about it. We got on well together and I reckon I could talk her into it.' Tom spoke the words as if he meant them, but Alice knew it was a ruse to see Callie again.

'Better still,' replied Alice, 'why don't we bring her down here and talk to her together? We can fly her down first class, make her feel special. You could take her out to lunch.' Alice watched Tom closely as she spoke. He picked up on the 'You could take her out to lunch.'

'Great idea. Why don't you phone her now?'

'It's not that urgent Tom, but I might as well get on with it anyway. She's probably quite busy.'

After locating Callie in her Contacts list, Alice punched in her number but it went to Voicemail on the first ring. She left a message asking Callie to call her when she got a chance.

'I might as well wait around until she phones back,' said Tom, trying hard not to seem too keen. At the same time, Alice thought to herself, *oh dear, he's very keen.*

'She may not get back to me today, but I don't mind if you've got nothing else to do. You can help me tidy up the office. I want to empty out that filing cabinet.'

Tom groaned inwardly. Emptying a filing cabinet was not his idea of the ideal way to fill in a couple of hours, but he smiled as best he could and said: 'Sure. Where would you like to start?'

'Well, why don't we start with another cup of tea?' replied Alice, kindly. But as she was filling the kettle in the kitchen, her phone rang.

'I'll get it. It's Callie,' yelled Tom, as he picked up Alice's phone. 'Hi Callie, it's Tom here. How are you?'

'I'm fine, thanks Tom. I'm returning Alice's call. Is she available?' *Well, that was short and sweet,* thought Tom. 'Sure, she's coming to the phone now.' He tried not to let his disappointment show as he handed the phone to Alice.

'Hello, Callie. Alice here. Thank you for your prompt email and attachments. Great pics by the way, and the article is exactly what I was looking for.' Alice let the compliments sink in before she continued: 'Callie, I'd like to discuss certain aspects of the article and the video with you in more detail. Would you have time to come down to L.A. within the next couple of days? Of course, we would cover all travel costs, plus any out-of-pocket expenses.'

'Glad you liked the interview, Alice, would you mind holding for a moment while I check my schedule?'

'Sure.' Alice looked at Tom and winked.

'Actually, Alice, I'm quite busy for the next ten days. Can you wait that long? Or, if you can manage it, I can do late Saturday morning.'

'Saturday is no problem,' said Alice. 'Why don't you organise your flights and bill me for all expenses. Shall we say here at my office, at 11 am Saturday? I'll email you the address.'

'Consider it done,' replied Callie. 'I look forward to catching up with you then.'

Chapter 26

It had been a long time since he'd gone to so much trouble to get dressed for a meeting in Alice's office. After shaving, showering, and changing his clothes twice so he looked good enough to take Callie out for lunch, it was still only nine fifty-five on the Saturday morning of the scheduled meeting. Alice would laugh at him if she ever found out about this. In days gone by, he would have poured himself a vodka, but that was the last thing he thought about right now. He was too busy considering changing his jeans for those new navy slacks. The sales guy had told him the navy pants looked great with the plain white tailored shirt, so why was he wearing jeans? It wasn't as if he didn't have time to change. So he did. At ten twenty-five, he decided to drive, slowly, to Alice's office. At least there, he could chat to Alice to while away another five minutes before Callie was due at eleven.

'Well, don't you look terrific!' said Alice when Tom tapped on the door and opened it.

'Thanks,' he grinned as he sauntered in and made himself comfortable in one of the new tub chairs. Alice had recently redecorated the office with new beige carpet and navy-blue upholstered visitors' chairs. The walls had been painted off-white and the window proudly displayed new cream shutters. *Shame she wouldn't part with that decrepit old table she uses as a desk*, thought Tom.

'Good timing,' said Alice. 'I've just made some tea. Would you like a cup now or would you prefer to wait until Callie gets here? It's nearly eleven.'

'I'll wait.' Tom replied and raised his eyebrows and smiled as the knock on the office door announced Callie's arrival.

The vision in the pink flowery, floaty, short dress and the high, strappy pink sandals which entered the office took most of Tom's breath away. He was left completely breathless when he caught a hint of her perfume as she shook hands with him and then, reaching across the desk, with Alice. The small diamond studs in her ears glittered in the light and scattered their brilliantly faceted colours around the room. The fine gold chain and diamond drop, which nestled seductively in the hollow of her throat, completed the look of total elegance.

'I'm very pleased to see you both again.' Again, the dazzling smile shone as she sat down and placed her small briefcase on the desk and removed her laptop.

'I don't always dress for my business meetings like I'm going to a wedding,' she paused and giggled, 'but I'm going to a wedding.' She laughed, a girly, tinkling sort of laugh, full of fun and mischief. 'Friends here in L.A. are getting married this afternoon so the timing worked out well. I appreciate your being available today. Now, what is it I can do for you?'

The look on Tom's face silently screamed disappointment when he realised his daydream of him and Callie, sitting in some intimate little restaurant, chatting, flirting, getting to know one another over lunch, had vanished.

Their discussions concerning the business of the media inter-view and the video began and continued until agreement was reached on the commission figure which would be paid to Callie if the video was used. Alice was delighted with the final figure, which was less than what she had budgeted, and Callie was happy with the result, particularly as she didn't even know they were thinking about using it—for any sort of fee! And to be credited on 60 Minutes was a huge bonus. Win, win.

As they finished and Callie packed her laptop away, Tom saw his opportunity to spend some time with her alone.

'Can I drive you to wherever you've got to go for the wedding?' enquired Tom. 'It's no trouble. My car's downstairs.'

'Oh, thank you all the same, Tom, but that's not necessary. A friend is going to pick me up as soon as I ring her and let her know the meeting is finished.'

Knocked back twice in the one day! That had never happened to Tom before, and he mentally tripped and stumbled. But he put on a smiling face and said,

'Oh. Great.'

Over the next few days, Tom's spare moments were spent recalling how Callie looked when she walked into Alice's office: the pink floaty dress that rustled as she moved, the perfect shape of her legs as she crossed one over the other when she sat, the brilliant smile, the sense of quiet confidence that emanated from her. If he thought about it, he could even recall the smell of the perfume she was wearing. He longed to hear her voice again.

By the third day, he was imagining what was under the dress, what the legs would look like, barefoot, on thick carpet. By the fifth day, he could wait no longer. He rang Callie's number, and she picked up on the second ring.

'Hi, Callie. Tom Watson here. How are you? Look, I'm going to be in Seattle for the weekend, and I was wondering if you'd like to have dinner with me on Friday or Saturday evening?'

'Oh, hello Tom. That's nice of you. Unfortunately, I'm busy both Friday and Saturday nights this weekend. I'm conducting a workshop for budding journos and I have dinner with them on the Friday and Saturday nights. Maybe the next time you're in Seattle?'

He paused. The sound of her voice had momentarily thrown him. It was softer and warmer than he remembered. Like velvet.

Undeterred, he ploughed on. 'How about Monday or Tuesday night?'

'They're the two nights I go to Uni. I'm doing an advanced course on the Stock Market. Sounds dry, and it is. But it's helping me get a handle on some businesses I deal with.' She hesitated before continuing: 'I thought you said you'd only be in Seattle for the weekend.'

'I'll be in Seattle any day, or night, you'll go out with me.' *Now you sound desperate,* thought Tom. *This'll end up a pity date if you're not careful!*

'Oh!'

Silence.

'I've never had anyone come from L.A. to Seattle to take me out before. Sorry if I sounded surprised. I am.' He could hear her smile through the phone. 'How about dinner, Friday of next week?'

'Great! If you'll email me your address, I'll pick you up at 7.30. I look forward to seeing you, Callie.'

'Thank you, Tom. I'll see you then.'

As he lay alone in the comfortable king-sized bed with the crisp white sheets in the Executive suite of the best hotel in Seattle, Tom thought back over his dinner date with Callie that evening, minute by delicious minute. There was no denying it—he was smitten. If looks alone were the main criteria, she was the most gorgeous woman he had ever met. But she was also clever and charming, and more importantly, she was not blinded by the manufactured aura of Tom Watson, Pop Star, that Golden Glow which had made parts of his life a misery. Tom was used to being fawned over, pandered to, and adored by female fans, particularly those who enjoyed bragging about how they had made out with Tom Watson. He got none of that from Callie. Her unaffectedness made her even more desirable. She was like a beautifully wrapped Christmas present, all sparkly and shiny; that one special present which stood out amongst all the others.

They had talked for hours. He had told her how important his music was to him, how it had always been fundamental to his feelings about his place in the world; of his friendship with Paul, how they had met at university in Melbourne all those years ago and how their friendship had stood the test of time, even though they lived eight thousand miles away from each other.

She told him of how her older parents, who adored her, had adopted her thirty years ago, about a happy childhood spent growing up in Boston, about obtaining her degree in journalism at Northwestern University in Illinois, and about subsequently starting work for a suburban newspaper on the outskirts of Boston before eventually signing a two-year contract with the Times in Seattle, which had then been extended for another two years.

She told him of how much she hated the cold weather during her years at university in Chicago, and that although it wasn't nearly as cold in Seattle, it never seemed to stop raining in winter. He said: 'You should try living in L.A.; the days are wonderful, when and if the smog clears.' And they both laughed, although at the back of his mind, Tom thought how great it would be if she lived in L.A..

They could have gone on talking forever, but the restaurant had emptied and suddenly, they were the only two people left. By 1 am, the manager had asked them to leave.

Tom smiled as he congratulated himself on his brilliant idea of booking the hotel for two nights.

He knew he was being presumptuous when, in the cab on the way home from the restaurant, he asked her if she would like to go out again tomorrow. He held his breath, waiting for her answer.

'I'd love to.'

He replied far too quickly, but still tried to sound casual.

'Great. Where would you like to go? We can go anywhere, do anything, you want.'

That didn't come out quite as he had planned. He hoped he hadn't sounded like an excited schoolboy.

'I know this may sound unusual, but I'd really love to go to the Museum of Flight. I've never been there but I believe it's fantastic and it's only about fifteen minutes out of town. They say it takes about three or four hours to go through it. Do you have that long?'

'For you, I've got all day.' *And night*, thought Tom, hopefully. 'Why don't I pick you up about noon. I'm sure we can get some lunch while we're there.'

And now he couldn't sleep.

The Museum of Flight was way better than either of them could have imagined. Tom had been apprehensive at the thought of spending a few hours looking at aircraft, anxious that Callie would get bored quickly, but that was not the case.

The open-air hangar was immense and contained some of the larger aircraft. They were transported to another era as they walked down the aisle of a Concorde, the first Boeing 747, JFK's Air Force One, listening intently as veterans related the history of each of the aircraft. They inspected the Space Shuttle and mock Air Traffic Control tower which overlooked Boeing Field.

Glad of a chance to sit down for a while, they stopped for lunch in the café in one of the exhibition hangers, but after four hours, both were happy to call it a day and Tom organised a cab to take them back into the city.

'I've really got to get these shoes off,' said Callie in the taxi on the way back to town. 'I should never have worn new shoes today.' She laughed. 'Would you like to come back to my place? I could make us a simple dinner if you haven't got anything else planned for tonight.'

'That would be great,' replied Tom. 'I was going to suggest we go out for dinner again, but I'd much rather a home-cooked meal at your place if it's not too much trouble.'

'Oh, don't expect anything grand. I'm not much of a cook. How would you feel about toasted sandwiches?'

'I **love** toasted sandwiches,' said Tom, as if they were his favourite thing. At this stage of the conversation, he would have agreed to any known food in the universe. The thought of spending the evening at Callie's place was a chance not to be missed.

As she closed the front door behind her, Callie kicked off her shoes in the hallway. 'Feel free to do the same.' she said. 'Make yourself comfortable while I put on some music and see what's in the fridge.'

He removed his shoes and followed her down the hall to the kitchen.

'Why don't you sit up at the kitchen counter and talk to me while I make us a fabulous repast.' She said, as she opened the fridge door and began removing the makings of sandwiches for toasting.

They chatted comfortably while she made their magnificent dinner. Callie set out plates and napkins on an obviously handmade and much-loved tray. Once it was ready, she carried the tray laden with food and Cokes into the living area and placed it on the coffee table. They sat on the sofa to eat.

'Great idea of yours,' said Tom, as he finished the last of his sandwich and wiped his mouth with the napkin. 'That was delicious.'

Callie had also finished her meal and sat looking at him. 'Can I ask you a question?'

'Of course. Ask away.'

'Um, do you have a timeframe in mind for when you're going to kiss me? I've been waiting more than 24 hours now. If nothing else, I think the sumptuous meal I just made for you deserves a reward.'

Tom laughed out loud and smacked his knee before he leaned in and kissed her modestly on the cheek. He sat back, looking pleased with himself.

'That's not really what I had in mind,' said Callie, slowly and deliberately.

Tom bent his head down and looked up at her with a sly smile. 'I know.'

Callie turned slightly to face him, took his face in her hands, and kissed him meaningfully on the mouth—one of those swoon-worthy kisses that increases the heart rate and triggers that warm sensation that starts somewhere in the belly and envelopes the entire body.

Tom thought he'd died and gone to heaven.

Eventually, they stopped kissing long enough for Callie to stand up and take his hand, helping him up from the sofa. 'Come with me,' she said as she led him down the hall to the bedroom.

Chapter 27

So, here they were, lying side by side in Callie's bed, under the covers, both naked, staring at the ceiling. Tom had been imagining, dreaming, and planning for this situation for weeks, and in those dreams, everything had gone like clockwork. But now that the moment had arrived, he was suddenly a schoolboy again. He felt gauche, awkward, worried he would seem clumsy, groping, immature. It had been so long since he'd been in this position, and back then, he would have been invariably high on something, and it would not have been important to him how he felt or what he did. Thoughts of riding a bike suddenly filled his mind. *They say it's like riding a bike, you never forget. It all comes back to you.* But even though his mind was working on this premise, he still felt insanely nervous.

Until Callie rolled onto one arm, leaned over him, and kissed him gently on the mouth again, her soft lips caressing his firmly, fervently, her bare breasts nestling against his chest.

Passion kicked in and all feelings of nerves disappeared as Tom returned her kiss, his spirits soaring, his soul coming alive. He didn't remember them getting undressed, getting into bed, even having dinner. All he could think about was the feel of her body against his, the warmth of her bare breasts, the feel of her mouth as her lips parted and their two bodies melded into one. He gently lifted her hips until she was completely on top of him. She straddled his body and slowly pushed herself down on him and as he entered her, his body and mind overflowed with pure joy. He gave himself up completely to the dual sensations of power and powerlessness.

She moved on him and he sighed in ecstasy as she increased the pressure, gaining momentum. Together they built to a climax, his feelings spiralling to an intensity he had never felt before. As he felt his world stop on its axis, it was suddenly over, and he lay still and spent.

Callie rolled over onto her back and sighed. She looked over at him, smiled wickedly, and said,

'Well, that wasn't so bad, was it?'

His feelings overwhelmed him momentarily, and he looked deep into her eyes and murmured, 'This is what I wanted from the moment I set eyes on you.'

OK, so maybe booking the hotel for two nights wasn't the best idea, in retrospect, thought Tom, as he sat in the airport lounge waiting to board his plane back to L.A. on Sunday. *But it's not like I can't afford the $600 or whatever the charge was for an unslept-in-bed in a swanky hotel.* He had taken no notice of the bill as he paid the account. The glow from last night and this morning still surrounded him, so much so that he had only just made it back to the hotel in time to pack and get to the airport. But at least Callie had agreed to go out with him again next weekend. The thing was, she hadn't suggested that he stay at her place and he couldn't really ask, so he'd booked the same hotel suite again for next weekend.

Worth every cent, whatever it costs, to see her again!

The fourth time he flew to Seattle for the weekend, Callie asked Tom if he would like to stay with her, so his investment in flights and hotel accommodation had been money well spent. He continued to fly to Seattle and stay with Callie each weekend for the next couple of months, and they more or less became a couple.

As they sat enjoying each other's company over dinner at a neighbourhood steakhouse, Callie explained that her contract with The Times was due to run out in three weeks.

'They only extend anyone's contract once; after that you become a consultant, which is not so secure. Besides that, I feel I've gone as far as I can go at The Times. I would really like to try another paper. I've sent my resume to nine major newspapers in various cities during the past two weeks but so far, I haven't heard back from any of them.' Tom could see his future with Callie becoming even more complicated than it was now, if she ended up working in New York, or Austin, or even Florida. On the other hand...

'Have you contacted The L.A. Times?' asked Tom.

'Not yet. They're in my second batch, if I don't get a job from the first lot.'

'Why don't you come down to L.A. and move in with me?' The words were out of his mouth before he had thought it through, but once spoken, it seemed like a fabulous idea to Tom and he continued.

'It would be super convenient if you applied to The L.A. Times while you're living there. Plus, there's a few other major newspapers and magazines in L.A. besides the Times. The Hollywood Reporter and Variety are significant entertainment industry papers with huge readership. And don't forget, you've already done one successful show-business interview.' Tom smiled and placed his hand over Callie's on the table and added,

'Admit it Callie, it's a good idea. We get on so well together; you know I'm crazy about you. Why don't we fly down to L.A. tomorrow and you can have a look at the house, see if you could live there.'

Callie reached over and picked up the menu, more to stall for time while she thought about what he had said than to choose a dessert.

'We haven't known each other for long, Tom, but you're right, we do get on well together. I really enjoy your company.' She smiled that wonderful smile at him and Tom's heart melted.

'Then it's agreed. You'll come to L.A. with me tomorrow and see what you think.'

His eyes held hers for a moment. Then, suddenly serious, he added,

'Do you want dessert? I don't want dessert. Please tell me you don't want dessert. Let's go home and 'get an early night,' He leaned over the table and kissed her ardently on the mouth as he took hold of her hand.

'Yes, let's do that. Let's go now.' She replied.

Callie fell in love with the house at first sight. L.A. had put on a golden day for them, and as Tom drove her around the hills, she became entranced with the place she had read about over the years: the Spanish-influenced architecture, the palm trees, and the art déco style. By Sunday afternoon, she was excited about moving in with Tom and living in L.A. when her contract with The Seattle Times expired.

When she declined the consultancy with the Times, Callie's boss was disappointed. However, after she explained she was moving to L.A., he offered to speak to a colleague of his at The L.A. Times for her, an offer she gratefully accepted. The subsequent arranged interview went well, and she signed a contract with the paper the following week.

It was an exciting time in the Watson/Williams household, made even more so when Tom told Callie that his closest friend, Paul, from Australia, was coming to stay for a few days, especially to meet Callie.

When Paul arrived in the US, he made Tom's place his first stop and was looking forward to meeting the Callie he had heard so much about. But equally important, he wanted to congratulate Tom on the way he was handling his sobriety. Paul had met several determined people on his travels and in his business dealings, but none as strong willed as Tom Watson. He had been convinced Tom would not be able to stay on the wagon when he left The Hermitage, but he had been proven wrong. He was sure Tom had endured some dire moments along the way but was so proud of his friend for his determination to stay sober and drug free.

It was a balmy Saturday morning on a cloudless L.A. day when a beaming Tom greeted Paul at the front door with genuine delight, and a warm hug. Paul noticed Tom had put on weight. He also had more colour in the face, which was accentuated by the streaks of grey in his black hair. He appeared to be in good health, happy and more content than Paul had seen him look in many, many years.

'I can't wait to introduce you to Callie,' said Tom, as he took Paul's bag from him and led him through to the kitchen. 'She's fixing us something for lunch.'

Callie, who was preparing food at the kitchen counter, stopped and smiled as Tom introduced them.

'Callie, this is the Paul you've heard all about. Paul, this is Callie, the light in my life.'

Rather than shake hands, Callie leaned in and kissed Paul on the cheek. 'I'm very pleased to meet you, Paul,' she said. 'You're exactly as I thought you would be.'

'And I'd recognise you anywhere,' replied Paul, smiling broadly.

Tom was touched by their reaction, as if they had known each other for years, and the three of them chatted comfortably together as Callie set lunch down on the dining table.

Lunch, and the rest of Paul's stay, was enjoyed equally by all three of them. Tom was especially glad that Paul and Callie seemed to genuinely like each other.

With Tom out of the house on Monday to attend a meeting with Alice, Paul and Callie sat and chatted freely about Tom, his health, and how he had turned his life around. Paul made a point of telling

Callie how pleased he was that Tom had met her, and he hoped they would have a happy and long life together.

As Callie hugged Paul goodbye at the house the following day before Tom drove him to LAX for his flight to New York, she put her hands on his shoulders and said,

'Please come back and see us any time you're in the US. It was really good to meet you. I can see why Tom thinks you're one of the good guys of this world.'

Paul replied: 'Tom struck gold the day he met you.'

Chapter 28

Thanks to Alice's talent for organisation, Callie's interview with Tom was broadcast on 60 Minutes. The same weekend, his new album of Jazz/R&B songs was released, and the music video of the first track hit TV screens all over America. How could this new album not be a success? And to add fuel to the bonfire that was the first week's sales, Alice had arranged for Tom to appear on the Ellen Show and on several evening talk shows. That week was a promoter's dream and sales reflected all the work Alice, Tom, and Callie had put into it over the preceding months. Although the album's first week's sales were not on the same scale as something new from Pants on Fire, Tom was happier with the album than anything he had ever done with the band.

The following month, Alice was approached by the Manager of the Mogambo, the leading jazz club in downtown L.A., who was interested in booking Tom on a regular basis. Alice's finely honed negotiating skills enabled her to sign him up to a very lucrative contract for the next two years. She was even able to re-draw the contract to allow Tom to do several concerts a year without affecting his gig at the Mogambo. She then arranged concerts starring

Tom Watson up and down the West Coast, as well as two major shows in New York.

'No doubt about it, Alice. You're a genius,' said Tom as they shook hands on the deal she had arranged.

'We work well together, Tom,' replied Alice, as she smiled and added, 'It's your reward for good behaviour. Mind you, it was a brilliant career move to change your style like that. Just when the rest of America thought you were all washed up, you came out smelling of roses. I admire anyone who can wrestle success from the jaws of disaster.'

Although Alice was aware the reclusive American billionaire, Abe Shapiro, owned the Mogambo, she knew virtually nothing about the man. She had heard he lived in South America but this had never been confirmed and apparently, nobody in the media had seen him for many years. So, it was a shock when six months into the second year of Tom's contract with the Club, the manager contacted Alice to see if she would agree to a meeting with Mr. Shapiro.

'As you know, Mr. Shapiro is an extremely private man. A condition of the meeting is that you agree to absolute confidentiality. It is imperative that no one else knows we have even spoken today. He will arrange for his private jet to take you to where he is and return you to L.A.. Do you understand?'

Alice was intrigued and replied: 'I can comply with Mr. Shapiro's request.'

'Mr. Shapiro's driver will pick you up from your office at ten o'clock next Tuesday morning. Bring an overnight bag and your passport.'

'Certainly.' Alice was surprised by this directive but was ready and waiting with her packed overnight bag, when the limo arrived the following Tuesday. She had spent most of Monday researching Abe Shapiro, but even with Alice's talent for uncovering information, she was no wiser by the end of the day. The lack of information on the man could mean he'd made his fortune from drugs. The thought of Tom associating with anyone involved with drugs disturbed her greatly, but she pushed it to the back of her mind and vowed to keep an open mind for the meeting.

The drive to Van Nuys Airport was silent; obviously the chauffeur was under orders not to leak information to any passengers. The plane was ready and waiting for them as they pulled up at the foot of the stairs leading up into the aircraft.

Alice appeared to be the only person in the beautifully crafted cabin of the luxurious jet. She made herself comfortable in one of the leather armchairs and adjusted the seat belt as a uniformed hostess approached her and smiled. 'Welcome to Mr. Shapiro's private aircraft, Ms. Weinberg. We'll be taking off in about five minutes and will arrive at our destination of Puerto Vallarta in a little over three hours. I hope you enjoy your flight. Can I get you a glass of champagne?'

'That would be very nice, thank you,' replied Alice. *Puerto Vallarta? Mexico? I wasn't expecting that!*

The flight was uneventful, the lunch delicious, and the champagne limitless. And, of course, a limo was waiting at the end of the tarmac when the plane touched down in Puerto Vallarta. Alice was pleasantly surprised when they drove up to a villa not unlike her own house in L.A., the major difference being that this one was set in acres of beautifully maintained gardens. The view out over the Pacific Ocean from the house's clifftop position was breath-taking.

A middle-aged Mexican woman in what looked like a housekeeper's uniform greeted Alice at the front door. She politely took Alice's overnight bag and led her into a large office on the ground floor of the house. 'Please take a seat. Mr. Shapiro will be with you shortly.' the woman said in a heavy Mexican accent.

Alice sat down in one of the two leather visitors' chairs facing the desk and took in her surroundings. She would love to have removed her shoes and wiggled her toes in the thick Aubusson rug underfoot, but decided against it, presuming there were probably CCT cameras everywhere. It was safer to just look around.

Strains of 'California Dreaming' played by Wes Montgomery, one of the finest jazz guitarists of all time, unobtrusively permeated the room from the seven or eight speakers dotted around the walls.

Sunlight streamed through the two floor-to-ceiling windows which overlooked the magnificent lawns surrounded by gardens of flowering shrubs. Wall-to-wall dark timber bookcases—packed with a variety of books, from expensive-looking leather-bound volumes to various popular paperbacks—covered the wall opposite the windows. The enormous desk in front of her appeared to be made from the same timber as the bookcases and was neat and tidy, recently polished, not a speck of dust anywhere to be seen. The fresh flowers in a small vase on the credenza had obviously been picked this morning, their fragrance still noticeable.

Somehow, the room did not give the impression of being the office of a drug lord. Although it was functional, the atmosphere was one of comfortable luxury. Alice smiled as she imagined what

Abe Shapiro would think of her office, had this meeting taken place there.

She was tempted to take a closer look at two of the magnificent paintings on the wall behind the desk, but the sound of the door opening put an end to that idea. She sat straighter in the chair and focussed her mind on the meeting about to take place.

A very tall, very thin man made his way across the office with the aid of a walking stick and extended his hand to Alice.

'Ms. Weinberg. I'm Abe Shapiro. I'm pleased to meet you and thank you for coming down here to meet with me.'

Alice stood and shook hands with the man. 'How do you do, Mr. Shapiro.' She smiled.

'Oh, please call me Abe. And I'll call you Alice.' He smiled the smile of a benevolent grandfather, and Alice felt an instant rapport with this spidery-looking man with dark sunken eyes and thinning hair. She knew also that he did not look well, his face the colour of putty, his hands, with their long, slender fingers, were covered in blue veins, his fingernails long and claw-like.

At the sound of the door opening again, Alice glanced in that direction to see the woman who had ushered her into the office, carrying a tray on which sat cups and saucers and a teapot.

'I thought we'd start with some tea,' said Abe. 'I know you like tea. And Maria has made us a Tres Leches cake.'

Maria set down the tray and poured tea for Abe and Alice before silently gliding out of the office, quietly closing the door on her way out.

'Let me tell you about the reason I wanted to speak to you today,' Abe began, as he handed Alice a delicate gold-rimmed porcelain plate on which sat a small piece of the delicious- looking cake. 'As you possibly know, I own the Mogambo jazz Club in Los Angeles.'

'I've been at the club and seen Tom a few times now and he's one of the best I've heard. And believe me, Alice, I know my jazz musicians. This man is exceptional.'

Alice made a mental note: how interesting to think that this man, about whom the media knew so little and of whom there were apparently no photos, had floated in and out of the club unnoticed.

Abe took a sip of his tea. For a moment, Alice thought he looked uncomfortable as he adjusted his posture slightly before continuing,

'Unfortunately, I have been diagnosed with a brain tumour and I'm not expected to live much longer.'

This was the reason he appeared unwell, and perhaps uncomfortable. Even though this man was seriously rich, his wealth made no difference. He had little or no control over his health or his lifespan. A feeling of sadness washed over Alice unexpectedly.

He paused as if the magnitude of that last statement had only just occurred to him and took a breath before continuing.

'Before I go, I'd like to sell the club to Tom, if he is interested.'

This was not what she had expected at all, and she hoped the shock didn't show on her face. She continued to sit, composed, drinking her tea, listening for whatever came next.

'The reason I'm discussing this now with you and not Tom is because I know you are his manager, and I also know that his movements would be followed closely by the press, something I studiously avoid.'

Alice sat, waiting, knowing that silence was the best way to handle any unusual situation, aware that all would be revealed eventually.

This was a most interesting proposition and one that had never crossed her mind.

'There are two provisos: the first is that any such action would be subject to non-disclosure and that the press know nothing of this at least until I'm gone. Then it would be up to you how you handle that.'

'The second is that the sale must be finalised by close of business tomorrow.'

Alice hadn't seen that coming either.

She poured a second cup of tea while her mind worked overtime. She was sure of two things: It would be a good move, and she could talk Tom into it. It would be difficult to keep it quiet. But not impossible.

'I'm very sorry to hear you are not well, Abe. I know you are getting the best treatment possible and I hope you don't have to suffer.'

'I need to talk to Tom about your proposal and I would like to do that today in view of your proviso.' She set her cup and saucer down on the desk and ran her hands down over her thighs to smooth her skirt.

She smiled. 'I realise now why I needed to bring an overnight bag.'

'Of course. Maria will show you to your room which has an adjoining living area. You can safely conduct any business from there. I need to rest now. Why don't we meet for breakfast in the dining room at eight o'clock tomorrow morning and you can let me know your decision?'

He took his time getting out of his chair and, with the aid of the walking stick, crossed the carpet to the door. His clothes hung loosely on his tall, thin frame, a sign of what a huge, powerful man he must have been before this dreadful disease took hold. As he opened the door, Maria entered and asked Alice to follow her to the guest room.

She sat at the desk in the adjoining living area and rang Tom.

'Hi Tom, Alice here. Before I go any further, I need your assurance that you will not repeat any part of this conversation to anyone.'

Unhesitatingly and immediately: 'You have it.'

'I've just had a meeting with the owner of the Mogambo. He wants to sell the club but he doesn't want to put it on the open market. He wants to sell it to you. For some reason, he thinks you're quite good.' Alice laughed, remembering Abe's expression—*'This man is exceptional.'*

'Are you interested in owning the best jazz club in L.A.?'

The silence at the other end of the phone was punctuated with heavy breathing, which continued for several seconds. Finally:

'What's your opinion, Alice?' Tom's voice was slightly shaky, as if someone was holding him back when really, he wanted to jump in the air. He was trying hard to be calm and businesslike, and it was almost working.

'I think it's a fantastic opportunity. We haven't discussed the price but his offer is genuine. Personally, I don't care what it costs; you will never get another chance like this. I believe you should grab it with both hands.'

'He wants the sale kept out of the press; nobody must know. Oh, and the sale needs to be completed by close of business tomorrow.'

There was a slight pause on the other end before Tom began talking excitedly.

'Come in it with me, Alice. You know you'll end up running it anyway. We've been more or less partners for years, what's one more venture? We could make this one 50/50.'

Alice was lost for words. This entire trip had been one of surprises, and here was another one that had slid in sideways and caught her unawares. She did some quick calculations in her head: this could cost her dearly if it went the wrong way. But then she considered the emotional and psychological aspects of Tom's offer and, for the first time in her life, Alice pondered the fact that life might be about more than dollars and profit and deals and making money. Whether or not it made money for them, this could be fun. Plus, they could both afford to take the risk and she knew that was the best basis for entering into a business deal: if you could afford to lose, you were sure to win.

'I think that's a brilliant idea, Tom. I'll talk to the owner tomorrow and cement the deal by this time tomorrow afternoon. And remember, not a word to anyone.'

Alice ended the call and sat thinking about her future as a co-owner of what could become the best jazz club in the United States. She would make damn sure of that. And the thought of being in business with Tom was surprisingly uplifting.

The following morning, she arrived for breakfast as Abe was sitting down at the table. Alice was saddened to see that he had deteriorated since yesterday. His eyes looked even more sunken, as if he hadn't slept, his left eye was closed, and she noticed he hadn't shaved. His hands shook slightly as he helped himself to coffee.

Not wanting to prolong his waiting for an answer, Alice came straight to the point:

'Abe, Tom and I would like to buy your club in a 50/50 partnership, if you'll agree. As Tom said, I'll probably end up running it for him anyway while he's busy drawing the crowds.'

And knowing full well that he would have calculated the price down to the cent, she added: 'Have you decided on a price?'

Another shock! The price he was asking was so much lower than Alice had expected, a clear indication of how much he wanted this sale to go ahead. She maintained a blank expression and said: 'On behalf of Tom and me, we accept your offer. I imagine you have a contract already drawn up?' She smiled at him knowingly.

'As a matter of fact, I've got two contracts drawn up—one in Tom's name and another in both of your names.' He smiled wanly. 'I was hoping that's what you would decide to do.' He stood and shook hands with her. 'You two will make an impressive combination to run the Mogambo. I hope you run it for many years.'

He didn't sit down again but collected his walking stick from its resting place and said: 'Why don't we meet in my office at eleven o'clock and finalize the sale? I'll have my pilot fly you back to L.A. after lunch.'

And with that, he left the room.

Chapter 29

During the following few years, the Mogambo became one of the major jazz clubs in the United States, developing a similar recipe for success as the famous Ronnie Scott's Jazz Club in London. Alice and Tom re-designed the basement club and gave it a sophisticated 1920s speakeasy vibe. The introduction of the 'Sunday Jam Night'—a late-night jazz jam session for musicians so inclined—elevated its position to the major jazz venue in America. When they renovated the two upstairs floors as a venue for other styles of live music, including Latin, blues, and even flamenco, it became the leading place for music lovers of all ages and tastes.

Tom continued to write music and lyrics and the crowd at the Mogambo welcomed his experimental stuff as well as his more traditional rhythm and blues/jazz numbers. He recorded another couple of albums, both of which were even more successful than his first solo album in the jazz/soul genre.

It was also during this period that Callie cemented her place in the newspaper and magazine world as a leading light on business and the entertainment industry, her knowledge and insight often expanded by Alice's vast experience gained over many years of being on the inside.

Life was good for Callie and Tom. They especially enjoyed it when Paul visited from Australia. Although he usually only stayed two or three days at a time, his business brought him to the States every couple of months. The bond between the three of them deepened, and they melded into a family—none of the three had ever had brothers or sisters.

Tragically, whilst driving home from dinner at a friend's house during a severe storm, Paul's wife was badly injured in a car accident and died from her injuries the following day. The tragedy was compounded by the fact that Paul was at their home in Melbourne and his wife was on holiday interstate where the accident happened.

The funeral was held a week later to allow Tom and Callie time to travel to Melbourne from L.A.. It was a sombre affair, although Paul was not as shattered as Tom had been expecting and seemed to hold up well under the circumstances. His demeanour at the service and later at his house was polite, pleasant, and almost jovial, which led Tom to wonder about the state of Paul's marriage over the last few years. Glenda had worked with Paul in the architect's office in the early days of Paul's career, and it was Tom who had encouraged Paul to ask her out. Over the many years since those early days, Paul rarely mentioned Glenda and Tom presumed their marriage was much like anyone else's. He also understood that Paul was a 'closed shop' on relationships, interpersonal situations, and anything remotely intimate. He didn't like to talk about that side of life. Callie was the only person who had ever drawn Paul out in a meaningful conversation.

Rooster flew down from Sydney for the funeral, and Tom couldn't wait to introduce him to Callie. It was during the gathering at Paul's house following the service that Tom convinced Rooster to come over to L.A. and play at the Mogambo. He didn't need much convincing.

Back home in L.A., as life returned to Tom and Callie's 'normal'—he worked at the Mogambo four or five nights a week and she worked at her reporting job most weekdays—they coincidentally slipped into a casual conversation about starting a family. It seemed so natural at the time, not in the least contrived, except that it led Tom to make one of the major decisions of his life.

The day after this conversation, while Callie was at work, Tom visited Harry Winston Jewellers on Rodeo Drive, Beverly Hills, and chose a classic 3-carat emerald-cut diamond engagement ring set in platinum with tapered baguette side stones.

Callie was usually home by about five-thirty, and Tom could hardly wait to give her the ring. But by about three o'clock, a feeling of apprehension began to envelop his psyche, like a spider web. *What if she didn't want to get married? Callie was a very independent woman. What if she thought the eighteen-year difference in their ages was too big a hurdle?* Their age difference crossed his mind occasionally, but Callie had never once mentioned it.

He quickly made himself a coffee to steady his nerves.

By four o'clock, he was feeling decidedly nervous. *What if she said no?* He would be devastated. *But they loved each other, didn't they?*

He made himself another coffee.

By five o'clock, he was pacing back and forth across the living room floor; the ring sitting snugly in its black velvet box on the coffee table, mocking him. For the first time in many years, he felt like a drink. *Don't be stupid*, he thought, *no you don't. Besides, there's no liquor in the house.*

He made himself yet another coffee.

He was feeling hot and sticky and was aware of the damp sweat patch down the centre of his back when he heard her car in the driveway. Moving quickly, he scooped up the ring and shoved it into his pants pocket, opening the front door as she walked up the front steps.

'Hello Darling,' said Callie, surprised to see him home at this time. 'I didn't think you'd be home tonight.'

'I'm not working tonight. Come in, come in. I've got something to tell you. Um, I mean ask you,' he stuttered, leading her into the living room. 'Sit down.' He almost pushed her down onto the sofa.

'Whatever is it?' she said. 'You look dreadful. Are you OK?'

He flopped down on the sofa next to her and, now sweating profusely, blurted out: 'Callie, I love you. And I know you love me. What are we waiting for? Will you marry me?'

A look of surprise and concern clouded her lovely face. 'Is that why you look so awful? The sweat is dripping off you.' Tom was taken aback by this reply.

Then she laughed—that delightful, tinkly, girly laugh he loved so much. 'Of course, I'll marry you. I can hardly wait to marry you.' And she kissed him long and hard on the lips, twining her arms around his neck and pulling him as close as she could. He wrapped his arms around her and returned her kiss. At last, they pulled apart, and looking deep into her eyes, Tom whispered,

'I love you, Callie Williams.'

'I love you, Tom Watson.'

'Let's go out to dinner to celebrate,' Tom added.

'But first, I need to shower and change into something special.' Callie laughed as she looked him up and down and added: 'You look like you've already done that.' And she raced upstairs to get ready.

Half an hour later she walked down the stairs, her sexy short red dress complimented by high-heel silver sandals. Her blonde hair gelled to pixie perfection set off by the ruby earrings he had given her last Christmas.

'You look fabulous,' said Tom as he glanced up at her. He held out his hand to take hers as she stepped off the last step.

'And I'm glad to see that you look much better than when I got home.' Callie smiled at him and took his hand.

Spago was buzzing as they arrived, but the Maître D' had no trouble finding the best table when Tom Watson entered the restaurant.

As they waited for their main meal to arrive, Callie asked: 'So, what's the timeframe?'

'For what?' Tom replied.

Callie frowned, wondering if he was being deliberately obtuse, but then she remembered—Tom was a man. 'The wedding.'

Tom grinned. 'That's completely up to you, Callie. I'll fit in with whatever you want to do, when you want to do it, where you want to do it. Just tell me where I've got to be and at what time and I'll be there. Oh, and you'll have to tell me what to wear too. But I would love to go to Italy for our honeymoon.'

'Sounds wonderful. I'd like to go to Boston and tell Mom and Dad as soon as possible, preferably before they read about it or hear it from anyone else.'

'Good idea. I'd also like to ring Paul tomorrow and ask him to be my best man. He's my oldest and dearest friend and I think he'll be thrilled when he knows we're getting married. Plus, I was his best man when he married Glenda.'

Callie beamed. 'What a lovely idea. Paul's my favourite person—after you, that is!' she added and winked at him across the table.

Later that evening, as they were undressing for bed, Tom pulled his shirt out of his slacks and over his head. The black velvet box was dislodged from its hiding place deep in his slacks pocket and fell on the floor. They both stared at the black lump on the floor.

'What's that?' enquired Callie, pointing at the floor.

'Oh, my God, Callie, I completely forgot.' Tom scooped the box up off the floor as he said: 'I bought you a present.'

Standing in slacks and socks, he threw his shirt on the floor and instantly bent down on one knee. Opening the box for Callie's inspection of its contents, he added,

'Callie Williams, will you marry me.'

They both started laughing as she replied: 'Well, I certainly will now.' And he took the ring from the box and placed it on her finger. 'Oh Tom, it's beautiful. Thank you.' And she began to cry.

I'll never understand women, thought Tom.

Two days later, in the taxi from Boston airport to her parents' home, Callie gripped Tom's hand and said,

'Maybe it was a mistake wanting to surprise them. Perhaps we should have let them know we were coming. What if they're not home?'

'Well, if they're not home, we'll sit on the front doorstep and wait for them to come home. Stop worrying, they'll be in and thrilled to see us,' he said kindly.

And they were. And absolutely thrilled to see them. Callie's mom, Linda, knew instantly why they were in Boston, visiting 'the parents', long before Callie proffered her hand and showed off the shiny, new diamond ring on her finger. Her father, Ben, beamed as he shook hands with Tom and wrapped his arms around Callie in a loving hug.

'Come in, come in,' said Linda as she wiped her eyes and dragged Callie into the hall. Ben put his arm around Tom's shoulders and once inside the house, stopped and looked fondly at both of them as he said,

'Ah, is there anything else you'd like to tell us?'

Callie replied, laughing: 'Oh Dad, give us a break. We're not even married yet. But that is one of the reasons we decided to get married. You two might end up with that grandchild you've always wanted.'

Ben picked up their suitcase and ushered them down the hall. 'Why don't you two make yourselves comfortable in the spare room while your mother makes us coffee and cake?'

Later that evening, the four of them sat around the table following a wonderful roast beef dinner, discussing the wedding. Linda had always been a fabulous cook, unfortunately, a trait which had not been passed onto Callie. Tom glanced around at the other three and realised how lucky he was to be marrying into this warm and welcoming family. His gratitude had increased tenfold when he discovered they didn't drink.

Linda stood, and thinking she was going to clear the table, Callie started to gather up the empty dishes. Instead, Linda took Callie by the hand and asked her to come with her as she headed for the door.

Once in the master bedroom, Linda told Callie to sit on the bed, that she had something for her. She opened the closet and, reaching up, retrieved a box from the topmost shelf. Placing the box on the bed, she removed the lid and gently took out a yellowed but pristine envelope. She turned it over lovingly in her hands and took a deep breath before handing it to Callie.

'Callie, this is your original birth certificate, the one that was issued when you were born, before we adopted you. I have never opened it. It's not mine to read.'

'However, with the possibility of your having children one day, I thought you might like to have it on hand in case you want to investigate your background for any health issues, or even to find out about your ancestry. Having children of your own may change how you think about these things. You know Ben and I have always loved you unconditionally and we are so happy that you've found a wonderful partner in Tom.' Linda dabbed at her eyes with a tissue she took from the box on the bedside table.

Callie was surprised at how unmoved she felt as she took the envelope. She glanced at it but didn't open it. 'Thank you, mom, for keeping this for me.' She smiled at her mother as she went on: 'You and Dad are my parents, the only parents I've ever known, ever wanted to know. I've never been interested in finding out about my birth parents, but you're right about the health thing. I hadn't thought of that. It's probably good to know if there's any issues we should be aware of.'

She hugged her mother and stood up. 'I'll put this away and be back to help you clear the table in a minute.'

From the moment Callie and Tom told her parents they were getting married, Linda had been concerned about Callie's reaction to the birth certificate. She realised now that she need not have worried. Callie was her own person, confident of her place in the world, and had always been unphased about being adopted. Why would she be any different now?

Callie went down to the spare room and found the handbag she had brought with her. She tucked the envelope into the zippered compartment and returned to the dining room as the men sauntered into the living area.

After a relaxing and happy three days spent with Linda and Ben in Boston, Tom and Callie boarded the plane for L.A., Callie's head full of ideas for the wedding, Tom wondering how the club had fared during his absence. As it was after ten at night when they finally arrived home, they decided to unpack and put everything away the following day.

The next morning, Callie walked into the large closet off the bedroom to return the now empty suitcase to its usual place. When she picked up her handbag to make more room for the suitcase, she remembered the envelope.

She took out the envelope and turned it over in her hands. *Wow*, she thought, *this envelope is thirty-five years old.* It was dry and had a slightly fragile feel to it.

She felt mildly curious and began to open it. The flap had originally been stuck down but now came away easily as soon as she began to prise it open. She carefully took out the neatly folded sheet of paper and opened it out to its full size. Staring at the heavy-duty official looking paper which was headed 'Certificate of Birth' in fancy letters, and with her heart beating ever so slightly faster, she read:

Child's name: Callie Ann Thompson

Date of birth: April 5, 1983

Sex: Female

Country of birth:United States of America

Mother's Maiden Name:Ann Meredith Thompson

Father's Name:Thomas McQuoid Watson

Date issued:April 5, 1983

Her breath caught in her throat and stayed there. She read it a second time before she let the breath go, her heart racing. She stared, unbelieving, at the father's name. Callie had only ever heard the name McQuoid once before, when Tom explained to her where his middle name came from—his mother had wanted her son to carry on her family name of McQuoid, so they had christened him Thomas McQuoid Watson.

Sally dropped to her knees and forced her trembling hands to hold the page still so she could read it again.

There couldn't possibly be two Thomas McQuoid Watsons in the world.

She felt faint as she realised—Tom was her father!!

Chapter 30

Callie sat on the floor of the closet staring at the certificate, willing the nausea to stop. She felt sick, faint, in shock. She could hear the thumping of her heart in her chest as she took deep breaths and focussed on the suitcase she had been putting away, staring at it whilst counting to ten, trying to calm the panic.

Her mind was racing and muddled as she tried to figure out what to do. She wanted to rush and tell Tom, make him assure her it wasn't him. But how could there be another Thomas McQuoin Watson? It had to be him. Why had he not told her he had fathered a child? This was a life-altering secret. Didn't he realise secrets have consequences?

She had been so happy in Boston. Her future lay before her like a golden light in the forest, leading the way to happy-ever-after.

But like all secrets, this revelation changed everything

For an instant, it crossed her mind that perhaps she should tear up the certificate, get rid of it, pretend she had never seen it. But she knew she couldn't do that. It was too important, the consequences of the information it contained too dire.

A moment later, Tom walked into the closet.

'It's very quiet in here. What's going on?' he asked, brightly. 'Would you like me to put that suitcase up on the shelf for you?'

She was sitting on the floor with her back to him and when he realised she was silent and unmoving, he asked,

'Callie, is everything alright? Callie?'

As she turned her head and looked up at him, Tom saw the tears rolling down her face as she sobbed, 'Oh, Tom, what have we done?' She thrust the certificate at him, explaining between sobs,

'This is my original birth certificate. Mom kept it for me in the event of me ever thinking about having children. It says that my father's name is Thomas McQuoin Watson. I'm your daughter, Tom.' And she put her head in her hands and wailed as he took it from her hand.

'WHAT?' replied Tom. He almost smiled as he squatted down on his haunches and, putting one arm around Callie's shoulders, read the certificate. The whole idea of his being Callie's father was too outlandish to take seriously.

As he read down the page: 'Who the hell is Ann Meredith Thompson?'

'My birth mother. You must have had a relationship with her when you were younger.'

Tom was silent for a minute before flopping down on the floor next to her. 'Callie, I honestly know nothing about this. I was at uni in Melbourne in 1983 but it's so long ago, and I have very little memory of those days thanks to the alcohol and drugs.'

He frowned and concentrated, straining to recover those memories of his uni days. 'I certainly don't remember any Ann Meredith Thompson.'

Tom sat on the floor massaging his forehead with his fingers as if that would clear his mind enough to remember those days at Uni. He could recall random bits of stuff—playing at one particular gig with the Dandy Rats, the day he first met Paul in calculus class, even the house he and his dad had lived in in Richmond when they lived in Melbourne—but nothing emerged out of the fog about any of the girls he had known, or more importantly, slept with. Flashes of one girl he had dated, a goth girl, faded in and out of his mind, but her name hadn't been Ann. He couldn't remember what it was, but it wasn't Ann.

Callie sat in stunned silence next to him, trying not to think about anything.

Suddenly, Tom jumped up.

'I'm going to phone Paul right now. I don't care what time it is in Australia. If anyone would know, it's Paul.' He ran to his office where his phone was charging and, yanking the cord out, quickly dialled Paul's number.

A groggy voice answered on about the seventh ring. 'Hi Paul, Tom here. I'm really sorry to disturb you at whatever time it is in Australia now, but it's important.'

'What's the problem?' replied Paul, instantly awake at the word 'important'. He looked at the bedside clock and saw that it was five-thirty in the morning. Something must be wrong for Tom to ring him at this time.

'Do you remember me dating a girl by the name of Ann Thompson when we were at uni?'

'Ann Thompson?' Paul sounded vague at first, but then, more definitively: 'Yes, I do. Why?'

'Callie and I have just seen her original birth certificate, you know, before she was adopted by Linda and Ben Williams, and it says her mother's name is Ann Meredith Thompson and her father's name is—get this—Thomas McGoin Watson. That's gotta be me. But I don't remember any Ann Meredith Thompson.' As he said the words out loud, Tom collapsed into his office chair.

There was a lengthy silence on the other end of the line before Paul said,

'You were going out with her for a few months, but she gave you the flick because you were too devoted to the band and drinking with your mates. She was devastated by the break-up even though she instigated it.'

This confirmed Tom's worst fears. He was so busy thinking about what to do, he hardly noticed the silence on the other end of the line until it had gone on for so long he thought Paul had hung up.

'Paul, are you still there?'

'Yes. Did you say Callie's birth certificate names you as the father?'

'Yes.'

By this time, Callie had come into the office and sat down opposite Tom. She looked dreadful—her red puffy eyes stark against her pale washed out complexion. The tissue in her hands was twisted into a small wet ball.

More silence at Paul's end of the phone line, then:

'Tom, there's something I never told you. I was too ashamed, and ordinarily I wouldn't have ever mentioned it, but this changes my perspective dramatically.'

'Ann rang me a few days after she'd told you to get lost. She was crying and upset and regretted her decision, I think. Anyway, I suggested we go out for a drink and she could get it off her chest.'

'We met at the Torrens Wine Bar and had a few drinks, then I drove her home. She asked me in for a coffee but instead of coffee, we had a few more drinks.' There was another brief silence as he swallowed, before continuing: 'and ended up having sex. I left immediately after and neither of us ever mentioned it again.'

'Ann and her parents left Australia a couple of weeks later and went to live in America as far as I know.'

After having overcome the hurdle of the confession, Paul gathered himself together and continue the conversation.

'Perhaps Ann genuinely believed you to be the father of her child, after all, you two were dating for a few months. Plus, the one time she and I had sex, it was not a memorable event for either of us. However, it is factually possible that either of us is Callie's father.'

Now it was Tom's turn to sit in stunned silence. Paul? Callie's father? He felt like a bucket of happiness had been poured over him.

'Tom. Tom, are you still there? Do you know what I think? I think I should come over to L.A. immediately and each of the three of us should have a DNA test, preferably done at the same lab. That way, we'll all know.'

Brought abruptly back to earth by the reality of the situation, Tom replied: 'Yes. Good idea. How quickly can you organise a flight? We're a mess over here. We need to know as quickly as possible.'

'I can be there tomorrow. I'll email you my ETA. See you tomorrow.'

As per usual, Alice weaved her magic—and paid somebody a large amount of money—to get the results of the DNA tests in record quick time. Mid-morning of the third day after Callie had first read her birth certificate, the three of them sat around in Tom's living room, drinking coffee, when the doorbell rang. It was the courier with their results.

Tom was the first one to rip open his envelope. He quickly scanned the contents until he got to the paragraph headed: CONCLUSION. His eyes focussed immediately on the words in bold, which he read out to the others:

'is excluded as the biological father.' followed by the words: 'the possible father **IS NOT** the biological father of the child as all data gathered from this test does not support a relationship of paternity.'

Callie's eyes filled with tears as she hugged and kissed Tom excitedly.

'God, I feel twenty years younger than I did ten minutes ago,' said Tom, laughing as he wrapped his arms around Callie. They both stopped abruptly and looked at Paul. 'Well? Open yours and tell us what it says.'

The magnitude of this moment had not escaped Paul, and he could feel the beads of sweat building up on his top lip. The envelope resisted his trembling fingers and, in frustration, he thrust it at Callie, who swiftly and neatly opened it and handed its contents back to him.

He silently read the complete document, but unconvinced, read it again, before clearing his throat and reading aloud:

'CONCLUSION: **this donor is not excluded as the biological father**. The data gathered from this test supports a relationship of paternity of 99.9% which means that this donor most likely **IS** the biological father of the child.'

As she clasped her hands over her chest, Callie exclaimed: 'You're my father!' and threw her arms around Paul, clinging to him as she cried in disbelief.

'Congratulations, you sly old dog,' said Tom, smiling broadly as he grasped Paul's hand and shook it wildly. Paul grinned as he looked at both of them in a new light. Grabbing Callie by the shoulders, he held her at arm's length and, in a trembling voice, said: 'A daughter! I can't believe it. A daughter!' He couldn't stop smiling.

'I always knew we had a special bond,' said Callie, smiling through her tears as she wiped her eyes with the wet ball of screwed-up tissue. 'Didn't I always say, Tom, that Paul was my favourite person? After you, of course.' she added quickly, grinning in Tom's direction.

'I can't think of anyone in the world I'd rather have as a daughter than you, Callie,' said Paul proudly. 'I can't believe how lucky I am today.'

'We are three very, very lucky people,' said Callie.

'Agreed,' added Tom.

Then: 'We must phone Alice and tell her the good news.'

'Yes,' said Callie. 'Ask her over for lunch and we can thank her for organising to get us out of our misery so quickly.'

Later, as the four of them sat around the big timber table by the pool after the delicious Caesar salad Callie and Paul had put together, Alice looked around the table as she said,

'Who would believe the odds of meeting up with your birth daughter, the daughter you didn't even know you had, 35 years later? The planets must have been aligned. Shows how good things happen to good people.' And she smiled at Paul.

Tom gently tapped his water glass with a fork, as if he was about to make some sort of announcement.

'Just had a thought. Paul, you know how I wanted you to be my best man? Well, perhaps you'd prefer to give the bride away.'

Callie looked uncomfortable, but Paul glanced at her reassuringly and smoothly answered on her behalf, as well as his own.

'That's a nice thought, Tom, but I wouldn't want to deprive Ben of that honour. I'm really pleased to be your best man, and I almost guarantee not to forget the rings.'

Relief washed over Callie and she smiled in gratitude at Paul as Alice added, 'Great. Now we can get on with the business of organising a wedding. What can I do to help, Callie?'

Tom was never so grateful to his good friends as he was at that moment. Alice would have been busting to organise a wedding but had instead offered her help rather than bulldozing her way into running everything, and Paul had handled the question of Father-of-the-bride with quiet diplomacy. The culmination of all those years of denial when he was sliding into the abyss of drugs and drink had nearly been the end of him, but thanks to his loyal friends, he was now happily sitting here planning his forthcoming wedding.

That evening, after Alice left and Paul had retired to the guest room to make some phone calls, Callie and Tom sat quietly in the big comfortable cane chairs in the sunroom drinking coffee. They were each thinking about the recent days full of drama and anxiety, which were now a thing of the past, when Callie said,

'I'll ring Mom tomorrow and tell her what's happened over the past few days.'

Tom nodded agreement. Callie placed her cup on the coffee table and thought for a moment before turning to Tom as she spoke:

'Also, Tom, I think I'd like to find my birth mother; tell her I'm getting married and thinking about starting a family. For whatever reason she may have decided to give me up, she might feel differently about grandchildren. What do you think?'

Tom reached over and took Callie's hand in his and held it. 'If that's what you want to do, then I'm behind you 100 %. Maybe you should mention that to your mother when you speak to her.'

'Of course.'

'You know, Callie, tracking down your birth mother might not be easy, but if there's one person who can help you with that...'

'It's Alice!' they said together, and they laughed and laughed.

The following day, Callie called her mother in Boston and filled her in on the drama of the past few days. She explained Paul had immediately flown over from Australia so the three of them could be together when the DNA test results were received.

Linda Williams was shocked when Callie told her that Paul's results showed he was her father. Linda and Ben had met Paul and had both liked him immensely, but to find out that he was their daughter's father was difficult to take in.

'There's something else I wanted to tell you, Mom. Discovering Paul is my birth father has not made me feel any differently about my *real* Dad, you know my adopted dad, but it has kindled my interest in meeting my birth mother. If it's possible, I would like to find her and meet her. I hope you can understand how I feel.'

Linda replied:

'Callie, we have loved you for 35 years, and we are secure in your love and affection for us. Just because you might meet your birth mother and father doesn't mean you would abandon us; it just means you will have two mothers and fathers, which sounds pretty fantastic to me. I think your dad will see it this way too.'

'So go ahead and find your birth mother. Invite her to the wedding if you'd like to, we'll leave that up to you.'

After another hour's chat with her mother about the wedding: the venue—Tom's beautiful home, of course; the guest list—Callie could get it up to two hundred without even thinking hard; the Wedding Planners—Alice will know the best one, etc. etc., Callie hung up from her mother and dialled Alice's number.

'Alice, Callie here. I have two special favours to ask of you: firstly, I'd like to find my birth mother and I don't know where to start. Will you help me please?

'Oh Callie, of course I'll help you find her. I know just the man who can track her down; he's a genius at finding people. Plus, I think it's a good idea—don't die with the music in you.'

'What's the second thing?'

'Will you be my attendant at the wedding?'

There was silence at the end of the phone. Then,

'My entire life has been made up of business—business deals, business contracts, arranging stuff to do with business. All my life, it's been business. Don't get me wrong, I'm not complaining. But nobody has ever asked me anything personal like that. I'm overwhelmed.' Pause. 'And I can think of nothing I'd rather do.'

'Fantastic!' replied Callie. 'Let's get together and discuss girly stuff.'

It took Alice's 'man' a little over two weeks to find Ann Meredith Thompson, a quest which would have probably taken Callie many months. Ann Thompson owned a successful horse training and agistment business in a rural area of Lexington, Kentucky, known as Cloudbase Ranch. As far as he could find out, Ms. Thompson had never married nor had any children, but had instead devoted her life to the training and agistment of racehorses ever since she had bought the ranch nearly thirty years ago.

Callie felt her pulse quicken as Alice told her what her 'man' had said in his report. However, in an attack of cold feet, Callie tucked the phone contact details for Ann Thompson into a drawer in her desk. During the next few weeks, she surreptitiously opened the drawer and looked at the phone number, but each time, would close the drawer quickly and walk away, frightened of actually speaking to the person who had given birth to her all those years ago.

Surely, she would have contacted me if she wanted to, thought Callie. *What if she doesn't like me? What if she won't even speak to me?* Negative thoughts crowded her mind every time she opened the drawer. Eventually, during one of their frequent phone conversations, Alice casually asked her if she had contacted Ann yet.

'Not yet,' replied Callie defensively. 'I'm trying to find the right time. To be honest, I'm scared. Scared she won't want to know me. I don't think I could take the rejection a second time.'

'Would you like me to act as an intermediary? I could contact her on your behalf. She might feel less intimidated speaking to me, rather than you ringing her out of the blue.'

Callie thought about this for a moment. She knew she was being a coward, but what Alice said made sense.

'Would you do that for me?' asked Callie.

'I'd love to,' replied Alice. 'I've got her number in my files somewhere. I'll do it now, it's nearly five in the afternoon here and Lexington is about three hours ahead of us so it should be about eight o'clock tonight there, probably a good time to get her.'

When her phone rang later that night, Callie answered it on the first ring. 'What did she say?'

'Callie, she sounds nice. She was surprised and extremely apprehensive at first. Like you, she was worried that you wouldn't like her and was wondering why you chose now to make contact. But when I explained about the upcoming wedding and the possibility of a family in the future, and that your adoptive parents were both happy for you to make contact with her after all these years, she came around.'

'It was she who suggested you two meet. I said I thought it might be a good idea to meet on neutral ground, somewhere between L.A. and Lexington. How do you feel about going to Oklahoma City? I can come with you if you want, but not to the actual meeting. I'll be there for moral support afterwards, but only if you want me to.'

'Oh, yes please, Alice, I would love you to come with me. I don't think I'd like to be there on my own but I don't want Tom or Paul there either. But you, you're different. You're so sensible Alice, so grounded. You're what I need right now.'

'I think I understand how you feel. I'll go ahead and organise it and let Ann know the details. I'll get back to you soon.'

The following week, in a shady area of a beautiful park in down-town Oklahoma City, Callie and Ann met and chatted for nearly three hours. Ann had to get back to the airport for her flight home. One of her client's thoroughbred horses had taken ill that morning and she needed to return home. Callie even asked Ann to the wedding and was delighted when Ann said she would love to come but would have to think about it. She would let her know.

When Callie returned to their suite, Alice was ready and waiting with a chilled bottle of champagne, and a small dark bottle bearing a label Alice had designed and printed which said 'Hemlock,' in case the meeting had not gone well. Callie giggled when she saw it.

'I won't be needing that, thank you,' she said as she kicked off her shoes and collapsed onto the sofa.

'Make yourself comfortable while I pour you a champagne,' Alice expertly popped the champagne cork and poured two glasses of champagne.

'So, how did it go?' enquired Alice as she handed a glass to Callie.

Callie took a big gulp of the icy liquid and sighed with pleasure as the bubbles slipped down her throat like tiny pins and needles.

'I got there first, and I was surprised at how calm I was. Even when she arrived and introduced herself, I still didn't feel anything. It wasn't as if I felt this huge rush or anything. She certainly didn't seem like my mom; I mean, she's almost 20 years older than me, but certainly doesn't look it. It was like meeting up with someone I knew from school.'

'But you're right, Alice, she is lovely and I think we could become good friends. She told me all about her relationship with Tom. When I explained about the DNA tests, she was as shocked as I was when I told her that Paul was my father. That was when she told me about her one-night stand with Paul. She had never disclosed the name of the father, whom she always presumed to be Tom, to anyone including her mother and father.

She said that even though she was tucked away on a horse ranch in Kentucky, she had heard of Tom Watson and Pants on Fire and their success over the years, but because she had put that part of her life behind her many years ago, she had no desire to contact him or to stir up the past for either of them.

Callie took a sip of her champagne before continuing,

'At first, I found this a bit hurtful, but then I thought about how I hadn't ever felt the urge to find out about her, so I guess we're even.'

'She's very forthright. I can understand how she would be a successful businesswoman. She seemed impressed with my career as a Journo. Seems she's had many dealings with the press, not always good, but that the good ones are memorable.'

Alice topped up their glasses, and as she placed her hand over Callie's, said,

'This has been a big day for you. How do you feel? What sort of impact has it had on you?'

'Today, I met someone I really liked, and who I'd like to get to know better. The world didn't stop on its axis, but I wasn't disappointed either. I feel pretty good actually.'

Callie's phone beeped and she picked it up and read the message:

'So lovely meeting you today. I look very forward to our next get together. And I'd love to come to your wedding. Love, Ann. xx'

She literally felt her heart swell in her chest and her throat tighten up as she read the message again. Unable to speak for a moment for fear she would cry, she handed the phone to Alice to read.

When Alice had read the message, she smiled at Callie. 'Everything considered, that's just about perfect, I reckon.'

The morning of October 14, 2018 dawned crystal clear and fresh, a sign of a perfect day to come.

Callie and Alice, and Callie's mom and dad, Linda and Ben, had checked into the Beverly Hills Hotel the day before. Callie had organised for the wedding planners to take over Tom's house today and knew that it would be chaotic there this morning in preparation for the 3 pm wedding, and they wanted to enjoy this day to the fullest.

Ann had flown in from Lexington the previous day and was staying at the Four Seasons, Beverly Hills, for the second time in a matter of weeks. When Callie had sent her an official invitation to the wedding, Ann had suggested she fly to L.A. well before the date so they could all meet prior to the wedding. The dinner Callie had arranged had taken place four weeks ago and had been a surprisingly pleasant evening, although Paul had been more quiet than usual. Often, when old friends meet up after many years apart, the conversation centres around the previous time they knew each other, but in her inimitable style, Alice kept things flowing nicely.

Tom and Paul had checked into the Beverley Wiltshire Four Seasons the day before the wedding, deciding to stay out of everyone's way on the day, until they had to be at the house for the ceremony at 3 pm, or as Alice put it—'3 pm sharp! That's not 3.01, or 3.10, Tom, that's 3 pm.'

Tom woke about eight o'clock, climbed out of bed, and sauntered into the adjoining suite where Paul was sitting at his laptop.

'Oh, you're awake. Want some coffee?'

'Good idea. I've just come in from my morning run. Didn't think you'd appreciate it if I woke you to run with me,' he said, grinning at Tom.

The two men sat sipping their coffee in silence. Tom, staring into the middle distance, spoke first. 'I can't believe I'm getting married today. Fifty-four years old and I'm getting married—for the first time! What was I thinking?'

'Smart man,' said Paul. 'Best thing you'll ever do.'

'Hmm,' Tom frowned.

He looked anxiously at Paul. 'Have you got the rings?'

'Yes, as I've assured you at least twenty times in the past couple of days, I've got the rings.'

'Do you think we should get ready yet?'

'I think getting ready at 8.30 in the morning for a 3 pm wedding is a bit premature, don't you.'

'You're quite right.'

'It's all a bit surreal, isn't it? I'm still getting my head around the fact that my best friend is the father of the woman I'm marrying. And that her mother, whom I dated all those years ago, will be at the wedding.'

'How do you think I feel? I only recently found out I've got a thirty-five-year-old daughter!'

Paul could see that Tom was a bit agitated. *Need to get his mind off the wedding*, thought Paul.

'Why don't we get dressed and go for a wander along Rodeo Drive and buy some presents for Callie and Alice?'

'Gee, you've got some good ideas,' replied Tom, downing the last of his coffee. 'Meet you downstairs in the lobby in thirty minutes.'

The wedding planners had done a wonderful job. The house looked spectacular, decked out in thousands of white roses, their scent filling the air. White candles in silver lanterns flickered on every highly polished surface. Outside, the gardener had coaxed the hundreds of white, and some pale blue, hydrangeas to bloom specially for today, and the lawns were manicured to perfection. As predicted, the day was flawless, weatherwise.

The white silk Armani gown Callie had chosen for her wedding dress glistened in the sunlight and was complemented by the half-dozen fresh white frangipani in her hair. Alice wore a pale blue silk Dior outfit and a 1920s style cloche in matching fabric. The beautifully tailored dark suits which Callie had chosen for the men contrasted dramatically with the delicate colours on the two women.

The Marriage Celebrant, a friend of Alice's from her acting days, made everyone cry, including the bride. Much laughter and cheering followed, as they were declared wife and husband.

It was following the ceremony, when the guests were enjoying French champagne and canapes on the upper terrace of the lawn, that Alice located her date for the wedding. He had blended in with the rest of the guests whilst Alice had been busy 'attending the bride.' Hand in hand, she led him over to where Callie and Tom were standing on one side as the official wedding photographer changed cameras.

'Tom, you remember Ivan, from The Hermitage? Callie, this is the man who is responsible for Tom's rescue from a life of addiction. Ivan, these are my two favourite people, Mr. and Mrs. Tom Watson.' Alice grinned wickedly at the look of surprise and pleasure on Tom and Callie's faces before adding: 'Ivan and I have been seeing each other for a while.'

All four of them laughed out loud with pleasure. And the photographer got the shot of the day!

Eventually, the bride and groom led their guests into the white silk marquee, which had been specially built on the lower terrace. The hanging crystal chandeliers and the abundance of white roses and silver candelabra belied the relaxed atmosphere within the marquee. People milled about, chatting to friends and colleagues, checking out name tags on the tables, until Rooster, who was M.C. for the evening, asked guests to be seated.

Once the dinner and speeches were over, people moved around the room, swapping seats with other guests. Paul sat down next to Ann and they began chatting.

The members of the 6-piece band, who had been playing quietly in the background whilst dinner was served, stood and played a rousing rendition of 'Love Will Keep Us Together' as the wait staff quickly moved the tables away from the centre of the room to expose a square dance floor.

When the music morphed into 'Can't Take My Eyes Off of You' Callie and Tom were first on the dance floor and as the spotlight fell on them, Tom whispered: 'This is about as good as it gets. I've never been happier.'

Callie replied, smiling into his eyes: 'And this is just the beginning.'

Jim sat alone at a table and smiled happily as he watched them, his only disappointment being that Tom's mother wasn't here to see the man Tom had become. At the same time, he was glad she had not been there to witness the dark times, when hope for Tom's recovery was all but gone; grateful that he had navigated his way through those dark times and was now enjoying the happiest day of his life.

Paul and Ann were watching Callie and Tom dancing, as were the rest of the guests, when Paul leaned in and whispered in Ann's ear,

'They make a terrific couple, don't they?'

Ann turned her head and looked at him, smiling. 'They certainly do. I think it's got a lot to do with the bride's genes.'

And they both laughed.

'So, how long are you in L.A.?' Asked Paul, looking at her over the rim of his glass as he took another sip of champagne.

'Two more days. I fly back to Lexington the day after tomorrow.'

'So, you'll be here long enough for me to take you to dinner tomorrow night?'

Ann smiled a cheeky smile, which she held for a moment before replying: 'I thought you'd never ask.'

ACKNOWLEDGEMENTS

Every endeavour involves many people—writing a book is no different.

The thing I like about researching, writing, and publishing a book is that you meet and speak to so many people, some of whom are known to you and some you've never met before—in fact, many more than I could list here. Their valued time and knowledge is much appreciated on this long and winding road. Without their help and support, this book would never have seen the light of day, but instead, here it is in its shiny new cover and pristine printing and binding.

To the members of my writers' group—Jacky, Jeremy, Paul, and Trevor—I am forever grateful. Thank you also to my ever-helpful team of beta readers whose feedback and advice made the book better—Carolyn, Deborah, Heather, Stephen, Rebecca, Bill, and Rod.

Many thanks also to fellow author and musician, David Atkinson, for his generosity and kindness, and whose advice and editing was so helpful, not to forget Tom from JamPot Recording Studios who answered my endless questions with patience and good humour.

Thanks to my friend, Geoff Saint, for his help and advice on several aspects of Tom Watson's life. Under Geoff's guidance, I graduated from completely ignorant to mildly knowledgeable on many facets of the lifestyle of the rich and famous.

There are so many more people and organisations I pestered during the writing of Tom's life, more than I can list here, who handled my many questions and inquiries with grace and candour.

But last and most, I would like to sincerely thank my long-suffering husband. Dearest Basil, I couldn't have done it without you. Thank you for your encouragement and support, especially when I needed it the most. You always told me I'd get it right in the end and of course, you were once again correct.

AUTHOR'S NOTES

Thank you for reading this book. There's a lot of choice out there and every time you, the reader, decide to read a book, it's a commitment of both faith and time. I'm a reader too, I understand.

I hope 'The Life and Times of Tom Watson' didn't disappoint. If you enjoyed it, I'd be grateful if you could leave a short review, perhaps on Amazon or Goodreads. It helps so much. I have no hope of matching the marketing budgets of the large publishers, and a good review really does make a difference. I do read them all, I promise.

There are some true bits of people's lives scattered throughout 'The Life and Times of Tom Watson', people I have met along life's path, but mainly it is a work of fiction. I started the manuscript way back, as I was writing the first book in the series, The Life and Loves of Karen Romano, when I became fixated on a secondary character in that book, Tom Watson. Even though he was only a minor player in Karen's story, I used to wonder how his life would turn out. I couldn't let him go, so I began to write his story, never thinking it would grow to cover 40 years of Tom's life.

So, it's more of a spin-off than a follow-on of the first book in the series – think Frasier as a spin-off of Cheers, those brilliantly successful TV series of the '80s and '90s. Although it would be helpful for you to read Karen's story first, The Life and Times of Tom Watson is a stand-alone story.

If you have any questions or comments, I'd love to hear from you. Feel free to email me at:

raynette@raynettemitchellauthor.com

And do have a look at my website –

www.raynettemitchellauthor.com –

for snippets of my next book in the 'Secrets Have Consequences' series.

<u>**ALSO BY RAYNETTE MITCHELL**</u>

The Life and Loves of Karen Romano -
Book 1 in the series: Secrets Have Consequences

AUTHOR BIO

Raynette Mitchell is an Australian author of contemporary literary fiction who enjoys writing about the complexities of the human condition, and how people handle life situations in good times and in bad.

After countless re-writes and edits, she completed the second book in the series 'Secrets Have Consequences' – The Life and Times of Tom Watson – following the successful release of the first book in the series –The Life and Loves of Karen Romano. The third book in the series will be released late in 2025.

Some of her favourite authors are Marian Keyes, Jodi Picoult, and Joy Dettman. However, she also enjoys reading classics by some of the renowned authors of our time - Winston Graham, John Irving, Ken Follett,John O'Hara, Guy Bellamy.

When she's not writing, Raynette thinks about writing, talks about writing, discusses writing with other authors, and sometimes occasionally even spends a bit of time gardening. Her husband has been a great help in all these endeavours, especially the gardening.

www.ingramcontent.com/pod-product-compliance
Lightning Source LLC
Chambersburg PA
CBHW050111120726
47904CB00004B/1308